A PHỞ LOVE story

LOAN LE

SIMON & SCHUSTER

First published in Great Britain in 2021 by Simon & Schuster UK Ltd

First published in the USA in 2021 by Simon & Schuster Books for Young Readers

Copyright © 2021 Loan Le

1 3 5 7 9 10 8 6 4 2

Simon & Schuster UK Ltd
1st Floor, 222 Gray's Inn Road
London
WC1X 8HB

www.simonandschuster.co.uk
www.simonandschuster.com.au
www.simonandschuster.co.in

Simon & Schuster Australia, Sydney
Simon & Schuster India, New Delhi

A CIP catalogue record for this book is available from the British Library.

PB ISBN 978-1-3985-0267-3
eBook ISBN 978-1-3985-0266-6

Printed and bound by CPI Group (UK) Ltd, Croydon, CR0 4YY

This book is dedicated to:

My parents Phung Le and Dong Pham
I love you so much

My sister An Le
I love you and I'm proud to be your little sister

My brother Dan Le
I love you still.

AUTHOR'S NOTE

Before escaping the country, my family lived in Nha Trang, a gorgeous coastal city in south central Vietnam. I grew up speaking the southern Vietnamese dialect, but given Nha Trang's location, some words may reflect a mixture of central and southern regions. For example, I call my dad *Ba* and my mom *Mẹ* while some readers might call theirs *Bố* and *Má*. The food featured in this novel also reflects the dishes that are commonly eaten in my family.

CHAPTER ONE

BẢO

Hoisin sauce is not paint.

We need a sign that says that, because our customers don't get it. Today's latest work is a misshapen star on the wall. A five out of ten, if you ask me. The kid's parent probably did a double take, snatched the bottle away, then paid the check and left before Mẹ could notice. To be honest, it's not like the sauce makes our wall look worse; it's just hard to wipe off when it dries. But I try, I really do—sometimes. Maybe.

Various relatives from both sides of my family judge me from their water-stained portraits that hang around the restaurant.

I sit down and look ahead at the five booths I still need to wipe clean, but this heat's unbearable and the main fan, the good fan, died last week. Break time. I brush off grains of rice that cling to my apron. Later, I'm sure I'll find a few that somehow end up under my socks at the end of each shift. On the opposite side, my best friend, Việt, goes at the same pace as me. His ears are plugged up, probably to block out the *Paris by Night*–like soundtrack blasting from the back room, songs on repeat about the Vietnam War, love, war, poverty, war.

Việt is the most chaotic neutral person I know. On any other day he wastes time by raving about the latest criminal-investigation show he's gotten hooked on. I consider that a trade-off; he's the one who suffers through my fascination with strange words. Once I was wiping down a front window from the inside, unknowingly overriding his work and adding more streaks than there were to begin with. I'd been mentioning the word "defenestrate," which made him calmly threaten me with that very word.

Ba stands behind the counter, punching in numbers at the cash register, then piercing receipts onto a spindle. I think he finds the routine satisfying.

The front door opens, the bell shattering the slowness in the restaurant, ushering in more sticky hot air. My mom's voice whips two other lingering, taskless waiters to attention, and I snatch up the towel and wipe off bean sprouts, leafless stems of herbs, and straw wrappers shaped as tiny accordions. Mẹ charges across the room. She drops her plastic shopping bags in the path toward the kitchen, a storm on her face. Everyone clears the way for her; they know Mẹ's mood. But Ba's expression is as indifferent as his look in their wedding pictures from the 2000s: Stone. Cold.

My mom slaps down a crumpled piece of paper before him. "Anh, do you know what they're doing across the street?"

Without looking up, speaking to his calculator, he asks, "Did you get more sriracha sauce?"

"On my way back, I saw these ugly posters all over the place."

"There was a sale. Did you get them on sale?"

It's always like this, their conversation misaligned, a *not much* to a *how are you* question.

"Lampposts, windows all over Bolsa Avenue!"

Glass shatters in the back kitchen. The line cooks start blaming each other, Spanish and Vietnamese mingling together. My guess: Bình did it. That guy sucks at his job more than me.

Mẹ ignores the noise. "Two-for-one. Two-for-one bowl of phở. *Trời ơi.*" Only one family can get her riled up like this. She pauses. "They're trying to steal all our customers. Why isn't Anh worried?"

Ba snorts. "Their phở is not good. They never have enough salt." Now *that* I can't verify. I've never stepped foot into the Mais' restaurant. Because what happens? Apparently my mom will cut my legs off.

Maybe they had one of the waiters pose as a customer . . .

Mẹ nods, dialing back her worry. After a moment, she says, "Two-for-one phở. Who wants to have phở *lạt*?" She laughs at her own joke about their phở's blandness. Ba joins, too.

Lately their preoccupation with the Mais has ratcheted, probably because they keep hearing about the changes the other

3

family's been making, changes that seem to be in direct response to our adjustments. We'd recently added new wood grain blinds that block out the sun—just because it looks like they replaced their blinds, too.

My mom zeroes in on me. *"Con đang làm gì đó?"* She side-eyes my tables. "Why are the tables still dirty?"

"I'm not finished yet."

"Why not? He's done." Mẹ points to the opposite side.

I look across the room at Việt—

And blink. The tables are shining, and the mirrors are fingerprint-less and—yes—hoisin-less. Kid's like an Asian Flash. "Oh, c'mon," I mutter.

"Giỏi quá!" she says to the traitor.

"Cảm ơn," Việt answers without a trace of an accent even though he was born here.

My mom turns back to me. "Hurry up!" She jabs a finger at me. "And fix your hair! It's so messy." I can't help it; my hair has a mind of its own.

The poster that Mẹ showed my dad floats to the ground in her wake. Curious, I pick it up, passing by Việt. Making sure my mom's a good distance away, I elbow him. "Suck-up."

Việt lands a punch to my stomach. "Lazy."

I pretend not to die; he's always been stronger than me.

Việt goes into the back room. I look down at the flyer. I'm not sure how anything like this can be considered ugly. It's awesome. There's no other word for it. Just really cool—some kind of collage of old and modern Vietnam: a woman wearing a traditional silk white dress and rice hat winking at a camera. You can see the sun and beachline—reminding me of Nha Trang, my parents' hometown—blazing behind her. An airplane flying above the woman spells out in the clouds OH MAI MAI PHỞ: TWO-FOR-ONE DEAL. With this kind of advertising from the Mai family, my parents should be worrying about *our* advertising. We don't have a Linh on our team.

I glance out the window. As if this poster summons her, Linh appears from Larkin Street's direction. She rushes into the restaurant, her flyaway hair alive, her large canvas bag, which she hauls everywhere, hitting her long legs. Over the entrance and below a pagoda-style eave hangs a South Việt flag just like ours—yellow with three red stripes—and it flutters in greeting to Linh. She's always a colorful blur—going to class, dashing down La Quinta's hallways when the bell lets out, running into the restaurant at 3:30 p.m.

I see her, but I know close to nothing about her. Maybe it's a good thing she's constantly moving, because if she ever stopped, we might have to talk to each other. And we haven't done that since we were kids.

Hypothetically, a Buddhist temple is not a place for insults or threats or a potential bloodbath.

I've gone to temple sporadically throughout my life, but the day I met Linh is the most memorable, for many reasons, aside from running into the rest of the Mais and being *thiiis* close to seeing bloodshed before Ông Phật.

Before meeting Linh, I'd never seen another seven-year-old kid stab paper with a crayon. Repeatedly. We were in the kids' room where the *chùa*'s volunteers babysat kids as the parents went to worship or at least get a moment of silence. Mine were catching up with friends upstairs. There were tables with finger paint, macaroni, glue, and paper, and another table with crayons and markers. I'm not sure why—maybe because it was less work—I went for the crayons.

The other kids sat so far away from Linh because they were afraid she might turn on them. But the look on her face was calm and concentrated—satisfied, even—and when she made sure all of the crayons were completely dull, she raised her white paper in triumph. I was closest to her, so she showed it to me.

The dots formed a complete picture: green grass, a yellow sun, and a red-and-blue swing set.

"Wow," I said, like any six-to-eight-year-old Asian kid with a bowl cut would say.

"It's the playground at my school," she answered proudly.

"Can you draw Spider-Man?" Because back then, that was the only thing that mattered to me.

"Maybe. I can't remember what he looks like. I need something to look at."

"I have one! I can get it!" I'd brought along my Spider-Man backpack, but it was upstairs in a cubby with our shoes. We raced out of the room, escaping the volunteers, who didn't really try to catch us. Up on the main floor, the temple membership was serving bowls of phở *chay* and a white-haired lady waved us over for a bowl of vegetarian soup.

Linh took her bowl with everything that my family always

taught me to use: hoisin sauce, thai basil, and bean sprouts. That told me she knew phở; she *came* from phở. It was confirmed when we both tried the phở at the same time and said, "BLECH." Salty as hell. We left our bowls, quick, then moved on to our destination.

Running, that's what I remember. I was chasing a girl I barely knew, but I really wanted that Spider-Man drawing. Before we could get to my backpack, though, Mẹ's sharp voice rang out. The one that still summons centuries' worth of furious Vietnamese mothers. I froze. Our families stood on opposite sides of the room, where Buddha was at the center, accepting gifts and praise from the visitors. Linh and I were caught in between. I waited for Buddha to come alive, chime in, like a referee, and bellow—while the ground vibrates forcibly— "Ready, set, FIGHTTT!"

But nothing like that happened.

Linh's mom took one step forward, like she was marking her territory. Her eldest daughter and husband were just behind her.

"Đến đây," my mom said to me. I thought she was angry at me for running in a temple. I couldn't say no and when I was with her again, she gripped my hand tight. Ba hung back, and I remember being confused by the fury barely contained on his face, so different from his usual passivity.

After that, they all but dragged me and Linh away from each other.

"You still haven't finished your tables."

Ba's voice from the front desk snaps me out of my memories. I'm still standing by the windows, but I notice the sky is a bit darker

7

and the lampposts are starting to turn on. The din of inside chatter fills my ears.

"Why do you have that flyer?"

"Sorry," I say. "I was thinking of how ugly it looked. Mẹ's right." I walk to the nearest trash can, hand poised over it.

The story of me and Linh at the temple could have been kept as a carefree memory, lost and dusty like an old book in the basement. And I did actually forget about it; she was just one of many kids I'd run around with and never saw again—best friends for an hour or two, instead of forever.

Then Linh's family opened their restaurant across from us five years ago, and I knew it was her. I knew she still drew, because she carried her portfolio with her everywhere, the size of it almost as big as her body.

I also knew that I couldn't go anywhere near her without risking my mom's wrath. Disdain was clear in my mom's voice whenever she talked about *that* restaurant, as if it were a person.

I heard that restaurant underpays its staff.

That restaurant is connected to a gang; they just moved from San Jose, after all.

That restaurant blackmailed Bác Xuân, pushed him out of his business.

That last reason might be why the neighbors didn't accept them so easily at first. Bác Xuân had basically helped the area flourish, connecting fellow business owners with the right people. Beloved, you can say. I don't think my mom's circle of friends made it any easier for *that restaurant*—social wolves who ran various businesses in the area: like Lien Hoa BBQ Deli, nail and hair salons, and even one travel agency. Back then advertising wasn't really a thing, so the good word of one of these women? Certified. You either get a *dở ẹc* or a *cũng được*, the latter being as close to great as you can get in terms of Vietnamese praise. Their group is led by Nhi Trưng, an older woman who constantly liked to brag that her name bears a similarity to one of the female military leaders to rebel against the Chinese domination centuries ago—as I discovered on Wikipedia. As if that was supposed to impress people these days. I think of her as the General, though the real-life Nhi Trưng was the general's daughter.

She had a special reason for hating the Mais; she'd always liked Bác Xuân's spot and said it'd gotten the most traffic. I bet she was planning to go for it right when the first opportunity came up.

Luckily gossip changes and some attention spans are short. Now the Mais' restaurant has become a fixture just like ours. But that doesn't stop my mom's competitive streak.

My parents—my mom, really—have now perfected the art of non-encounters, knowing their schedule right down to when they close and when they leave. In a way, their schedule has become ours. We're background characters in each other's stories.

As I look at the poster in my hands, though, I wonder if it's possible for us to change up our scripts. What would happen if our families came face-to-face with each other like that time at the temple? What would me and Linh say to each other?

"*Tại sao mày đứng đó vậy?*"

"Sorry!" I shout to my mom. Back to work.

I fold up Linh's poster and pocket it, not knowing why.

CHAPTER TWO

LINH

"Maybe I just won't take the SATs again. Maybe I'll just drop out right now and become the next best American novelist."

I give my best friend, Allison, my *You're annoying me again* look, since this is the third time she's interrupted me as I worked on my latest sketch. "C'mon."

"No, really. What's the point of the SATs? There's no real-life application that we can get here." She twirls her curly hazel hair with a finger. Her foot kicks my left ankle. "And your legs are in my space again."

I fold them just a bit more, but there's not much I can do in this booth. "You're going to do fine. They were fine the first time around. So what if your math scores aren't perfect? They're still great. And you'll ace the writing part, Ms. Editor in Chief. I know it."

"And you're going to ace all of it. Because you're Linh fucking Mai," Ali says. She pretends to take an angry slurp of her *cà phê sữa đá*, condensation leaving a puddle next to her. Since middle school we've always had iced coffee to get us through the mountain of homework we have. Senior year just started but I already feel as if I'm buried.

Some of my coffee spills onto the table, soaks the edges of my cream-colored sketch pad. I don't clean it up. Ms. Yamamoto is in my head, saying, *If you want to be an artist, you'll need to get messy.* I focus on my sketch.

Downtime at the restaurant is actually a nice time to draw. The empty seat next to me to balances my Prismacolors. My eraser, an ugly blend of all the colors I've been using, sits beside them. The sketch isn't going that bad. The assignment: *Draw your memories.* Instructions: *Why the hell should I tell you what to do?* Or at least that's what Yamamoto always says to our art class.

I'm drawing a beach scene, remembering the time Ba taught me how to float on my back, and where Mẹ taught me how to "cook" with sand—or play make-believe as I dug concave dents in the sand, poured water in them to make *bánh bèo ngọt*, a sweet steamed treat you can hold in the palm of your hand and eat.

My older sister, Evelyn, stayed under the shade of our umbrella, reading—of all things—a book about the human skeleton. Guess who's now majoring in biology at UC Davis?

The tip of my colored pencil breaks as I shade an area under my beach umbrella.

"What is it?" Ali says, reaches over her SAT book to touch the picture—but I quickly slap her hand away. *Jesus*, you're a beast when you're drawing, you know that?"

I pull back my sketch pad. "It's not ready yet." And it won't be if I keep losing focus, or let Ali distract me with her talking.

And that's what she does best.

Luckily, I'm used to it. Ali is a fixture in the restaurant after school, and for years, it was me, Evie, and Ali, and nothing really changed, unless you count the fact that now Ali steals the last egg roll, always shooting me an impish grin.

There was a time for a year when her parents were going through a divorce, and as strong as she was, home was more like a battlefield. The divorce eventually happened, and everything's more stable now. She's back to being the Ali who likes my artwork so much that she always has to take a peek at it. She says that one day we're going to dominate the world—her as a writer, me as an artist.

"What's with your dad today?" Ali tips her chin toward the front of the restaurant, where Ba takes up his own booth. The light from the front windows streams in, turning his normally salt-and-pepper hair a blinding white. He's writing the checks for the week, but keeps looking up at the Nguyễns' restaurant. Best guess is that he's keeping an eye on the Nguyễns. Ba's weird like that.

"I dunno."

The Nguyễns can't *not* see him. My dad isn't the most discreet person or the stealthiest; every part of him—his walk, his breathing—

makes noise. My mom, though, is the opposite. She slips in and out of any social gathering, from any room, any conversation, like a ghost. But she's loudest when she's cooking; the spices and flavors in her phở, *bún bò*, and *bún riêu* are her way of announcing, *I'm here*.

Our plan to do a two-for-one deal combines Ba's talent for advertising and Mẹ's cooking, or so Ba claims. But I'm already dreading the flood of people who'll come. We're understaffed as it is; we had to say goodbye to three servers who were seniors off to college. We hired replacements, but only one of them seems like they'll last.

Before I realize it, Ba appears at our table. He sets down a plate of hot, crispy egg rolls that Mẹ sent out from the kitchen. Ali literally *ooh*s, like she hasn't eaten a gazillion in the lifetime we've known each other.

"*Cảm ơn*, Ba."

He reaches for my sketch, appraises it. "*Con vẽ này hả?*" he asks evenly. I nod and he dips his chin in acknowledgment. I know he sees I can draw. He wouldn't have asked me to make the flyers if he didn't at least approve of my work. "Did you do your homework already?"

"*Dạ*, Ba."

Ba nods, satisfied, and walks back into the kitchen.

There used to be a time where I brought home every single art project in elementary school and middle school, and they would take it, hang it up. A picture of flowers in a vase still hangs in the kitchen by the in-and-out door. I knew they were proud.

But high school is different. In my freshman year, regulars would come in daily, updating my parents on their kid who went to Harvard, or won a prestigious award, or graduated with honors, or bought them a house. That was when my parents really started paying attention to my grades—the ones that actually mattered and could get me into a good school.

Toward the end of junior year, I'd brought home a physics exam that I aced and it was only because I studied without sleeping, abandoning an art project I had at the time. The test was worth too much. Mẹ had mentioned it to a regular customer who mentioned a niece who was good at physics and now works as an engineer. Somehow that idea has stuck, and my parents have been pushing engineering as a path for me ever since.

I'd never seen them look so eager.

"Have you told them yet?" Ali pulls me from my thoughts. She is watching me. She's one of the few who can guess my moods, read me instantly.

"About coffee with Quyền Thành? No, it's pretty much all set. I can't back out now."

My parents don't usually ask for favors from regulars or their friends. Here's how it goes: If something is broken in the restaurant and a friend offers to fix it, they protest. That same friend shows up with a toolbox anyway, and my parents grudgingly let them in. When all things are fixed, my parents offer to pay them, but their friend protests and argues all the way to the door.

In that case, an envelope of money might mysteriously end up under their doormat, or in a pocket of their jacket they might hang up inside the restaurant.

But my parents had pulled in a favor when Evie was deciding

among schools, and called a few friends of friends to help weigh in. This time they used up another favor, arranging a coffee meeting with that niece who was an engineer. They tell me it's a chance to ask questions and learn more about "my future."

How can I say no?

"Con," Ba calls for me. He's halfway into the kitchen but he gestures to the front where a family of four are waiting to be seated. I slip into my role as waitress, something I've done since freshman year—and even before that. When we'd just opened the restaurant, I remember tagging along with other servers, armed with my own notepad and pen—or was it a crayon?—the customers indulging me with smiles.

"Table for four? No problem. Just follow me." I lead the family to one of the center tables, until Jonathan, the most competent of our new hires, easily swoops in.

I slip back into my booth with Ali. She's chewing on the end of her pencil, stuck with an article she's writing.

It kills my parents, even now, to have Evie a day trip away instead of at home. Evie was the better server out of us, calm and cool under service. Orderly. Mẹ never had to tell Evie to fill up the napkin dispensers or the bottles holding *tương phở*, because they were probably already filled.

And she's definitely more charismatic, like Ali, with the other customers. It's unsaid, but I know, in the way they ask after Evie, that some longtime customers must be disappointed to have me replace her—me who would much rather be in my head or in front of a canvas. They tell my parents how proud they should be of her.

"She'll be a doctor in no time," these customers say fondly. Then they look significantly at me. "And maybe you can be the same."

Perhaps in other families it would have worked out. I mean, me and Evie are only two years apart, but if anyone didn't know better, we might as well have been raised under two separate households.

Mentioning that I want to major in anything remotely creative? Impossible. Back in freshman year, when the idea of doing something with art just came into mind, we had a regular who had one daughter who couldn't be more perfect. Straight As, active in everything in her life, her hair always in a perfect bun. She was also one of the best seniors on the dance team and naturally decided to major in dance at college. Supposedly, the dad was more lenient, hence why she was even allowed to, I don't know, *live* after announcing her decision. Her mother's reaction, though, stays with me: "I want to die sometimes! She'll be poor her entire life. It'll never work out."

And my mom just consoled her as if she had lost a child, agreeing with every word. The woman and her daughter used to be close; now the girl's a choreographer and rarely comes home. Whenever her mom drops by the restaurant, loneliness comes off her in waves.

Now I glance around the restaurant, my eyes landing on the familiar parts that make up a place that's been like a second home for years: our red shrine greeting customers; our private shrine in the back room, where the ceiling is black with soot after so many years of joss sticks lit for worship; the people who come here for breakfast, lunch, and dinner, people from way back, like Mẹ and Ba's refugee camp days, who apparently remember everything about me as a child, even if I don't remember them. I mix them up half the time.

Nothing is bad. Nothing is *wrong*, really.

But it doesn't feel enough. There's something urging me to go a bit farther than here. Am I just being selfish?

Ali has gotten up to stretch her legs. She stands by the window with Ba and has started talking to him. Leave it to her to talk to someone who doesn't like to talk unless he has reason to. Off-and-on charisma. Ali laughs at something, but Ba looks serious. I leave my sketch and join them, curious.

"I can always sneak in, you know. Pose as a customer and steal some recipes."

Ba doesn't answer right away. It even looks like he's considering. I roll my eyes. "Ba, no way."

Anything the Nguyễns do, we have to do better. They knock down their *chả giò* price to four dollars for two rolls, we have to do three dollars and fifty cents for the same number of egg rolls. They have five flavors of *sinh tố*; we have six flavors. I'm never sure who's winning.

My parents are still trying to catch up to the others in the area, like the Nguyễns, still cognizant of how hard it was to open a new restaurant in the place of one that had, for all purposes, looked successful.

I remember Bác Xuân, the previous owner, coming over to our old San Jose apartment whenever he had a free weekend—stopping by after seeing his only daughter and his four grandchildren. The oldest, Fay, is getting married later this fall. I remember the slow way he'd shuffled inside and given a satisfied sigh as he sunk into our only comfortable La-Z-Boy chair. He told my parents he wanted to retire and that his daughter, a coworker of my mom's from a nail salon where she used to work, would rave about my mom's phở.

If you make good phở, you can open this restaurant, he'd said.

Things happened so quickly after that. We moved. I transferred schools. The restaurant opened ... and suddenly I was only a few feet away from that boy who'd asked me to draw him a Spider-Man. It would have been a good coincidence, and I could have made a friend—if only it wasn't made clear that I should never step near their place.

"Gia đình đó thì dữ lắm, lại rất là xấu."

"But how are they mean?"

"They don't pay their staff anything. They owe their suppliers too much money. They—"

"Just don't ever associate with them." My mom had cut my dad off, rarely doing so.

I know Vietnamese people like to judge one person based on the whole family, and to my parents, the Nguyễns are the worst, but Bảo is a mystery to me. There, but not. In four years of high school, with more than 2,500 students, we haven't had one class together. As if our school administrators know of the rivalry and have conspired to keep us apart.

And high school will be over before I know it and we'll lead even more disparate lives.

"Mr. Mai," Ali says in a mockingly grave tone, "I am more than happy to spy on our enemy if it helps the restaurant biz. Just tell me when." She goes back to the booth to pack up. "Think I'm about to head home now. I'm on deadline." She puts on her backpack, groaning at the weight of her books. She stops by the pass-through shelf and pops her head in. "Can I take home some broth, Mrs. Phạm?" Pro tip to getting on my mom's side: Address her by her maiden name, which she kept instead of taking Ba's. "My mom's *dying* for her next phở fix."

Perfect pronunciation, thanks to me.

It's like you're confused and asking, "Huh?" except there's an f.

Oh. Yeah, I get it. In the pitch that kind of loops around, right? But it's also like if you're swearing and saying, "Fu—"

Okay, yeah, you got it.

In Vietnamese, my dad mutters in awe and confusion about how he's never seen a *mỹ trắng* —a white person—eat phở so many times a week.

I hear my mom's pleased smile in her voice. "Of course!"

Her hair tied in a loose bun—with a pencil, which I can't ever figure out how to do—Mẹ appears from the back, wipes a hand on her apron. She offers Ali a plastic cylinder filled with our signature homemade chicken and beef bone broth.

Ali beams at her. "Awesome. Thanks so much, Mrs. Phạm!"

We both watch Ali leave the restaurant until Mẹ gushes, "Allison is so *dễ thương*!" She's proud that I have a friend who likes her cooking.

Ba shakes his head. "*Con đó khùng*." I laugh. According to my parents Ali can only be cute or a bit weird. I'll take my dad's side this time.

"You're not eating?" She points to the egg rolls.

If I say I don't have the stomach for it now, she'll be worried. "Yeah, working on it." Remembering Ba's reaction to my sketch, I close my pad and stash it in my backpack, rustling the paper tucked inside.

Ms. Yamamoto gave me that flyer two days ago. It's for an exhibition at the Asian Art Museum that will only be there for one night and morning. Chang Dai-Chien's piece will be displayed, donated by his living family members. He'd been one of the first to elevate ink painting and traveled all around the world before focusing on perfecting the art of Buddhist paintings. Yamamoto thought I'd be interested. She's always telling me how it seems I like capturing memories—rather than something posed—in my artwork.

'Just check it out," she said, as class was letting out. I was already late for work and ran out the door after grabbing the flyer with a quick thanks. But as I looked at it on the walk from La Quinta, I knew I couldn't miss out on it.

Mẹ disappears, then returns from the kitchen with her own bowl of phở. She likes to eat before the dinner rush. My insides sigh at the smell: star anise, cinnamon, the earthy tones of chicken and beef bones. She dresses it with shredded thai basil and fresh bean sprouts, a spritz of lime here and there, and finishes it with a generous swirl of hoisin sauce, glossy under our lights. A work of art.

'Beautiful, isn't it?" She inhales, a small smile on her face. Mẹ's loud when she's cooking—and she's happiest when she's eating. And I love her for it. I always want her to stay this way.

She gets sad sometimes—mornings when she doesn't let the sun in, leaving the window shades closed so that only slivers of yellow peek through. She buries her head in her pillow, both temples dotted with dabs of *dầu xanh* to soothe her headache. I hate the smell.

It reminds me of sickness and tummy aches, because that's what they used on me as a kid. Ba cooks on these days. Dinner is always a simple *canh sườn bí*, which always has less salt than it should, and never measures up to Mẹ's cooking.

It's worst whenever it hits the anniversary of her escape in 1983 or when a relative's death anniversary is just around the corner. Mẹ's story about her boat escape to the Philippines is the stuff of nightmares. I grew up listening to these tales. I'm not sure why—a lesson, maybe? Like in a *hey, listen to the hell I went through so you can have a good life* kind of way. But should an eight-year-old have dreams about a pitch-black sea and a boat packed with thirty-nine people, including crying, starving babies?

It's not depression, I don't think. Sometimes, she checks out. That's all. Like she's remembering something and can't get it out of her mind.

It helps when she calls my aunt, her older sister by six years, the one who stayed behind in Vietnam. She'd planned to escape with my mom in tow, along with their older cousins. But the officials had gotten to her, so she pushed my mom ahead, trusting their cousins from there on. They eventually made it to a camp in Palawan, Phillipines. My aunt wasn't held back in Vietnam for long, and might have bribed her way out.

But she understood then that she wouldn't be as lucky the second time.

Mẹ says I remind her of Dì Vàng because we both like to draw and sketch. My aunt had visited us when we lived in San Jose. I was five. I remember thinking she was like a colorful painting come to life, and when I saw a Kandinsky painting in my sophomore-year art theory class—one of his *Compositions*—I thought: *This is her*. Kandinsky had always talked about a connection between himself and the viewer, how the role of the artist was to not only excite the senses but trigger the viewer's soul. Colors and soul—I saw that in my aunt.

When my mom and my aunt get on the phone, I know things will be okay. They took care of each other back in Vietnam—since my grandparents had passed away when my mom was eleven—and they still take care of each other now. The almost nine thousand miles between them is insignificant.

Mẹ smiles as a young couple comes in—Vietnamese, by the way she greets them. Ba shows them to a table. Charisma on. He's already pushing the upcoming phở deal by handing out my flyer along with the menu. Dad's latest marketing scheme might work, but it's going to be hell working during those nights. It will track in a bunch of other Vietnamese people, who were trained by their chopstick-wielding mothers to eat what's in front of them, *then* eat some more even if they're full.

The sight of the flyer tickles something in the back of my mind.

"When is it again?"

"Hmm?"

"Phở Day." *Or whatever you call it.*

"September thirtieth, remember? We'll need your help that day."

Until three weeks ago, we were down three waiters and waitresses. Julia, Kingston, and Huy were a grade above me and left for college. But to say that the new workers were making things easier would be a complete lie. Jonathan was just okay. Lisa, the hostess, gets flustered too easily. And Tài has slippery fingers.

I lean back in my chair. Some of the air in the padding squeezes out.

Of course it's September thirtieth. The same day as the exhibition.

"Is Evie coming back to help?" My sister texted the other day and sent me a long string of pictures of her dorm room, a selfie with her new roommate, and a sunrise view of the campus after a morning run.

Maybe if she comes back, she can help out like she used to and I can sneak out . . .

My mom frowns. "Con, you know your sister is busy with school."

What about me? I'm busy. I have other things to do. I have a life.

But I can't say those things. "Yeah, right, I remember now."

Mẹ sighs as she mixes up her phở. "I know this is not the best situation. I know this isn't how you want to spend your time." I try protesting, but she only adds, "You are not so hard to read. Your face always tells me everything. I just know.

"But we want this to go well. We need it to go well. Or else your father will be grumpy for days." She glances over at Ba, who's taking a couple's orders to the kitchen.

There's no way I'll be able to see the exhibition. No way at all.

I tuck a strand of hair behind my ear. I bite into my egg roll. Soggy.

CHAPTER THREE

BẢO

I regret many things in life, and I know I'll regret many more at the rate I'm going. But my number-one regret *now* is taking journalism as my elective. Astronomy, the easiest class any senior can take, was already filled up. Việt was lucky enough to get in. I thought journalism was the second easiest. Since freshman year, *Hawkview*'s been filled with crossword puzzles, sudoku games, and What's the Difference? games, and always ended up stuffed in toilets or cafeteria trash cans.

Then Allison Dale became the editor in chief. I swear she's tougher than any staff member at the *Los Angeles Times*. She's not even *in* this class—she has study hall last period, which means she can technically leave school early, but doesn't. Even though this is our first journalism class, Allison's already expecting us to chase news stories from things like the chess team embezzling money from their joint fundraiser with the checkers team—how Allison sniffed that lead out, I'm not even sure.

The adviser, Ben Rowan, should step in more often, but he seems more like a glorified babysitter. Rowan lets Allison run everything on the newspaper. He's the kind of guy who looks like he says "sorry" a lot.

We're at the tail end of our editorial meeting about assignment statuses. I take the back seat at this meeting and try not to fall asleep, since it's the end of the school day. But a part of me is still recovering from being accosted by theater nerds at the club fair during lunch period. Traumatic. They were demonstrating some circle game in the quad, but to me, it looked like they were trying to summon demons. Other clubs were less intimidating. Apparently there's a new TikTok club? I even managed to dodge the Vietnamese Student Association.

The president, Kelly Tran, still hasn't forgiven me for oversleeping and missing one Saturday service day during sophomore year. Actually, it was three.

The newspaper room used to be an art room, so the walls have posters about journalism ethics and one blow-up portrait of a younger Woodward and Bernstein posing together—not sure where that came from—but also a deep sink with an annoying drip and leftover jugs of neon green and yellow paint from last semester. Macs surround the perimeter of the room, all asleep. I'm basically silent because I don't have anything to show. I forgot my article about upcoming school field trips.

Kind of.

The truth is, I started to write it. I really did. I'd talked to the people Allison told me to seek out: the bus drivers, the teachers, and some random students that she found somewhere, and I jotted down everything they had to say—nothing interesting, of course.

But the moment I started to type them out during the last class, my words stopped making sense. I remember thinking in that moment: *What's the* point? *Will anyone read this?* Then my words and sentences froze onscreen until nothing was coming out, and I was stuck trying to find a way to string them together into something remotely reasonable.

Meanwhile, everyone around me was zoned in, typing without pause, putting their stories into those "pyramids" or whatever that Rowan had taught us when we first started classes.

So I say that I "forgot" my article, and Rowan just sighs—

Did he just write Loser *on his pad?*

Honestly, I don't know where Allison gets her energy from. What does she eat? What did her parents *do* to her? She stands at the center of the desks, which are flush against each other in a perfect square. She's more like a lion at the zoo looking out at gawkers. Her hair is in a braid. I think of Katniss Everdeen.

She squints at me. Of course she knows that I lied, that I actually hate writing. Why isn't she saying anything? I squirm. I see her at school with Linh in the hallways. What if Linh talks about me or my family—and what stories has she heard? Maybe she and the rest of the Mais throw darts at pictures of us. That could explain why Allison looks like she's devising a way to meticulously murder me and stash my body.

"Fine. Since you don't have anything to write about, I'm putting you on proofreading duty. Do you have an *AP Stylebook*?"

I shake my head.

Smack. Allison tosses me a tome that lands on my desk.

Fingerprints smear the glossy front cover. "Thanks," I mumble. Awesome. All I've ever edited was our restaurant menu where the letter *s* mysteriously dropped from plural nouns. I just added them back in if I thought they looked weird.

Finally, Allison's focus shifts to another kid named Ernie, who smells like wintergreen gum even though he never chews gum. He fiddles with his round glasses that are down to his nose. Looking at him makes me feel anxious.

"Ernie, you're two days late with the article on the recycling scandal. Where is it?"

"Mr. Allen hasn't gotten back to me." From what I remember, Mr. Allen, the marine biology teacher, was caught putting trash into his recycling bin—by Allison herself. That's a "scandal," apparently.

Allison sighs. "Did you talk to him?"

"I e-mailed him."

"I want you to chase him, okay?"

"O-okay," he stutters.

"Wait for his class to let out. Show him that I have proof that he broke the rules."

"Hang on, Allison, you saved the contents of a *recycling bin*?" Rowan interjects.

She looks confused. "Yes, why?"

Is she for real?

Rowan starts laughing but he hides it behind a cough. "Good. A journalist always needs to back up their claims." He shakes his sleeve up to show his wristwatch. "Why don't we finish the meeting now and get right into it? Bảo, here's something for you to start proofreading. Try to finish it." He offers me a manila folder, which I get up and take.

Try?

Asshole.

We still have more than a half hour left and Rowan doesn't think I can get through a five-hundred-word article. Oblivious to the insult, he retreats into his office abutting the newsroom.

Allison pushes away a desk with her hip, creating an exit. She pulls aside Luigi, the managing editor, so she can come up with a way to fill what used to be the comics section. Apparently the comics artist showed up to one class, was given an assignment by Allison, and then switched over to graphic design class.

I dive into Allison's article about bullying issues and how our statistics compare to nationwide statistics. She knows how to write, knows when she's said enough, knows when to punch the details. She's good. She quotes Hal, the janitor who's one of the main advocates for stronger anti-bullying policies because he sees it happening all the time in the hallways, and Allison writes him so well that it's like he's right there in the room, leaning against his mop, a watchful eye on bullies.

I only fix a few commas and start a new paragraph when one of them looks too long. At the last sentence, though, I stop. I read the sentence over and over again and it just feels . . . weird to me. I can't put my finger on it, so I let my pen linger there, a red dot bleeding through the page. But still, it's one word. One word won't ruin a piece. And Allison's probably not going to like the fact that I'm questioning—even if it's a small bit—her article.

The hallway bell dismisses us, thankfully. Allison is yelling out the next deadline for articles. When she walks past me, I hand back her article.

"It's really good." Then I'm free, but not really, since I have work.

"Wait."

I turn.

"You're lying." She peers at the paper . . . at the red dot that I left. "You hesitated here. Why?"

It's unnerving to see a girl my age use the same withering glance as my mom.

"I don't know."

"What do you mean, you don't know?" she demands.

Now she's annoying me. I snatch the paper back and stab at the paper. "Maybe cut this word and replace it with an adjective. I just think you need a stronger one. Plus the word is repeated earlier in the article."

A long pause falls between us. I swear I hear the clock ticking. *Did I just say that?* "Thank you," Allison says. She looks like she's trying not to grimace.

I grab my things. My adrenaline's pumping, like I just finished a mile. I feel good—being right about something for once.

I'm the only one left in the room, so I leave ... before running into someone.

"Sorry!" a girl says.

Linh.

"Uh, no that's fine." My mouth feels numb. I can't find any other words to say because of the way she's looking at me, wide-eyed, indecisive—everything that I'm probably feeling right now.

I do the only thing I can think of:

I run away.

CHAPTER FOUR

LINH

"Hey, what are you doing here?" Ali asks as she leaves room 436 with her backpack. Strands of her hair have escaped her braid, but she hurriedly brushes them aside. I didn't expect to see her because I knew she had study hall; she should be home right now, which makes me jealous even thinking about it. I would have given anything to have a break before going to work. A time where I can just think and not be around people, like I am all day.

"Grabbing paint for Yamamoto," I tell Ali. When I'd gotten to the studio upstairs, she shouted from the back, asking me to drop by the old art room downstairs because she left behind a few things during the move.

Thinking everyone had emptied from the room by now, I walk through the door . . . until I collide with Bảo. His eyes widen.

"Sorry!"

Why do I sound like a squeaky first grader? He's a head taller than me, which shouldn't surprise me—puberty and all—but having always seen him across the street from the restaurant, I never noticed his height.

"Uh, no that's fine." He slips past me, then nearly bolts down the hallway, away from us. Away from me. Which shouldn't bother me so much, since I would probably do the same in his shoes, but it does. I glance at Allison to see if she noticed the weird exchange—she usually does with things like this—but surprisingly, she's watching Bảo, looking like she has something to say.

"I'm not sure I like that kid."

"Bảo?" I spot the canary-yellow paint by the sink and grab it while Allison talks at me.

"Yeah, him. On one hand, he's clearly lazy and doesn't give a shit about journalism. On the other hand, he found a mistake in my article that even *I* missed."

"Oh, wow, he found a *mistake*," I say mockingly. We walk down the hall together, toward the art room. With school letting out at the end of the day, it's chaotic. Elbows and shoulders crash against me, and the smells of Axe, sweat, and sweet Victoria's Secret perfume hit me all at once. Loud rap and pop music float from the earbuds of my classmates. Teachers fast-walk with their heads down and dodge students TikToking random sketches.

"I'm serious! It's been read, like, three times by Rowan. Bảo has a good eye. But I don't think he cares—or knows. Which is annoying."

"His parents own that restaurant across from me, you know." I've told Allison about the feud in general, how it doesn't really make sense and all that, but I've never really mentioned Bảo. Or our time at the temple together. Some things aren't worth mentioning; they sound and feel better as memories locked inside your brain.

"No way! He's *that* Nguyễn? No wonder you guys freaked out." I smile. I knew it; even if she didn't react in the moment, of course she'd catch that. "That's a tragedy. He's kind of cute. And he's taller than you, which is good."

Good? She doesn't explain why. "One minute you say you hate him—"

"Obviously you're not listening. I said I don't *know* if I like him. But I know how to appreciate someone's aesthetics."

"Aesthetics?"

"C'mon. That hair?"

Silently, I agree.

Yamamoto's room is a forest of easels, with white canvases of all sizes, their pictures all works-in-progress. This side of the school gets the best lighting, not only for drawing, but also for feeding the hanging plants by the windows. Yamamoto is closer to the back and sits cross-legged on a stool, yet manages to look completely relaxed. Her nose practically touching the canvas, she dabs whatever she's working on with a wet sponge. She has a streak of forest-green paint on her cheek.

A tattooed Asian wasn't a familiar concept growing up, so meeting someone like her was so cool. She's not posing, either; the tattoos fit her. She can say the word "bullshit" in a classroom without a problem.

"Here you go," I say, handing her the jug.

"Ah, perfect. Canary yellow, just what I need." She sets it down on the ground. "How's my old lair lookin'?"

"Weird to see all the computers there. And the room looks smaller."

"That's what I think too. You know, even though I complained a lot last semester, the move was actually a good thing. Look at all the space!" She opens her arms wide. I laugh because I love it when she smiles. Not that she's so serious in class, even if she has the authority to be. But when it's just us, she acts like an older sister—sans the weird, unnecessary biological facts Evie likes to point out.

She claps her hands together. "Okay. Give it here."

I let her see my homework assignment again. I ended up finishing it after work, at midnight. That's when I usually do my art—with a desk lamp as my only light source and bass-heavy electronica thrumming in my ears. It makes me feel peaceful and zoned in.

"So are you going to the exhibition?"

Left turn.

"Wait, what?"

She sets down my sketchpad and I follow the movement. Suddenly the conversation is turning to me.

"At the museum I mentioned. It'd be good for you. You should really go."

"Um, yeah. I think I will." I bite my lip at the lie.

"Your parents don't know, do they." A statement, not a question.

The flyer that I made floats back into my mind, September thirtieth haunting me. I sigh. "No. I still haven't asked my parents."

Yamamoto knows a bit about my family and what it's like to work at a restaurant, since she's lived some of it. Her mother owned a Japanese fusion restaurant for half of her childhood before retiring. But because her parents were also artists on the side, she can't truly relate to my dilemma.

I lean in on my elbows, listening as she continues with her critique. Yamamoto shares the same language as me. No one else in my life can teach me about light and shadow and how they fall on objects. Ba's unlikely to sit still long enough to watch shadows. He'd only think of it as wasting time. *Ba không có thì giờ!*" Which is actually his usual excuse for things he'd rather avoid doing, like fixing something broken at home or running errands for the restaurant. My mom *loves* that.

And the few times I've talked about art class with my mom, there's some words and feelings that I can't translate into Vietnamese. Like, orange is *màu cam*, but then there's also burnt orange and cider orange. Direct translations don't work.

My phone vibrates in my pocket, bursting the bubble ensconcing me and Yamamoto. "Ugh, sorry, I'm late for work."

"Okay, but wait." Yamamoto crosses the room to her desk and removes a packet from her drawer. "I know I've mentioned this before, but I wanted to make sure you don't forget about it."

The Scholastic Awards. Each year, high school students submit their best works in art and writing. There are local awards, then there are national ones called Gold Keys, judged by the best in the business, and the winner gets recognition at Carnegie Hall in New York, and even some scholarships.

"I'm telling you. Keep your eye on this. You have a chance."

"Really?"

Yamamoto smiles. "Absolutely. And, hey, maybe it'll help your parents see the value in what you're doing. They can't say no to money. But first step: Just make sure you check out the exhibition, okay? I know you have a lot of things riding on you, but I don't want you to forget about yourself. About what *you* want. This is *your* year."

"Yeah, sure." Dread sits at the bottom of my stomach, and her heavy gaze on my back pushes me through the door, out into the hallway.

CHAPTER FIVE

BẢO

"*Con ăn giống như mèo,*" Mẹ says. According to her, I'm eating like a cat right now. I look down at the meal before me: a nearly finished *bánh xèo* in a bowl, floating in *nước mắm*—my fifth serving in twenty minutes. Other times, Mẹ accuses me of eating too much like Ba.

Three hours ago, my parents were in the kitchen checking on their Powerball numbers, their concentration resembling scientists working toward a breakthrough cure. After each ticket failed to yield winning numbers, they placed it in a pile that goes into the "everything drawer" in their bedroom. *Everything*'s there: keys with no locks to fit them in; nail clippers; prescribed medicine for their high cholesterol (which they trade sometimes, and I'm pretty sure they're not supposed to do that); and pictures of me at various ages. Mẹ had glanced through the kitchen screen door. "Oh look, it's raining." She nodded to herself. "A good day to have *bánh xèo*."

"Ah," Ba said in agreement, before striking out another losing ticket.

And here we are.

Why does *bánh xèo* taste good when it rains? Every time I ask my parents they always start to explain— "*Tại vì . . .*"—and then something else grabs their attention. I've come up with my own explanation. I'm not sure there's a scientific reason, but I do know that *bánh xèo* tastes like a good fire when the outside pavement is wet, the air ripe with earth and cement. I found a word for that smell: "petrichor." In this kind of weather, nothing tastes better than rice flour, made yellow by turmeric powder, cooked crisp, packed with chewy pork belly, shrimp, bean sprouts, in one megabite.

Thinking that we need another batch, Mẹ disappears outside in her raincoat, fishing out another piece. She noisily slides the screen door open, returning with a giddy smile. A perfectly cooked *bánh xèo* sizzles on the plate. My body a half hour ago would have been like, *Oh* yes. She gestures for our bowls, filled with salty *nước mắm*, and lets those babies sink in.

Ba gestures for it, chewing on his piece, as if to say, *Lay it on me, woman.*

"How is school going? College applications?" Mẹ asks.

Nonexistent, my brain answers, but I say, "Good."

We'd done our road-tripping last year, visiting mostly state schools so that it's cheaper. My scores might be able to get me into some of them, though there aren't any guarantees. At least my parents know that.

"Just make sure your grades are steady and you don't go under."

"Sure."

Mẹ lets out another sigh.

"Con, do you have any idea what you want to do? What major yet?"

"Mẹ, that's, like, a year away."

"But isn't it better to know now?"

"Plenty of students go into college undecided. It's perfectly normal."

"Dì Nhi"—the General— "said her son knew right away that he wanted to do premed before going to Stanford."

"Premed's not a major, though."

"I know! But what I mean is, he knew what he wanted to do."

I shift when I realize I'm sitting exactly like my mom, one leg bent on the chair. I stretch out both legs and cross my arms. But then I notice that's how Ba sits.

"A year will come quickly," my mom continues.

"I'm thinking of a lot of things." Strangely, today's journalism class pops into my mind. The feeling of my grip around my pen, seeing the changes I made on the page, the moment I made Allison shut up for once. I haven't felt this way before.

"Thinking is not the same as doing!" She leans back and turns to Ba. "Anh, tell him."

"*Ừ*," he says in agreement. My mom stares at him reproachfully, probably hoping he'll say something more inspiring.

She gives a long-suffering sigh. "*Mẹ* wonder what Việt is planning to major in."

Given his attention to criminal TV shows and his near-obsession with getting into forensic science class, I'd figured that was his intention. But he hasn't really said anything, even though it shouldn't be an issue with him. The kid doesn't study and has probably never studied, because his pores just absorb all the knowledge on a page. "I don't know. Ask him next time you see him."

"Việt is so smart." My mom nods in approval.

"Brilliant," Ba agrees.

"His parents must be so proud."

Not for the first time, I wonder if my parents would be happier to have him as a son. Their eyes are practically glazed over at the mention of him.

Annoyed, I say, "Maybe you can adopt him, then."

"*Con*," my mother says, her voice turning sweet in a way that bugs me. Pleading, almost. "We just think you can do anything. And you have to *cố gắng*." She pauses to inhale.

Here we go.

"You know, con, when we die—"

"*Mẹ*—" I plead.

"When we die—"

"In, like, fifty years!"

Mẹ talks louder. "Ba Mẹ just want con to be able to support yourself. But that means trying." She gestures to her and Ba, who

40

nods like he's confirming, *Yes, I will die, son*. "Con don't know how lucky you are. When Mẹ arrived in this country back in 1982, Mẹ was three years younger than you. Only *mười bốn tuổi*! *Không biết* what was going to happen. But Mẹ learned. Mẹ adapted. Same with Ba. We trusted our education and we only want you to do the same."

I duck my head, eating the last bit of *bánh xèo*, and feeling like the biggest asshole. But low blow, using her escape story. I can't really say anything in response to that. How can I, when she mentioned everything she'd lost? Her home, plenty of relatives—including her older brother, who attempted escape before her, but died during the passage.

In rare moments, she would say that I look like him, like Cậu Cam. We have the same hair, she says. I can tell how much it hurts her to mention him because she either goes silent or quickly moves on to mention something else. I never know what to say when that happens.

Before my mom goes on to talk about her night of the escape— the last recitation having been one hour and forty minutes long—I relent with an "Okay. Okay. I promise I'll focus." I breathe in. "I'll do better."

Mẹ brightens and shares a look with Ba, her guilt trip a success. It's like I solved all her worries—past, present, and future. "You can be anything!"

"Maybe a doctor," my dad offers, finally edging a word in.

... with the most malpractice lawsuits, I finish as I carry my plates to the sink.

My mom starts clearing away the other dishes, and she's already on to the next task on her list, a nonstop machine. She asks me if I want to take anything to school tomorrow. *No? Why? It wasn't good enough?* I relent and tell her maybe a few pieces of *bánh xèo*, sans fish sauce. Turning to my dad, who's still digging away at his teeth with a *tăm*, she reminds him that they'll need to wake at five in the morning to receive Việt's parents' delivery, so the alarm needs to be set. Ba tells her to stop reminding him: *Bà nói điếc lỗ tai.* Which only means she'll continue to pester him to purposefully get on his nerves. Her type of revenge.

I leave them, the thoughts about my promise to them—*to do better*—running rampant in my mind.

CHAPTER SIX

LINH

One of my earliest memories of learning Vietnamese at home and at the temple with other kids has to do with a traditional folk poem. If I close my eyes, I'm back in that basement room, surrounded by our teacher's singsong voice, loud over the overhead ceiling fans fighting off a July heat: *Công cha như núi Thái Sơn / Nghĩa mẹ như nước trong nguồn chảy ra . . .*

I was more enthralled by the image that went with the folk poem: a towering, majestic mountain wrapped inside a delicate fog. Father. A pool of glistening water gushing from the same mountain. Mother. The next lines talked of honoring their labor and love; the lesson was clear enough: Everything I do is in their reflection.

Now alone in my bedroom, I lie flat on my back, staring at the ceiling fan turning at the slowest speed possible no matter how far right I turn the knob. I thought the room would feel more spacious since I wasn't sharing with Evie anymore, as I've done for sixteen years. That I can decorate however I want, make it however messy I want. But my body became used to another person in the room, and any desire to rearrange things is forgotten.

Anyone walking in would see two distinct personalities—one wall immaculately decorated with cute thrift-shop finds—Evie can sniff out discounts like no one else's business. My side, while it might be just as clean, holds years of my artwork, no rhyme or reason to the colors, from drawings showing my childhood obsession with goats and llamas, to my more recent work.

On my Picasso desk calendar, I marked the thirtieth but somehow didn't mark Phở Day. I trace it with my finger—it's not the end of the world if I don't go. I know that. But am I giving something up? Missing out?

I sit up quickly and my vision spins. Sometimes when I think too much, I make myself sadder, which doesn't help at all. I find refuge in art, escaping thoughts like this, to regain control when life throws another obstacle my way. When I work, magic happens; for a few hours at a time, the world just slips away. I don't have to listen to customers comparing me to Evie. Any worries about upcoming tests or working a shift at the restaurant—that all takes second place in my mind. My attention fixates on an image or an idea that doesn't exist just yet, and can't exist without me.

I first saw art in action when my family and I took a trip to

Huntington Beach. We were walking along the boardwalk; I was still young, because I remember holding my mom's hand when *it* happened. A small crowd had formed, a sketch artist ensconced inside, his canvas before him. His muse, a little boy, sat in a chair, feet dangling. The boy tried and failed to look serious as the artist captured his likeness on the canvas. He kept grinning at his parents. It was only five bucks for a portrait, yet the artist treated him like the most important being in the world.

I stayed there the entire time, counting the artist's deliberate strokes. My mom waited alongside me, half interested and half ready to move. We would have if only we hadn't reached the end of the boardwalk.

The artist's still there these days, though his hands look more shriveled and sun-spotted than they did over a decade ago.

I breathe out, letting go of my memories, replacing my thoughts with a nicer reality: *Maybe no one will show up and I won't need to work that night. Maybe my parents will be in such a good mood that they'll let me go.* Their moods are always good indicators of whether or not I can do anything. *This is your year*, Yamamoto's voice says in my head.

I'm choosing to believe that can be true.

Our home has only one floor, with a long hallway connected to each room. I pad lightly across the tiled floor to the opposite end, where Mẹ and Ba's room sits.

At the door, I hear only whispers. I'm seven again, eavesdropping on my parents like I used to with Evie. Evie would be right across from me, mouthing, *What are they saying?* because she was never the stealthy type, didn't have good hearing, and completely sucked at reading lips. Through the slit of the door, I see my father lying prone, shirt off. In the morning, he's usually half naked, baring his stomach, and wakes up before everyone else, then shuffles through each room, lifting up all the window blinds.

Mẹ stands next to the bed, a tube of Bengay in plastic-gloved hands. She scolds him in Vietnamese. I lean back against the wall, out of view.

"You should have let someone else carry it. You're not young anymore, Anh."

"Hmm? One of our cooks? They can barely lift anything. I'm the only one who lifts things back there."

"The only one," Mẹ repeats sarcastically. "Are you sure?"

Ba, ever the stubborn one, answers, "Yes." He hisses as she slathers Bengay on his back. She then tells him calmly that if he keeps complaining, she'll actually break his back. I hide a smile even if I don't have to. Ba stems his protests and Mẹ takes off her gloves. I hear her go into the bathroom, the creak of the mirror as she puts back the Bengay.

"Will we need to hire someone for the day?" Her voice echoes. "I can ask Duy-Loan's cousin to work."

He doesn't answer right away, as if he's waiting for her words to subside. "We have Linh."

He says my name like I'm the solution. A flash of anger courses through me. Why do I always have to be the solution?

"You know we can't afford more people," Ba continues. "I think it will be fine. I can still help."

Wait. What does he mean?

"If you say so."

They haven't told me about any financial problems. My stomach drops as I remember how anxious my mom looked yesterday, the hope in her voice that the special will work. Of course. But then I remember they wouldn't have told me something like this. They don't want me to worry about things that *they're* supposed to be worried about. Typical.

Later, sitting down for dinner at the kitchen table, I smell the Bengay, but Ba doesn't complain, only winces as he slowly sits down at the head of the table. I slide over our bowls, which Mẹ just filled with rice—mine full to the brim, while hers is half. She eats the side dishes more than the rice.

"*Mời Ba ăn cơm. Mời Mẹ ăn cơm,*" I say before we start eating.

We don't immediately talk, each of us lost in our thoughts. Our chopsticks ding the sides of our bowls. The waves of steam from the *canh chua* rise up, swirled away by the ceiling fan. It's one of my favorite dishes—sour soup, but not the kind sold in Asian restaurants. It's made sweet from pineapple chunks, and balanced out with simmering tomatoes and tamarind. Mẹ asks if I want more catfish. I shake my head.

I swallow a clump of rice and muster as much eagerness into my voice as I can. "Phở Day will be fun."

By Saturday, Ba's back problems are worse, and now he can barely move. Mẹ and I leave around noon to start prepping for the rush, but before we do, Mẹ reminds Ba not to do anything too strenuous.

Ba lies across the living room couch, TV remote in hand, which is his preferred state whenever he has time off, but he wants to work tonight. As much pain as he's in, he's still thinking about the restaurant.

Mom's having none of it.

He continues his protest in Vietnamese. "No, you need me tonight. Who's working the stand?"

"Lisa."

Ba snorts. "Lisa! She doesn't know how to do anything!" Lisa's been working for us for three weeks, a replacement for the outgoing seniors.

Mẹ answers, "Ba say that about her all the time. And Jonathan—"

"Everyone, basically," I mumble. "And you're the one who hired them."

Ba just glares. He lies back down, staring at the ceiling.

"But what if something goes wrong?"

My entire morning was spent alone in my room, preparing myself for tonight's rush. I was so tense that I couldn't concentrate, couldn't even sketch in my note pad or pick up a brush. Ba complaining throughout the house didn't help things.

Yet now, I hear the genuine worry in his voice, the worry that everything he had masterminded would undo itself.

Mẹ pats his head as she passes by, keys in hand. *Đừng lo.*

The simple truth is that he can't get up; all three of us know this. He falls silent. Or more accurately, Mẹ silences him by shutting out any response with the front door.

One thing that people forget when they're yelling at waiters or complaining about meal prices is the realities of how much prep goes into the menu. It's hours. I learned that the hard way when I was young, hanging out in the kitchen, waiting for Mẹ to be done because she said she was "only doing prep." *Only doing*. No. That meant watching the outside go from incandescent yellow to midnight blue with specks of white from the street lamps. But it was fun back then. I always had my crayons with me. The waiters and line cooks took their turns watching after me or cooking up something sweet—caramelized plantains sort of became my drug. Evie took it upon herself to refill all of the hoisin bottles.

Now in the kitchen, my mom has two large pots cooking on the stovetop, all containing the broth for tonight. Four small pots sit on the prep table, ready to be reheated once the orders come through. Mẹ strides with purpose in the kitchen while the other line cooks chop green onions, limes, and jalapeño peppers, and wash bean sprouts and Thai basil that makes the anise in the phở broth pop even more. It's all a rhythm; they follow the beat set by Mẹ because they've done this for forever. She's the most methodical in the kitchen, though whatever method she uses here can't be replicated or measured. It's instinctive. My art and her cooking are kind of the same, when I think about it. Our hands move before our brains. But I never say this out loud, because the retort would be: "But will it support you?"

"How's everyone on the outside?" she asks when she notices me watching by the door.

I double-knot my apron strings, then sweep my hair into a

high ponytail. "Good. Everything's in place." Servers are setting out the soup spoons, chopsticks, and sauces.

Mẹ wipes her forehead with the back of her gloved hands. "Good," she repeats. I wonder if she's trying to make herself feel better about tonight. Like I am.

The first wave of customers are young college students. Lisa greets them, clumsily grabbing the menus. I hope she can pull it together before the real challenge begins.

Within a half hour, our tables are booked and a line has formed, a sight that would make Ba giddy—as giddy as he can get, at least. Instead, my body pings with a sense of foreboding. As I move to table six with plates of egg rolls, a chatty group of three passes by, Jonathan leading the way. He mouths, *Help!* before plastering on a fake smile to the group, who seat themselves at table eight—which I'm sure is reserved.

I make a beeline toward the booth and sort through the table management system. I'm right. Lisa comes back from seating another group, playing with her hands. She does this when she's nervous. "Lisa, did you check the system just now?"

"Why?"

"Table eight. Someone had a reservation and we were going to seat them there."

Lisa glances down and blanches. "I'm *so* sorry, I didn't see it!"

I tamp down my instinct to shout, like Ba would. "Just find a way to fix it." I turn sharply and control my breathing. It's not my usual job to greet the guests, only serve them. Lisa will need to do it.

Passing by table four, I see a little kid, age six or seven, reach for a bottle of hoisin while his mother chats with a friend. I summon the Mai and Phạm women's stare—*Mày đang làm gì?*—and the kid retracts his hand. As he should.

The sound of pots and pans from the kitchen grates on my nerves, threatening to send a headache my way. But there's nothing I can do to stop it, so I hand in my orders, then circle back to the stand to make sure Lisa hasn't messed up again—I can't help it.

If possible, the line outside has gotten longer. More college students. Families. Couples. They stare back at me as I pop my head out, a sea of eyes reminding me of a surrealist painting.

"Uh, excuse me, miss," a guy wearing cargo shorts asks. He's third in line. "How long will it be until we're seated?"

"About a half hour."

"Half hour, whoa." He sends a look to his friend who stands behind him.

I tamp down my annoyance as best I can. "As you can see, it's quite busy now."

"This is ridiculous," he mutters to his friend.

"We apologize for the wait, but there's nothing more we can do."

"What's taking so long?"

The. Nerve.

"Hey! We're having a special! So of course there will be a line!" I snap. The guy reels back for a second, rendered speechless. He's too shocked to be angry. Before a mortified apology can slip past my lips, Lisa sidles up to my side, taking control of things. She shoots me a concerned look and says a few things that I can't

51

make out. The fact that Lisa needs to save me pisses me off even more.

I stalk back to the kitchen. Pine for the art exhibition. I pretend I'm there right now—me with other patrons. Whenever I'm at a museum, seeing the work of geniuses before me, I imagine a cloud of quiet reverence settling over me. In the room, there's a bunch of people looking to art for answers, who examine pieces just to *feel* something.

One day, I want to be that artist who sees this, who knows that what she created made them feel completely content, filling a void they didn't know they were seeking.

I want to be there . . .

. . . but I'm here. The ticket machine pushing out food orders at crank speed yanks me back into my reality. Its chirping will stay in my nightmares forever. From the dining room, Vietnamese, English, Spanish, and other languages and laughter swell up, crashing into me like a tsunami wave. The back room now feels like a sauna.

"Con?"

My mom pops her head out when she realizes no one's picked up the three bowls of phở she just placed at the window.

"I just need some air," I say.

"But—"

"Just one minute!" I say. Using my whole body, I push through the back door, my mom's question chasing after me.

I duck into the alley. I don't care that it smells like fish and sewage or that the ground might be dirty; it's the best sanctuary I can find in the moment. I slide down, bring my legs to my chest, and rest my forehead on my knees. *Breathe, Linh. Breathe.*

I'm not sure how long I sit there. At least I'm alone. At least no one's here to see me fall apart like Jenga pieces.

"Um, hey."

I peer down at the scuffed edges of red Converse.

Oh no.

CHAPTER SEVEN

BẢO

It's always hard to work when your best friend is summarizing a rerun episode of *Law & Order: SVU*. Even when we're not in the same area, Việt's shouting across the room.

"You always know it's the good-looking celebrity guy who's the perp." He uses the term like he's a well-seasoned cop.

"Uh-huh."

"I just wish that for *one* episode, the perp would be the ugly one. You know?"

"Yeah."

"I mean, the *moment* John Stamos came on screen, I was like— *hello*, it's him. The bad guy."

We're running through our checklist of things to do at closing at ten, only a few minutes away. Cold items in the fridge. Cutting boards washed down, then turned over. Each bottle of hoisin and sriracha sauce filled. Eduardo, one of the line cooks, fist-bumps me on his way out. He's usually the last one to go and first to show up every morning, on the dot. He sends me a rictus of pity, having been on the receiving end of Việt's recap before.

Việt has his quirks—his obsession with all the weirdest police procedural or forensic science shows and his near-perfect ability to quote the dialogue from them—but I can't imagine Việt without them. He's been in my life for that long. His parents and mine would get together at the restaurant—mostly after the shift ended, or when Việt's parents were done delivering supplies to various restaurants—to unwind or rant about other store owners in the area. Heineken would come in at some point. While the adults talked, we'd sit underneath the tables trading imaginary stories—playing cops and robbers—sharing toys with each other. Sometimes we didn't even need to talk.

I thought him joining the cross-country team in freshman year would be the end of Việt and Bảo. That he would find more coordinated friends who didn't wheeze after running a quarter of a mile. But I was still his best friend.

And as Việt launches into another recap, I think: *For better or for worse.*

The night passed easily, the two of us having already established a rhythm with the other servers. Mẹ had put a line cook's mom, Trần's, in charge of the kitchen so she didn't have to come in. It's different with the server situation, though. She's pairing me up with Việt because we know each other and make decent partners. She trusts Việt to do his job, as well as make sure I do mine. The concept's not perfect: We're the same age, and letting him watch over me makes as much sense as letting a horse and a pony run the show. But somehow it works.

Trần's mom leaves before us. I make sure the front is locked from the inside. As I'm closing the blinds, I see Linh's place is packed with customers at ten. Just for today, for that special, it's staying open for two more hours. A line wraps around the corner. Something that I'm sure our place has never seen before. I'm glad Mẹ is home tonight or else she'd come and just sit here and spy on people coming and going, scaring not only their customers but our own.

Việt joins me to peer through the blinds. "What people do for specials." He shakes his head. "We gotta one-up them, man."

"How?"

"Put something special on the menu."

"What else should we make?"

Việt shrugs. "Mom's always telling me your mom makes the best *bánh xèo*—why not work with that? Like an anything-you-want-in-your-crepe kind of deal. I mean, my mom has talked multiple times of poisoning her to get the recipe. Which could be effective, if you think about it, since your mom needs to taste a lot of things in the kitchen."

I glance over at my best friend. His mom's known for being hawk-eyed and competitive. She didn't get to be one of the most sought-after suppliers by doing any favors. But poison?

Việt backtracks. "But she won't—you know, poison her. It was a joke."

I can't ever imagine his mother—or his father—joking.

"That's appreciated," I reply dryly. I almost drop my blinds. Then a blur bursts from the back door.

Linh. She escapes into the alley. "What the hell?" The customers waiting in line watch her go before facing frontward again—shrugging or just shaking their heads. I glance back at Việt, who'd already gone back to the kitchen. He notices no one had thought to restock the fridge with beverages yet.

"That was probably Trần's fault," I say, still distracted.

That alley's one-way. Where could she possibly go? And why was she running?

"Of course," Việt scoffs, the sound distant, before reemerging with a carton of Arrowhead and kicking along another one half full of different sodas. He crouches down to start filling up the fridge's compartments. My attention alternates between him and the alley. "You gonna make me do all the work here?"

Linh's been out there for a while now. Three minutes?

I've never worked so fast. We recycle the leftover boxes, turn off the lights, then go outside to lock up. As Việt pulls down the doors over the storefront, I turn toward the alley, imagining Linh there, no one knowing where she'd gone. What made her run away?

An unnamable feeling washes over me—similar to when I was looking at Ali's article, knowing, *just knowing*, there was a piece that did not fit. I'd tried to pass it over without fixing it, until Ali confronted me, forcing it out of me.

This time, though, maybe I can fix what's wrong . . . whatever that is.

Right on the dot, I get the ten o'clock text from Ba—but really from Mẹ—asking if I was finally on my way home. My thumbs hover over the keypad, my vertical bar blinking slowly.

"Take the long route home," I tell Việt.

"Uh, why?"

"Because I'm going to need to buy some more time, and I don't want my mom wondering why I'm late getting home."

"Why are you going to be late?"

"I can't really say." Because even I don't know what I'm going to do.

Việt regards me in silence and I imagine that he gets the intensity of his stare from his mother. He's not going to do it. He's going to ask why and what I'm doing, and Linh's never going to get out of that alley.

"Tell her you stopped by my house to get a copy of a homework assignment. I'll cover for you."

I blink. "Really?"

"Yeah." He shrugs. I've never been more thankful for his laissez-faire attitude. "But you're gonna have to tell me later what's up."

With a small wave, he's off. I quickly type out my excuse to Ba, who answers with a simple "Okay." And I know it's really Ba, because his answers are always short and right to the point.

Just before I hit the opposite street, I think about turning around again. *What am I doing? Maybe this is a bad idea to come over here.* It feels like I've just walked past enemy lines and might step on a mine.

But now a few feet away from the alley, I hear her whispering, "Keep it together, Linh! It's not the end of the world." She's crouching, breathing deeply, forehead to her knees.

I clear my throat when I'm in front of her. "Um, hey. Are you okay?"

"Um, yeah." She sounds like she's about to cry. I shuffle my feet.

"I didn't mean to bother you. I'm Bảo, from across the street. I don't know if you remember me, but we met that one time—" I stop. It was ages ago; she wouldn't remember. I was just a blip in her childhood . . .

"I remember you," she says slowly, blinking a few times. The question of why I'm here sits heavy between us.

"Rough night?" I ask, my voice catching slightly. Why do I sound like that guy in about every romantic comedy? Next thing I'm going to ask is *Wanna talk about it*? "I mean, it seems like things are busy over here."

Linh sighs. "It's just hectic in there. My dad hurt his back, so we're short one person. I couldn't breathe for a moment, and totally just ran out on the customers." She adds, almost to herself, "I feel so useless right now." She sounds miserable. I don't have to know her to know that.

I crouch down to her level. Linh inches away instinctively, but she doesn't leave. I try to find the right words to help her, to make her feel better, but who am I to do that? I'm mostly a stranger to her. Before I can get a word out, Linh inhales deeply.

"Never mind." She furiously wipes away her tears. "I'll have to go back inside."

Back when we were kids at the temple, I could have gone to any other table, sat with any other kid. Instead, I ended up with her. I wonder if it wasn't just the crafts that drew me in, and if it was also her, Linh Mai, in the zone, in her natural habitat. So sure of herself, while other kids were only fooling around and passing time.

This isn't the Linh I remember.

I look at the alleyway door, imagining that it would lead us into a kitchen. I assume her mother is in the kitchen, cooking, delegating tasks to the other cooks—just like mine would. That's her domain and unless an issue manifests, she usually stays there during serving time. Linh's mom wouldn't have a reason to go up front. A plan starts to form in my head. An impossible one that I hesitate to even voice. "I can help?" I clear my throat. "I mean, I can help you. You know, with customers and stuff. Just for tonight."

"But your restaurant—"

"Closed a few minutes ago."

"I don't know if my mom—" She pauses, though I know what she's suggesting. "I just don't know."

"It's a win-win. I won't need to be trained," I try to joke.

She cracks a smile, but it disappears. "If my mom or my dad were hearing this, they'd think you're just trying to spy on us."

That type of thinking echoes what my mom would say. It's the same kind of gossip that's passed around by my mom, the General, and her Vietnamese watch group. The truth of it pierces the bubble enveloping us; the noise from inside the restaurant intrudes.

I'm instigating some sort of plan that Linh clearly doesn't want to take part in. I shouldn't have even come. Annoyance runs through me—at Linh for bringing up this confusing feud when I was only trying to help; at me for thoughtlessly running into this whole situation that had nothing to do with me—for reasons

60

I'm not capable of understanding right now. I should just go back, return to our separate stories as background characters in each other's small worlds.

"I'm not trying to spy. And I'm not my mom *or* my dad. I'm just . . . Bảo." I back away, shoving my hands in my pockets. "You know what, it's okay. Sorry for bothering you and for butting in. Good luck."

Tomorrow, when Việt asks where I'd gone, I'll make up a shitty excuse.

Tomorrow, everything will be back to normal, this encounter between us erased from our minds.

"Bảo, wait." I pivot at my name. "Are you really serious? About helping me?"

The despondence already clouding my mind eases just slightly. She still sounds distrustful, but there's a note in her voice pulling me back. I retrace my steps, standing in front of her just like before, and I offer my hand—my sweaty hand. "Tonight I'm Bảo Nguyễn, some guy just trying to help out on what's clearly a stressful night."

She stares at my hand, shaking her head slightly, realizing how ridiculous it is for me to do this in some alley. Still, her hand, showing traces of washed-out paint, accepts mine—and releases.

Linh wipes her hand on her jeans.

Great.

"What's the plan?" she asks.

"I can serve in the dining area. Your mom's probably cooking in the back, right? She won't even see me. And the waiters—" I stop. *Shit. I haven't thought of that.* At our restaurant, Bình and the others have suffered hours of my mom's rants—about them, about customers, and especially about the Mais. They've been indoctrinated. So it's likely that Linh's fellow servers have gone through the same thing. They *could* recognize me.

"We have new waiters," she adds quietly. "Which might work in our favor."

She looks away for a second. Then she pulls back her hair. I'm shocked by how long it is as she hurriedly ties it all up, not caring that some strands have escaped. As the moonlight hits her, as I see the tightness of her jaw set in determination, the fierceness in her eyes that makes me breathless for a second, I realize—

The Linh from the temple is here.

She draws back her shoulders, looking like she's ready for battle. Which I guess is accurate. "Okay, let's do this."

We're doing it. We're really doing this.

Please work out, I think, as I follow Linh inside.

The smell of phở is ubiquitous. If I close my eyes, I'm back inside my family's restaurant. We're in a narrow hallway where employees store their bags and jackets. To the right is the kitchen, bustling with the clang of pots and pans, water running, shouts from the line cooks. Linh gestures for me to crouch as we get to the serving window. A woman's voice calls her name.

Without warning, Linh shoves me back and I backpedal into the alley.

"Jesus," I mutter as I regain my footing. Is everyone stronger than me? I need to work out.

"*Dạ*, Mẹ! I'm good. Sorry, things were just . . ." The door cuts me off.

A pause. For one frightening moment, I imagine her mom emerging from the kitchen, kicking the door open—as my mom would do—and seeing me, recognizing me on sight.

Brandishing a pair of chopsticks.

I know what Vietnamese mothers are capable of doing with chopsticks. And my butt cheeks definitely remember '10 when I drank ginger ale for dessert without asking Mẹ and Ba first.

A few seconds later, Linh pulls me back in by the hand. "Sorry," she whispers. I nod numbly, my mind suddenly still, feeling her hand in mine again. She looks down, then snatches her hand away.

Trying to push past the awkwardness, I say, "I'm ready. Just tell me what needs to be done."

"Follow me. Act normal."

I crouch-walk past the window again. The moment I walk into the dining room, I regret every step that I'd taken to get here. Though the front-of-house staff might not recognize me as the enemy's son, they're going to notice a new guy miraculously starting on the job when they needed the help the most.

But I'm wrong. They're busy with their tables; one guy shoots past us, muttering that he'd forgotten the drinks. Linh brings me to the reservation system to teach me the layout. We use the same system, I realize, and my mind zones in, keyed to the language we've grown up with just a street apart from each other. It's not as hard as I thought it would be, the restaurant practically being a mirror of ours.

Unbidden, Linh's earlier insinuation and my mom's accusing

voice come through: *They spied on us to learn our ways!*

I shake away that thought. Not helping. Unlike our restaurant, though, whose walls and floors have seen better days, this one has a grand statement wall with mirrors and art that might have been done by Linh. I feel a flicker of jealousy before Linh pulls me back to reality.

"I'll stick around in the back of the room to keep an eye on the food coming out. Just look for me—if you don't see me, I'm at the window and will probably need to get dishes out. But if you hear the bell and I'm not there to grab whatever's ready, just come find me."

"Got it."

"Linh?"

I freeze, not turning for a second. A girl our age steps in front of the stand. She's wringing her hands, eyes beseeching Linh. "I'm so sorry about earlier. I should have remembered to check the reservation, but now everything's fine, I think."

"It's fine. Mistakes happen, but thanks for fixing it, Lisa," Linh answers quickly, already grabbing my arm, but the movement catches Lisa's eyes.

"Wait—have you been working this whole time?" Lisa asks, more curious than suspicious.

"Yes, I was ... prepping in the back." I glance at Linh, who gives me the barest of nods. "But her mom noticed things were getting hectic, so I'm just jumping in."

"Oh, thank God." The girl smiles like I just saved her life.

A customer steps up to ask for a table, allowing me and Linh to escape.

"Nice!" she whispers. I hold back a smile as she points me to table four by the statement wall, a couple looking to order dessert.

Working at a restaurant over the years, the customers themselves become a pattern, types with issues and demands you learn to manage. I always spot the let's-do-something-different-tonight crowd—the moms who think they're being adventurous by deviating from ladies' night at Olive Garden. They're always asking for our opinion: What's the crowd favorite? What do *you* suggest? What's the most *authentic*? Ignorance is the same no matter where you eat. When I do bother to give answers, they don't even take my suggestions.

There are assholes who come in as a party of eight and expect to be seated within five minutes; Vietnamese women dressed up way too fancy for this type of restaurant, like Bà An who comes on Tuesdays— *"Bà ngu,"* my mom spits out whenever she comes in— and people who didn't learn how to use chopsticks at a pliable age, but make a valiant effort, only to search helplessly for a server so they can flag down forks and spoons.

Then, there are customers who don't even need to order; they walk right in—or at least shuffle in—a tide of gray and salt-and-pepper heads, and my parents know immediately what they need. Most of the time, these people and my parents go way back, some even from the refugee days. It's all easier for us; they're the least fussy of the customers.

Tonight, I'm not spotting any here, maybe because they'd know to avoid this huge crowd.

If I have an order in there, Linh slides it down to me to grab. I'm an hour in and I swing to the back to get my next order. Linh's there,

65

elbows on the order table, speaking to someone in the window. She spots me and her eyes widen, which tells me to hide, and I step back into the eating area, out of view.

"… another order of *gỏi cuốn*?"

"Yeah, third order for the same table."

"Third!" Her mom sounds delighted. She addresses one of the cooks, joking, "What did we put in there? We're doing good, yes?"

"We're doing awesome, Mẹ!" Linh answers, catching my eye again.

She smiles briefly before bringing her order to the table.

In my section, I field questions about the menu, but that's no big deal since we sell similar food items. Customers ask me how many shakes we sell, and of course that's five—

Wait, the Mais have six?

"Excuse me, can I get another order of *chả giò*?"

"Sure, let me just—"

Oh shit.

"Frank," I breathe.

Frank's five years older than me. His mom used to work at the nail salon on the same strip as us and we'd suffered through hours of their lunchtime gossip by playing games on his Nintendo DS, which I'd never owned. But they'd moved somewhere else and I hadn't seen Frank in years.

We're at a standstill, lost for excuses as to why we're both in a competitor's restaurant. We start speaking over each other.

"I'm just helping out a friend—"

"Don't tell your mom I—"

'But it's no big—"

'I just wanted some *chả giò*!"

We blink at each other.

My shoulders relax when I see Frank looking sheepish. His group of friends watch the exchange, amused. 'Look, I know your mom would have my ass if she knew I was here. Well, first my mom would. And I'm not sure what *you're* doing here, but I won't tell if you won't."

In any other situation, I'd laugh at the idea that a grown-ass man is still terrified of getting in trouble with two Vietnamese mothers. But now's not the time. 'Deal," I say.

"Thank God. I've been craving these egg rolls. They're the best in the area—er, I mean, no offense to your mom."

Good decision.

Apparently Linh was watching us, and as soon as we pass each other, she leans in, a hand on my elbow. 'Everything okay?" This is the third time she's touching me, and I'm finding that I don't mind at all. I was lucky and partly thankful that my mom has the skills to intimidate people even if they don't live in the area anymore.

'I think so."

Time passes quickly. Customers have finished and left at a steady pace, allowing the line to grow shorter and shorter. The deal has probably given the place a profit. I remember my mom's snide comments about the Mais' phở, how it's all too bland, but from the smiles on the customers' faces as they leave, I'm sure that's not the case.

We have five tickets left at this point. The restaurant closes soon, at midnight, and my time here will end. Maybe we'll never see each other again after tonight. Maybe this will just be a fluke incident. But I don't think anyone can deny that we made a good team.

From across the room, over a sea of heads and laughter, I catch Linh's eye.

We got this.

I sneak out once the servers have said goodbye to the last customers. Linh gestures that she will follow in a few minutes. I wait by the alley while cleanup happens. The back door opens now and again as some of the bus boys dump the trash or empty boxes. They see me, but just nod indifferently, not caring that some weird guy is just waiting there in near-darkness.

Linh appears at the alley's opening having gone through the front. She's carrying her messenger bag. "My mom's just cleaning up a few things. You're safe."

Out by the curb, some feet to the right of the restaurant's facade, we wordlessly sit down. I watch her shoulders move as she breathes, until I realize I've timed my breathing with hers.

She speaks first. "Tonight was . . ."

She trails off, a smile playing on her lips. My brain has gone to mush. More strands have fallen out of her ponytail and I get the urge to move them out of her face, behind her ear. They shine, like the hair of a violin bow just polished.

My hand rises of its own accord. Linh freezes; her body stills, then my brain yells, *WHAT ARE YOU DOING?* And my hand goes off course and before I realize it . . .

I pat her shoulder.

CHAPTER EIGHT

LINH

Did he just pat my shoulder?

CHAPTER NINE

BẢO

"We were awesome today!" I say with more enthusiasm than I have in that moment. I look down at my knees, my face burning. And I'm pretty sure I'm sitting on gum. After not hearing anything for a few seconds, I risk a glance at Linh—and feel light-headed when I see her smiling. We lose it, our laughs echoing down the street, vibrating with the other late-night sounds. Ecstasy.

CHAPTER TEN

LINH

Okay, so that pat on the shoulder was weird, but I forget it soon enough.

"That was intense!"

Bảo laughs, a deep, husky kind of laugh—God, what a nice sound.

"I thought I was finished when your mom called you—"

"And Lisa came by—"

"Then that guy Frank who I did *not* expect to see there at all!"

We're like little kids full of sugar. Or like the kids we were back at temple. This time we didn't get caught. "Never thought that would work," I say after calming down. The smell of rain is faint in the air. Couples stroll past us, their shoes squeaking. Cars crawl by. "But we did an awesome job." I register the parts of us that are touching—our thighs and shoulders.

I'd shut down his offer before and watched him close up and turn his back on me. Waves of regret overcome me, not only because of what I said about him spying on us, but because I was ashamed that he was only trying to reach out to help and I denied him. He didn't have to check on me. He could have gone home just like every other week. But he didn't turn *his* back on *me*.

I sneak a look at him now. Bảo stares the opposite way, resting his forearms on his knees. He's, well, *hot*. He doesn't have a bowl cut anymore. There's quietness to him as well, reminding me of my mom when she's concentrating on a new recipe—the opposite of the energy around Ba or Ali. I shift, discomfited by these unexpected emotions warring inside me. We don't know each other. *We can't.*

"Thanks for tonight." I gesture toward the alley. "I'm not usually like that, you know. Freaking out."

"It's cool. I'd be like that if our restaurant was ever that busy."

"It wasn't just that." I exhale. "There's this exhibition I wanted to go to. I just found out about it recently, but then remembered it fell on the same day as this whole thing."

"Oh."

"Yeah." I'm rubbing my thumb against the bump on my middle finger—made callused after years of resting my pencil against it—not understanding why I want to explain everything to him in the moment, or if he wants to hear it. "I was going to ask my parents if I could have the night off. But my dad hurt his back, and like I said before, we're short-staffed."

"How do you feel now?"

I'd wanted to run far away. I'd wanted to be anywhere but in that restaurant. Then Bảo reached out to me, looking so solid, so earnest, and just one touch shocked me so much that I had to pull away. It seems silly to think about it now . . . but he was real! He was right there, and now right here.

"I'm okay," I answer honestly. "Now, at least."

Bảo nods. "That's good. I mean, tonight was challenging, and you survived it. And there will always be another exhibition." He pauses. "Was it some kind of avant-garde exhibition?"

"Avant-garde?" I say teasingly. "Wow, most people default to cubism. Picasso."

"Sorry, who?" Then he smiles and shrugs one shoulder. I forget what I'm thinking about for a breath. "I know nothing about art. I just thought 'avant-garde' sounded smart."

"You *almost* convinced me."

We smile at each other, not knowing what to say next, which I guess is expected. We haven't had enough time to work out a true rhythm in our conversation.

"Shit, I think I just saw your mom by the window." Bảo scrambles to his feet, brushes off his bottom. I remember now— this isn't supposed to happen. "I guess that's my cue to leave," he says, walking backward toward Lemare Street.

"I'll see you around?" I call out.

Did I just—?

He nearly trips over a raised part of the sidewalk and shoots me a sheepish smile that makes me woozy—even though I'm still sitting down. "Definitely! Let's not wait another six years, though."

And he's gone.

The door rings as it opens. Mẹ is behind me, locking the doors.

"Who was that?"

"Someone was just asking for directions."

Mẹ smiles. She looks younger than I've ever seen her.

Any other day, she would have pestered me about who I was talking to, but she's too elated. She lifts a bulging plastic bag. "I'm bringing home *chè Thái*. Three for all of us."

"Nice." I stand up and snuggle under her arm when she gestures for me.

She presses her nose against my cheek and squeezes me tight, like she used to when I was younger. She'd say she "just wanted to eat me up."

Today went well. I want to paint us just like this.

"C'mon," my mom says. "Let's see if Ba is still alive at home."

Ba forgets about his back pain the moment we unlock the door. The television shuts off. My mom dangles the bag of desserts before him like she's a baiting dog and he shoots her a mock expression of anger before taking it and undoing the knot. This isn't the first time we've had dessert at midnight. When me and Evie were younger—and probably still too young to stay home by ourselves—we would fall asleep on the couch, curled up against one another, waiting for them to finish at the restaurant. They'd bring us leftovers—always something sweet.

We're missing one person now, but we still move in unison toward the kitchen.

"Did it work?" Ba asks almost warily. Playing with his hesitation even more, my mom ignores him. She digs into the drawer for spoons, closing it with her right hip, grabs ice from the freezer, and crushes it in a ziplock bag with a pestle. She pours the ice into three cups, then spoons the *chè* over it: coconut milk, sweet, plump longan pieces, cubes of grass jelly that snap under your teeth, red-dyed tapioca pearls made from water chestnuts. It's one of my favorite summer desserts—and one of the best late-night desserts to have without feeling so guilty.

She's taking too long for Ba. *"Bà này,"* he says, and clicks his tongue with real annoyance. He just wants to hear about tonight.

Finally, Mẹ gives in. "It was perfect."

Ba accepts the spoon handed to him. Then he just nods. He tries to hide it, but I can tell by the way he's straightened his posture that he's glad to hear it. "Of course it worked. It's all because of me."

My mom smacks him on the shoulder. *"Ông quỷ,"* this wouldn't be possible if the food wasn't good, and that's because of me." She sends me a shining look. "Not to mention Linh, who took care of the front and the customers."

"Of course. This is Linh we're talking about."

I smile weakly. If they were able to read my thoughts, review all the events from tonight, they wouldn't be praising me. I wouldn't be able to explain how I didn't want to work tonight. How I wanted to give up. And of course I can't do that, shouldn't do it. It'll ruin just about everything.

75

CHAPTER ELEVEN

BẢO

"Infestation." The word is usually negative, referring to bugs or something else that causes illnesses, but it accurately describes how thoughts of Linh swarm my mind lately. Yesterday after school, as I was wiping down tables, my thoughts drifted to Linh and last week's encounter. Then, noticing I wasn't doing any work, Mẹ whacked me good on the head, propelling the image of Linh—hair tied up like that night and that damned smile—from me. Việt laughed, watching me recover. He knew what was distracting me because I'd already given him a recap in our forensic science class together, waiting for our teacher to get here.

"Linh Mai."

"Yes."

"You talked to Linh Mai."

"Yes."

"Linh—"

"Okay, you can stop saying her name like that."

"It's just hard to believe. You actually helped the enemy."

"Do *you* see her as an enemy?"

"Yes, but that's what I know your mom would want me to say." A slow smirk began to form on his face. "The question is: Do *you* see Linh as the enemy?"

"I never did," I answered quickly, almost marveling at the truth of it. Việt arched an eyebrow, which I'd never seen him do.

"I still can't believe you actually talked to her. I never thought that'd happen. I mean, way to go!" I was somewhat amazed and bolstered by his enthusiastic reaction . . . like he was cheering me on.

"You're strangely happy about this. Meanwhile, I'm dead if my mom ever finds out about this."

"I don't know. It's just . . . you're taking a risk. Going out of your comfort zone. And you don't usually do that."

All of this was true, but it was something I'd never heard coming from my best friend.

Now, I'm debating the possibility that my school schedule is conspiring to keep me and Linh separated. When I do "see" her, it's just the usual flash of her hair as she turns the corner. I can never seem to find her during passing time or lunchtime.

A nagging thought comes to mind: What if Linh's actually dodging me? Did something happen after I left her? Maybe her mother *did* see us and told her off. Maybe Linh agreed not to speak to me because of that. It's not hard to imagine what she's heard about me and my family over the years.

A few minutes before sixth period—journalism class—I reach into my locker to exchange books. Allison basically said she was "a bit" disappointed by the quality of our recent articles, so there's going to be a long lesson on how to write. Is Rowan ever going to step up and remind Allison that she's still a student? I mentally and emotionally prepare myself, when I sense someone next to me. I close my locker.

My day hasn't completely gone to shit. "Linh. Hey."

Linh leans her shoulder against the lockers. "Here." She hands me a carton of chocolate milk.

Her hair's down past her shoulders, longer than I remember, and she looks like the Linh post-Phở Day instead of the one I'd checked in on in that alley. My throat feels dry. "What's this for?"

"I didn't get to it at lunch but didn't want to throw it away. Consider it a small token for helping me out last week."

"You really know the way to a guy's heart." *Okay, Bảo, okay! That was smooth ... maybe?* We start walking. I try to remember if I'm actually going the right way. "How's it going?" That's the question I ask after a WEEK of thinking about her?

"Good, I'm glad it's almost over. I feel like it's been one assignment after another." Linh then grimaces. "APs especially."

"How many do you have?"

"Three."

My stomach clenches. Three? And she's still alive?

"Plus I have to work tonight."

"I do too. Maybe we'll see each other?" I say this as casually as possible, not wanting to seem like I'm suggesting anything other than, well, just seeing each other.

"Sure, maybe I can help out this time," she says conspiratorially, adding a smile. I'm feeling the effects of it—maybe it's because she's so much clearer under the lights—a nice faintness that I've only felt after waking from a long, good nap.

"There's no chance we can get away with that again," I say weakly, half as a joke, until it registers that isn't a joke. It's the truth. Things just worked out over at Linh's, but he can't ever expect that to repeat.

Some of the laughter leaves Linh's eyes, and we walk in quiet silence, our bodies remembering to feel unaccustomed to each other's company. That feeling, back when I thought she'd rejected my help, takes over again, until she says, so quietly that I might have imagined it:

"That's sad to think about . . . because we worked great together. Like we were meant to be partners."

Partners.

Yeah, it sounds right to me.

Eager to just keep talking until we can't anymore, I ask more about her classes. She asks if Allison is *still* attending our classes instead of using her study hall time to go home. She seems to talk about Allison with a teasing smile, so I don't tell her that I'm truly terrified of her in certain moments.

We make it to journalism class, where—no surprise—Allison

sits in Rowan's seat, next to her the biggest Blue Bottle cup of iced coffee I've ever seen. In a disorienting move, she smiles at Linh. She looks different when she does that.

"Hey, lady!" Her eyes fall to me, then flicker over to Linh. If possible, her lips widen. "Didn't think I'd see you two together."

Linh clears her throat. "Ali, I told you about how he helped me out last week? Right?"

"*Rightttt*. That was sweet of him. Well, good timing that you're here. Because I have an idea." *Ali* spins in her chair before rising like a villain who finally settled on a plan for world domination.

"Oh no," Linh says, earning a glance that is both withering and playful from Ali.

"So, in one of my classes, some girls were complaining that their boyfriends are taking them to all the wrong places. Boring vibe. Expensive, etcetera, etcetera. So what if we created a whole new beat for the newspaper? Assign a reporter to visit new places that any high school student can go to *and* actually afford, and tell the real deal about it."

"Will restaurants let us do that?" We're not exactly the *Los Angeles Times*. Who cares about what someone from La Quinta says about their establishment?

"I'm sure I can spin something," she tells me confidently. "It's basically free publicity for the restaurants."

"Okay, yeah, it's not a bad idea," Linh says. "Do you have someone in mind?"

"Good question." She points both fingers at me. "Bảo, I'd want you on this beat."

In what way does any of this sound good or helpful to the newspaper? Me who's been delegated to proofreading duties. Me who consistently gets Bs on his English Lit essays.

"Why me?"

"Because you're better than you think you are, as much as it pains me to say." Ali watches me closely; there's a gleam in her eyes telling me she likes that she can shock—and disturb—me with her compliments. "And Linh, you can help, too."

Her eyes shift to me. "Um . . ."

"Hear me out: Bảo puts words to the scene, rates the food, describes it. Since he grew up in restaurants like you and knows food, he should *hypothetically* be capable of doing this—"

"Hey!" I interject.

"—and you can sketch the environment. Or paint it. I've watched you sketch for years, Linh. You'd be perfect for this. The newspaper desperately needs your talent. It needs something entirely new." Her voice has taken on a tone I've never heard from Ali before—something more earnest. She's turning a bit softer, gifting me a glimpse of her normal self, and of their friendship.

Linh looks away, deep in thought. She said she was taking three APs just earlier, not to mention juggling after-school work at the restaurant. I'm brought back to last week, seeing her in that alley alone, looking overwhelmed, looking lost. Something inside had pulled me toward her then. I just knew I needed to see if she was all right.

That feeling rises again, and the words are out before I can stop them. "I'll do it."

The girls look at me—Ali, triumphantly and maybe even a little approvingly; Linh just confused.

I know there's a lot against me. It'll take away some of my weekends, most likely. But as long as my parents don't find out *who* I'm working with, this project might work. "And for what it's worth, Linh, I know you'd be awesome for this, too."

"I don't know if I can do this. It's not just the workload—it's the fact that I haven't done something like this, let alone had my work published in a newspaper. What if I just *think* I'm good and it turns out I'm not?" Her question comes out quietly, laced with uncertainty.

"Yeah, no," Ali counters immediately. "I don't think anyone could think that. I've seen what you've done ever since we were twelve."

"And the flyers. They're great!" I interject. "If anything, it's another chance to show just how good you are."

"Linh," Ali says. "You have two people here saying you can do this!"

"How—" She pauses. She's aiming that half-said question at me. I read her mind like that night. We're part of a long history; we might not be directly involved like our parents, but nothing can change the fact that our families and our restaurants are considered rivals.

So I keep my answer simple. "We can make it work." We have *worked* together and it turned out great. Because it wasn't anyone's family against someone. It was just me and Linh then. I want to believe that can happen again.

After a few beats, Linh looks away. "Let me think about it some more."

"That's not a no, so yay!" Ali claps her hands together and hugs her, then turns to do the same to me before remembering herself. Linh still appears unsure, maybe a bit exhausted in her thoughts, but she still musters a smile.

When we're alone, Linh says, "Ali only asks for help when she absolutely needs it. So you've earned some Ali points."

"That's good, because I was in the negative for a while."

Linh heads off to her art class. When the last of my classmates walks in, Ali closes the door, game face on. The lights dim abruptly, freaking some kids out, but it's only Rowan being complicit in whatever torture Allison has cooked up for today. Turns out I don't really care about that. Linh and I might get to be partners.

I open the chocolate milk carton and sip from it. *Partners.*

CHAPTER TWELVE

LINH

Of course, when I was walking with Bảo, I didn't mean to give the chocolate milk to him. I didn't finish it at lunch, felt guilty throwing it away—my parents' voices reprimanding me—so I carried it for my next class. Then I saw Bảo at his locker, and before I even knew it, my legs were carrying me across the hallway and suddenly: chocolate milk. If Ali saw that, she would've never let me live it down.

I dip my brush into a jar of water, washing it of cadmium yellow. Yamamoto's voice is on background as she talks to the class, weaving in between each student to check on their work.

Bảo has snuck his way into my brain for the last few days. I turn into a mess every time I see him, which is more than I can ever remember. There's a theory that we've talked about in my psychology class called red car syndrome, where you hear or see something once, like a red car, and suddenly you see red cars everywhere. I don't remember seeing Bảo so many times in the hallway—or maybe I've trained myself to see past him—but I've turned a corner several times before pivoting in the opposite direction. Just the other day at work, while my dad was passing along details on where to meet Quyền Thành, which happens to be today, I was sneaking looks at the window, hoping to catch sight of Bảo through his. My mom wondered aloud if I should dress up for the interview.

"Linh."

Could we really work together?

Had Ali planned to pair us the moment the idea came to mind, or was it after I told her about Bảo and Phở Day? I make a note to bring it up later.

"Linhhhh."

But the question is: *How are we ever going to do this?*

"Linh!"

Yamamoto is right by my ear. I yelp and my brush falls out of my hand and clatters on the floor. Classmates, now busy packing up, snicker. Yamamoto stands before me, arms akimbo, but while other teachers would be pissed off, she only appears amused, a stampede of questions probably in her mind.

"You know, I've seen you get lost inside your brain before, but never like this. I mean, you were *far* gone," she says teasingly.

Blushing, I hurriedly fold up my tarp and place my canvas on a tabletop by other day-old canvases. Just a bunch of fruits in baskets and flowers—beginning paint classes. I wash my brushes with an odorless thinner—I hate the citrus kind—before wiping them dry, then running them under water with some linseed soap. The usual next step is futile. I wash my hands until most of the paint has disappeared. I've stopped worrying about the rest on my fingers; it all eventually just fades. The bell rings and I push my way out into the hallway.

Inside my jeans pocket, my phone buzzes. I have a half hour until I have to meet with Quyền Thành, learn about the *fascinating* world of engineering.

"Hey, lady," my best friend says casually at my locker. But I know her better and read the gleam in her eyes. She wants to talk about Bảo. I don't think she'd ever been more excited than after hearing me tell her about Phở Day. "Wow, I didn't know he had it in him," Ali had said in mock surprise.

"How was art class?"

I roll my eyes at her. "Is that the question you really want to ask?"

"No, but I'm a journalist. I have to throw out questions to warm you up. But now that you mention it: What do you think? Are you going to work with Bảo?"

"Ali."

"C'mon, it'll be *fun*."

"Wouldn't use that word."

"What would you use?"

"Full of dread. Confused. Perplexed—"

"That's a synonym." She waits for me to switch out my textbooks, smoothly catching one that jumps out at her. She reads the title before shelving it. "Psychology—well, that's saying something."

"My question is: How the hell will this work? Our families hate each other. We know *nothing* about each other. I feel like I'm breaking several rules just by agreeing to this—"

She holds up two hands, telling me to slow down. "I already worked out the first question. I'll just find restaurants that are a little farther outside the radius of where your parents tend to go. Aren't you always telling me that your parents or people they know never eat out because your mom—"

"—says she can make anything at home." Evie and I used to beg our parents to take us to McDonalds for Happy Meals.

"Exactly." She signs the number two. "Second, I'm well aware of this feud. I don't get it, but I'm not supposed to. But it's your families who despise each other. What about you? For once, let's just remove the whole family situation—if it's just you and Bảo standing across from each other, would you say that you like him?"

"It'd be very easy to like him."

She smiles knowingly. After a few seconds of delay, my words catch up to me. My face warms up. "Seems like you already do like him." She pauses dramatically. "Maybe even more than that."

I close my mouth, reaching out to shut my locker door that dangled between us. The afternoon rush around us seems more muted than it usually is, the crowd flowing naturally around us.

Like him.

My phone buzzes again. Fifteen minutes until the meeting.

I don't have time for this right now.

Ali nods in agreement, like she's just read my mind. "Things like this don't really wait for you to catch up. Like the way you end up drawing something you never intended to draw. Just think about it: When you *like* an art piece, how much of it is thinking and how much of it is feeling?"

There are artists and fans interested in artwork on an intellectual level; they consider the message of the piece, the intention of the artist, the connotations of the time and place of its creation. Yamamoto's one of those artists, which makes all of her lessons interesting. But I'm different from that—in art that I like, in the pieces I create. It's always a memory or feeling that I start with. Ali knows this by now.

"You're using way too many art metaphors today."

"How else will I actually get through to you?" Ali nudges me by the shoulder and we walk outside together, heading to her car. She'd told me she would drop me off at a nearby Starbucks.

A jock runs by, jostling me as he tries catching up with his teammates off to practice. The buses full of students depart one by one, leaving little trails of smog. Everything's moving, but, somehow, inside me is still.

"Why don't you just feel things out?" she asks me finally as she unlocks her Nissan, and we slide into our seats. "There's so much in your life that you can't control, Linh, as much as I *totally* want things to be different for you. So maybe you can use this chance to do something for yourself. Forget everyone—your family, Bảo—this is about you. No rules but your own."

I buckle my seat belt. A reminder pops up on my phone: ten minutes until my coffee with Quyền. Without words I show it to Ali, who brushes the notice away, saying there's no reason to worry.

"I thought you didn't like Bảo," I finally say.

"I said that I didn't *know* if I liked him or disliked him. But he has an eye for words. I think he's better than he realizes." She makes a right but too widely, and she needs to adjust before straightening in the lane. "You know, I feel like I can write a whole human-interest piece about you, Bảo, and your families."

"I strongly disapprove."

"Can you imagine the headline?" To my horror, she releases her hands from the steering wheel, doing what I'll now call the Banner Move. "Two students from rival families and restaurants? Like *Romeo and Juliet*—"

A car honks at us and her hands snap back onto the wheel.

"Just drive."

As I walk into the restaurant after an exhausting half hour with Quyền Thành, I try to gather enough enthusiasm to convince my parents they didn't waste a favor on me. Even though they did.

Quyền Thành had shown up before me. She sat straight-backed, on a stool no less, her badge from the firm proudly pinned to her chest. She was on her laptop looking focused as she sent off e-mail after e-mail. She wore a gray business suit—which I won't mention to my mom because then she'll despair, "I knew it! You should have worn one to make an impression." While Quyền was petite and smaller than me, the strength of her handshake took me by surprise. Her eyes, framed by black thick-rimmed glasses, were strikingly clear and I felt that she was somehow scanning my body for answers.

I had questions that I looked up the night before, pulled off some college website about informational interviews. She had clear, precise, straightforward answers; I had to wonder if she was used to doing this type of favor.

She was a mechanical engineer but she was 'told that I liked art," and knew tons of friends who were 'Into that thing, but it's not really My Thing."

Our meeting was interspersed with inconvenient pauses, long sips of cold coffee, and me finding it hard to maintain eye contact because I was afraid she'd see the truth about how little interest I really had in engineering.

By the end of it, though, she smiled sympathetically. She even hugged me as I thanked her for her time.

'I know I bored you."

'No, I—"

'You're sort of easy to read."

I hate my face. But Quyền Thành just laughed. "Trust me: You're not the only one who's had to suffer through hearing about my work. As much as I love what I do, I know it's not for some people." She was being so nice that I wish I could have pretended to feel something. But as Ali mentioned, that's not the way I work—I either have to feel something . . .

Or I don't.

"Some advice. I don't think I'd enjoy this career as much as I do if it wasn't *mine*. And what I mean by that is it's something I can claim as my own. If my parents were forcing me to be a physicist, I would not be okay. So, do you have something that's *yours*?"

I don't nod or answer, still hesitant to prove how I've wasted her time. But maybe she saw something in me because she merely nodded, saying, "Good. Then protect it."

We parted and she promised not to say anything to her parents.

Back in the restaurant, my parents don't jump on me right away about the coffee interview. Instead, Mẹ is wrangling a box free from tape. Ba is sitting in a corner booth that my mom banished him to. While his back is better, he's still wearing his back brace and looks completely miserable, like a dog in his flea cone. I set down my backpack and slip into Mẹ's booth, inching closer for a look at what's inside the box. It's a flower vase, cerulean with specks the color of the jade bracelets she and just about every woman in my family wear. When I was younger, I thought it was something every Việt woman had to wear, some rite of passage.

"Whoa." It's handmade, that's for sure. "That's so cool. Where's it from?"

"Dì Vàng." Mẹ sighs. My aunt always seems to evoke that kind of sigh from my mom. She hands over the vase; I weigh it, feel the slight bumps alternating with smooth curves. I took a pottery class once in freshman year but couldn't control the speed of my spin, or get the clay into the shape that I wanted. But Dì Vàng does this

91

for a living, which is mind-boggling to think about, something I can only dream of.

She likes sending my mom things, and I know Mẹ likes them, as much as she doesn't approve of her sister's career choice, since she displays them everywhere: the mantel under the TV, the night-stand in my parents' bedroom. I have an elephant-shaped piggy bank that Dì Vàng made for my fifth birthday and hand-delivered when she was last in America.

Since the Vietnam War, and especially after the fall of Saigon, which was what forced our family to scatter, most of my extended family relocated to Washington, Louisiana, Florida, and Texas. It wasn't exactly cheap to fly over here, and the government has strict rules, so my aunt must have made the right friends to be able to visit for a little while. I imagined how cool it'd be for her to live per-manently nearby and how she could teach me more about her art.

I'd asked my mom why Dì Vàng didn't want to just move here.

Mẹ just waved her hand. Her usual gesture and non-answer. "I've tried to convince her, but she says she's happy there." Then my mom turned her attention to something seemingly more important, ignoring my question.

She and Ba tell childhood stories about Vietnam all the time, but they often conflict with each other: the good times, when Mẹ talks about running carefree along the beach with her friends, the sun rising behind them, or when Ba would play soccer with American soldiers stationed nearby. Then there are the dark days—funerals, saying goodbye to family members, losing everything on their way here. It's something I can't ever understand.

"Aren't you supposed to be working?" Ba says grumpily from his booth. Mẹ and I roll our eyes, then pack up the vase again ever so carefully. "Ah, your coffee meeting!" she suddenly remembers. "How was it? Isn't Quyền Thành so nice?"

"She was really nice. Really helpful." I pick at the flap of the box the vase came in. I wonder if she can pick up on the dullness in my voice.

Mẹ nods approvingly. "Perfect. It's all working out."

Just like Phở Day. Just like anything that doesn't make them worry too much.

As I'm tying up my hair, readying myself for my shift, Ali's words from earlier came back to me.

There's so much in your life that you can't control . . . So maybe you can use this chance to do something for yourself.

Something just for me.

I take out my phone and text Ali.

CHAPTER THIRTEEN

BẢO

I groan the moment I walk into work. My mom and her circle are planted in one of the side booths, cackling about something. The General's telling the story, her face pink with laughter. I'm sure this is *after* she brags about her son at Stanford and her *other* son at MIT, both of whom rarely come home.

"The meats they use are never fresh! One day I'm sure they'll poison their customers."

"You shouldn't say things like that," one of the women says while laughing, her voice nasal.

"But it's true. I swear. I'm surprised *that restaurant* is still standing."

Of course that's why they're laughing.

Biting back my disgust, I quickly walk to the back, though not before registering my mom's laugh, dimmed compared to the General's. I wonder—considering how much she talks shit about the restaurant to me and my dad—does she really want Linh's family gone that much? Does she truly want the other restaurant to fail so badly?

I nod absentmindedly at one of the line cooks, Trần, who goes into a series of coughs as he breaks down cardboard boxes. Eddie's prepping vegetables, his knife-chopping at warp-speed. A pile of onions takes over the prep table and newly washed aprons sit nearby for the taking.

Before, I would have let these thoughts slide; they were normal things to hear. Not now, though. I remember Linh, her near breakdown in the alley, the pleasure in her mother's voice as she heard how customers complimented her cooking.

Maybe there's good reason for the Mais to hate us.

"God save us," Việt groans as he enters the kitchen, backpack hanging off one shoulder. "Bà Nhi's voice gives me the worst headaches."

I smirk. I call her the General, but Việt calls her by the term usually reserved for older people. *Bà Nhi, bà quỷ.*

"At least she's going to leave soon."

"How would you know that?"

Việt swipes through his phone. "My mom says she heard from Tracy's cousin's uncle that Bà Nhi's planning to get a nose job. So she has an appointment." It takes a minute for me to connect

95

the dots. "The uncle at Star Nails." Still doesn't help, but if Việt's mom is the source, I'll believe her. She's judicious about the people around her.

Trần, still dealing with the boxes, coughs so hard that spit flies from his mouth.

"You okay, man?" I ask.

"Ugh, I've been so sick. But I can't miss out on work. Got some bills to pay."

My mom comes into the kitchen. *"Mày bệnh hả?"* she asks Trần. She doesn't wait for an answer. Despite the usually threatening-sounding *"mày,"* she steps closer and rests the back of her hand against his forehead. "Why are you working? You are burning up."

"But—"

"Go home. Sleep."

"I know but I kind of need the money and—"

"Go home. You will get the money." She pivots on her feet and heads to the stove where broth simmers in two pots. "Here, take some of this home. It'll be good for your throat. *Bệnh mà còn đi làm.*" She tsks. Then she calls him an idiot.

Again he tries to protest, but Mẹ steamrolls over him. She won't take no for an answer. Giving up, Trần thanks my mom as he backs out of the kitchen.

A few years ago, Trần's wife had had their first daughter, but she couldn't take off more work—her company didn't have maternity leave—so on certain days, Mẹ let them leave the baby in the room with air-conditioning. The other servers and I would rotate shifts, poking our head in. Ba had worn the baby monitor on his belt like it was some fashion accessory. But my mom mostly looked after her, cooed at her in a pitch I'd never heard from her.

I watch now as my mom gives Việt a to-do list for today, her voice sharp and leaving no room for arguments. This is the mom I see all the time. But she's also the type of person who'd give a sick man a container of broth, who'd babysit a kid at a busy restaurant.

My mom is still a kind person, even though she hangs around the General, and listens to jokes at the Mais' expense. She has to be.

It's 8:00 p.m. on the dot, and I'm finishing up to go home to do homework. My mom made a point to let me out early even though the shop closes at ten.

I spot Linh's door creeping open. *That's right. She also leaves at this time.* She's too busy stuffing something into her messenger bag to notice me at first. A week ago, I'd count the seconds until she was gone. Today, though . . .

Risk. Once I think about it, I've never really taken a risk. But I'm taking a risk today. Seized by an emotion I can't place, I'm out my own door in a split second.

"Hey, Linh!" I shout.

Alarmed, she looks up, then her expression melts into recognition. She says something, but a beat-up sedan decides to struggle through at the exact moment, dragging away her words. We smile when it's gone. I realize my parents also have a clear view of us enemies fraternizing with each other.

Getting the same idea, Linh gestures to a spot out of window

97

view. She's tied back her hair into two small buns, exposing her face so that when she's smiling at me, like now, her left dimple shows. My stomach does a dismount. I recover and smile back as best I can.

"So, there's this boba place that I love," Linh says, as if we're just continuing a conversation. "7 Leaves."

"Yeah!" *Hold back, Bảo.* I clear my throat. "I mean, I've gone there all the time."

"You wanna meet there? We need to figure out some sort of plan if we're going to work together."

"We are?"

"Yes. I've decided, why not have some fun?"

My heartbeat spikes in excitement. "Yes, a plan." Apparently I can only say monosyllabic words. "I mean, that sounds great. Copacetic."

I wince. *I just said that, didn't I?*

Luckily Linh laughs. "Meet you there in an hour? Just want to change. I smell like fish sauce."

That gives me an hour to get ready. I probably smell like fish sauce too.

I sniff myself.

Yep.

Once Linh disappears around the corner, I bolt in the opposite direction toward home.

I will be "studying with Việt." The normal translation is that we'd just play games at his house. But now that's changed. Việt texts me that I need to pay him each time I use him as my cover. When

I respond with a GIF of Stephen Colbert lifting a certain finger, Việt merely sends back a kiss emoji. But really, any activity that was Việt-related was okay in my parents' book and they barely acknowledged me as I flew out of the house, Mẹ occupied with a Korean drama because she's all about the drama. Ba waved me aside, more preoccupied by his bowl of warm, sugary *chè xôi nước*.

Linh is outside 7 Leaves, her hair free around her shoulders, dressed in jeans and a white tee.

I never thought walking to the cashier would cause an internal freak-out, but it did. I order milk tea while Linh orders a strawberry. *Do I pay? I should pay, right?* The counter person, some twentysomething bored-as-hell guy glances between Linh and me, looking like he pities us. Awkward teenagers, he must be thinking. Then he sighs out loud. Definitely thinking about us. Just to relieve us from his gaze, I pull out my wallet and the cashier nods almost approvingly, like, *Good on you, bud.*

"You didn't have to do that."

"Consider it payment for the chocolate milk the other day."

We get our drinks and sit down at a table sandwiched between two others: one table with a couple, Chinese from my guess, who act all lovey-dovey with each other, and another table with a grandpa sleeping on a stool—impressive—wearing a fishing hat, a black vest over a plaid long-sleeve shirt, and beige cargo shorts. A fisherman who doesn't fish. The cashier says something, but the grandpa has zero reaction. Probably the owner or the owner's father.

The upside of meeting here is that it's easy to see who's here and who's not. Especially if anyone is a part of Mẹ and the General's group.

The seat beneath me is chilly. My stomach gets jittery the moment we sit down together. The quiet in the room, the hum of the fridge, accent our proximity. Our ankles touch, and all of my body—I mean, *all* of it—wakes up.

Linh's taking out a notebook and pen; she's serious about coming up with a plan, and maybe that's the only reason she suggested meeting here. To get something off her checklist. I try to tell myself I'd be okay if all we talked about was the new beat.

Only thing is, I'd be lying.

"I'm nervous."

I glance over at her, but she has her eyes to the table, her fingers playing with the edge of her notebook.

Maybe I should have played it off, thinking about how guys are *supposed* to be cool and charming—like the male leads of so many films: Chris Pine, Will Smith, Henry Golding. In reality I'm more of a Randall Park character. "Me too. I keep thinking someone we know will pop up and see us, and word will get around."

"Like spies wearing sunglasses."

Instantly, the image of my mom popping out from behind the serving counter, in sunglasses and some funny hat, nearly makes me choke on my drink. "I think we're safe."

Linh cups her drink. "Part of me chose this place for that reason." We smile sympathetically at each other. "But if you're having second thoughts, you don't have to do this. Ali can be pushy sometimes, but I can let her know this isn't your thing."

"This could be my *thing*," I joke. "It might even be my favorite thing out of all the things I like."

Linh catches on. "Careful or Ali might volunteer you for other *things*."

I pretend to shudder. "Don't tell her." The tension lets up and I want it to stay that way, so I rush through. "Look, I would honestly not be here if I didn't want to be. But it's sounding like you might be second-guessing all this."

This time, she raises her chin, like she's accepting a challenge. "I'm not. Not anymore." She fiddles with her straw. "Why are *you* here?"

"Because I've been thinking that it's ridiculous we grew up across from each other and never truly met. Because the night we worked together proved that you aren't like what I've been told. Well, at least what I've heard about your family."

"What have you heard about us?"

I hesitate to answer. It might cut this meeting short. "You really want to know?"

Linh nods.

"Gang members."

"*What?* That's what my parents have said about *you*!"

I try to picture my parents as gang members—my mom might actually be a believable leader—but I keep that to myself. "They also said . . . that you drove out Bác Xuân from his place." Linh's mouth drops open at that. She looks truly offended, and I wish I could take it back. "I mean, that's what I've *heard*. I'm not saying I believe it."

"We would never! He was a family friend. I was there the

101

moment he told my parents that he wanted to retire. That he wanted to spend more time with his grandchildren! Did your mom say that to you?" My face must have given me away. "Honestly, your mom can be brutal."

I bristle. It's never a good feeling to hear someone you know get called out. "You think she's brutal? Haven't you met Nhi Trưng? She's the real leader. *She*'s the worst."

Something we can agree on. A part of me is relieved the attention's off my mom; I'm not sure I want to hear more about what may have been said against us.

"Oh, we know about her," Linh says. "She wanted the restaurant so badly that she wanted to drive us out to get it. I'm sure she's still trying."

I shrug helplessly. I have nothing to use as a counterargument, because it's true.

"Sorry," I manage, worried that I've ruined things before we could even start working together. In my mind, this newspaper project is like an old rickety bridge above a roaring waterfall. One false move and we'll tumble over.

"I'm not mad at you. It's just—" She has a faraway look in her eyes. "I wonder what else we've been told that turns out to have been a simple rumor that grew into something else."

I lean forward. Careful. "We can agree that our parents are both protective of the businesses and maybe that's why they're like this. I know my parents have spent everything on the restaurant. I can't tell you how many times they've worked through nights just to make ends meet."

Linh grimaces. "I know. Nights when they probably left us alone more often than they should have."

"And when we were too young to stay home by ourselves."

"It's one of the best-kept secrets in this community."

The bridge is stable again.

"What was it like for you, growing up in a restaurant?" I ask. "All of my childhood memories seem to have taken place there."

Linh's eyes light up. "Let me guess: It's where you've watched all segments of *Paris by Night*? Played lava across the tiles?"

"Yes! Getting side-eyed by the regular customers whenever I took over a whole booth."

"Did you have a nap room, too?"

"You mean the place where we stored our bags of rice?"

It was really like parallel lives. The storage room, with all the rice and nonperishable foods, was where I napped as a kid, and as weird as it was, it still brought me comfort whenever I walked in to grab something. I remember it now—the hot summers when I wasn't yet in school, sleeping on a small cot while my parents were working in the kitchen. A pink fan near the end of its life jaggedly blowing cool air at me. A tiny dictionary that my parents kept there just in case they needed to look up words from the customers—I'd look through it when I was bored being out in the main room. A small stool for Mẹ to sit on when she fed me lunch, which happened after naptime.

"I guess to answer your question about growing up in the business: It hasn't been completely bad. I mean, sometimes I'd rather be drawing instead of working, but"—Linh shrugs— "It's such a

103

part of my life that I can't separate myself from it . . . as much as I try to."

Underneath Linh's writing notebook, I spot a sketchbook— white with a bunch of doodles on it: her artwork. Ignoring her questioning look, I take it from under her arm, examining the drawing, which is similar in style to her family restaurant's flyer, only this time it's of a couple strolling down a brightly lit boulevard in some city. It feels like I'm there with the couple.

"Nice. It's cool. Looks like New York." I slide the sketchbook back at her.

"I've never been. It's just something I pulled from Google images." She mumbles the last part, as if she's embarrassed.

"Do you want to go to New York?"

"I don't know, really. I feel like that's what real artists are supposed to do, and I can see why. It's probably cool to see all the skyscrapers, stand in Times Square, just seeing all sorts of different people and cultures. But I can't even think about that yet. I first have to figure out a way to tell my parents that I don't want to do engineering."

I make a face. Engineering. It seems too boring for Linh. Where would her colors go?

"So your parents are the typical Asian parents."

She nods almost morosely.

"I think you should be an artist."

A short laugh escapes her and some tension leaves her face. "Okay, sure, that solves *everything*."

"You're really serious about art. Even when I met you that day. You did some damage to that paper with your crayons."

104

"You were the kid with the bowl cut and weird Spider-Man obsession," she recalls, the corners of her eyes crinkling. She's smiling.

I raise my hands in defense. "Don't tell me you weren't obsessed with *something* when you were younger. Mine just happened to be Spider-Man. You apparently had something against art supplies. Poor crayons."

"It was a pointillist drawing!"

There's a look that people get when they're excited—a spark, I guess, in their eyes. I see it when Việt's face lights up, talking about the latest *SVU* episode. In Mẹ when she's cooking *bánh xèo*. In Ba whenever good food is involved. Even Allison's focused gleam as we're in the newsroom comes to mind. Here, with Linh, she has that sort of light behind her eyes. Makes me want to know what that's like.

"Can you tell me about it? Your art—like, what it's like when you're working on something?"

Linh sits back, chewing on a boba. "It's like I go away from my body for a second. It's not an out-of-body experience, exactly. Like, I'm not hovering over my body or anything like that. But I guess I'm zoned in. And nothing can distract me. Whenever I'm working on a piece, my mom always complains that I don't hear her when it's time for dinner."

Then the gleam kind of disappears and she has a faraway look in her eyes. She shakes her head, coming back, not telling me where she went, even though I think I know. Her parents probably popped into her mind. "What about you? What do you like? Are your parents bugging you to do something you don't want to do?"

"I'm basically a failure and they'd be happy if I just found *something* to do." *Let's get right to the truth of it.*

"Oh, c'mon."

"No, really, I'm nothing compared to Linh Mai of the Oh Mai Mai family."

"Be serious."

I shift in my seat. She thinks I'm kidding, but how do I tell her I'm not? "I'm not good at anything. I'm not sure I will ever be."

"There must be something. Cooking?"

"There's a reason why I'm not allowed to stay long in the kitchen."

"Singing?"

"Sure, I can sing a song now, but I wouldn't want to traumatize you."

"Sports?" At my look, Linh stifles a laugh. "Well, who cares if you're *good* at anything? What do you *love*? What can't you live without?"

I shrug and sip my boba loudly. Nothing's coming up. "I'm not bothered by mediocrity."

"You can't be serious."

"Mediocrity has allowed me to float by without too much pressure or judgment. Being mediocre at school is great. No one bothers you! No one even looks at you."

"You're lying. You *so* care," Linh says it matter-of-factly. Her aim is perfect.

"How can you know that?"

"Your voice went up a pitch." That's a very Việt-like observation.

"My voice—"

Linh takes a dainty sip of her tea but humor lights up her eyes. Her very *nice* eyes—I'm getting distracted. "Yup."

I remember the other night at dinner, when my parents believed in me, maybe too much. I haven't done anything so far to give them that much confidence in me. Nothing to make me look good to their customers who always seem to brag about their freakishly talented kids.

So I give in to Linh. Scratching the back of my neck, I admit, "Okay, fine. I'll try to explain. I look at my parents. I know what they've done to get here. It's never been easy. And lately I think I've been failing them. I haven't done completely great in school. And I'm not breaking any records at sports like my friend Việt."

"Cross-country runner?"

That's a shocker. "Yeah, that's him. You follow sports?"

Linh explains after grimacing, "You haven't been forced to listen to Ali reread newspaper articles to you."

"I would rather run a cross-country race," I deadpan. "Anyway, I'm feeling the pressure more than usual. It's our last year and I guess ..." I breathe out. *How should I say this?* "I feel like I've ignored all the chances around me, and now I don't have much to go on."

"That's not true!" Linh says forcefully, leaning forward. "Ali and I were talking earlier—"

"Hold on, you were talking about me?"

Not gonna lie: My self-esteem shoots up.

"She was deciding whether or not she hates you." She laughs.

107

And my self-esteem plummets. 'I'm just joking. She mentioned how you had a good eye for words. Which makes sense, because, you know, not a lot of guys out there say 'copacetic.'"

She tries to mimic my lower voice, and we both know she fails, so we burst out laughing, so loud that we wake the grandpa slumbering in the corner. He glares, then leans his head back again.

'Maybe you just need to find something worth writing about. Something that you're interested in … Maybe this"—Linh gestures not to us but to the idea of what we've agreed to do— 'Is your chance to stand out." The future. What a dampener it can be.

Linh reads the look on my face right away, because she laughs and drops questions about the future.

We finished with our drinks, and the grandpa is actually still awake, now staring at us through suspicious eyes. The place is closing soon. *Okay, I get the hint.* I lift my cup with the remaining boba and ask Linh, 'So how much should I pay you for this life coaching?"

Linh gives me *that* smile.

'Free bobas would work just fine."

CHAPTER FOURTEEN

LINH

Once outside, the silence is comforting and warm, like a good bowl of wonton soup on a rainy day. I feel Bảo's heat beside me, my hand a whisper away from his. During the summer, with tourists flooding in, this part of the neighborhood gets packed with squatting old Vietnamese women, dressed in countryside outfits. It's not as heavy as Bolsa Avenue traffic, especially when the night market's up, but it's still a tourist trap. You're likely to get bullied into buying jackfruit in Styrofoam trays, rambutan or longan, or—if the woman's a *really good* seller—durian. Sometimes I wonder if they ever sell all of their items, and when that doesn't happen, where they go.

The sight of Bảo passing under a lamplight stops me. It's as if he's just stepped into a Caravaggio painting. The light throws off shadows, darkening half of his body. The lines of his face seem sharper.

"What?" Bảo brushes his hand through his hair. "Do I have something on my face?"

"Nothing. The lighting. It was just perfect for a second."

"You notice things like that?"

I shrug, embarrassed that I was caught staring this time.

Bảo hops on a nearby cinder block wall, walking down the length before jumping down, back at my side again. "Remember that bowl of phở? How bad it was? It's probably from—"

"Phở Bác Hồ. My parents hated that place."

"Same." At least our parents seem to agree on one thing—a universal distaste for anything that refers to Hồ Chí Minh in name. Reminds them too much of the war. The owners made some poor excuse when they opened—saying they were referring to an elderly relative. But you have to be so ignorant to open something like that here. It closed not long after me and Bảo met.

"But I never got to see you draw Spider-Man, did I?"

"Because of our parents."

Something passes in his eyes that makes me shiver. "Did you ever think about what it would have been like if our restaurants weren't competing against each other?"

It's a loaded question to wrap up our time together, but I answer as honestly as I can.

"I think I thought about the idea of you, if that makes sense. But this is different. I finally get a chance to know you—and you seem nice."

"Don't worry, the nice-guy act disappears once we meet for the fourth time."

"Great. I was really sensing asshole vibes back there."

It feels like an hour before we finally get to Ward Street, where our paths diverge. This is what I'll remember: his bashful wave and the shadows swallowing him up as he heads home.

When I'm inside the house, only Ba is up. Back problems, most likely. I can smell the Bengay emanating from him again. He sits in the dark living room, TV on, but with the cable off. The static from the screen lights up his sleeping face, a hypnotizing pattern.

"Oh, *con về rồi*?" he asks groggily, stating the obvious. "How was studying?"

"*Dạ*. It went well." The lie leaves me a bit too easily, though I feel the weight of it in my stomach. But it has to be done. I take off my shoes, then make my way to my bedroom. "The test will be easy. Now go to sleep."

"Ah." I'll give him two more hours before he drags himself to bed and wakes up early to start his routine again.

My mom's knock wakes me up the next morning. My mouth's parched, and the light almost hurts my eyes. I remember that I didn't drink any water after drinking boba. Is it possible to be hungover from too much boba?

I hear Mẹ lightly pad across my room. Her shampoo—Head & Shoulders, which she shares with Ba—tickles my nose. The bed sags just a bit when she sits by me, patting my side. This was how she'd wake me and Evie up before heading off to a long day at the restaurant.

"Con, dậy đi. Chín giờ rồi," she whispers, her voice as smooth as the glide of a brushstroke across a well-primed canvas.

I twist my head to the right and check the actual time: eight o'clock, instead of an hour later like she just said.

"Five more minutes."

"Mẹ just made *bánh paté sô*. Just hot out of the oven. It's only good when it's eaten hot."

I breathe in hints of her promise. Buttery puff pastry. Tender, flavorful chicken at the center. And then my ultimate favorite: earthy Vietnamese coffee just waiting to be paired off with sweetened condensed milk.

Okay, I'm up.

Mẹ knows she has me. I hear a smile in her voice. "See you soon."

Once in the kitchen, I see that it's not just pastry or coffee that she's made. She must be experimenting with recipes. Several pots are cooking on the stove, and on the outside patio, there are two larger pots, which tells me whatever she's cooking there might stink up the house. Various herbs are soaking in tubs of water. At last five bottles and jars of *gia vị* are opened on the kitchen table. Ever-methodical in the restaurant kitchen, she's the complete opposite in our own kitchen.

Still, I love mornings like this.

The pastry is waiting just for me. I sink my teeth into it, flakes falling into my lap. Mẹ has me taste the coffee and milk level, then pours ice over it. As Mẹ busies herself around the kitchen, I

FaceTime Evie, who complains that while other parents have sent their kids care packages, Mẹ and Ba haven't.

"Care package, what is that?" Mẹ asks—or shouts, as the blender breaks down some spices. Evie quickly explains the concept, to which Mẹ says that Vietnamese food, the good kind, can't ever be mailed.

Meanwhile my hands are getting tired holding the phone so they can see each other.

"What about *bánh tai heo*? I'm craving it." My sister loves eating pig ears. Not real pig ears, but sugary biscuits that are shaped like them.

"Okay, if you want, I will make them."

"Don't do it if you're too busy." She points out that Mẹ shouldn't be cooking on her day off. "Weekends are for fun. For people to do a hobby or something."

"Yeah, like gardening," I say.

"No way. Every time Mẹ tries to grow something, she kills it."

"Something is wrong with our soil," Mẹ protests lightly as she grabs something from the drawer.

Evie and I exchange knowing looks. Makes me feel like she's not hours away. In our small backyard, there's a graveyard of plants Mẹ tried to grow: tomatoes, cucumbers, peppers. The only thing that has survived are herbs, though it's only a small selection.

"Sure, Mẹ. Sure."

Evie says she's going on a run next and would text later. Once she's gone, Mẹ asks me worriedly, "Does she sound happy? Does she look thinner to you? Maybe she doesn't have enough to eat."

When we moved Evie into the dorms, we had more food than anything else for her. Luckily her roommate is Filipino, so she and her parents merely congratulated my parents on their preparedness. Then Ba told them to stop by our restaurant if they were ever in the area. That was when Evie decided it was time to say goodbye.

"Mẹ, she's fine. She seems really happy. Don't worry."

"Mà Mẹ là Mẹ. Mẹ phải lo."

I get up from the table, finished with breakfast. I hug my mom from behind. "Yeah, but Evie's got this. She can take care of herself. You know how she is." At that, Mẹ only sighs deeply, and my body mimics the movement.

"Do you miss her?" she asks me.

"Sometimes." And that's the truth of it. I thought it'd be much weirder to go home to a half-empty bedroom. But over the past few weeks, I've gotten used to it. I think of my aunt and the packages she sends Mẹ. I look at her longingly staring out the window over the sink, the light showing that Mẹ seems to have a few more gray hairs than I remember. "Do you miss Dì Vàng?"

"Sometimes," she says quietly. She doesn't elaborate, and I'm wondering if she's going into one of her moods.

I let go and ask if I can help with anything.

"No, there's too much to do. I should do it myself. Why don't you do your homework and if you have finished, go to your *hobby*," Mẹ says, trying to mimic the way Evie says it, but she ends up sounding nasally.

I bite my tongue, feeling like that's how my parents will always see painting for me.

It's just a suggestion, she probably thinks nothing of it, but the easy dismissal of my hobby makes the taste of *pate so* linger uncomfortably on my tongue.

"You really should find something else to do, Mẹ. You work too much."

"And work is good. Work makes money." As she opens the blender to peer at its contents, she says, "I haven't had a hobby since I was a teenager. Your age."

"What did you like to do?"

A wistful look passes through her eyes. "Travel. When I wasn't at school or helping out around the house, I'd go around Nha Trang to places I'd never been. I would travel to Saigon and Đà Lạt. Oh, Đà Lạt was so beautiful! So romantic!" She laughs. "And when we escaped, my first wish was that we'd land somewhere in Europe."

"Have you traveled since?"

"No, no. Where was the money? *Đời sống đã rất là khó.* I had to work in factories, the nail salon, wherever I could get work. School wasn't a priority since we needed money. Traveling was a foolish idea. An impossible idea." She shakes her head.

"That is why I'm happy to see Evie find her way. She will live a life that's not *khó*. Unlike I had. Unlike your aunt." Her tone shifts to one of disapproval. "And soon enough you will have a good life too."

A good life. A good life only comes if you have security—that's what my mom's basically saying. Anything beyond that is just a pipe dream.

CHAPTER FIFTEEN

BẢO

My phone buzzes as a text comes in. I lift my head from the pillow, my bleary eyes searching for my alarm clock, which tells me the time is eight thirty. Who's texting me *now*? Despite having the uncanny ability to wake up early—probably drilled in by his parents, who took him on morning delivery routes all his life—Việt's never the one to text first; he only responds to them, three days too late. The only other person who texts me consistently is Mẹ, through Ba, and if she wanted me to actually wake up, she wouldn't be this discreet.

Nothing is more efficient at waking you from a dead sleep—while also drawing out an involuntary, undignified high-pitched scream—than a Vietnamese mother bursting through the door without warning.

I grapple for my phone and squint down at my screen.

hey! it's linh. i got your number from ali.

Linh. Last night's events trickle through my hazy mind. Boba. Our walk. Partners.

I sit up immediately.

sorry to bother you so early.

Should I tell her I don't recall ever giving Ali my phone number—and part of me is perplexed at how she managed that? Another time.

no worries! i'm up anyway.

The bubbles appear. An exclamation point! **are you an early riser, too?**

yeah—I start typing, then change my mind. Why would I want to lie about that? **only when my mom's threatening my life.**

she doesn't knock either?

I grin, leaning against the headboard.

very unfamiliar with the concept . . . are you usually up this early on weekends?

sometimes it's the only chance for me to draw.

wow, that's commitment.

anyways, just wanted to let you know our lovely boss—I laugh at this—**has given us our first restaurant. they responded right away when ali emailed some places. kami, it's a japanese**

**restaurant in santa ana. i could do next weekend. i'm not work-
ing. you?**

I grow more awake with each word. We're doing this! We're
making plans, together!

totally. My thumb hovers over my next sentence. **can't wait!**

Bubbles appear. Those damn bubbles.

Now I can go back to sleep.

It's nearing ten when I finally wake up again. Strangely my mom
hasn't barreled in to scream at me. When I go down still in my
sweats and T-shirt, I see my parents sitting at the table, like they've
convened for a meeting. They're already dressed.

"You're not working?" I ask, fighting past a big yawn.

"We're going in the afternoon. But we thought we'd eat out
today."

We never eat out. Which can only mean: We're going on a spying mission.

I don't remember when it started, but this isn't the first time
we've gone to a competing restaurant to see if it's really any competition to ours. Only my parents would do this. Really. Because
they're weird and obsessed, and they like to bring me into their odd
hobbies. And maybe, in an odd way, it's their attempt to compro-
mise. I'd always wanted to eat out: McDonald's. KFC. Red Robin.
When I begged and begged, my mom's reply was always the same.
That it was a waste of money and—

"I can make that. And I can make it even better!"

So far, my parents have managed not to bicker over the GPS and we haven't gotten lost yet. That tells me Ba probably did advance research.

"Anh, slow down," my mom says. She's in the passenger seat, death-gripping the handlebar just over her head.

I look at the meter. Forty-five miles per hour.

"How'd you hear about the place?" I ask my parents, resigned to my fate.

"One of our customers mentioned it in passing," Mẹ says. "But don't worry: That customer is loyal to us."

Oh, I was so worried.

We pull into the parking lot of a plaza. The restaurant's surrounded by upscale jewelry stores and "elite" nail salons, and that confirms—at least to me—that the restaurant won't be legit. It's all too … new. Too shiny. Where are the errant shopping bags rolling along with the breeze? Discarded rinds from clementines or lychees?

This is what happens when we step inside "photastic." Purposely all lowercase.

"*Trời Đất,*" my mom mutters first. Usually it's an "Oh my god," but in this case it means, *What shit is this?*

Everything in the restaurant is white: the walls, the tiles, the tables, and chairs.

Even the host is white, wearing a T-shirt printed with a poorly drawn BÁNH MÌ.

Where's the shrine? What kind of Vietnamese restaurant doesn't have a shrine? Where's the red? And yellow? Fake flowers? The floor that's seen better days?

119

'Chao, Bac!' says the host, missing the tones completely. He has the audacity to bow. "Table for three?"

Dumbstruck, my parents nod. Even though the waiter's annoying me, I almost laugh at my parents being speechless for once.

Not for long, at least.

"A white waiter?" Mẹ hisses after we get our menus. We sit in the center at a round table that Ba moves around to see if it's lopsided. It's not, which, to me, makes this place even more inauthentic. "Speaking horrible Vietnamese, too."

"We can always turn around," I say.

"No," Ba says firmly and calmly, pushing a menu to me and Mẹ. "This is competition."

"Barely!" my mom protests.

He overrides her. "Let's see why that customer is talking to you about this place."

We fall silent when the waiter—John, because of course—returns again. He asks if we're ready to order and Ba *actually* pulls out a list of menu items and reads them off.

See: research.

When the confusion dawns on John's face, my stomach drops.

"I'm sorry, sir. Can you repeat that?" John looks to me, like I'm expected to translate for Ba. I look away from him, wanting to prolong his misery. We get this a lot when we go out to non-Vietnamese places—and maybe this is why we don't go out often. Obviously, my dad's accent gives him away. He wasn't born here like me. But even though I understand him perfectly, sometimes he gets nervous—but doesn't want to say so—and he speaks quickly. When I was a kid—bowl-cut me, let's just say—it was embarrassing. Maybe it was the look others gave him, or the visible discomfort in my parents.

Now I'm just annoyed by people like John.

Ba clears his throat, sits up straighter in his seat. "Coffee. For the three of us." He slows his words as he relays the rest.

"Oh, yes, sorry." The red in the waiter's ears—now he's embarrassed—fades while he jots down the order.

The time waiting for our food consists of my mom and dad's airing their complaints against the place. Seems like we're the only Vietnamese family here. The lights are too bright. They gave us "organic" *cà phe sữa đá* that was already served in a glass with ice. Real Vietnamese restaurants make the customers do their own work. The only concession is good-looking waiters—one, as my mom points out, resembles a K-pop star.

Then the food comes. Turns out, even a kid who didn't grow up in a restaurant could tell this wasn't any legit Vietnamese restaurant. General atmosphere aside, the kitchen was only doing a poor imitation of the Việt food I recognize. The *cơm chiên* doesn't have Chinese sausage—what kind of fried rice dish is this? Other crimes include oversalting the phở and not crisping up the fish enough.

"*Dở ẹc!*" my mother says, a look of disgust on her face as she sorts through the mushy fish. She'd already removed the bones and they slid off suspiciously cleanly. If it were really done well, the bones would refuse to come off, and you'd have no choice but to use a hand and chopstick pair to remove them.

"No doubt, this restaurant will close within a few months," Ba finally says, pushing away his unfinished plate. I repeat: unfinished.

Linh's text about our first assignment comes to mind. I ask my parents if I could duck out of my shift early next week. And then the interrogation happens.

"Why?"

"I have a newspaper assignment."

"Newspaper? When?"

"Just this year. I'm writing food reviews."

"You?" my parents ask, simultaneously stunned and incredulous.

"Yes," I answer exasperatedly. "It's something I started doing."

"You are writing about food?" Ba asks for confirmation.

"He does eat like Ba," Mẹ mutters, still staring at me. "But why?"

Because Linh's going to do it too. Not the best answer to give. "Because it's something to do. I thought you'd be more excited that I'm doing, you know, something." Using my chopsticks, I stuff a bite of white rice in my mouth, trying to act casual. Too *ngảo*. Mushy.

"Writing ... You never said you liked it," my mom says.

"Just because I never talked about it doesn't mean I didn't like it."

"You did like reading dictionaries as a kid," Ba concedes. Turning to my mom, his tone shifts to a joking one. "Maybe he's seeing his girlfriend."

Mẹ catches on, her preoccupation flying away. "Ha! Like that would happen."

"Funny, guys. Funny. Girls like me!" I decide to play along. "There's at least one girl in each class who likes me. Kelly Tran. Fiona Su. Cindy Jackson." The idea of these girls liking me sends my parents laughing. Even I'm joining in. Me and Kelly, the girl who despises me for avoiding VSA duties like the plague?

Later, I won't be able to explain why I said what I said next. Maybe it's a slip of the tongue, or because it's a notion even more ridiculous than Kelly, Fiona, or Cindy having a crush on me. Right after Cindy, Linh's name slips through my lips.

A dark expression crosses my mom's face, like clouds engulfing the sun. "Linh Mai?"

There's a dangerous tone in her question, and I immediately retreat. "Just kidding. I've never talked to her in my life."

"Good."

"I mean, she's, like, really weird. Like, really, *really* weird. No one likes her at school," I say. "And she smells!"

Acting: not my career path. My parents continue glaring at me stonily, the playful mood from before gone. "Seriously, I'm not seeing anyone. I really am on assignment for the newspaper."

This causes my mother to lean back, shoulders relaxing.

A different waiter has come back—mixed, Vietnamese and white, maybe. Her grin falters when she notices my mom's fury.

"Can I get you anything else, *cô*?"

My mom softens her expression, musters a smile. Maybe she's consoled in seeing another Vietnamese person in the room. "Yes, we're ready." She cracks open the menu again. "Let's try the dessert."

◇ ◇ ◇

All the guys here have perfect hair.

That's my first observation as I walk into the restaurant that Ali had assigned us. The host disarms me with his bright smile as he greets me in Japanese. Average height, he's still made tiny by the large wooden desk that he stands behind. The divider's just low enough to let me see the waiters walking around, their polished hair—many of them with the hair of a Silicon Valley guy post-startup phase. Many immaculate man-buns, which the host also has. I'd look ridiculous if I tried wearing my hair like that.

Linh hasn't arrived yet, and in various hand gestures, I let the host know that I'll wait for a few seconds. Looking up: stalactites—thin wooden structures jutting down from the ceiling, painted to mimic the top parts of northern Japanese hemlocks. Somewhere in my research about this place, I remember seeing that the chef is from Kyushu, specifically Fukuoka. Maybe this art was inspired by his home. I sneak my notepad from my back jeans pocket—Ali forced it on me, saying it'd make me look more "legit."

I turn to the mirrors functioning as walls. Strands of hair still stick out no matter how much gel I use. I'm so preoccupied that I don't notice Linh sneaking up on me.

She arches an eyebrow. "Everything okay?"

"Um . . . hair," I manage to articulate.

Her mouth moves like she's fighting words back. Or a smile. "It looks fine."

We let the host know that we're from La Quinta, and as Ali promised, the restaurant was expecting us. Ken, the host, leads us past the dividers. While the waiting room transports you to a different height, the main dining room brings you back to the ground, literally. The floor takes on the cool colors of a modern city; the walls, the outlines of high-rise buildings, adorned and labeled with the sleekness of kanji. Japanese pop music brings an intimate, personal vibe that calms me immediately. It reminds me of seeing out the last customers for the day, of the feeling right before I throw myself into bed.

The other diners are mostly Asian—a good sign—and aged young. We don't recognize anyone, which makes sense since it's a city away. We get seated, and I sneak a look at Linh smiling and nodding at the waitress who swooped in. Linh asks about the artwork, sparking life into the waitress's eyes. Maybe she's an artist, too. I take down parts of the conversation: her uncle's the chef and yes, he wanted the restaurant decor to be an homage to his home island.

"We were just fixated on the idea that art can say so much about family history."

"I totally understand! I'm working on something similar."

I make a note to ask about that. When the waitress leaves, though, we're alone, forced to look at each other, and suddenly my ability to speak has retreated somewhere else. Our time at the boba shop might as well have been a dream. I resist the urge to straighten the bottle of soy sauce between us, just to do *something*.

"You've been taking notes already?" Linh nods at the notepad next to me. "I brought mine, too."

From her small backpack, she pulls out her sketchbook that I saw in the boba shop. I watch her hands, faint paint still on her fingers. A trademark. Linh notices, glancing down, and tries to hide it. 'Sorry, I was trying to fit in some painting time before and probably should have washed it off better."

'No, it's all good. It's very ... you. You know, being an artist and all that." I see the same expression from before, like she doesn't quite know how to read me, so I rush to add, 'Anyway, yeah, I only took a few notes so far. I had to Google how to write a food review. That's the level of confidence I have right now."

Linh laughs, sitting back. 'Here's a tip. I've learned in reading art reviews that the best reviews aren't just about the art or whether it's good or not. It's also how other patrons will react to it. What meaning the art piece might have to others."

'Good to know."

'You won't have any issue at all on the food part, though. I mean, we grew up in the business. We know good food, don't we?"

Her words summon into memory our first meeting—the first time we reviewed something together in a way. I crack a smile, relaxing a bit more. We take a few minutes with the menu before ordering a tempura assortment, shrimp and vegetable, to share, then ordering ramen—*tonkatsu* ramen for me and spicy miso ramen for Linh.

'So," Linh says, stitching together her fingers and leaning forward. 'What kind of place is perfect for a date? Maybe it'd help to think about that as you review it."

Of course, to contribute to my under-qualifications—add the fact that I've never been on a date, either. Unless you count one lunch with a girl at Burger King during a sixth-grade field trip.

Which I tell Linh, and she just laughs. She'd probably gone on more dates than me. Most of my classmates probably have, too. So it shocks me when she says, "I've never been on a date either. So I guess we're even."

"That's comforting." I pick up my pencil, tapping it against my notebook. "Dates have to be somewhere you can actually get to know someone. Like us right now." I wish I could take the words back. *Does she think that* I *think this is a date?*

But Linh doesn't seem to notice, adding, "The noise level has to be just right so that it's an actual conversation. Like, if someone is speaking quietly, you should still be able to hear that person."

"Dimly lit atmosphere with a noise level that's perfect for conversations and whispers," I say aloud as I write.

I feel like she means it. We go back and forth with other requirements of a "perfect date": a nice seating or standing arrangement; an activity that both people like and could talk about later. The waitress drops by with our appetizer, then disappears again.

"Ultimately, I think both people on the date need to be comfortable, as if you could literally share everything and anything. Which is why the setting matters," Linh says.

Our waitress shows up again with a bowl, her fellow waiter tagging along with another bowl. I make a note about the short waiting time. I start salivating the moment the aroma wafts from my ramen—intense and smoky. It doesn't disappoint. The first spoonful of broth coats my tongue in a silky layer, and the noodles are still firm yet give way easily under my teeth. The egg is sweet and salty, soaked in umami.

"Remind me to thank Ali," Linh says into her spoon. "It's not like most other ramen, which goes overboard with the salt."

"Good ramen doesn't feel like you're drowning in a bowl of salt," I pretend to write. "You want to trade for a second?"

We exchange bowls, keeping our utensils. Linh pauses and blows on her broth. *"Ăn đi, con,"* I say, mimicking countless cousins or aunts at family gatherings who are almost always chasing an impossible toddler to feed.

Linh's now midbite but she laughs, then covers her mouth. "Don't! You just made me spit!"

"On a date, it's important not to sit across from anyone who spits," I add to my invisible list.

Linh telepathically lets me know to shut up. Her ramen is pleasantly spicy, the texture of the broth similar to mine, the kind that sits comfortably on the tongue, doesn't attack you.

My earlier nervousness is completely gone now as we alternate the time eating, describing our food, and complaining about school and balancing working at the restaurants. She talks about how her parents set her up with an engineering student they know so she can ask questions. Which is a good idea—and I hope my parents don't think of it. I'm fine with limiting the times I disappoint someone.

Linh takes pictures of her ramen, and she starts with her sketch of the restaurant, outlining the most prominent parts: the walls, tables, and chairs. "For size comparison." Her pencil seems to float above the page instead of touching it and she falls silent now, locked in her world. A world I'm finally getting a look at.

Watching Linh's thoughts play across her face is … interesting. I remember how she looked that night, distress rippling across her face, the indecision as her eyes flitted between me and the restaurant.

For years, my parents' issues with her family were a separate, weird thing that I'd accepted, one of their many oddities—like their near-worship of lottery numbers, their insistence with each wrong number that they were *just* about to give that number. Or Mẹ's tendency to use me or my dad to get a double-tasting of samples at the supermarket.

"How can your parents *not* want you to be an artist?"

I don't mean to disrupt her, but it pulls her out of her head.

"I guess it doesn't feel stable to them. My parents aren't really about making tons of money. It's about making just enough to sustain themselves. They didn't have that when they came over, so they wanted it for me."

"They escaped too?"

"They escaped," she confirms. "By boat."

I spoon some of my remaining broth, watching the surface ripple. All my life, I thought it was normal that my mom and dad had left by sea. They'd known each other growing up and left in the same boat owned by the second cousin of a mutual friend. Their connection to this boat owner might have been loose, but they were past caring. Trustworthiness during this time was a messy ideal anyway. They just had to leave. But after hearing conversations from my mom's friends, conversations with other Việt kids at school, families came another way: through sponsorship, through marriage.

But I feel like it does say something about the type of people my parents are—Linh's parents, too—to put trust in the unknowable sea, in the people who navigated the boats to the ultimate destination. Survivors.

'So you don't tell your parents about wanting to be an artist because they don't see it as a viable career.'

Linh nods. 'That's why I have to keep it a secret. Some secrets are good. They can be helpful.'

'Still, it's hard to keep a secret.'

'*You're* keeping a secret. You haven't exactly told your parents that you're working with me on this newspaper assignment.'

It's not the same thing, but I can't figure out how to say it.

'Me and my art—I'm not really lying. I'm downplaying it,' Linh continues. She fiddles with the end of a chopstick, not looking at me now. Somehow I feel as if I've stepped over an invisible line. 'Okay, I guess it's hiding. But it's necessary!' She directs the last line at me, suddenly insistent. 'First of all, you're a guy, so you probably get away with a lot of things.'

I open my mouth to argue, but I remember a cousin at a gathering complaining that her brother had a later curfew because he was a guy. 'Okay, I see that.'

'But my parents are pretty much insistent that I do *anything* but be an artist. To do this, I have to lie. There's no other way, really,' Linh says, defensiveness seeping in at the edges. 'I'm not usually a liar.'

'I'm not calling you a—I'm just saying.'

It's my fault things went a little sour. Linh's now avoiding

130

further conversation by zoning in on her sketchbook. "It's fine."

Later, our goodbye is less hopeful than our last one the night we had boba.

This isn't a date, so why does it feel like I messed everything up?

CHAPTER SIXTEEN

LINH

It's not that I didn't know I was liar. But to hear someone else agree with that? It's piercing. Especially coming from Bảo, because as much as I dislike the label, I know he's right. Lying to maintain stability. Lying to make sure my parents aren't worrying about me or nagging me because they already have to do that as parents. In a way, isn't this saving my parents from grief? He's doing it, too. That's the only reason why we're able to do this whole food beat.

But it's never going to stop if you go on like this, says a voice unusually like Bảo's.

I yell in frustration, glad to have the house to myself for an hour. My parents are still at the restaurant. My sketch from earlier tonight is beside me, nearly done. I just have to add more depth perception. I run my hand across its rough texture.

Bảo can't know the pressure. From what I can tell, his parents aren't forcing him to be something—they just want him to find his path, which he said he couldn't see, but observing him tonight, writing seems to come naturally to him.

I force down the sudden spike of jealousy; his parents are clearly different from mine.

It felt normal in the beginning. If other people were looking in, we probably seemed like two high school students on a real date. When I'm with Ali, I can talk about a lot of things, but she can't understand being raised the way me and Evie were. We grew up differently.

I smile at the memory of watching him try to tame his hair. He didn't know I was there. I can't be sure, but I feel as if his hair is the type to grow faster than it should. I like it long, better than his bowl cut—for obvious reasons. It's the kind of hair that'd be easy to run through with your hands.

My hand. I glance down.

In my reverie, I was starting to outline the shape of his head. I rub at the image, smudging the lines.

But of course I botched the conversation. I panicked when he pressed me about lying. The moment he mentioned lying, I denied it, but I was denying the truth. I shouldn't have shut down. I wouldn't be surprised if Bảo told Ali the next day that he can't work the beat anymore.

It'd be another lie to say that that wouldn't hurt me.

"How was dinner with Ali?"

Flipping over my sketchbook, even though there's nothing to give me away, I look up. Right: my excuse. Mẹ had come back from work at some point. I hear Ba over in their room, opening and closing drawers, getting ready for bed.

"Good. We ate ramen."

Mẹ makes a face. She's not a huge fan, claiming it's too salty for her taste. As she comes over, I shove the sketchbook under my pillow.

"Mẹ missed a call from Dì Vàng. Let's see why she called." Mẹ sits on my bed, and scoots back so that she's against the wall like me.

After a few rings on Viber, my aunt appears onscreen in all of her familiar late-morning, *I was sculpting all last night for fun* grogginess. Her large black-rimmed glasses sit at the end of her nose. She's still in her pajamas, light green elephants printed on the sleeves. My mom has a similar set; the material is perfect for the heat here, too. Dì Vàng is in her apartment's kitchen, a cup of *cà phê đen* beside her. If I strain enough I might be able to hear the motorcycles outside her window, some neighborhood women laughing, loitering on the sidewalk, or a vendor hawking fish or fresh veggies.

"Did you just wake up?" my mom asks. It's eleven in the morning over there, too late for Mẹ's typical wake-up time at dawn.

"Maybe." *Knew it.* My aunt makes a show of yawning and stretching. "What did you eat for dinner?"

"Leftovers. And you?"

I roll my eyes. They say hi and immediately ask about food? My aunt points the phone downward to show her plate of *ốp la*—fried eggs, the yolk runny once pierced—with *bánh mì*, likely fresh from next door.

"Where's the *xì dầu*?" Mẹ asks almost accusingly.

"Chị trying to diet. Less salt. It's perfectly fine without it."

"You sound Mỹ," Mẹ says. I grin, thinking about how much my mom acts like the older sister even though she isn't. My aunt knows how to take it, though, shooting back playful replies. Oh yes, I can see it.

"So, what's happening? You don't usually call me. It's the other way around."

"Did you get my vase?"

"Yes. You shouldn't have sent it. It costs so much money to ship things over."

"I wanted to give you something nice! But if you're that worried about money, maybe I should just deliver my next one to you myself." Dì Vàng leans closer, grinning now. Her eyes are alive.

Does she mean...?

"Are you coming here?"

"Are you?" I ask, pulling the phone from Mẹ's hand. She snatches it back.

"You're coming here, really?" she asks again.

"Yes, it's been way too long. Twelve, thirteen years?"

"When are you coming?"

"Around Tết."

"You're leaving around Tết? But why? It's the best holiday. Traffic will be horrible."

Dì Vàng laughs. "Of course you're already worrying about the

135

travel schedule! Anyway, I've seen so many Tết; I live here. Plus it's been so long! I want to see you. I want to hug Evie and Linh!"

"That can't be the only reason."

"I also might be visiting some artist friends on the West Coast."

"You have friends here?" I ask, though I shouldn't be surprised. When she visited the last time, she managed to make conversation with everyone on the floor of our old apartment building, people my parents and I never even interacted with. She even met Bác Xuân when he came by, and in no time they were trading hypotheticals on what he would do when he retired and moved closer to his adult children and their families.

"I have friends all over the place. I'm international."

"I can't believe you're coming," I say excitedly. It'll be two artists under one roof. We'll go to museums, I'll show her my work. Someone who will understand my language. And support it.

"Do you have enough money to go traveling?"

Dì Vàng tuts at my mom. "Of course I do. My business is good over here; I wish you believed me." She leans in again, seeing something in my mom's expression that I must have missed. "I am no longer a struggling artist, as you seem to think I will always be."

"You've struggled for a long time, I remember."

"I know; I remember too. But I am fine. You shouldn't worry too much, *em*."

Mẹ holds back whatever thought she has and they move on to talking about old friends, some woman they knew who'd eloped in Hội An, then came back without the husband recently. I sit there, silent, content to listen, eyes tracking the level of my aunt's coffee as she sips away at it. Then Mẹ notices my eyes closing slowly. The ramen is finally kicking in, lulling me to sleep.

"Okay, *cho* Linh *đi ngủ*." They exchange goodbyes, my aunt saying she'd circle back with more info about her visit next year.

Mẹ only sighs as she maneuvers herself off my bed.

"Be happy, Mẹ!" I say, holding on to my mom's arm before she leaves, trying to get her not to worry already. "Your sister's coming over." I see a hint of a smile blooming on her face, though she stops herself, shooing away my hand.

"I really don't know what she's thinking. She's so unpredictable. And she shouldn't spend her money so freely."

"Was it really that bad? Dì Vàng and her sculpting business."

"She'd just started it when she was seventeen right after leaving school. Then rationings were happening and the government was watching anyone who was against *cộng sản* very closely. They stole part of our land, leaving little to us." My mom fiddles with the back of her phone cover. "Many times Dì Vàng would come home without making any sales."

"So what happened?"

"Luckily, we had older aunts and uncles who would come in and out, making sure we were fed. That is the Vietnamese way. But still, Mẹ *biết nghề nghiệp của* Dì Vàng would not help us. Art was only for fun. And during that time, there was no time for playing.

"At the camps, when Mẹ finally made it—just *mười hai tuổi*—I promised I would work hard. So that we would suffer less. So that Mẹ could help your aunt back home."

My mom was fourteen by the time they left the camps and

were accepted into the United States with her cousins and two other refugees they'd grown close to. But she couldn't depend on her cousins alone—they too were thrust into an unfamiliar place with minimal English—and finding work was hard. So, when she wasn't studying to catch up at school, she was working odd jobs. Some of the money went to their daily expenses. Whatever was left over she'd send back to Vietnam, to help my aunt.

"Ah, *Mẹ nhức đầu*," she says, massaging her temples, worries about my aunt plaguing her mind. Then she's off to the next room, muttering about how much she'll need to clean up to accommodate her sister coming over, despite us having plenty of time to prepare.

I still don't understand. My aunt seems so happy, and she's managed to get this far, and it can't all be because she gets some money now and then from America. She's not struggling like before, so why can't my mom see that it all turned out okay in the end? It's like the memories of my aunt's struggle keep her from seeing the good sides to art.

I pull out my sketchpad from its hiding place and trace over the image of Bảo. I barely remember doing this drawing; I was just lost in the act of doing it. It's a type of forgetting that I love, that I can't get anywhere else. Inside my head, I can just *be*. My aunt must know this too.

I text Evie about our aunt coming over, and she texts back, jokingly, great, there will be two of you.

CHAPTER SEVENTEEN

BẢO

It's not really unusual for kids who grew up in restaurants to eat in record time. Mẹ had to feed us before the rush hour or else there wouldn't be another opportunity. And now, working at the restaurant, when noon hits, when customers come flowing in, we need to eat quickly.

"So, what, you think she's mad at you, then?" Việt asks, scraping the last of his egg noodles from his Styrofoam plate. An apple sits on his left, a strawberry yogurt that he won't eat to his right. He hates artificial sugar. I'd told him about the restaurant, how things had started out fine. Fun, even, until Linh shut down on me.

"I guess so. Maybe because I basically called her a liar."

Việt shakes his head, like, *You poor kid.* "I don't know, man. It's hypocritical. I mean, you're lying about where you're going and who you're spending time with, too. And why's that?"

I see his point now. "So my parents don't blow up on me. My mom, especially."

"Exactly," Việt says.

"I didn't mean it like that, though. I was just saying . . . I wish her parents could see what she's doing. Because she's an artist. She can't be anything else."

"And you know this after only a few weeks of talking to her."

Okay, he's looking at me like I'm obsessed with her. "Shut up."

Việt grins in return, biting into an apple. "This is the first time I've heard you talk about a girl, let alone the daughter of your family's worst enemy."

"I didn't think you'd ever give me advice about talking to a girl."

My best friend merely shrugs. "Whenever I take a break from watching *Law & Order* or *Criminal Minds*, I sometimes flip to *The Bachelor*, which tells me exactly what not to do when talking to a girl you like."

Sure, very reliable.

"I don't know, dude. Maybe next time you see her, try to apologize. Let her deal with her parents at her own pace."

When Việt's cross-country friends join our table, our abnormal conversation ends. It's a brief respite since I have my limits with their circular conversations about sprint times, better sprint times, and plans for another pasta party before a meet. And I've never seen anyone eat as many bananas in one sitting as Steve, the team captain. Because of Việt, they tolerate my complete un-athleticism, acknowledge me with a slight nod and a "What's up, man."

"C'mon, how long has it been since you washed your uniform?" Steve asks one of the guys.

His friend, who has a watch tan, shrugs. "I dunno. A week?"

Việt's friends are the definition of riveting.

But as different as Việt is from his teammates, at least from what I can see, it makes sense to see him with them. Việt's always been precise and stuck close to regimens, and I guess that's why he and his teammates hang out outside of practice.

I look around and spot Ali and her Viking braid. She's laughing along with some of her friends—didn't think she was capable of that—but I scan her table and don't find Linh anywhere.

Where's Linh now?

Next time I see her, I'll apologize. I stand up, gathering my things. Việt asks where I'm heading. "Gotta finish some homework." The strawberry yogurt that he set aside conjures the memory of Linh ordering her strawberry-flavored boba tea. And the chocolate milk she slipped into my hand.

"Can I grab this?"

A caution cone blocks off the guys' bathroom, where puddles of water glisten on the floor. Old, torn posters and flyers have fallen from their fastenings. Home Economics is having a bake sale. The Vietnamese Student Association is having a carwash fundraiser in a week.

I have to make sure *not* to be available.

Voices volley off the walls outside the cafeteria, but the hallway itself is silent, absent of rustling clothes and slamming lockers. Where does Linh go during lunch?

Then, of course, I know. The art room. Where else would an artist find refuge? I'm there in a few minutes, standing just by the threshold, where we nearly collided a few weeks back. She's crossing the room to sit on a stool by the window, dressed in paint-splattered overalls that I imagine she'd changed into.

I clear my throat. Linh turns. "Oh, hi. What's up? You're not eating lunch?"

"I already did. You?"

"Yeah, I eat pretty quickly. Habit, I guess."

"Of course. We're restaurant kids."

Taking this as sign to come in, I hide the yogurt behind my back, walk into the room. "What are you working on?" I'm close enough to see the canvas now, with just a few strokes of color, a shape yet to be determined.

"I really don't know. Sometimes I come in, grab some tubes, and start mixing colors just because."

I reach up to touch the canvas, but her hand goes around my wrist.

"No touching." Her voice is threatening, but she's suppressing a smile.

I hold up a hand in surrender. There's a different energy to Linh now. A more protective Linh.

I like it.

"Is this where you always go during lunch? I never see you." Of course, I'm admitting I'm a stalker—a shitty one, since I never *can* find her—so that's great.

But Linh turns back, dipping her brush into a jar of water, before answering: "It's nice down here."

Unable to find other things to say, I hand over the yogurt. Her brow furrows in confusion before she glances up. She accepts it, her fingers lingering against my palm. *Breathe.*

Linh says "Hmmm" before setting it down. "What's this for?"

"To apologize." I seize the moment. "Or try to. Look, when we were at the restaurant, I might have asked some questions that you clearly didn't want to answer. I didn't mean to push you or accuse you. I guess I realized only after that I was being hypocritical too."

"And you think a yogurt's enough to make it up to me?" She faces the canvas again, her tone monotonous.

Oh shit, should I run?

"N-no," I stutter. "It's—well—"

Her laughter splits the air. She faces me again, and her eyes soften. "That's nice of you to say. A part of me knows you're right, and I don't like it either. Lying is not who I am. But—" She shrugs. "I don't see another way to do this without lying."

"We'll be partners *and* liars."

"We're pathetic," Linh groans, laughing into her hands covering her face.

"You just realized that?" I ask. "I meant what I said, though." I pause because, when Linh looks at me suddenly like that, words escape me. So I stare at the floor. "I really wish your parents liked the idea of you as an artist. Your work, it has a way of drawing

143

people in. I'm the least artistic person on earth, and I just wish you could feel freer to do it."

"Thanks."

"Okay, I guess I'll just leave you alone now." I start backing away, even though my legs don't want to move.

"No, you can stay. I don't mind. But only if you're quiet." She gives me a pointed but playful look.

I take the invitation. "I'll be over there." I wince when the stool I pull out squeaks against the floor. My backpack slams against the table. "I need to start on my article anyway." I remember how I shoved my notepad to the bottom of my backpack. I'll need to dig it out.

"You haven't started it yet?" she asks incredulously.

"Um . . . no."

"Use this for inspiration." She's right next to me now, opening up a see-through folder and sliding a page to me. A sketch, all inked up. I know what this is.

"How did you do it so quickly?"

"I just did." She shrugs. Am I cursed to surround myself with casual geniuses? Việt's tolerable, he doesn't rub it in my face that school comes easily to him, and here's Linh basically saying, but not bragging, *I'm just naturally talented.*

"Oh, come on." I glance down at her sketch of the restaurant. It captures the dimness of the room, the structures hanging down from the ceiling, the columns of Japan's cityscapes. It looks print-ready.

"Better get started on your end of the deal," she teases me, right by my ear. "Or else you'll have to answer to Ali."

"Teach me how," I say, boldness coming from nowhere. I stay as still as possible.

"How to what?" she asks, a hint of amusement in her voice. Disappointing me, she takes a step back.

"To get inside my head. Like what happens when you paint."

"Close your eyes, then."

"Are we going to meditate?"

"Just do it."

A few seconds pass and soon I feel her prying my fingers open, placing something wooden in my palm. I feel it: It's long and there's rubber at the end; it's a—

I open my eyes.

Linh's trying to hold back a laugh, looking down at the pencil in my hand. "I can't teach you something like this. You have to do it yourself because writing is personal to you. So"—she gestures with her fingers, her tone becoming stern— "turn around and just do it."

"*Now* I see why you and Ali are friends."

"Thank you," she answers proudly. And she turns to walk back to her easel.

And this is how I spend the rest of my lunch, hidden away, just the two of us.

The cool metal under me, the hum of the air-conditioning. I listen to Linh washing her brush periodically in water, the brush hitting against glass, sending out a ringing sound, the scratch of brush bristles. And the sway of her ponytail when she tilts her head to examine her work.

I zone in on her sketch, the colors perfectly capturing the decor.

I can even smell salt in the ramen. I close my eyes, tight. The warm broth layers my tongue in flavor. The chewiness of the noodles. Linh's laugh as she tried mine.

I begin to write.

CHAPTER EIGHTEEN

LINH

The next day, Bảo barges into the art room without any announcement, as if he'd always spent his lunches here and he was running just a bit behind. His hair is windswept and fashionable at the same time, like a breeze purposefully styled his hair. But it's his gaze I notice the most. Last year in an art theory lesson, we were taught about the gaze—or "the Gaze," as my art teacher wrote on the board and underlined three times. There are many definitions of a gaze—it could be the spectator or the patron's, or one person in the art piece looking at another person in the same frame, or, more disconcerting, the art looking back at the spectator. It's what's fascinated critics about *Mona Lisa* for centuries—how her outward gaze appears both superior and subdued, defiant and diminutive. That gaze, that look, can carry the whole artwork.

Now, I can only describe Bảo's gaze as shining. Vibrant. Made even more intense since he's looking straight at me. He was looking for me.

I set down my brush and palette when he offers a piece of paper to me. "It's my article," he says in a rush. I wonder how much caffeine he's had. "I worked on it last night. Can you read it?"

"Me?"

"Yes."

Hesitantly, I take his paper, which he really did write. His handwriting is solid and straight, nothing like the chicken scratch I'd seen from other classmates.

"You *actually* hand-wrote this."

"At first I was just jotting random things down, and then, I don't know, it turned into sentences. Didn't even realize how much I was writing." He grins. "I think I actually understand what you meant, when we were talking at 7 Leaves. I was outside my body."

"Ali never lets me read her things," I start saying, though I'm pleased that he remembers what I said. I never have an issue with what Ali writes. I just know she's good. Secretly, maybe she's always wanted a person to challenge her, find the mistakes that she can't spot herself.

Bảo looks so eager that I wouldn't want to turn him down anyway. "That's Ali. This is me. And I want you, specifically, to read this."

"Why?" I say, laughter bubbling in my throat.

"Because I've never written something like this. So I want you to be the first one to read my first article."

"Since I'm not a writer, I'll probably just say it's good. And even if it's bad, I'll probably lie."

"I think I'll know if you don't like it."

"How? I *can* lie." I pretend to think. "Didn't we talk about this before?"

"All right. Let's test it out."

Suddenly, from his seat, he hooks his foot around one leg of my stool, pulls me closer so that our knees touch. His eyes are fixed on me, and I want to look down, but I force my gaze ahead. I won't let him win. His hands loosely hold my wrists.

"Do you like phở?"

I almost burst out in laughter. He's being so ridiculous. "Isn't that an obvious answer?"

"Do you think I'm annoying?"

"Again, obvious."

He glances down. Strands of his hair fall into his eyes as he pauses deep in thought. His knee bumps against mine. "Do you think I'm handsome?"

That came out of nowhere. My eyes widen.

"Oh, I see," he says dramatically, beaming widely. "Your face just told me everything."

My heart is *racing*. "That proved nothing. I wasn't expecting that question. And you were only making broad interpretations anyway. My reaction doesn't mean that I think—"

"So I'm handsome, got it," he says cheekily. He easily ruffles his hair, a direct attack on my nerves right now.

I *have* to look away. I can't deal.

"You want me to read your article or not?" I ask.

Bảo raises both hands in defense.

I shake my head, trying not to smile, before turning my attention to his review.

As a visual person, I like his opening, his descriptive language painting the scene. I remember the wooden stalactites hanging from the ceiling, the intimidating sensation of gazing up at them, only to be transported to the forests they were emulating. I grin when he describes the staff's hair as "perfectly coiffed."

But the food is where I can understand why Ali chose him for this beat. He knows just the right words to describe the ramen and its broth (*full-bodied, tinged with enough salt just for the tip of your tongue*), the spiciness of my ramen (*happy tears, not fiery tears*), and by the end I forget that I've already eaten lunch. I have a craving for Japanese food again.

Bảo's staring intently at me when I look back up.

"Well?" he prompts me.

"It's horrible," I say. But he sees my face—reading it, as he said. And a beautiful smile comes to life.

Ali takes offense when I tell her I let Bảo into the room while I was working on an art piece. It's something I never let Ali do. For a good reason.

I'm in the newspaper room, her domain, waiting for the warning bell to signal me to leave. She has her curly hair tied up high in a messy bun on top of her head, a pen buried in there somewhere. Her feet are on the teacher's desk, and Rowan, entering the room to disappear into his office, points at them, then to the floor. Ali does exactly that ... until his door closes and her feet are back on his desk.

"You barely tolerate me when I'm in the room," she says with a fake pout.

"Yeah, because you're distracting!" I shoot back. "You can't sit still *and* you won't stop talking. I need to concentrate."

"Oh and Bảo isn't distracting."

"He's not, actually," I quickly say. Then I remember him "reading" me. "He's really ... considerate."

I thought I wouldn't be able to work with Bảo in the room, conscious of my every movement, the slouch that I've picked up over the years, the mess of my ponytail, how unattractive I must look in my overalls. I felt his gaze on me at times, but when I got the nerve to look around, he was turned away, preoccupied with writing.

Then I forgot about him. I abandoned thoughts about what image I want to make. Yamamoto likes to tell us that it's not always about what we want to put on canvas, that we should let our brushes, pencils, or whatever utensil we use, guide us on unexpected paths. I fool around with colors because most of my memories come up from color. The yogurt that Bảo handed to me brings me back to the first moment I tried strawberry cotton candy at Huntington Beach.

"You like him distracting you," Ali says mischievously. She

brings her feet to the floor, scooting closer, but I avoid her comment, pulling out the sketch that I made for her. Really, I was prolonging my time here. I wanted to see her reaction when Bảo handed in his review. I wanted her to say it's as good as I thought it was.

"*Anddd* here's your sketch—"

"Come on, Linh! Tell me more—"

"Oh, perfect, you're here too." Bảo's at the threshold, one backpack strap slung over his shoulder. His hair is messy again; he must have been rushing over. I *have* to stop fixating on his hair. He hands a USB stick to Ali.

"There, my article. *And* it's on time." We share a look, nearly laughing. I guess he took what I said to heart.

"Have you ever heard of e-mail?" Ali mutters.

As Ali turns to her screen, Bảo moves closer to me.

"I've imagined many scenarios of how she'd react if I handed her what I handed you. One: She'll rip my pages to pieces." He pauses. "Actually, that's the only scenario," he admits. He's cute when he worries.

"You'll be fine."

Ali doesn't say anything immediately during her review. It goes on for two more minutes. The dripping sound of the sink from its art room days starts irritating me. Anxiety radiates from Bảo's shifting stance.

"Okay." Ali whirls around, slowly crossing her legs. I envision her as a big-shot editor poised to tear apart some poor journalist's article. "Linh drew this?"

"Yes."

"And you wrote this article."

"Yeah."

She folds her hands together and twiddles her thumbs. Slowly, a smile spreads on her face, one I've never seen directed at Bảo. "This is good. No, this is *great*. You two really did it."

Bảo scratches the back of his neck, a blush rising in his cheeks. "Really?"

"There's this one line about not spitting at the person across from you when you're on a date, but I don't get it, so we'll need to cut that line." I throw Bảo a look—I hadn't read that line, so he must have added it after—and he winks. Winks!

"But we'll run it this issue," Ali finishes.

Fast forward to a week later.

Bảo and I didn't break new ground with our review and sketch. It's not on the front page, either. It's not going to change anything, and no one is treating us differently or even acknowledging us as the writer and artist. But I notice that there are fewer stacks of newspapers around the school.

I'm in the quad packed with students. The temperature's nicer today; people are playing Frisbee, couples are lounging on the grass together, and some dancers are trying out new moves, staying inside their exclusive circle.

"This! Why can't Alex take me to places like this?" says a girl whose name is Lilly. She's on the swim team with her brother Ben.

"Because he thinks getting boba is an adequate date," her friend points out.

Yamamoto was happy to learn I was the artist. Turns out she was planning to use discarded newspaper copies for her paper-mache unit—which I will definitely never tell Ali—then unexpectedly caught my name in the byline.

"I didn't know you were part of the newspaper, too."

"It's a favor for a friend," I said, a bit embarrassed.

"I like it! And the writer. Wow, it's a great pairing. You're full of surprises, Linh."

"Looks like people are *actually* reading the newspaper," Bảo says, now sneaking up behind me. "For once."

"Careful, Ali might be around."

This feeling that I have whenever I'm around him—energy zapping through my veins, the warmth in my cheeks, a never-ending want to watch him without being obvious—doesn't seem to be going away. At the restaurant, I'm glancing more often at the window—not to watch him, like Ba, but just to steal another look at him.

Hidden away in the art room, we're not as jittery. It's our sanctuary. We've fallen into an unspoken pattern, me painting while Bảo works on an assignment for the newspaper or some other homework.

Ali's right. This is becoming something more, but like many things in my life, it can't all happen at once. These feelings, this crush, whatever you call it, they're something to keep to myself. To contain before it gets reckless.

We find Ali eating her own lunch, a neatly cut egg salad sandwich. There's a stack of newspapers next to her. Leave it to her to pass around newspapers during her break.

"Look!" she squeals.

"Yeah, it's great. Just what you hoped for, right?"

"I *knew* the front-page article would be a hit." From what I recall, the front page is about the school's lack of cybersecurity, authored by my indomitably spirited best friend.

Bảo gives me a look before throwing his bag onto the ground. We won't ruin her joy. He stretches onto his back and lies there for a moment, the sun shining strong down on him, highlighting the lines of his face again. What *is* it with his face and light? It's just too perfect. I sit on my hands to stop myself from sketching him . . . again.

Another part of me itches to join him, lie right next to him and take in the sun. I settle for sitting, stretching out my legs so that my shoes are just by his ear. Just one touch away.

Bảo's best friend, Việt, finds us a few moments later, and introduces himself to me and Ali. Ali's already trying to recruit him to be a reviewer after hearing that he's obsessed with dark, gritty television shows.

"Think about it," she says. "If you start now, you can be the next Roger Ebert."

"I'm not really a writer. I can't write like Bảo," Việt answers simply.

Bảo, now sitting, looks genuinely shocked to hear the comment, but Việt doesn't seem to notice. "Thanks, man."

"Knew all those words you collect would pay off someday."

I can tell from Ali's expression that she's not done trying to recruit Việt. She means well; she just wants to leave a mark when she graduates, but some people don't see that as easily and might stay clear of her. A wave of sympathy washes over me until I remember what Bảo said about Việt. He's cool and collected and seems to do his own thing. Maybe he'll be the first one to really handle Ali's assertiveness.

The four of us are a little weird together, but somehow ... I can't ask for a better group to eat lunch with today.

"Oh, great!" Ali's staring at her phone. "We already have our next restaurant. Are you two ready?"

Instantly, I look to Bảo, and I know his answer, because it's mine, too.

"Ready."

Days later, I get home and see another set of shoes by the door. A guest? It's a weird time, and usually if people come over, they come over at night. I sniff the air, picking up a familiar scent: oil, so food's being fried, and as I follow the scent, it clicks: Mẹ's making egg rolls. As I walk closer, I recognize the guest's voice.

"Mẹ, I don't *need* another set of dishes. Where can I put them? I don't even have a kitchen."

"You have a communal kitchen, don't you?" my mom asks in Vietnamese.

"Yeah, but other people in my dorm are shitty and they'll probably steal all my things."

Mẹ and Evie, wearing a UC Davis hoodie, sit at the round table, spooning meat into defrosted egg roll wrappers while my dad carefully peels each of them away. Seeing me, he beckons me, probably wanting me to take his place, but I ignore him for now—

"Evie!" I squeal, going in for a hug.

My big sister laughs as we nearly fall over. She hugs me without her hands touching me. "Please rescue me. Mẹ's forcing me to take *all* of this back with me." She points to the kitchen counter filled with Costco-size food and pots and pans. Probably from the basement, where she keeps so many on-sale things, saying that one day we'll need them. The Bounty rolls I can understand, but four types of wooden chopping boards?

"I didn't know you were coming home."

"There's only so many text messages from Mẹ that my phone can hold. *Con ăn chưa? Con có muốn về tuần tới không?*" She softens her voice to mimic our mom.

"*Mẹ nhớ con,*" our mom says defensively.

"Yes, I know you miss me, but can you miss me less?" my sister says, jokingly rolling her eyes.

"You should have told me, or else I wouldn't have stayed so long at school," I say, taking a seat.

"Linh is always staying late," Ba chimes in. "Too many times, I think, for her art classes. You have to think about school, not art. Good grades will get you into school, not art."

I lean back into my chair, stomach dropping. Not again. Across the table, Evie gives me a sympathetic look. It hits me then how much I miss her. She's usually the one saying, "Art isn't always painting and drawing. It has a lot to do with creative thinking and not a lot of people can think that way, think like Linh." She always had a way of explaining things to make them sound so much easier, sound like it could work in an ideal world.

Like now: "Well, it's cool that Linh does this. And she's good. And there's *tons* of people who do art in college."

"Yes, but have you met one with a job?" Mẹ asks.

"No, but that's because I don't hang out with—"

"See!" Ba interrupts her. "See, artists don't get jobs."

"You *can* get a job," I finally say, my voice loud. "It might take a while, but it's not impossible." My parents glance at me at the same time. Something behind my dad's eyes makes me bite my tongue.

"Art is fun," he says shortly. "But that's just it: It can only be fun. It can never support you. Con, Mẹ and Ba have worked so hard so that you can have a better life." My sister and I exchange suffering looks, knowing where our parents are going. Ba catches the exchange and merely tsks, though it might be because the layer he's trying to peel isn't complying. "Evelyn is on the right track, so we don't have to worry as much about her."

"The texts from Mẹ about my eating habits prove otherwise," Evie mutters.

"Now it's your turn," Ba finishes. He gestures for me to start filling the wrappers. The key is to put a modest spoonful of meat inside, then roll up tight enough and seal it with egg wash so that it doesn't uncurl when the roll hits oil, which happens too many times to mine.

"First batch is out!" Mẹ emerges, shows us a batch of crispy, golden egg rolls in a sieve, layered with a paper towel to catch excess oil. "Try one."

My sister bites into one, then beams at Mẹ. "Just what I needed."

We fall into a familiar pattern as we work together. Evie regales us with tales of college so far. I try not to laugh whenever her recollection gets interrupted by Mẹ and Ba as they ask about her friends, about their nationality, if they're *mập hay ốm*, where they live, what their parents are like. But my sister answers each question patiently, already anticipating their questions. I make a note to do background checks when I get to college.

I stay quiet, still stung by my parents' tone when they said I could never make a living from my art. They don't get it.

That feeling of missing having my sister around? Disappears in not even two hours, especially since Evie's back to sharing a room with me for the weekend. She's already dismayed by how messy I've made it. "If I find one thing missing, I'll kill you," she says casually as she searches her drawer for something. I actually think she's taking inventory until she pulls out Q-tips. She just emerged from the shower and has her long hair wrapped up in a towel turban.

Evie bends over to examine a sketch of mine. "This one's great. Did you just draw it?"

"Yep."

"I don't understand how you can do things like this. See something, then put it on paper. I can barely do stick drawings." She's only teasing me; she's remembering the kitchen table conversation.

"Tell that to Mẹ and Ba."

She sits down on the edge of my bed. "They told me about your interview with that engineer. I almost didn't believe it. How'd it go?"

"Horrible."

"Figured. Engineering's not for you." She says it like an undisputed fact, though I wish it were my parents stating that. "I have tons of friends majoring in engineering. They're logical, *organized*—" I throw my pillow at her, which Evie deftly catches with a grin. "Hey, I'm not finished! What I mean to add is a 'but.' They can't look at a painting and see what you see. And they can't create things like you do. Not instinctively like you do."

Now I want to take back my pillow. She's being nice. She's always nice.

"I think about telling them. But I have this feeling that it won't go well."

In a better reality, Evie would dispute that fact, would tell me to "go for it." But Evie is Evie. She grew up with me. She knows our parents. She knows what they've said about having art as a career. So thoughtful silence is the expected response.

"I lied about it going well," I admit.

"Figured. You know how your face gives you away."

"You're, like, the fourth person to say that about me!"

She lifts her chin, appearing haughty. "I'm your sister, so I know. I always knew whenever you stole one of my shirts."

I roll my eyes. "That only happened twice."

She points at me. "Lie."

I shrug. I might have stolen from her a couple more times, but at least she's older and she won't enact revenge against— "Oof!" The pillow slams in my face.

"Evie!" I protest loudly.

From their bedroom, where Ba was probably trying to fall asleep, he yells for us to quiet down.

We laugh mutedly and fall back into bed. Evie cuddles closer to me, while I pretend to kick her away, telling her to go back to her bed. But we only have a day or two together, and then she'll be back at UC Davis, miles away, living a completely different life from me. I don't mean it. I want her close by.

In one perfect move, Evie launches the pillow at the light switch, and we fall under darkness. We lie in silence. I'm counting each time the ceiling fan makes a complete turn, signaled by a nearly indescribable screech.

"UC Davis is good?"

"It's better than I could have ever imagined, Linh. The campus is beautiful. And the science lab—" She sighs. It sounds like she fell in love with her lab instead of, like, a person.

I envy her. She's where she wanted to be. Where she always dreamed of going. Plus, while she and my parents have disagreed on things—curfew and sleeping over at a friend's house—they've never argued about Evie's future. They never had an issue with it.

"I wish I could like what you like," I whisper in the dark.

Evie's foot touches mine; it's cold and I kick her. I can feel her smile in the dark. "If you liked what I liked, you wouldn't be Linh."

"Life would be so much easier if I liked what you liked, though."

"Easier?" I imagine her lifting herself into a sitting position. "How would that have made it easier?"

"It's something safe. It's something our parents approve of."

"Safe. Huh."

I sense Evie's mood shifting, then I replay what I just said. "I don't mean that in a bad way, Evie. It's just, you're doing something that Mẹ and Ba approve of. Meanwhile, I want to be an artist. Definitely what they wouldn't want me to do."

She doesn't answer right away and it's making me uneasy. I have half a mind to get up from bed and turn on the lights, just so that I can see her expression.

Then she sighs. "It's not easy, Linh. It's never been easy."

She's speaking not at me, but to me. "If I'd ever taken an art class in high school, I'd get an earful. Whenever I asked them to hang out with a friend after school, they'd say no, there were too many things I needed to do. I had to wear them down. But for you, it's different. They treat you differently. They allow you to do more things.

"And there are some moments where I think about how I decided on biology. Am I doing this because Ba and Mẹ pushed me toward it? Or did I always like biology? Where does the line between what I want and what our parents want end?" I had to think, too. I'm not so sure. "See, I don't know. It's different for you, though. Two years makes a whole lot of difference."

"I'm sorry," I say in the dark. "I didn't ... well, I guess I didn't notice." But I was only younger by two years, and I lived in the same house, so how could I have missed this?

Evie eases back into bed. She throws her leg over mine. "It's generally accepted that in families like ours, the older kids have it way harder. We're the guinea pigs in a real-world lab." Her tone shifts to something more playful. "What did Hasan Minhaj say one time? Older siblings 'go to war' for their younger siblings? Because that's what it was like. That's what I did. So that really means, you owe me everything."

I shove her lightly by the shoulder. "For what it's worth, I think you're made for biology. I don't remember you ever liking anything else."

"That could be." Evie sighs, and yawns.

CHAPTER NINETEEN

BẢO

Slowly, I'm getting used to being on the newspaper, being a part of a team. After the success of my first review, Ali's not so on top of me anymore. In her eyes, I've stepped up; she's still delegating proofreading tasks to me, but she's giving me multiple articles—more than anyone else on the editing team.

My classmates are coming by to talk about their edits, having revised what they wrote and asking me to look them over. One side of me wonders if they ask me because Ali can be a little intense— "passionate" was Linh's word—but I like to think that they truly want my help. Even if my classmates are using me to avoid Ali, it feels good to be approached like this. To have them trust me with their work.

Each writer looks at language so differently. Ali focuses on the message in writing—is the point getting across? Where can the writer be clearer in their intention? Me, I like the writer's style. One person can say something that's been said before but in a way that's completely different; their unique experiences and personality infuse their words, their sentences.

I'm working with Ernie's article summarizing the National Honor Society's induction of new members. Ernie shrinks under attention in person, so whether he knows it or not, he uses a lot of passive voice in his writing. Things are done to the subject; the subject isn't taking action. The budget cut to the arts was cut *by* the budget committee—not the budget committee cut the budget for the arts program. Compared to Ali's writing, which gets straight to the point, Ernie lacks confidence.

"I couldn't get into astronomy; that's the only reason why I'm here," he says glumly, reading my edits.

"I didn't want to take this class either," I say, trying to cheer him up.

"Yeah, but you're good at it. And Ali doesn't go after you." As if she were right behind us, Ernie glances over his shoulder.

Ali's sandwiched between two designers huddling around her. They're going over proofs for the next issue. I might not understand their process, though I don't have to. It's hers, it's theirs, something only they can understand.

Ernie's eyebrows scrunch together like he's reading a different language. I know where he's coming from.

"Journalism might not be for everyone, but you're not bad at all. Maybe you just need to find something you like writing about," I finally say, channeling Linh. "What are you interested in?"

"I dunno. I like skateboarding. Reading comics."

"Anything else?"

"I guess I watch a lot of Netflix. TV stuff."

I remember Ali trying to recruit Việt as a writer. This might be perfect. "Would you want to write about a show? You can ask Ali if you can do it. She's looking for a reviewer."

"Really?" he asks hesitantly. "Do you think she'll let me?"

Looks like I'm not the only person who's intimidated by her. I laugh. "I'll talk to her."

Later, as the dismissal bell rings and students fly out of the classroom, I stop by Ali as she's scrolling through her phone, answering texts. "Oh, hey, Bảo. Did you work through Ernie's article? Thought it needed to be tightened but otherwise it's good to print."

"Yeah, everything worked out. I heard Ernie's into TV shows. Watches a lot of Netflix. Maybe he should try the entertainment section."

"Really? He never told me that."

"He didn't know we had an open spot."

Ali nods, calculating something in her head. "Sure. Why not?" The alarm clock on her phone goes off. "Shit, I'm gonna be late."

"Where are you going?"

"Part-time gig at a local newspaper."

"You work at a school newspaper *and* a real newspaper too?"

"Of course, what else would I do with my time?" she says simply. I pretend not to look so shocked but, first she doesn't use study hall in favor of heading the newspaper here. And now I learned that she also works part-time. She must really love the newspaper.

Imagine my surprise when one of Việt's friends sits down in front of me at lunch. It's miserable and raining outside so most people are in the cafeteria. Việt hasn't even sat yet, but Steve, the banana-eating captain, takes a seat across from me. He's grown out his brown hair, tied it into a little ponytail—to be ironic? In all our time together, we haven't really held a conversation.

"Hey, you busy?"

"Uh, no."

"I wanted to see if you can do something for me."

"You're asking *me*?"

"Yeah, Việt said you're on the newspaper or something. Said you edit shit."

"Uh, yeah, I edit shit."

He digs into his backpack that almost looks Army-issued. Removes his brown-bag lunch. Used tissues. A paperback and dog-eared Carnegie's *How to Win Friends and Influence People.*

My eyebrows go up.

Steve clears his throat. "My mom wanted me to read it," he mumbles.

Fascinating. "Right. Uh, you needed my help on what, exactly?"

Finally, he yanks out a crumpled, lined piece of paper with his chicken scratch all over it. He smooths it out against the table's edge, like you would with dollar bills at a vending machine. "I'm working on my personal statement for some college applications, and I have an essay, but I can't really make the first paragraph stick. My sisters read it and liked the essay in general, but they say the introduction makes me sound like a fifth grader."

"Ouch."

"I know." He grimaces. "But I think they're right. I know we always have to open something with a strong statement, but I can't come up with anything. Can you help?"

If Ali were in my seat, she'd have a few more words to say to Steve, probably things worse than his own sisters. But me, I try to be more sympathetic.

I feel for my red pen in my backpack and blow out some air. "Okay, what are you trying to say here, exactly?"

His essay is about his love of running. How it's not just a physical thing, but a mental thing for him. When he's stressed out or upset about something, he puts on his shoes and just runs, no destination in mind. As I switch between listening to him talk and reading his words, I'm starting to understand what his sisters said about the introduction. It doesn't even sound like him. It sounds mechanical, forced.

"Start with a feeling," I tell Steve finally, circling his paragraph. "I like what you said about letting your mind take you on a trip and how you like being surprised by where the run's taking you." Kind of like how Linh talks about painting. "So why not open with that?"

"Yeah, but shouldn't I write some sort of thesis statement, too?"

"In a way, yeah. But to call it a thesis statement makes it sound like a school paper. You're writing a personal statement, a personal essay, about something personal to you: running."

Steve nods, looking down at his pages.

I add, "So be honest and open with that. Make the readers feel what you feel when you run."

Steve doesn't say anything immediately. I re-cap my pen just so that I can have something to do. Maybe I'm not even helping. Maybe I've made him more confused.

Việt finally arrives, saying something about waiting for more Sloppy Joes. By then, Steve's nodding to himself, reading my edits. When he looks up, he's a bit more reenergized. "Thanks, man." He fist-bumps me before sneaking away to the library to type up his new introduction.

"So, did you help him?" Việt asks through a mouthful of ground beef.

"I think so. Why'd you tell him I was good at editing?"

He shrugs. "Because you are."

"How would you know?"

"Ali."

"You've been talking to Ali?"

"Yeah, she's cool. She keeps trying to recruit me for the entertainment section, and I keep telling her no."

Việt: My best friend with nerves of steel.

"Well, I think we might have someone for that section now and I just told her. Maybe she'll leave you alone."

169

'It's all good. She doesn't really bother me."

A sense of unease settles inside me. They're talking to each other, which means they must *like* being around each other, which means . . . "What else do you talk about?"

The saying "Waiting for the other shoe to drop" has never felt more pertinent as I lean forward, expecting Việt's admission of feelings for Linh's best friend.

"We talk about when you and Linh are getting together."

That shoe, from who knows where, never falls.

"What?"

Việt grins. "Yup. Ali's saying after the fourth review. I'm saying way before that."

"*Why* are you even making bets?"

"Something to pass the time."

"Who do you think is gonna win?"

"I am, which is why I'm telling you now that this all needs to happen after the second restaurant review. So hurry up."

Việt's more invested than I thought he'd be and—Ali.

Oh God. Has she said anything to Linh?

Before I can even ask these important questions, a plethora of bright colors blocks my field of vision. I look up to see pin-straight bangs against a prominent forehead.

Kelly Tran, president of VSA, the club I've ditched way too many times.

"Bảo. It's been a while."

"Uh-huh." This cold reception is expected, given how I skipped duty on a Saturday because *it was a Saturday*.

Việt quickly excuses himself from the table.

He also skipped along with me.

"You know, I've been meaning to find you. I'm feeling like you're not taking your membership seriously. If you continue to miss more meetings, I'm afraid you can't be in the club anymore." There's a threat to her voice, but it's entirely ineffective since I wasn't even aware I was still a member.

Movement behind Kelly's head brings my focus to Linh, and my heart leaps. An excuse! An escape.

"Oh, hey, Linh. Great, you finally came. I know we have to go to that thing."

"Thing?" Linh asks, an eyebrow quirked. Then with a familiar smile, she says, "Hey, Kelly."

I say, "That thing, yeah."

"Oh." A pause. A side glance at Kelly. "*Oh*. Yeah, totally. Let's go."

Kelly's looking between us, probably wondering how we even know each other. "Wait, since you're both here: How about you join our table at the Thuận Phát next weekend? We're raising money for the club."

Damn it.

"Um," Linh says, hesitating only a little. "Sure, I think I can do it."

"Awesome!" Kelly does a French exit, relieving me of her colors. "Thanks, Linh. Thanks, Bảo!"

"I guess I'll be there, too," I say grudgingly.

"Sorry, I didn't think *you'd* be roped in," Linh says sympathetically.

"Yeah. Well, you're too nice. You could have said no to Kelly."

"I like her. We had some classes together and she was always nice. And this club is her baby, so of course I want to help." She bumps shoulders with me. We'd started walking together without thinking. "C'mon, I'll be there. It'll be fun."

"You're forgetting one thing. This is public. Way public. My mom, her friends—hell, everyone who owns a business near us—shop there. Weren't we trying to avoid being seen together?"

"Now you're just trying to get out of volunteering."

Yes and no.

Well, mostly yes.

"Wear a disguise," she says somewhat cheekily. "We'll figure something out."

Baseball cap and sunglasses. That'll be my disguise for today.

"Who are you? Are you trying to be a gangster?" Mẹ asks immediately when I come down from my room in the morning.

"No, I'm protecting myself from the sun."

"Well, you don't look like yourself."

Perfect.

My mom had been happy to hear me mention an effort to volunteer. Maybe it's something to share with her gossip circle. *Bảo is such a good person. He thinks of other people.* Ha.

While clearing the dishes at breakfast, she offers to drive me. Well, have Ba drive me as she rides along. That would meet two of her goals for the weekend: (1) force her son to do something and (2) get some grocery shopping done. Mẹ doesn't go to Thuận Phát too often, maybe every month or so. I guess she hasn't been there in a few weeks.

I immediately object, imagining her seeing Linh at the table outside Thuận Phát. She'd *flip* the table, most likely.

"I'll take the bus. Don't want to bother you—"

"No, it's fine—"

"Really. Anyway, there isn't anything on sale today. I checked." I grasp for an excuse. "But Saigon City Marketplace has sales." I mention the one that's a bit closer, and I must have said the magic words, which land on Ba as he sets down *Người Việt* at the table. What's the point of going when nothing is on sale?

"*Thoi, để nó đi đi,*" he says. "*Mình sẽ đi* Saigon City."

My mom relents. "*Mẹ did* want to go to Saigon City to see what herbs are on sale . . . Maybe I will go today."

"Great."

"Don't come back too late. Or eat anything for lunch. I'm making something."

"Got it."

I get on bus sixty-six and it drops me off at McFadden. I walk a few minutes to the supermarket. The parking lot is already packed like sardines, Camrys and Highlanders cruising to find the first open spot. Mothers marching like they're on a mission, their kids dragging their feet. Older shoppers walk with the help of their adult daughter or son and others rely on their canes and walkers.

I see the sign first: HELP VSA, made with enough glitter to stop traffic. Kelly's doing, most likely. Linh sits at the table, glancing around. She's dressed in a simple white tee and jeans, sunglasses on top. I slide into the empty seat next to her.

"Ta-da."

"Bảo?" She laughs and taps on the bill of my ball cap. "Nice disguise."

"Thank you. I think it was your suggestion."

Linh scrutinizes me. "I guess it'll work. I almost didn't recognize you."

"That good, huh?"

"Usually your giveaway is your hair. So yeah."

"How's it going so far? Kelly putting you to work?"

Together we watch Kelly, who has stopped a disheveled-looking man who must have been forced to do a last-minute grocery run by his wife. He attempts to escape, to no avail.

"More like she's doing it herself. Which I think is why not a lot of people want to do this."

"Can I tell you a secret?" I lean in, beckoning her, and she follows with a smile playing on her lips. "I'm glad you're here. Because I wouldn't want to be alone with her; she despises me."

Her laugh catches the other volunteers' attention.

"Why are you laughing? It's true."

"First it's Ali who hates you. Then it's Kelly. Now what did you do to her?"

"I skipped volunteering."

"Okay . . .?"

"Three times."

"Bảo! No wonder she loathes you."

"Sorry, that was all back when I wasn't as motivated."

"What's motivating you now?"

A couple of shoppers have come by, inquiring about our table, and Linh greets them automatically, putting on a smile like she did this all the time. Her energy is palpable and contagious.

"No one in particular," I answer her question, more to myself than to her.

Meanwhile, Kelly passes down another pile of flyers to replenish our stack. She sips a boba from Boba Corner 2. "What's with the ball cap?"

"Bad haircut."

Time passes slowly, but it's not so bad with Linh next to me. We pass commentary about Kelly's determined efforts to solicit money while we hand out flyers about VSA's upcoming events. I spot faint paint marks on the back of her hand, which weren't there yesterday. She must have fit in some painting time this morning.

"Were you painting?"

"Oh, yeah," she says, sheepish again. "Trying to, at least. I need to submit something to the Gold Key competition. I'm realizing that the deadline is getting closer and closer."

"What are you going to do?"

"I'm working on a few things about memory. Good memories. The kind that last a while and show up unexpectedly."

"Like?"

"A restaurant scene. Just me and my parents as we were closing up in the first year. It was a tough year, that first year. People were hard on them." Linh looks over at me and I know what she's thinking. My mom. The General and the others, the snide remarks they made at the restaurant and also freely in public—

"I'm sorry."

Linh shakes her head. "Anyway, my sister and I never really saw our parents because they were always working. But that night, we finished and it'd gone well, and I remember seeing my parents standing by the front windows, just chatting, saying goodbye to some customers. A totally normal scene."

I'm there with her, can feel the window's smooth glass against my hand and its warmth after facing the sun for the whole day. Linh's tone changes into something like reverence and she lifts her hand, gesturing as if she were smearing paint all over a canvas. "But the sky behind them was swathes of blush red and purple and yellow. It took my breath away. It was really beautiful. So I'm working on a small canvas for that."

"That sounds nice."

"Yeah, it was." She looks over at me. "How about you? Still okay with mediocrity?" she says teasingly, leaning forward. A piece of her hair has caught itself on the neck of her T-shirt and I feel like I want to move it away.

"Hey, I've advanced a little." I copy Linh, moving closer even though there's no reason to. "Someone asked for my help the other day. One of Việt's friends needed help. So I helped."

"Did it go well?"

"Yeah. It doesn't happen often—someone asking me for help. Especially with writing. So I was kind of surprised."

"I'm not." She looks deep in thought. "There are people out

176

there who don't have the energy to help people get better. They just accept the other person's flaws, and sure, there's less conflict to deal with, but it's almost like living out a lie. *Then* there are people who aren't afraid to point out something's wrong—even something as little as a typo. In the end, you're making *something* better, and that's more than other people are willing to do."

I clear my throat, trying to quell my emotions fighting against one another. "That's about the nicest thing anyone's ever said to me. Isn't that sad?"

"Sad and true for all kids with demanding Asian parents." Warmth spreads through me. Other curious shoppers have come to the table, but, not for the first time, I see only Linh in front of me. Beaming. I have to blink a few times to remember where I am.

CHAPTER TWENTY

LINH

"My middle finger can't be that big."

"It's not big. It's normal size."

"On the page, it's big," Bảo says in protest. "It's offensively big."

I laugh, turning my pencil upside down and erasing the lines of his "offensive finger" until it *looks* thinner—but not true to size. I was using the back of an extra flyer to sketch Bảo's hand. "Better?"

"Yes."

"I didn't know you were so sensitive about your fingers."

It's easy, when you're having fun, to forget about matters that seemed important only an hour ago. Or at least pretend that they don't exist. The canvas of the restaurant—more of a portrait of my parents—drying at home, one of many I need to finish if I want to even have a chance at the competition.

The deadline is coming, and in moments when I imagine I'm keeping that date far away, it creeps up on me. There's so little time.

Great. I promised myself that I would leave some of my worries at home, and now I'm just buried in thoughts.

I glance at Bảo. At least we're having fun together. We're not looking over our shoulders. But that thought doesn't last long.

I'm the one who spots her first.

And by "her," I mean *them.*

Our mothers, walking down separate parking lanes. Mine is looking through her purse. This morning, before heading to the restaurant, she mentioned she might need to run to the market, but I didn't think it'd be this market. She doesn't like Thuận Phát because of the size. Plus they never have enough of the fish she likes to use.

Bảo's mom walks forward, but squints with the sun in her eyes. I nudge Bảo, cutting him off mid-conversation with another class-mate, and in a second, understanding—and panic—manifests in the visible parts of his face.

"Shit."

"Let's go," I say, pulling him along inside, my heart beating madly. Bảo lowers the bill over his eyes.

Through the automatic sliding doors, the market's smells rush at me: fried pork, herbs, and lingering incense from the owner's shrine. I'm brought back to my childhood, when weekends often meant wandering the aisles, riding on abandoned shopping carts, climbing piles of sacks of rice, and begging my parents to buy me strawberry Hello Pandas and Marukawa gum packets.

The two of us dash into one of the aisles—the one with all the dried fruits, seeds, and peanuts. An older woman catches sight of us and narrows her eyes, before wheeling her cart and turning right at the end.

"Out of all the days," Bảo moans. His phone vibrates in his hand. His mom. "Should I answer?"

"Yes, pick up. You don't want her to be suspicious."

"Hi, Mẹ," he answers, forcing cheeriness into his voice. "Yeah, that was me. I was just taking a break." Pause. "Where did I go? I'm in the . . . snacks aisle. You're heading—where? The peanuts aisle?"

An alarm goes off inside me. I make a split-second decision and dash into the aisle to the left, where sriracha and other Asian sauces are stocked. The lady from before huffs in annoyance when I nearly ram in her. She mutters under her breath about teenagers these days being *mất dạy*, yet continues shopping.

Then I hear Bảo's mom. Her voice is loud as she addresses Bảo, jolting me. I don't think I've heard it since that day at the temple. I duck, catching a glimpse of her through the shelves low on stock. "Bảo?"

"Yep," he answers hoarsely before clearing his throat. "It's me."

"Mẹ almost forgot con wore that hat today. Look *kỳ*. Mẹ thought con want snacks."

"Well, I thought I'd just meet you here." He glances at me swiftly, then uses his back to block me—and my line of vision. "You couldn't find anything at Saigon City?"

"No, there was nothing much on sale. But there's plenty of things on sale here."

"Uh, sorry, I guess I read an old flyer."

"Do con want a snack?"

His reply is quick. "Oh, no I think I'm—"

"Con?" I pivot sharply. Mẹ. "What are you doing?"

"Oh, I'm just . . . I'm hungry." Meanwhile, I try to listen to the conversation on the other side, to see if they're moving. Bảo and his mom are walking to the back. Too close. Our mothers can't see each other—who knows what will happen! So I steer my mother the opposite way, into the nuts aisle, moving us like a revolving door would. "But never mind, I figured I would just wait for lunch to eat."

"Mẹ can buy you something if you need it."

"No, no, I think I'll be fine for now—let's just—" Unfathomably, Bảo's mom is walking past our aisle, him trailing behind, probably thinking we'd have moved by then. He freezes, then runs ahead, grabbing a random snack. I hear him ask if he could get this.

Thankful for the distraction, I loop my arm through my mom's. "Actually, can I get an egg tart?" That, on any other occasion, would have been a normal request. It was always a reward for me and Evie for behaving while our mother completed her shopping.

Mẹ smiles slightly, the corners of her eyes wrinkling. "Some things never change."

Even though we're a good distance away from Bảo and his mom, I keep an eye out for them as Mẹ points at the pastries—the guy at the counter only speaks Malaysian. My mom ends up buying enough for the volunteers, and when she finishes checking out her groceries—watching the prices climb closely—she waves good-bye at me and leaves none the wiser.

I run into Bảo around the corner of the exit. He stops me from going further, grabbing my wrist, and I hear his mom complaining to him about the final receipt before telling him she'll see him back at home. "Don't eat too much," she says, though she's shoving another bag of snacks his way. The other volunteers are going to love us.

Then Bảo's mom is gone.

And we're both alive.

Returning to the entrance, Bảo and I plop down at the volunteering table, exhausted. Kelly asks why we just disappeared, but we hold up the box of pastries as an excuse. The volunteers eagerly dig in, and Bảo gladly reaches for an egg tart.

"See?" he says in between bites. "This is why I don't volunteer." A triumphant grin starts forming until he looks down at our knotted hands.

I don't pull away.

He doesn't pull away.

I'm staring at our hands together, trying to pretend that they aren't ours, just like I did to Bảo's hand before. I was studying his fingers objectively, sketching them as nothing more than a prop.

But I can't do that now. Because it *is* our hands, and neither of us is letting go. My heart pounds. Adrenaline from before or now? I'm not sure. His thumb caresses my knuckles in a move that seems natural, like he'd always held my hand like this. I inhale sharply. In different circumstances, this could happen. This is possible in an alternate reality.

My other hand, I realize, is resting on the table, exactly on top of the sketch of his hand.

We don't say anything, and we don't move until someone down the table asks me to hand them extra flyers, so I have to let go, and I do it like I've been scorched. *Don't look at him*.

The rest of volunteering for us is spent in silence, and I'm lost in how to handle this impossible, unsaid thing sitting between us.

CHAPTER TWENTY-ONE

BẢO

I've been thinking about Linh's hand a lot, her paint-marked hand fitting into my palm. I remember it like it was a living heart, pulsing. I've replayed that moment we noticed what was happening and decided not to care, the moment that I knew we'd stepped into a new place without planning to. I wish there was a word stronger than "palpable," but I guess that was sufficient for now.

When she let go, I wanted so badly to snatch her hand back. When she muttered a quick goodbye to me, I wanted to tell her not to leave. We couldn't just ignore what happened.

She didn't pull away. She could have, but she didn't. Does that mean she feels the same way as me?

Việt and Ali had seen it before us, apparently.

The next week, to my disappointment, unfolds like the days before our worlds collided on Phở Day. Our schedule consists of way too many misses. At lunch, when I stop by the art room, I don't find her there. I know for a fact that Linh's avoiding me, because she skipped the next restaurant coverage, mentioning it to Ali, who told me she was overwhelmed by work and painting. There's truth in that, I'm sure, but not completely.

She's scared, and I wish I could tell her that I am, too. That I don't know how things will work. But if we could hold hands a bit longer, maybe we'll figure it out.

I had to go alone to a Malaysian restaurant, while most of the customers enjoyed meals among large families. They must have felt sorry for me, a high school boy, dining out alone. The chef gave me a doggy bag of some kind of cookies that Ba demolished later in the night.

As we sit across the table at 10:00 p.m., feeling Mẹ's absence as she was still at a friend's house for a mani and pedi, I have this ridiculous thought to ask for advice. *Ba is a man. Ba has experienced things like this . . . right?* Then I stop the idea almost immediately. I must be getting desperate if I think it's a good pick to ask my dad, stone-cold Dad, for girl advice when we don't exactly enjoy small talk in general.

Tonight must be different, because Ba starts the small talk anyway. Those cookies must be good.

"We're going to need your help in the next few weeks at the restaurant."

"Oh, okay. What's happening?"

"Your mom and I are planning a *Bánh Xèo* Day to introduce different kinds of *bánh xèo* to the menu. So things will be busy."

Just like Việt had suggested.

"Did Việt mention anything to you?"

"Why would he?"

"Never mind." I think about the special. Linh's family—Linh—are going to see it as a direct response to their Phở Day. Great: One more reason for our parents to despise one another.

"Why now?" I ask warily.

"To make sure our customers don't get tired of our menus."

"Will it work? We don't usually do different kinds of *bánh xèo*."

"We never really know when things will work. We weren't sure a restaurant would work, but here we are. There is no use playing it safe when it comes to our restaurant." Ba gets up and puts on the teakettle. He shuffles to the cabinet where we keep various tins of tea leaves. *"Muốn trà không?"*

I shake my head, thinking tea will only keep me up later than I should.

Playing it safe.

If my dad's willing to do something that might not bring him any sure result, maybe I can do the same.

Later I stared for longer than I'd like to admit at a text to send to Linh. A text asking her to meet again, face-to-face. I wasn't as blunt; I had a good reason to text her, since Ali sent me another restaurant to visit. So I mentioned that to her.

186

Then her bubbles begin to appear, so I shut down the Messages app, until a ring tells me to read it.

sorry to be MIA. your article on that malaysian place was great.

thanks! do you think you can make the next one?

i think so.

CHAPTER TWENTY-TWO

LINH

I've been thinking about Bảo's hand a lot, his thumb unthinkingly brushing the top of mine. A moment brimming with potential, but neither of us could say a word about it. Because we know. We both know the risks that we were taking, just sitting next to each other. We barely escaped our mothers back then.

"What do you think, con?"

It's after dinner; the dishes have been cleared and a pot of freshly brewed Jasmine tea sits between us. Ba and Mẹ push a large binder of fabric toward me. They're thinking of ordering newer place mats and tablecloths for the restaurant, eager to keep up the momentum from Phở Day. Usually they don't bring me into business decisions about the restaurant, but I've "always been good with colors," Ba said. One of the only occasions he'd acknowledge my art abilities as an asset, like the ad that I'd done for the restaurant.

I touch one that is the lightest green available, which might soften the harsh lights in our restaurant. We can find a light beige place mat to match it. Add a small vase of flowers, and I can see it happening. "This could work."

My parents lift it up, assessing it. There's a glint in my mom's eyes that I've only seen for food. She's having a vision for the restaurant, just like my dad. Things are going so well. They're happy. I'm happy too, even though I have a list of things to do. This . . . thing with Bảo has to be kept safe, confined to what we do in the art room, secreting moments away from everyone's eyes.

I can't do anything to upset the balance.

"Good, con," Ba says in approval. "Good."

I got the text from Bảo asking if I could go to the next restaurant. There's a blank feeling to his message, a straightforward ask, and I wonder if Bảo's determined to pretend that our hand-holding didn't happen, too.

I told everything to Ali, about volunteering, our near escape, our held hands. She said it's like we're in some romantic comedy or something, but also freely expresses how she thinks we're both being ridiculous. In fact, she hasn't shut up about it, even as we're trying to finish some homework at the restaurant. Ba's out running errands, specifically finding a saucepan to replace one of ours with a broken handle. I glance at the tables that used to have our worn white tablecloths, which have now been replaced with the pastel green I liked, the beige place mats to follow soon.

"Linh, is that why you missed out on the Malaysian restaurant the other day?" Ali asks, light bulb turning on. She asked this after Bảo handed in his review and she noticed I hadn't sketched anything. I told her how busy I was, mentioning the Gold Keys, and she understood; now my friend rather than the editor in chief was asking me.

"Yes," I say finally. "But it would have been so awkward."

"So what are you going to say to Bảo's text? No? Then he'll really think something is up. Don't avoid this, Linh." She grabs my hand. "I know you. I know you want to disappear into your paintings." I try pulling away. "I know you want to keep things inside. Bảo seems to want to explore more with you, but if you don't want that, you have to tell him."

I look around to make sure my mom isn't nearby. She's in the kitchen. "That's the problem, Ali. I do want him."

Her expression doesn't change. "Then talk it out, at least."

"But our families—"

"Again, I'm not going to pretend I know everything about your families. But sitting here avoiding him will not help at all."

She reaches for my phone and places it between us. "Call him. Or text him. But silence isn't the answer. It'll make things worse."

"What will make things worse?" Mẹ comes by with two glasses of iced coffee for us. She glances between me and Ali expectantly, but neither of us answers. Wants to answer.

190

As always, Ali's right. Avoiding Bảo isn't the right way to handle this. And I miss having him in the art room with me.

"If we didn't get our iced coffees, which we seriously need if we want to stay awake. So much homework," Ali says, suddenly perky. She takes a loud sip of her drink. "Tastes great, Mrs. Phạm."

CHAPTER TWENTY-THREE

BẢO

Chơi Ơi is the opposite of a traditional Việt restaurant. The restaurant name itself parodies *"trời ơi,"* an expression my mom likes to use when she's annoyed at me or at my dad. But the name turns the exclamation into something more playful—literally, "Play!"

Inside, the restaurant, located just at the edge of Fountain Valley, has a high-vaulted ceiling and deep red walls brightened by lanterns. Columns are decorated with eye-catching nighttime cityscapes of what looks like Vietnamese cities, rendered from photos.

Linh had arrived a few minutes before me and was inspecting one of the photos. Of course.

"See something interesting?"

Linh jumps, then brushes back her hair sheepishly. The movement brings my attention to her hand, the one that I held.

"Didn't think you'd make it," I say, watching her closely.

We'd almost had to reschedule again, though, because things at work were getting busy for me and Linh. Lisa, the girl who'd seemed too nervous to work at a restaurant, had called out sick, so Linh had to pick up a shift. I also know the deadline for the Gold Keys was drawing closer and closer. In my texts to her, I wasn't sure what to do or say to help—lethologica: the inability to find the right words—but being here seems to bring back some spark in her eyes.

She knows how I feel now. Ball's in her court.

"Figured you needed me," she answers simply. "Unless you already have another artist friend lined up."

As the host shows us to our seats, I'm hoping her emphasis on "friend" isn't purposeful.

I focus on the restaurant instead. According to the existing interviews I'd read online, the owner and executive chef Brian Lê had trained in Paris, then Italy, but as much as he loved European cuisine, he always considered Vietnamese his first love—thanks to his father, who's a retired chef. So he came back to the States and opened up his restaurant, which has been reviewed by the *New York Times* and the *Los Angeles Times*, which praise his specialty: his *bún bò Huế*. Not for the first time, I wonder how Ali managed to be so persuasive that someone with this much notoriety and posh training had agreed to invite two high school students to taste his food.

But the moment Chef Lê bounds out of the kitchen into the dining room, it all makes sense. Maybe in his late thirties, he wears a worn ball cap backward and his chef's jacket is opened to reveal a T-shirt that says, ALLOW ME TO EXPLAIN THROUGH INTERPRETIVE DANCE. And his wide grin—kind of like a kid who was told he could have as much candy as he wanted—coaxes a smile from us.

"What's good, little ones?" He gathers each of us into a bear hug. "Glad you're here. Brian Lê. Or Chef Lê." *Now* he shakes our hands.

"My mom's maiden name is Lê," I say.

"Maybe we were related way back when, who knows." He winks.

I like him. "Thanks for letting us stop by. Just tell us where we should sit. We won't be in anyone's way."

"Sit?"

"Um yeah, we're here to review your menu," Linh says.

"Don't you want a tour, too?"

We didn't get a chance to walk around at any other restaurant. Do reviewers usually get this kind of access?

"Come on, let's take you guys to the back where all the magic happens." Without waiting for us, he turns and we stand helpless for a few beats until we follow him into his labyrinthine kitchen. It's like Mẹ's kitchen, only cleaner and probably more organized. And probably staffed with more people who are less apt to mess up.

So, not like our kitchen.

The cooks give us a quick look before focusing back on their dishes. One cook sprinkles chopped raw green onions over a platter of freshly cooked *cá chiên*, the snapper still sizzling from its quick fry in a sauté pan. Another guy uses a ladle the size of my hand to transfer bubbling broth into graphite-colored bowls. Even the cooked rice, which someone's spooning into bowls, looks better than usual, gleaming under the restaurant's expensive lights. I'm glad my parents aren't here to see this.

Another chef yells, "Behind!" before passing us with a large pot smelling of pineapples—*canh chua*, most likely. Meanwhile, Chef Lê points to different cooks and their specialties. Picks up ingredients that he insists are totally "high-grade." Narrowly crashes into his employees as they busily rush around, though it's all done in odd synchronicity like they're used to his chaotic energy.

Chef Lê stops before one large pot in particular. With a flourish, he lifts the lid and beckons us to lean in. "Smell that shit and tell me no one will want to eat it." Seeing his expectant look, we do as we're told.

"That smells—"

"—delicious."

Linh and I lock eyes before releasing immediately.

Bún bò. An earthy, fatty broth, a powerful punch of citrus from lemongrass. It's familiar. It's home in one punch. Chef Lê shoots us a smile, likes seeing us confirm how good it smells and *looks* without us wasting words. Maybe he's a bit smug about it.

"This is just a preview, of course. Wait until you taste everything."

Somehow I wonder if he mistook us for someone else. Linh thinks the same, saying as much to him.

"Nope, I know who you are: Badass high school students." He points to us with both index fingers. Me and Linh share another glance, nearly bursting out laughing. What a weird guy. "I was your age once upon a time. When I was in Paris and in Rome, I made things that cost even more than I could afford. I hated that. And sometimes the food wasn't even good. If I can make any Việt kid your age happy and wanna come to this restaurant, then I guess I did my job." He directs us back to where we came in. "Now that you got the tour, let's get you back and you can taste all the magic that happens here. You and your girlfriend will love this."

"She's not—well—" I know I'm stammering.

"What if he's *my* boyfriend and *he's* just tagging along?" Linh says.

Chef Lê smiles again. "Oh, touché. She's got some spice!"

"We're partners," I quickly clarify, saying anything so that Chef Lê doesn't get the wrong idea and keep going with the joke, making things even more uncomfortable between me and Linh.

Back at the table in the center of the room— "Newly renovated! So you can experience everything," Chef Lê says—Linh and I sit across from each other, absorbing the flurry around us.

"Settle down and food's going to come out in a sec."

I turn to Linh. "Did we even order?"

"Nope, but I don't think we're going to have a bad meal here," Linh says.

A line of servers brings out the appetizers and immediately our table goes from empty to crowded. A good thing, since it makes me less aware of how I'm sitting, holding myself. How far away my hands are from hers and how weird it'd be if I reached for her again.

Turns out Linh and I have nothing to say to each other. For good reason.

The reason being we're more preoccupied with the food that may or may not be better than my mom's.

"If my parents were here . . .," Linh begins to say into her bowl of *bún bò Huế*.

"They'd steal this recipe. Mine would do the same."

"Sorry, this recipe is legit sealed," says Chef Lê, who'd come back five minutes ago to check in on us but sat down as if he was part of the party. I guess this isn't unusual for him because the servers set up a plate for him right away. "My dad would chase me out of California if it somehow leaked."

I grin as I write down his quote. I'm already five pages in with my notes—most of the pages filled with details from the kitchen and atmosphere instead of the actual food. Linh has started some sketches of the appetizers and entrees. "Is your dad the cook in the family?"

"Yeah, Poppa Lê had a small place in Santa Monica about half the size of this place. I basically grew up there."

"Our families have restaurants, too," Linh offers.

"No surprise—you two have healthy appetites," Chef Lê teases us.

"Where did the idea of opening up a restaurant come from?" I ask.

"Probably from my dad. Loved what he did with the place. He just wanted to make customers happy." Chef Lê laughs, now with a faraway glint in his eyes. "I was always tagging around at his place and he'd yell at me because there was legit no space. My mom, though, she completely disagreed with me going into a culinary career. Even culinary school! It wasn't exactly . . . stable, you know."

Linh shifts in her seat, catching the message. Seems like a theme with Việt mothers.

"So when I told her I wanted to open a restaurant, she went off on me. I know she was worried then, but we said some stuff to each other. Lot of angry words."

"What happened after?" Linh asks quietly.

"My mom didn't talk to me for two years. But it's not like we weren't a part of each other's lives. They lived just a few minutes away from me. I'd talk to my dad, who always updated me on my mom and what she was doing. *Always*. I mean, I knew what she'd bought for groceries because he'd tell me! It was the same thing for me. I bet my mom knew what I was up to each week."

Chef Lê points at the entrance as if someone would make an appearance. "Then, the day after I got that *Los Angeles Times* review was the day my mom appeared at the door. My dad had dropped her off! He was tired of the fighting and called us the two most stubborn people he'd ever met." He lets out a loud laugh. "And we made up, just like that. After that she was always showing up here, playing host but also correcting my chefs' mistakes, correcting *my* recipes."

"Two years," Linh whispers in dismay.

Chef Lê nods knowingly. "We lost some time. I think about that all the time now that she's gone." He pauses. "It's been six and a half months."

That last bit shocks me—I didn't come across that in any of the articles—and I put down my pencil. "I'm sorry," I say, hearing Linh offer the same condolences. The sentence sounds so canned; something I'm not used to saying. I don't know anyone who's actually lost a parent. I've heard about it, but the concept seems so far away. So impossible.

"Do you think about her a lot?" I ask.

"Legit the other day. I was creating a recipe, something that I had as a little kid and only my mom could make it. I just wished I'd asked when she was alive. And then I just had a kid, too, so I'm wondering how to tell him about my mom. There's still so much history that I don't know. My dad casually mentioned the other day that he'd lost a sister when he was six and she was two. Seven siblings I knew about, but not his sister. . . ." Chef Lê trails off, looking back at the kitchen. "History, man. There's a lot hidden." Then he perks up, remembering where he is. "Anyway, I'm still glad we came back into each other's lives. We had a good time together."

A server comes by with a message for Chef Lê from the kitchen. He needs to go back, so he does, leaving me and Linh to ourselves again. A busboy stops by with his bin to clear the plates and we hand them over, too accustomed to doing it ourselves.

"He's nice," I tell Linh as she packs up her things.

"One of a kind." She turns her notebook upside down, showing me her quick sketch of him, ball cap and T-shirt captured perfectly. Much like my notes, her focus is Chef Lê and his dynamic personality. "There's a lot to unpack."

"Right, his mom."

"And going two years because she didn't like what he was doing. That's hard to even imagine." She sighs loudly, shoving her colored pencils into her messenger bag. "That's another reason I don't ever see myself telling my mom the truth."

Now that we don't have any food to distract us, or Chef Lê to dominate the conversation, or anything else between us, the elephant in the room comes back, the reason for how hesitant we seem to be acting toward each other.

"Hey," I say as gently as possible. "Can we talk?"

"We are." All of her emotions have shut off.

"Linh, I mean about the other day."

"I don't think I can stay longer," she says in apology. Her expression is twisted, like it's physically hurting her being here. "Can we talk another time?"

"I know what you're thinking."

"Believe me, you don't know half of it, Bảo," she says firmly.

"Well, you can tell me, then. Because I'm here. I'm all ears. Even if you don't want—" *Us.* My thoughts pause. What if I'd misread everything up until now? What if I thought she liked me because I liked her too much and Linh was being too nice to say something? Like how she was nice to Kelly even though she didn't have time to volunteer? Like now, how she's avoiding it so that she doesn't reject me outright?

She's barely looking at me. Maybe I'm closer to the truth than I thought I'd be.

"I can be here as a friend," I finally say. "Really, no hard feelings."

"Thank you," she says with such relief that it hurts. "I'm sorry."

There is a painful pause as Linh pretends to check the table to make sure she hasn't forgotten her belongings. I squeeze the back of my chair, fighting the urge to just say something—anything to make her look at me. Before I can think of anything, Linh says a quiet goodbye and leaves.

I exhale. *So that's it. She doesn't feel what I feel.*

I head to the front, thanking a Black woman with the name tag Saffron—which I had to look at twice; it was too perfect for someone in the business. The way she stands tall reminds me of my mom when she's fired up and of Linh when she's excited about light or some obscure painting that I wouldn't know about unless she told me. I feel like I should fix my hair and anything else on my body that's out of place.

"Brian made the best food for you tonight. Usually it's not this good," she jokes, her French accent apparent.

"Hey, do you want to keep your job?" Chef Lê says, emerging from behind a divider, wiping his hands on a hand towel.

"That's not for you to decide," she retorts, "since I own half the place."

This doesn't faze him and now he merely sports a smile. "Mr. Nguyễn, meet my partner and wife."

"Partner but his boss," she playfully chastises him. "Oh, and also his wife."

"Yeah, yeah. Anyway, Saff, this boy here, he's going to be big one day. I can feel it. He's like Anthony Bourdain, rest in peace."

I blink at his unexpected compliment. This is what it means when someone gushes, I guess. "Thanks."

"You made me think, you know. Not a lot of people know how to do that," Chef Lê says, looking serious.

I brush the back of my neck. "I was just asking questions."

"That's the best type of interview. You gave me room to just talk." He claps me on the shoulder, and I sway from the weight of it. "Come back anytime. You and Linh. I saw some of what she's sketching. She seems great, too."

"She is."

"But she's *really* not your girlfriend?" He makes a show of looking over his shoulder. "Or, I'm sorry, you're not really her boyfriend?"

"No, she isn't."

"Yooo," he says with a slow-forming smirk, "you like her, don't you?"

Saffron elbows him. "Bry! Stop teasing him."

"It's complicated."

Chef Lê just laughs. "Good luck, man."

"Con!" My mom calls for me the moment I step into the house. *Biểu đấy.*

I'm home on time, so that's not why she's calling for me. *Shit, did I leave the toilet seat up again?* I take the steps slowly, trying to figure out what I must have done wrong. Running through me, though, something I can't ignore, is an urge to sit down and just *write*. Because Chef Lê is more interesting than I thought he'd be. Because I'd rather get lost in writing than think about the failed attempt to talk to Linh about us . . . about her rejection.

Mẹ, just showered, stands in front of the bathroom sink. She leans toward the mirror—her mirror counterpart looks at me. A Vietnamese ballad spills out from her bedroom. Ba must be at the restaurant still.

"Here," she says, and hands the tweezers over. "I need you to pull out a white hair."

My mom likes to complain that she has so many because of me. I guess I probably shouldn't tell her it's because she's just old.

Sighing, I take the tweezers from her, agreeing to a task that I've been subjugated to since I was old enough to hold these things and also since my mom spotted her first one back when I was in sixth grade. I'm not the only one, though. Việt's had to do this too.

"Where?"

"*Nè.*" She holds it up and I squint. Got one. "Did you finish your project?"

"Yep."

"Good." I feel her gaze through the mirror. "You are out a lot these days." I accidentally pull out a black hair. "Ah, *mày làm gì vậy?*"

"Sorry." I do it more gently. "The newspaper keeps me busy."

"Con still writing reviews."

"I am, yeah." I'm not sure why but Chef Lê comes into mind again, about his early struggles with his mom. Two years. I wonder if me and my mom can ever stop talking for that long. And who would instigate it? "There's this guy I met on my assignment. Brian Lê."

"Vietnamese. What does he do?" she asks almost immediately.

"He's the executive chef and owner. He's pretty young."

"It is hard," she answers sagely. "But impressive for his age."

"He was talking about his parents and the things he wanted to ask them."

"Oh?"

"His mother died in the past few months."

Mẹ clicks her tongue. *"Tội quá."* Poor guy.

"Yeah, and he mentioned not knowing everything he could have known about her while she was alive." I thread my fingers through her hair, rechecking my work. "Why don't you talk about Vietnam more?"

"I do! I talk about it all the time." She looks at me directly through the mirror.

"Yeah, I know, but more specific things. I know where you lived, what my grandparents did. That you escaped at night. But that's more like an overview. Why don't you tell me the smaller things?"

"Because you don't ask. But the things I do tell you, you always say, 'Oh, I don't want to hear it, I don't have time, Mẹ, I heard you say this already.'" She mimics what she thinks I sound like.

"My voice can't go that high," I say grudgingly. I *have* said those things, though.

"I am your mother, so I don't have to tell you anything most of the time. Some matters are too adult for you," Mẹ starts to say in a familiar *There's no use arguing* voice.

"Okay."

"But, if you do want to know more, Mẹ will try to answer you. But my memory isn't so good anymore and things are just from so long ago. Mẹ wonder if the past should stay in the past."

"Maybe, but maybe not." Silence eases in as I concentrate on her hair.

"All of this writing business is making you different." Our eyes meet in the mirror again. She tilts her head, regarding me like she would with a recipe that was missing one crucial ingredient.

"Good different?"

"Maybe. You seem less weak."

I refrain from rolling my eyes. "Thanks."

"What is making con write?"

I don't expect that kind of question from Me, so I wonder if it's a mistranslation. "Like, why am I writing?"

"Yes."

"I don't know. I'll get a good grade, I guess." Even my answer, said out loud, doesn't sit right in my head. I couldn't care less about the actual journalism class and getting good grades and all that. But I have to admit, I feel more and more solid when I have a pen in hand. When there's an article that needs fixing and it's up to me to make everything sound right. I did that for Steve and Ernie. I did it for myself.

Linh had said I'd find something to be passionate about. What if she's right?

"Who is right?"

Oops, I'd said that last line out loud. My mom gazes expectantly at me.

"Me," I begin. "Weren't you saying earlier in the year that you wanted me to find something? Be more motivated?"

"Con want to be a writer?"

In my mind's eye, far into the future, I'm seeing myself in a news-room, a big one. In some big city. I see nights working under desk lamps. Ink staining my shirt cuffs, eyes tight and bleary from unrest. I see words flowing from my fingertips.

"I'm thinking about it."

"Writing is hard. Con might not find a job." Mẹ, always blunt.

"I know."

"You might need to live in our basement."

"What—I won't."

"You can if you will need to."

"It's all cement."

"We will work on renovating it. Just for you."

"So much confidence," I mutter.

Mẹ pats my hand, holding the tweezers. "Mẹ saying the basement is yours if you need it. You can stay as long as you want."

I imagine thirty-five-year-old me, journalist, writer, or whatever, living in the dungeons of our basement. Maybe some people would be okay staying with family, but I don't think that's for me. As I look back at my mom, I see her contented smile, and the corners of my mouth tilt up. All that nagging she's done over the years finally paid off, she's likely thinking. And now she can worry less, have less gray hairs.

I wince at the idea of her satisfaction swiftly turning to anger once she realizes who's been a part of this change inside me. Linh's apologetic face appears suddenly. *I'm sorry.*

I say nothing more and continue to scout for the rest of Mẹ's rebellious hair strands.

CHAPTER TWENTY-FOUR

LINH

Two years. Two years that Chef Lê went without speaking to his mom, despite having the bravery that I lack to follow what he wanted. He's made a career of it, yet it took a while for his mother to come back, and that was only by his father's doing.

I'm sitting at my desk, finessing my sketch of Chef Lê, who's now grinning back at me. I'll need to redraw it so that it's publishable. Other pieces of paper are scattered across my desk, some homework sheets and different drafts of the Scholastic Art Award application. The essay still needs filling out, but everything's turning into hieroglyphics and my eyes must be red after me rubbing at them so much. I've been struggling to put words to paper, and now

I think I've highly underestimated what Ali and Bảo do seemingly so easily.

My thoughts turn ugly, too many colors mixed together. *Would it even matter if I ended up getting this award? Would it do anything? Would it change much?* I guess this is what it means to tear your hair out.

I wouldn't know how to stand it—me and my mom not talking, for whatever reason. I've only done this with Evie; growing up we've had a few arguments that all seem childish now, but back then we'd go days without talking. Instead of trading nasty words, we'd fight by turning the bedroom lights on and off at inopportune times, seizing control of the washer and dryer even when a load wasn't finished, and completely ignoring the car-sharing schedule. The longest silence between us had lasted a week, broken only when Ba had done something ridiculous at the restaurant, and me and Evie accidentally met eyes, stifling our laughs.

But a laugh wouldn't solve how much I'd already lied to my parents.

And then there's Bảo and that moment outside the supermarket. His questions while we were at Chơi Ơi.

If I were anyone other than Linh Mai, someone *not* from a family who despises his, I'd be excited. There'd be no hesitation.

But I can't be. Hence why I practically ran away when Bảo broached the topic just as we were leaving.

What am I even doing anymore?

My phone buzzes in my pocket.

"Bảo?"

"Hey, Linh."

He never calls me this late. We've only texted so far. The deep pitch of his voice through the phone sounds more intimate.

"Is everything okay?" I hold my breath. Not the question I want to ask, because obviously, something happened between us. Something I hope he doesn't bring up again, because I can't deal with it right now.

"I wanted to let you know: I'm going to be a writer."

"What?"

"Yeah, I've figured it out. It's what I want to do. And I wanted you to know because you're the one responsible for it."

I lean back in my chair. In the mirror I look at when applying makeup in the morning, I'm smiling. "Bảo, I did nothing. It's all you."

"Lies." He pauses. "I told my mom, too. I can't tell how excited she is, but she's not complaining about it, at least."

"So your mom's accepting?"

"She offered the basement to me in case I can't find work after college, so I guess so."

"Lucky you." I try but I can't keep the bitterness from my tone. Immediately, I feel horrible. "I'm sorry. Imagine me saying that but without the vitriol." He only laughs, clearly in a good mood. "No, seriously. This is great. I'm not surprised. So whatever I did to influence you, I guess I'll take it."

"Ever since we met, you haven't said I can't do it. You've just accepted that I was starting to write, and I think you're the first person in my life to do that."

209

I turn in my swivel chair, smiling against the mouthpiece.

"What are you doing now?"

I hear Bảo typing away on the other side, and I'm sure he'll hear my eraser squeaking against the desk as I write another grammatically incorrect sentence.

"It's taking me ages to write my statement for the Gold Key application. *How* do you write?"

He snickers. "That's like me asking how you paint."

"Seriously, if there's a secret, tell me. My Gold Key statement still needs to be written."

"Be honest."

Is it a comment, in a not-so-subtle way, on what I haven't been honest about? Annoyance spikes within me. "Bảo—"

"What I mean is, you spend so much time worrying about your parents, how to tell them about the real you, that this is your chance to have a conversation only with the one reading your essay. You don't have to worry about your parents. Or anyone else." *Like you?* I ask silently. "Think about what you want. What you want to make and add to the world." He stops suddenly. "Wow, I sound like Ali, don't I? All of this motivational talk."

I smile, hearing genuine awe in his voice. Ali was my number-one fan before I knew I needed one.

"She'd be honored to hear you say that. You know she likes you now." I don't tell him that if Ali had an issue with him, it wouldn't be so subtle.

"Sure. Deep down."

"Exactly."

"Deep, deep, *deep* down."

I roll my eyes.

"Don't roll your eyes." I hear his smile.

"I'm not!"

"You are. It's not too hard to imagine you right now."

"Oh? And what are you imagining?"

Bảo exhales into the phone. I wait. My pencil hangs loose from my fingers as I rest my elbows on the desk. Outside it's completely dark, save for the streetlamps that've dimmed to save energy; they'll return to full force in a few minutes. Somewhere a dog growls and barks, and on the opposite side, a smaller dog chirps back. Talking to each other with a fence—maybe many—in between them.

"You're at your desk. You have your hair in a ponytail. You're leaning all the way forward in your chair because you're deep into your work. That's how you always are, especially when painting." I exhale a shaky breath. *This guy.* "Whenever you're thinking you rub your thumb on that bump on your middle finger, where your pencil's usually resting. The desk lamp is giving you a warm glow; it's the type of light you like—not too bright, not too dim." Then he lets out a half laugh. "Am I right?"

I hear the creak of his chair as he leans back. Probably looking smug.

"You're wrong."

"Am I?"

"My hair's down, not in a ponytail."

"Sorry for the gross assumption." He lets out a deep sigh. "Sorry, I'm taking up your time. You want me to go?"

I keep drawing. "No, it's fine. You can stay." It's comforting just to have him on the line, made even better by knowing he's not pressing me.

By the time my mom comes in without knocking, Bảo's off the phone, but not before I texted him my sketch of Chef Lê. I cover it up with some loose chemistry notes. Her wet hair is wrapped in a towel and she's already applied her Crabtree & Evelyn body lotion, which signals she's about to turn in. Her eyes sweep the room—the dim lighting, various half-finished homework sheets scattered on my bed, and the rainbow of papers across my writing desk. I shift to the left to hide my Gold Key essay drafts out of sight.

"We're doing another Phở Day."

"When was this decided?"

"A week ago."

"But why?"

Mẹ removes her towel and rubs out the water in her hair. "*That* restaurant is having a *Bánh Xèo* Day, so your father decided we should have our own. So we will need you in a couple of weeks."

I've already cut my time for art in half and am no closer to finishing my pieces for the Gold Keys. And now this. "Mẹ, I can't. I have so much to do."

My mom glances down at the papers across my desk. "You have a lot of homework?"

"Yeah, but it's more homework than usual."

"But you have always managed to do your homework on time. You shouldn't worry—"

"Just because I've managed before doesn't mean I can't be stressed out." I'd cut her off without realizing it, a harsh tone ringing in my ears. I bite my lower lip.

Perhaps she's really tired or just disappointed; she doesn't press me. "We can talk more tomorrow, but *con phải ngủ đi*." Mẹ runs her hand through my hair, telling me to sleep. She runs a hand on my shoulder before leaving the room.

The drive over to the restaurant is silent. My mom must have said something to my dad about my reaction last night, because he's not saying much either. A Vietnamese song plays low in the background, a crooning one that my mom likes to play in the house at nighttime, something like a lullaby. The sun is just peeking out over the arched roofs of restaurants and stores, as if wary of the people below it.

Ba yawns. I yawn back. He switches on the blinker, and we turn onto the street. We pass Bảo's restaurant and it's dark inside, but any minute now, his parents will turn the OPEN plaque around, and Bảo will be there, too. I think he mentioned having to work on Sunday.

"*Sao mà thấy con mặt bực mình vậy?*" Ba asks, his voice still gruff with sleep.

"I'm not angry," I mutter, which, of course, gives me away. "I'm just stressed."

"Schoolwork?" Ba asks.

I nod.

"Why is it stressful now? Last year was more stressful." Which is true, in a way. I was busy worrying about SATs and didn't have much time to work on my paintings then, either, but now . . . everything is happening at once.

I deflect. "Why do we never have enough people at work?"

"Lisa quit. It was unexpected."

"Then hire people who won't quit."

I meet Ba's furious eyes in the rearview mirror. *"Con này,"* he starts to say. Mẹ shushes him, probably knowing his anger will not help here. But the tightness of her posture shows that this argument isn't finished.

Mẹ takes the back entrance while I help Ba lift the security grilles up front, walking in once the front door unlocks. The fans begin to turn, working against the heat. But instead of telling me to grab an apron like usual, or delegating tasks to me, like refilling the napkins or getting ice from the freezer or unwrapping the bins of herbs we'll need for the day, my mom nods for me to join her in the kitchen. Ba goes his own way to check last night's sales and the timesheets.

The two of us are in the kitchen, our steps echoing off the walls. I take a stool.

She dons kitchen gloves and pulls out her wooden cutting board, starts slicing onions. Next to her is a vinegar bath that the cooks made, so Mẹ just needs to complete the pickling process. She dips her finger into the vinegar bath, then adds a spoonful of sugar before dumping in the onions. I watch her stir it, then taste it, before she pushes the bowl toward me. My turn to try it.

"Vừa không?"

I ignore her question, staring resolutely at the tabletop. Heaving a sigh, my mom leans forward, resting her elbows on the prep table. Her hair has already loosened from its bun. I see bags under her eyes. The guilt that's become all too familiar nowadays flares up. But I still hate the idea that I'm expected to be the replacement when someone else isn't available. And the last special would have failed if it weren't for Bảo's help—which will not happen again.

So I look away. I hear my mom's lips part, then close. Maybe I've made her angry too. Aside from three or four blowups—including the time when she stumbled across me and Evie drawing pictures with crayons on our old apartment walls—she's been decidedly calmer than Ba.

Instead, her voice takes on its usual soft quality, with an indiscernible tinge. "Con, I know this isn't how you want to spend your time. And Mẹ and Ba hate having to ask you to work.

"But you don't know how hard it was to start up this restaurant. It wasn't about inheriting customers, finding new customers. It was inheriting a whole neighborhood of people who didn't want us." Mẹ's voice cracks. Anguish, that's the note I'd heard. "You don't know how that feels."

"You never told me," I retort, though my intent to sound annoyed is weak. I've never heard Mẹ sound this way. It tugs the same part of my heart storing all the hugs and kisses and laughs she's given me through so many sacrifices.

"Because you shouldn't have to know those things. We wanted to protect you." A spike of anger rushes through me. I'd hate to say it was in response to Bảo's parents, because that would mean I was angry with him, too. Still, it's clear that the cold welcoming had hurt my parents, made them feel less than welcome.

Mẹ shakes her head like she's denying the memories brought up. "The gossip was horrible, not just from that restaurant. Everywhere. But if I addressed it, people would add something else to the mix and there'd be no ending to it. So I ignored it. I put my everything into the food here, to make it speak for itself. Then your dad made friends and we made loyal customers." She gestures to the restaurant. "Phở Day made me so happy because it worked out. And now we're doing well. But it is always a game here. It's always a game to win, to maintain that we belong here."

I wonder if Mẹ means not just this community but in America in general.

I keep my head down. "Will the gossip ever stop? Will we always need to fight B—" I catch myself before saying "Bảo's parents." "—the Nguyễns' restaurant?"

Thankfully, Mẹ doesn't seem to notice. "Gossip and rumors never stop. They always come back in different forms." The knowingness in her voice—and the palpable feeling that there's something more she's holding back—triggers me to glance at her.

"Like when?"

It takes a few beats for Mẹ to make her decision. When she sits down across from me, I lean forward on my stool. "When I was eleven. Back in Vietnam," my mom starts, "Dì Vàng was ready to marry a neighbor who grew up with her. They were always together, and when our families realized what would happen, we began to set up our meetings to talk about expectations and the

216

future for the two of them. The man was smart, nice, and always put the family first."

"Was he an artist too?" I try to picture my aunt with a boyfriend or a husband, but I only see her as I do now: her blurry face enlarged on the computer when we'd speak, her loud, assured voice when she talks about art. That's her true love; I can't imagine someone else in her life.

"Of course not," Mẹ answers quickly. "One of the reasons why your grandparents liked the man, before they passed, was because he was a logical person. He was going to inherit the family business, too. They knew that he would be able to support her when she couldn't do that herself with her art." I hold back from protesting. She said that as if it were a fact. As if my aunt weren't doing well for herself now.

"One day, though, he left, apologizing to everyone through a letter. But oh, the gossip! His family and the whole neighborhood were blaming Dì Vàng, as if she had done something, when it was actually him who'd run away from his promises. His responsibilities."

"What happened then?" I ask. "With the guy and with your sister?"

"I learned that he died." That can mean many things: during a battle, during one of the bombings, or during the escape, the same route that my family miraculously survived. "It is horrible, yes. All of it. He was, at the end of the day, good, and he would have made a good match for my sister." I sit back, cupping my tea for warmth, feeling as if a part of me has turned inside out. Her art. That's why her art always feels so sad. In each artwork she produces, she leaves that melancholic imprint behind.

"Why I haven't heard of this before?"

Mẹ sighs as she pushes back her hair. "There was no reason for it to come up. And it is something of the past—what good will it do to bring it up? Your aunt certainly doesn't mention it. We are in the present now—we look to the future." She takes an apron off the hook and offers me my apron. "We ignore all gossip and do our best.

"Con, I know you are busy. But you did such a good job last time. You can do it again. And you will survive your schoolwork. Because you are my daughter."

I take the apron from Mẹ. She smiles, and it's so grateful and so understanding that I muster up a smile, the weight on my shoulders even more insistent.

CHAPTER TWENTY-FIVE

BẢO

In the newsroom, just as the dismissal bell rings to let out class, the phone rings, too. Shouldering past our classmates flooding out of the room, Ali answers with a brisk tone. I can see her in the future now, poised over the phone, a notepad and pen in hand. She waits for a few minutes until she turns, fixing me with a look. I start walking past her, but she stops me.

"Bảo, it's for you."

That's new. I take the phone as cautiously as if I was just asked to take care of some dangerous creature. "Hello?"

"Yo, *em*!" Chef Lê. I know it immediately from his voice. "It's me: Chef Lê from Chơi Ơi! What's good?"

"Uh, hi. I'm in school right now." Is he calling about the article? It doesn't sound like he's calling to yell about how bad it was. I picture him at the same table, his chef jacket's sleeves rolled up. Maybe with his feet propped on the seat across from him until his wife, Saffron, comes by to smack them off.

"Yeah, sorry, I was looking for a way to contact you and figured this was the best way. I saw the article online. It's legit the best review I've ever gotten. Thank you so much."

"Oh, thanks."

"What, you thought I'd hate it?"

"I had that thought."

"No way, the review is great and I appreciate it, dude. But I'm actually calling because I saw your girlfriend's—"

"She's not my girlfriend—"

"—artwork with the piece," he says over me on purpose. "I dig it and was wondering if she did things like that on the side. Either draw or paint on a large-scale."

"She's actually a painter. That's her main medium."

"Fantastic. So here's the thing: A lot of the decor at my restaurant is pretty modern, but I have this one column in the back of the restaurant that needs some TLC. I was thinking a big-ass mural. You got her number?"

"Uh, sure. Hold on." I pull out my phone and read out the number. "So, you're going to pay her?"

"What, are you an agent now?" He laughs. "Yes, dude, I'll totally pay her. There's no such thing as free labor."

Ali watches me expectantly, arms crossed. I hang up a few

seconds later and face Ali, who asks almost immediately, "Are we in trouble?"

Dazed by the quick turn of events—from Chef Lê's praise, which I wish I could have recorded for posterity, and his offer to Linh—I shake my head. "I think Linh just got offered her first gig."

On a Sunday, we drive to the other side of Westminster to celebrate one of my second (or third?) cousins' first birthdays. Walking into the house, we see a layer of shoes swamping the front door: Nikes, Crocs, loafers from various relatives who've flocked there for the celebration. Cousins and nieces and nephews, or second cousins if you want to be technical, dash through the hallways only to stop when my aunt—one of my father's many cousins—emerges from the kitchen with a pair of chopsticks in hand that foretells their fate if they misbehave. A mom chases after her toddler, who dashes around with Usain Bolt–like speed, as if knowing that his mom will give up if she's too tired. I give her maybe fifteen minutes and she'll start bargaining food for her love: *Ăn đi con. Ăn đi con để cho Mẹ thương.*

My mom made *chè Thái* as a sweet treat, a punch-bowl worth that she fretted over last night. But the kitchen table, as we discover, is already covered end to end with food that no one was asked to make but brought anyway. Somehow, with gatherings like this, no one ever brings duplicate items. I see someone already provided the egg rolls: crispy and hot from their oil bath.

Tinfoil trays of *bánh bèo*, disks of rice cakes just small enough to fit your palm, are paired with jugs of fish sauce ranging from

221

mild to burning off your tongue, which is what most of the men here like.

Cậu Trí, who I'm glad I only have to see occasionally, makes a point to serve me the mildest fish sauce. Asshole. After a round of mandatory greetings and pretending to recognize all of the guests, I sit down at the men's table—a bunch of tucked-in polos, belts, and a few Bluetooths glued to their ears. They're red-faced after a few bottles of Heineken and Corona and don't even know I'm there.

So I end up drifting toward the kitchen to grab a drink. Việt's already there, and you'd think I'd be shocked to find him surrounded by women forty years older than him, gossiping and cooking together. Yet, still, it looks like he's been there all along. He stirs vinegar and sugar in a bowl. The conversation sounds heated, and I catch a few harsh words in rapid Vietnamese.

"So how did you get roped into this?" I ask.

He tastes the dressing. "My mom knows one of the other moms or something. One of the delivery customers." Which is the answer you would expect at this type of gathering.

Việt quickly catches me up on the gossip getting swapped around.

Apparently some guy they all knew couldn't find a wife here, so he went back home to Vietnam and miraculously got married. They're due to come back in five weeks, but *where will they stay? What are they going to do?* The wife doesn't speak basic English, from what they're saying. From the snide comments and the tsk-ing, I don't think the new couple's gonna have it easy here.

"C'mon, let's grab something to eat," he says, shaking out his wrists. How long has he been stirring?

We leave the kitchen. I think Việt's mom calls his name, but he doesn't react, so maybe that's my imagination.

Việt and I are relegated to sit at the kids' table. I'm pretty sure I'll be at this table until I'm married, whenever that happens. Việt is across from me, while twelve-year-old twins—maybe directly related to me?—violently elbow each other, then stab each other with chopsticks, until their mother comes over and hisses at them to behave. Another cousin, five years old, stares at me with a mouthful of rice, snot running down her nose. She uses her tongue to wipe some clean, even as her own mother tries to shove another spoonful into her mouth.

Not the best seasoning.

Other kids continue to wreak havoc, seizing an escape from supervision. "He farted!" yells a little girl as she dashes across the living room, earning bemused looks from the adults.

Seconds later: "I didn't địt! I didn't địt!" a boy, maybe her brother, screams, running in the same direction.

"Kids are fascinating," Việt deadpans.

My dad's other cousin comes over, tells us to stand up, that she hasn't seen us for ages. I lean on my toes to look taller than Việt, but he beats me by standing straight, for once. Then the subject, as always, turns to where we're planning to apply to school.

"Your mom tells me you are going for the big schools," she says to Việt, impressed.

He answers dutifully. "Trying for it. I want to major in biology and then become a doctor." But why does he sound so dulled by it?

"Your mom tells me you have the grades for it, too!" Then her eyes slide over to me. "And ... con?" This aunt knows by now that my chances of going to the same schools as Việt are close to nonexistent.

"I'm still deciding."

Her smile fades. She saves herself by plastering on a fake one. As if my self-esteem weren't already low enough.

Here's Việt, who can probably get in anywhere. And me. Then again, I don't think Việt's ever said if he liked any particular college, let alone the idea of going to med school.

"You serious about majoring in biology?" I ask once the aunt disappears.

Việt shrugs, picks at his papaya salad. "It's an answer that gets them to stop asking."

I'd use that answer if only I knew people wouldn't immediately call me a liar.

"Seriously, what *do* you want to do?"

"Forensic science."

"No surprise there," I joke. He stares at his food, not saying anything for a moment. He's usually not this quiet, not with me. "You okay?"

"Mentioned the idea of it to my parents the other day. They yelled at me for hours. My ears kept ringing after."

Maybe that's why he avoided his mom before. When he talks about his parents, I don't exactly think of the word "empathetic." It's his mother's shrewdness that my mom admires. Việt's father's honesty has earned my paranoid father's trust. But emotionally, they're not the people to rely on. And they're strict when it comes to Việt's studies.

"Exactly," he says, reading my look. "That's just another reason for my parents to fight. They've been doing that for way too long."

"But forensic science is still a type of science. It has a lot to do with biology, right? Shouldn't they be happy? I mean ... maybe they'll come around to it?" I say unconvincingly. I always assumed Việt's situation was better than mine. But then again, these days, I'm assuming a lot. Especially when it comes to Linh.

Việt smiles. It's the quiet kind. The sad kind. Because he knows that my words can't be much help now, can't change things. "They're never happy these days."

We sit in silence, scraping our paper plates clean. I want to fill it with something, so I tell him, "I kind of told my mom that I wanted to be a writer."

"A writer." Việt stares blankly at me, and I swallow, realizing that he'd just told me how his parents were shutting down his dream. I'm an asshole. This was what Việt was talking about before about me, him, and Linh having different variations of parents. Different circumstances in which we are either allowed to go for our dreams ... or not.

I breathe easier when a genuine smile blooms across his face. He punches my shoulder. *Fuck.*

"Dude, no way! What did she say?"

I rub my shoulder. "She didn't blow up on me. She said I could use the basement if I didn't get a job." Which isn't so nice when you say it out loud. But Việt knows my mom and her weird sense of humor.

"The fact that she didn't get angry is something big!"

"It's not serious or anything."

"C'mon, you know that's the best you can get from them." He shakes his head at a thought he doesn't voice to me. "Sometimes I can't believe how fast things move.

"It's like this. We were in our own worlds. Me with cross country. You with . . . um. Actually I don't know which world you really belonged to."

"That makes me feel really good about myself."

"Obviously you've found your shit. We're growing up. You're becoming a writer, falling in love—" My heart wheezes at his choice of words. I haven't told him about Linh essentially rejecting me.

I hadn't even had a chance to talk to Linh one-on-one, or mention Chef Lê, who's trying to reach her. Last I heard, she hasn't responded to his calls.

"When are you going to make the Grand Gesture?"

"Grand Gesture?"

"Dude, like on *The Bachelor*. It's the thing you do to signal that you're serious about someone."

"Right. And what does *The Bachelor* do exactly to show that?"

"Helicopter rides. Day trips to a beautiful winery. Farm visits. Which actually doesn't really make sense to me."

Someone please help me.

226

There were many failed attempts at singing karaoke. Plus, the little ones needed to go to sleep soon, including the birthday boy. So, the night ends with a tradition. Twelve items are laid out before him, all of them somehow representing a possible career. Whatever he'd choose would be his profession in the future. I'm sure it's all for fun, but I think the parents are secretly betting everything on the kid's final choice.

My cousin, bib just removed, stares wide-eyed at the crowd around him, mesmerized by the camera lights shining on him. Then he glances at the items: a calculator, a fork, a toy stethoscope, and other random things from around the house. After a few minutes of goading and laughing from his audience, he scrabbles for the stethoscope, causing everyone to cheer. He sucks on the diaphragm.

Mẹ is seated, surrounded by her cousins and friends, also rocking the Asian glow, though I'm sure she's only had one drink. There are traces of laughter on her face.

"Mẹ, what did I choose?"

"Huh, con?"

"When I turned one, what did I choose?"

She has to think about it for a few seconds, and my aunts chime in with answers that are all wrong. An emotion dawns on my mom's face and her answer finally comes, sending my mind reeling— possibilities feeling an inch closer to reality.

"A pencil."

There's a whisper of a word inside my brain as Mẹ reveals this

227

fact, this forgotten memory. Serendipity. It was just a game back then; I was a child who picked the most interesting thing to me. Or something I could bite on.

Now, it's real. The word is "serendipity."

Things are falling into place. The possibility that I can be a writer. My mom's acceptance, or something close to it.

The only other piece is Linh.

It's a reckless idea, me wanting to be with Linh. My mom wouldn't like it as much as she likes the idea of my writing. There's also no way it can ever come true.

So maybe it's okay for me to feel this way. As long as nothing happens. As long as I can still be her friend.

CHAPTER TWENTY-SIX

LINH

Gold Key. Phở Day Part II. Gold Key. Bảo. Gold Key. Bảo. There are so many things competing for purchase in my mind. I want to shut off these rivaling thoughts, but my normal way of coping—painting or sketching—isn't happening as easily. I'm fidgeting, my attention straying. I made the mistake of looking in the mirror this morning and could have sworn that a ghoul was staring back at me.

I'm in the art room during lunch, as usual, feeling Bảo's absence. The window curtains are drawn to block the afternoon light, but not enough to block the rays completely. The room is awash with pale blue and it calms me so much. I'm in the center of the room, earplugs in to try to get myself to focus, though I end up preoccupied by the motes of dust seemingly suspended in the air.

My phone vibrates once. I look over and see that unfamiliar number again. I've gotten it two times already. Probably spam, so I've been ignoring it.

"Hey, Linh."

I pause, wanting to see if I have to turn to greet him. He'll see the ghoul that was me this morning. When I do turn around, his expression doesn't change. "You busy? Need to talk to you—"

I brush back my hair, nervous. "Bảo—"

He holds up a hand. A sheepish smile is on his face. "Not about *that*. It's actually something that Chef Lê mentioned to me. Did he call you?"

"Chef Lê?" Now I'm confused.

"Yeah—" His eyes catch on something to his right. He laughs.

"What?"

He points to his hair, then to mine. I mimic the gesture and thread my fingers through mine, feeling something wet—it's *paint*.

"Oh, shoot." I whirl around, trying to spot the roll of Bounty that I always keep around, but I can't find it. Embarrassment flushes my face. *Great.*

When I turn back, Bảo is there, gently grabbing the wet piece of hair and dabbing it with a paper towel. I hold my breath, relishing the feel of him close to me, the feel of his eyes on me. His touch. Tender.

"There," he whispers. "All better."

230

He steps away and I feel my shoulders fall. My heart pumps at an indecent pace.

Bảo realizes what he's done and he drops the towel on the nearest stool. "Um, anyway. Chef Lê's been trying to reach you."

"Oh!" I glance at my phone. The strange number. "What does he want?"

His smile looks strained. "Give him a call back. He'll explain. But I think it'll be good news. It might actually be fun, you know. It's perfect for you."

He stands, shoulders slightly hunched, unsure. Before, he would have made himself comfortable at his own table. Might have even hovered nearby to peek at my work.

I hate that I did this. The stilted conversation, the pauses. It'd been easy before. Now everything's changed because of these feelings—because of all that's working against us.

"I guess . . . I guess I'll see you later, Linh," Bảo finally says.

The room is awash in more shadows than I realized.

If I looked tired earlier, I can only imagine how I look now, even more so with the mystery of Chef Lê's message weighing heavily in my mind. My parents aren't as tactful about my appearance when I come to work. Ba's straightening the tablecloths that just came in. I was right. It made the light inside less piercing to the eyes. It's almost like spring has come to the restaurant. The fake daisies that we bought complete the picture.

My dad stares at me a little longer. *Con bệnh hả?* He uses the back of his hand to feel my forehead, checking if I'm sick.

"*Mẹ sẽ* make ginger tea," Mẹ says, standing up from her booth, where she was eating an early dinner.

"*Ngồi xuống đi*," Ba suggests to me.

"Ba, Mẹ, I'm fine." I brush away his hand. "I just … didn't put on makeup this morning." *And I also have too much to worry about.* But the closeness allows me to see the bags under his eyes. He must be worried about Phở Day again. We're all worrying, them more than me. My issues pale by comparison to theirs.

"You look worse than that." Ba turns to Mẹ. "Perhaps she should go home and sleep."

"No, I'm okay," I grumble, even as the thought of bed is enticing. A chance to be alone and recharge.

"Right, she should sleep."

Ba says firmly, having Mẹ's agreement, "Sleep. We want you to be rested for Phở Day."

But I don't go home, not right away, at least. Instead, I'm sitting in my car outside Chơi Ơi. After leaving my parents' restaurant, I drove around mindlessly, taking the longer route home, an excuse to clear my mind. But then I remembered the missed calls from Chef Lê's number. I shoved my phone away in hopes that I wouldn't need to think about it. Or think about Bảo. Before I knew it, though, I reached down for it, and started driving.

The parking lot is relatively bare, but I expect it to fill up around dinnertime, which is within an hour.

Why does he want to see me?

I meet Saffron, his wife, at the front. "My husband was raving about your sketch!"

"Oh, thank you, I'm glad he liked it." My voice comes out flat. *Did I sound like this the whole day?*

Her smile falters by a fraction. "Are you okay?"

I sidestep the question. "Um, is Chef Lê around?"

"Oh! He'll be happy to see you. The column's been something of a sore spot for us, and he couldn't figure out what to do until he saw your work. He knew you'd be the right person to dress it up."

Column? It hits me then, that I hadn't even thought to listen to his voicemail. But now it all connects.

At her words, the first spark of warmth comes back to me. Chef Lê actually wants to hire me? A high school student?

"Go ahead, you can find him in the back."

I'm heading in that direction until I see the tape cutting off a section of the restaurant, a curtain shrouding that part in mystery, keeping it out of sight from wandering customers. Curiosity getting the best of me, I cross the room and part the curtains to face the white column. It's a good size, with a lot of space to work with. Done right, it could make a nice splash.

"Miss Mai!" Chef Lê says, dropping a towel that he was using to wipe his hands. "Glad you got my message."

"Is this—"

He nods, slapping the column. "Yep, the real estate."

A vision of what it could be surges forward in my mind. This column is in the center of the room, so it should naturally draw the eye. It needs bold colors, ones that won't clash with the rest of the walls, but complement them. Mostly, the decor already shows off landscapes. What we need now are people. Faces as vivid as the discerning ones who will come to dine here.

Emerging from my thoughts, I almost miss the amount he's offering to pay me. I ask him to repeat himself. "If you're gonna try to say that's too much, I'm not going to listen," he says good-humoredly. He reminds me of my parents, how they don't let anyone refuse payment.

"Why me?" I manage to ask.

Chef Lê tips his head back and his laugh bounces off the walls.

"Like I told Bảo, I know talent. You're talented, Linh."

Talent.

A wave of sadness catches me off guard. It travels up inside me, splitting into tendrils. There are people who have faith in me, and they shouldn't. I'm not the person they need. I'm always second-guessing myself, running away scared.

I touch the column with my fingertips; it's damp and newly painted with base coat. I spot the tarp and drops of white, and I see a pair of Converse. Red.

Bảo. Saffron appears right behind him, carrying some towels. "Chef Lê, where do you want—Linh?"

I look closer. The edges of his sleeves appear as if they'd been dipped in white as well. Some specks are on his jeans.

Did Bảo do this? Was Bảo actually painting?

"Right over there's good. You came just in time. I'm trying to strike a deal with Linh."

"Oh." Bảo stays put, glancing between the column and me.

"You're supposed to paint the column, not yourself," I say, fighting back a smile. He offers an uncertain one in return. Another pause, one that Saffron appears to notice, because she sets down the towels, then coughs delicately.

"Bry, I need to talk to you for a sec. Over there?" She's already walking back out toward the curtains.

"What, now?"

"Yup." She disappears outside.

Chef Lê follows half in, half out. "But, Saff—" There's some whispering, growing more insistent. "What do you mean, leave them alone? We're just—" A hand grabs his collar, yanking him through the curtains, out of view. I look over at Bảo, who's watching in bewildered amusement. He catches me peeking and normally we'd laugh together, but he sobers up immediately.

He examines his sleeves. "Shouldn't you be at work?"

"My parents sent me home. They think I might be getting sick."

He frowns in worry, and walks closer, less hesitantly then he had before. My heart leaps when he touches me on the forehead. That doesn't help things. "I knew you looked off before. Shouldn't you be in bed, then?"

"I'm not sick. I'm just tired."

"You have a lot going on," he murmurs. His hand curves around my jaw, his thumb lingering on my cheek. He stays like this longer than I think he realizes.

And when he does, he takes a wide step back. "Sorry."

"No, it's—" Again, the air between us tightens. "Why are you here, Bảo?"

"I had a day off. So I decided to stop by and give a hard copy of my piece to Chef Lê. And then we just got to talking and he wanted to get the column ready." He quickly rushes to add, "But I told him you didn't say yes yet. He just got excited and pulled out all of this and before I knew it—" He gestures to the mess on his clothes. "When Chef Lê wants something, he just does it, apparently."

I circle the column, my fingers tracing the parts that are relatively dry. Bảo follows close behind like there's a string loosely connecting us.

"A small part of me, I guess, was still hoping you'd show up."

"But you couldn't have known I'd come here."

Still, he came. "I know." The earnestness of his statement moves the ground beneath me.

The column. Big and vast. There are so many designs it can take. So many possibilities in every way. I can paint another cityscape. I can paint the people that Chef Lê holds closest to him: his wife, his dad, his late mom. I can make the colors as bright as they can be—I can use normal colors; I can mix my own. I can make something beautiful out of this.

Inside, the tendrils of anxiety settle down. I take a deep breath.

Bảo's offering these options to me. Just like the night he stepped over enemy lines to help me. He always wants to help me. I'm always the one to turn him away, always having a reason to keep a distance. This understanding touches me in a way I can't voice with words, and God, I wish I could paint my feelings right here for him.

Yet, words—my inadequate words—are all I have in this moment. So I choose.

"Hypothetically, if I accept Chef Lê's offer, it'd take a lot of work to get this mural done."

A handsome smile graces his face. "You could do this. I've seen your work."

"It'd be hard, too. I probably won't know what to do with it half the time."

"That's fine. Inspiration doesn't come that easily."

"It's something just for me."

Bảo nods again. "After all the things you're doing, you deserve a break sometimes."

"Even though I still wouldn't know what to do about our families."

"It's oka—" He levels his gaze at me. "Linh?"

"Thank you," I say in a rush, before tackling him with a side-hug that coaxes a short laugh from him. After hesitating for a millisecond, his arms come around me, and we lean into each other.

When I paint, there's always a moment where I *just know* that I'm finally finished. The colors and textures come together to depict a feeling of *rightness*.

Us, here, is that rightness.

I breathe him in. I nestle my head into the crook of his neck, fitting myself into him like a piece of puzzle.

Yes, I want him. I want us.

Him loosening his hold on me and the sharp catch in his breath tell me he finally gets it. Still, he leans back to confirm the answer.

A hand that circled my waist slides up my arm. The other gently, so gently, remains on my hip. A fine shiver passes through me and I hold my breath, but my heart hiccups. He cups my cheek with a hand and his face inches forward.

"Can I?" he asks.

I meet him there.

Ecstatic colors surround us, the happiest of colors, yellow, orange, pink swirling. Blooming. Like we're in Monet's *Water Lilies*.

No. This is all mine. This is *my painting*. I want to memorize this feeling and make my own masterpiece.

I press my lips against his more insistently. He makes a small noise of surprise, but I feel his smile. It's surreal, us kissing here. I've tried to tamp down all of these feelings for the wrong reason, but now I can show them. This, *this* feels so right: the quiet smack of lips parting before coming together, the exhaling out of noses, and his hand light against my neck, keeping me in place—not that I ever, ever want to move away. All I care about right now is his arms around me, his lips on mine, and the utter freedom I feel to slide my hands through his hair. Finally.

CHAPTER TWENTY-SEVEN

BẢO

I'd showed up here without any expectations and just started painting. Everything was already there; Chef Lê had already bought everything Linh would need, so sure that she'd answer his call and accept the offer. I didn't have the heart to tell him that Linh was already busy, and this was the last thing she needed to add to her pile.

Then she appeared. The white of the column glowed under the light and she was entranced. I was entranced by her. But I tried to hide it. Act like we're just friends because that's what we are. Just friends.

Is it possible to be this happy?

Our kiss steals the air from my lungs, and that's the only reason I eventually pull away from Linh. I rest my forehead against hers, disoriented. I never thought I'd ever feel weak-kneed—that was for damsels in distress or elderly people with low blood pressure—but I guess it's the same for first kisses.

Linh's eyes are hazy when I look into them, then I watch them clear up, reality rushing back with a vengeance. I read all of this easily because I know her worries. Some of them are mine exactly. She opens her mouth. "Just pause," I say, desperate to keep the moment to ourselves. Her mouth closes. "We can delay it for a few more minutes."

"You're acting like me," she says, half teasingly. "But once we step outside, nothing's changed. We'll still be Bảo Nguyễn and Linh Mai, whose families hate each other."

"But here," I counter, arms going around her waist, "even if it's just for a little while, we're Bảo Nguyễn and Linh Mai, food reviewer and artist. And we've made it work for the past few months," I try saying.

Linh smiles sadly because she knows I'm stalling. Her hand goes back into my hair, and if I could ever pick a moment to freeze, it'd be now, with that tender look in her eyes. Tired, yet hopeful. Indulgent. Actually, just one adjective wouldn't be enough to explain it.

"Hey." I touch her chin, marveling that I'm allowed to do this. How easily it comes to me. "We'll figure it out. One step at a time."

"Okay," she says before kissing me. "What's the next step?"

I try to think of lighter things that don't have to do with our families, a breach we'll need to figure out how to navigate.

"I'm your boyfriend."

"I would think that was obvious."

"I guess Ali and Việt saw this coming before us. We'll need to let them know."

"What do you mean? Ali knew how I felt, but Việt did, too?"

"Apparently they talk to each other. About us."

"Oh God." Linh rests her forehead against my chest. She mumbles something that I can't hear.

"What's that?"

"Romeo and Juliet. Ali's not going to shut up about us being Romeo and Juliet now."

"We kind of are," I say. "Our parents hate each other. Our secret meetings. This column looks like it'd even fit the time period."

"Are you saying you're going to poison yourself? Will I need to find a dagger somewhere?"

"And a tomb. We need to be prepared."

She laughs, but doesn't say anything. Just lets me hold her. Or she's holding me. It's all the same at this point.

From behind the curtain, I hear Chef Lê and Saffron whisper-arguing. "So should I knock, then?"

"Bry, baby, it's a curtain. You can't knock."

After letting Chef Lê bear-hug us—Saffron shaking her head all the while—and tell us how he "knew it," we talk about the column and his initial vision. He wants it to complement the red wall yet act like a statement piece—something to lure people when they come into the dining room. He hands Linh a couple of photos of his family—many of them of his mother from throughout her life. They remind me of the black-and-white photos on our wall and our family altars. When my relatives were posing for those portraits, I wonder if they knew what they'd be used for, if their sober stares were made on purpose.

Ultimately, Chef Lê says, he's leaving other elements up to Linh but he'd like to have his family incorporated somehow.

"I have a few ideas," Linh says, holding the photo while doing another walk around the column, taking in how much space she has to work with. She's very much an artist at work, not some high school student playing around.

And she's my girlfriend. *Girlfriend.* I beam at her, even if she's not paying me any attention. I think about the kiss. I think about her worries. And of course, thoughts of my mom and dad seep in, threatening to taint these new feelings, but I hold on to the memory of our kiss.

Chef Lê spreads out the photos, moving them around like puzzle pieces. He's explaining what he knows about them so that Linh can decide which ones to work with.

When we first met him, he talked about the questions he had that will never be answered. He talked about discovering parts of his past in innocuous, unexpected ways.

If I look into my family's past, could I find an answer that would explain today?

Linh is arranging times to start on the mural and unexpectedly throws a question my way. "Are you free for the next couple of Thursdays? Chef Lê says that works for him."

"Do you want me here too?"

"Of course I want you here."

"Like . . . paint?" I gesture to my clothing. Linh's face twists. Ah. That's an obvious answer.

Saffron steps in smoothly. "You're welcome to just hang around. Do homework and the like. Bry will try not to bother you too much."

"Always trying to insult me, isn't she?"

"Really?" I ask, ignoring Chef Lê. Linh squeezes my arm excitedly. "Sure, I can do that."

In an irreverent move that only Chef Lê could manage, he finger-guns me. And I guess we have a deal.

CHAPTER TWENTY-EIGHT

LINH

The next morning, my alarm clock doesn't wake me. No, it's someone tickling me awake, pulling me out of pleasant dreams. I was stuck in a painting of my own, but I was happy. I could paint with my hands, no brush needed, and everything I touched took on color. I walked into a little cabin at the end of a long rainbow road, and opened the door, and I think it might have been Bảo standing with his back to me. I reached out to tap his shoulder, but a pair of hands got me from behind—

I jerk out of bed and flip the light switch on.

Evie.

"What are you doing here so early?" I exclaim, launching myself at her as she catches me, laughing. She smells like a brand-new car.

Ba was supposed to leave in an hour to drive her here. "I rented a car to drive in myself. Didn't think Ba needed to be up this early," she says. That explains the smell. "But here you are, sleeping in. How lazy."

I glance at the alarm clock. Seven in the morning. "Hardly." I push back my hair, mussed from sleep, and focus on her. She's wearing her UC Davis sweatshirt again, the hood covering her hair. Her eyes are alive, probably hyped from the coffee she must have guzzled down during the long trip. "I'm glad you're here."

"I couldn't leave you three to fend for yourselves."

I hug her again, the strength of it surprising me and her. But she doesn't say anything else.

I'd been so mad for the past few weeks, busy with the Gold Key submissions, my feelings for Bảo—just having so many thoughts weigh me down. I know it was selfish. I know I could have handled it all better. If Evie were in my place, she would have handled it differently for sure.

But now that I was honest with Bảo, that's one thing off my chest. As for the other things?

"Ouch, Linh. You're hugging me way too tightly!"

It's rare for me to wake up before my parents, but it's all worth it, watching Evie tiptoe into their bedroom down the hall, leaning down close and blowing air into Ba's left ear. He lets out a snort, lurches over. His arm swings up until he realizes who's right beside him. "Con!"

"Gì?" Mẹ says blearily. Then she's instantly awake.

Mẹ playfully slaps my sister's arm, scolding her for driving all night and not letting any of us know. What could have happened on the road? And she was alone! But her wide smile undercuts her rebuke; she's happy to see Evie here. I'm reminded of past Sundays when my sister and I would sneak into their bed, crawling like toddlers until we could sandwich Mẹ and nearly knock Ba off his side. We're older now, all grown up.

We could still knock Ba over, if we really wanted to.

After showering, I walk down to the kitchen. Mẹ makes a feast for breakfast like she's preparing soldiers for battle: cooking eggs *ốp la*, *cà phê sữa đá*, and some leftover *bánh ướt* from the restaurant. They're talking about Bảo's restaurant, especially their plans for later tonight.

"*Bánh Xèo* Day," Ba remarks. "Why didn't we ever think of that?"

"Making *bánh xèo* was never my strong suit," Mẹ says.

"Maybe you should practice," Ba replies.

"Maybe *you* should," she retorts, before turning her attention to the sauté pan, where another serving of over easy eggs is ready to be flipped. Evie and I grin at each other.

I look down, realizing that my mom had set before me a bowl of *cháo gà*, warm rice porridge with chicken meat, freshly chopped parsley, and a few turns of ground pepper. My mom must have made it late last night at some point. A rush of warmth washes over me, and I haven't even taken a bite.

She settles into her seat to my left. Ba's at my right, and Evie's across from me. The seating that we'd had as we shared countless dinners. "Let's hope today goes off as well as last time," Mẹ says.

I thread my fingers through hers. I hope so too, but I also would hate that to mean that Bảo's family somehow fails, and maybe that makes me a traitor. I brush aside the thought, focusing on my mom and the rest of my family.

"We'll be fine."

CHAPTER TWENTY-NINE

BẢO

The weather is dreary and gray, but it bodes well for tonight, my mom proclaims. It means rain is coming—the perfect excuse for *bánh xèo*.

At home in our kitchen, my mom woke up early to prep. I shuffle into the kitchen in my sweats, trying to compute what my eyes are seeing. On every surface available—the table, the counters, the top of our rice cooker—sit metal food buckets, each holding the food items that would go in each batch of *bánh xèo*: shrimp, pork belly, bean sprouts, and more. I see another batter that's not as yellow; it might be the desserts she's trying out, something that resembles a crepe, ready for fixings of strawberry, Nutella, and banana.

Mẹ comes in from outside, raincoat on, her PJs underneath. She shakes out her wet hair. From her morning shower or from outside, I'm not sure. Behind her on the outside stove, whatever's inside the pan sizzles and pops.

"Need help?"

"No touching," Mẹ answers tersely. She tries to clean but all she's really doing is moving from one bucket to the next. I haven't seen her fretting like this since she found out about the Mais' first Phở Day. And it all makes sense.

"Mẹ, are you nervous?"

"Nervous? Mẹ not nervous."

"What's the Vietnamese word for 'nervous'?"

"*Lo lắng*, but Mẹ not *lo lắng*," my mom counters. "*Chết cha*." She does a double take toward the outdoor stove, cursing when she sees something I can't. I watch from inside as she scoops the batter from the pan and dumps it onto a plate—with other failed attempts, I guess.

"Mẹ," I say firmly once she gets back in. "What can I do?"

Mẹ sighs and glances down at her bowl half full of batter. "I've done a couple of batters. But something is not right. I'm about to put in another layer right now. Here, let's use another pan. Everything else is almost cooked."

She lets the pan sit for a few seconds over the fire before instructing me to douse it with two bottle-squirts of oil. She adds shrimp and pork belly. After waiting a couple more beats, using her chopsticks to mix the batter, she deftly pours in a thin layer and it slides into the pan with a satisfying sizzle.

249

"It's tricky, getting the layer just right," Mẹ says, adding in bean sprouts. "Too much and it won't be crispy. *Không giòn*."

"How do you know when it's crispy?"

"The edges look as if they want to peel off." Seconds pass and she has her spatula ready. She folds the pancake in half, the other side golden brown. I grin. If she were in Chef Lê's kitchen, he'd probably be praising her. *This is the shit*, he'd say.

The *bánh xèo* slides off easily onto the plate that I'm holding. The rain has let up, but water from the gutter drips by my feet. I'm about to head inside again to actually get a raincoat, when I hear Mẹ speaking.

"I used to love *bánh xèo* as a child. During the monsoon seasons. Your uncle and I would eat this up whenever our parents made them," she says. "We would leave the door open and watch the rain from the kitchen."

"Cậu Cam?" The uncle who I resembled. The one who didn't make it.

"When I cook things like this, I remember him. I'm sure he'd be surprised by how good of a cook I've become. He was always so critical of my skills," she says fondly.

After a moment, realizing that's all she's going to say, I mention, "*Everyone* says your *bánh xèo* is the best one, you know."

Mẹ tsks, pretending to shun the idea. "I wish people will say that to my face." But she smiles at me, her hood covering most of her face. I know her, though; I know she likes to hear praise like this. She glances up at the sky, watching for something I can't see. "I'm hoping the rain doesn't make everyone stay inside. If so, both

250

restaurants might lose, which can't be helped. But until then, we think this deal will get a lot of customers. Even more than *that* restaurant."

Later at the restaurant, Linh texts me.

how are you doing?

you spying on us?

why do you think I kissed you?

i knew it

thinking about you

I look over my shoulder. My mom's busy cleaning up.

me too

also you're going down tonight

oh, it's going to be like that?

game on

After a few hours of prepping, service is about to begin. The line doesn't compare to Linh's, not at this hour, but still, there are people waiting outside the restaurant, umbrellas up. So far, no one looks upset that they're in the rain. Ba walks down the line, handing out menus for consideration and even some samples of *bánh xèo*. One guy takes a bite and says, "Dude. This is the best thing I've ever tasted. Even my mom doesn't make it this good."

I only saw the back of my dad's head, so I have to imagine his reaction to being called a "dude."

"Game on, man," Việt says, standing right next to me as he ties his apron strings behind his back. He was here earlier with us, his parents tagging along as they dropped off a fresh batch of shrimp for tonight's service.

In the flurry of everything, I remember that Việt doesn't know about me and Linh yet.

"How's the bet with Ali going?"

"No changes from last time."

"I don't think it's necessary anymore." After making sure no one's nearby, I tell Việt everything about my visit to Linh in the art room, my note to her, and then our meetup at Chef Lê's place and our decision to test out our relationship.

Clearly, I catch him off guard; he blinks but doesn't say anything for a few beats. Suddenly, he's thumping me on the back—channeling Chef Lê's strength—congratulating me.

"And there's no better way to test a relationship than competition."

"Thanks for the reminder, Việt."

"Personally, I don't think anyone can really win. Both restaurants are doing different specials, so it's going to draw different people. Don't tell your mom I said this, though. She wouldn't like it."

"Who wouldn't like what?" Mẹ asks, appearing behind us as she dons a pair of kitchen gloves. "Why are you talking instead of working?"

"Nothing, we're just wondering if anyone's ever going to make *bánh xèo* the way you do. What if the other restaurant tries to

252

copy us?" Việt answers, so sweetly that Mẹ might see through him.

Mẹ doesn't even bat an eyelash as she says, "They're no good at making *bánh xèo*."

"You've had theirs before or something?" I ask, surprised that she would know how it tasted. Or at least it sounds like it. She used to call their other foods bland, especially the phở, and I always thought it was an assumption on her part. A way to mock them.

Mẹ waves her hand. "I just know it."

"Oh." Her quick answer bothers me, though. It's more of a feeling than anything. But there isn't time to think about it more, because Ba is shouting for us to get into formation up front and seat everyone he's about to let in.

The deal started out as a combination special—phở plus a free mini pancake. It was going fine until the first ticket for one complete order of *bánh xèo* emerges, and then another, and then another. Soon enough, we find tables ordering *only* pancakes and not phở.

The customers are mostly Việt, with a few stragglers who probably spotted a flyer at a Vietnamese market.

One woman—strikingly blond—with a hint of some European accent asks me to describe *bánh xèo* to her. She's in charge of ordering for her family of five who look the most out of place in the restaurant—and I'm guessing Bolsa in general.

"Have you ever had a crepe?"

"Yes."

"Well this is kind of a like a crepe, except it's mostly savory. Think about the crispiest thing you've ever eaten. Got it?" The customer nods, looking like she's hanging on to my every word. I feel suddenly powerful, and I go with this feeling.

"You're sitting outside under a storefront's umbrella. It's raining, but not pouring, and you can smell soil, gasoline from a motorbike just passing through. Someone places this bright yellow pancake in front of you. It has turmeric, juicy pork belly, soft prawns, and crunchy bean sprouts tucked inside, and you drizzle salty and spicy fish sauce all over it. One bite . . . and you're gone."

The customer blinks twice and sits back. "You sold me. One for everyone at the table."

"You won't regret it."

Back in the kitchen, I hand over my slip to Mẹ, who does a double take. "Five?"

"Five," I repeat with a wide grin.

"Did you tell them we put gold in it or something?" she mutters. I catch a hint of a smile as she turns back toward the kitchen line to bark an order.

Over the years, my parents have had to deal with various levels of nasty customers. Abhorrent. Unconscionable. Sometimes, the criticism comes from other Vietnamese people. The broth's too bland or the egg rolls haven't been cooked enough or the *nước mắm* doesn't have enough lime. Mẹ's quick to have a word with them, her voice turning firm when she's speaking in her language. By the end, they always agree to disagree about the recipes.

"Every Vietnamese person is different. Our family may be different according to region."

But some customers are on a different level. Like today.

Around four in the afternoon, Việt comes up to me by the service window looking, for once, concerned.

"What's up with you?"

"Dude, it's ridiculous. Some guy's saying we haven't given him enough egg rolls."

"How many did he order?"

"One side."

"And we gave him two?" At Việt's nod, I ask, "So what's the deal?"

"He doesn't believe me, thinks we're scamming him. He wants to speak to the manager." I hesitate then. That would be my mom. It's fine for my mom to berate Vietnamese customers—somehow she manages to win them over by cracking a joke or two, then she gives them an extra side of something. But in English, she's different. I can see it in her face when she struggles to find the right word, the right retort. It's one of her biggest insecurities. Then she loses her cool, getting angry mostly at herself.

I search the room and find the trouble immediately. His face is sunburned and he has his sunglasses on top of his head. His hair's all spiked up. While he waits for attention, he leans back, arms crossed, fingers tapping away his impatience. It looks like he's with his wife or girlfriend and their kids. The woman's leaning in, whispering something, but he just stares straight ahead, jaw clenched. I wonder how the kids must be feeling.

Mẹ makes her way from the front desk to the table—and steps back when the man rises slowly. He towers over her in a way that reminds me that my mom's actually under five feet. It's always her voice and manner that make her seem taller than she is.

"Shit. I have a bad feeling about this." Việt and I get closer to the table.

"—if you're dissatisfied with the taste of it, we will happily make another order for you."

"Jared," the woman next to him whispers. "Let's just have our meal. It's fine."

"It's *not* fine, Beth." He looks down at my mom. "I wanna know why you're scamming us."

"A scam?" Mẹ asks.

"What, that word not clicking for you? Do you even know English?"

"What the fuck, man," Việt whispers to me.

"Mister," Mẹ starts over, regulating her voice. She speaks slowly, but clearly, "We always serve two egg rolls for each order. Look around at the other tables."

She gestures to other tables, where customers have stopped eating or are trying not to look interested in the drama. The man can't help but look around too, and he lets his arms fall loose. From my place, I breathe out. There. It's just a misunderstanding. He's going to apologize soon, and then everything will go okay.

But that doesn't happen.

"This place is shit. Shitty food. Shitty owners who can't even speak fucking English." His voice is booming and if the customers weren't listening before, they're listening now. "I'm not paying for this," Jared declares.

"What—" My mom's sputtering now, shocked by his declaration. As am I.

Before another word can be said, the guy forcefully pushes his chair in and barks at his children to get up too, which they do, eyes on the ground. Embarrassed, maybe. I would be. The little girl looks close to tears, even. "Hey," I jump in. "That's not cool, man. You already ate, like, everything." Which is true. The phở, the *bánh xèo*—save for the side order of egg rolls—are all cleared. But my protest goes unheard. Beth scrabbles for her purse hanging on her chair and almost hesitates to follow Jared. Mouth opening, then closing, she finally heads toward the door.

I'm the first to move. "What the hell!" I try moving past my mom, planning on calling the police on them, or *something* that would make them pay, but Mẹ quickly catches me by the wrist.

"Con, it's not worth it."

I'm shaking with anger. "But—"

"We have to get back to work." Mẹ gives me a hard look. "There are other customers to take care of. This family won't make a difference." To the remaining customers, she turns and smiles diplomatically. "Please, return to your meals. Sorry for the disturbance." She repeats it in Vietnamese.

My mom saves her complaints about Jared and his family for the kitchen. I'm sure this has happened before but it was the first time I'd seen it in person. I grew up here, living around people who looked like me. We belonged to the same temple, our parents knew each other. I didn't expect to see someone from the outside look so sure of themselves as they spouted hate.

I lean forward, elbows on a prep table, and say, 'Do you think that guy's going to come back?"

'No, I won't let him."

'Shouldn't you report him?"

'There's many men like him. Are we going to report all of them?"

'Yeah, but . . ." I trail off; I don't have a real solution. I guess I just don't like the feeling of some guy treating my parents—and other owners in the area—like this. It was more painful than hearing the waiter at photastic ask my dad to repeat himself. This guy basically attacked them. 'I don't know, it just seems wrong."

'We are not new to this," Ba says shortly. 'We have lived in other places before Little Saigon. There are much worse people."

'He won't come back, con. *Đồ quỷ.*" Somehow she makes swear words sound like a natural part of our language.

'He's an asshole," I agree. Now she scolds me for using a bad word, but I press on.

'Let's get back to work."

CHAPTER THIRTY

LINH

My phone chirps. A text from Bảo. My parents are finally sitting down with friends who'd stopped by at the tail end of service hours. The men brought out Heineken, signaling that it'll be a bit longer until we get to leave the restaurant. Evie is busy with cleanup tasks, though from what I can see, she's catching up with the line cooks who looked after us when we were younger, and the less senior servers are taking care of clearing the tables. I sneak out, promising myself ten minutes of my own time.

The air is cool enough for me to wear my jacket outside. I use the lamplights to guide me away from the restaurant, to the small park usually populated by skateboarders and people exercising outside. Bảo's there, sitting on a graffiti-ridden bench. He sets a Styrofoam container on the bench and stands when he sees me. His smile is weary, a perfect reflection of mine. He kisses me.

"Peace offering," he says, handing me a container. I laugh and hand him my own, which I had hidden behind my back. Inside Bảo's box, he'd packed away a small slice of *bánh xèo,* while I gave him egg rolls nicked from the kitchen. We sit there, eating food cooked by our family's respective enemy. I wish I could say I understood why their food is considered a threat, a reason for my dad's competitiveness when it comes to them, but I can't really taste the difference, even if the *bánh xèo* is good.

"Do you think it's possible that our parents actually know each other?" Bảo asks. "Like, actually interacted with each other? Maybe way before us. Vietnam, or sometime after their escapes?"

"Wouldn't they have said something, though?"

"Come on, it wouldn't be unusual for them to hold back a few things from us."

I think about the comments my mom and dad have made about his family. *Have I missed signs?*

"What makes you say that?" I ask.

"My mom mentioned something about your mom's cooking. About her *bánh xèo* not being good, but she sounded like she *knew.* Like she's had it before."

"Okay . . .?"

"How much do we really know? Like Chef Lê said, there's stuff that they don't tell us because it isn't relevant to us."

"So, what, you want to ask your parents about us?"

"Nothing too direct. Nothing to raise suspicion. You okay?" Hands together, he runs his thumb over my hand. I wonder if he knows what he's doing. "It's a lot, I know."

I don't want to run away again.

"For now," I say.

"My mom just texted. She's wondering where I've gone off to; they're heading home."

"I know," I sigh. I hate thinking that the moments we spend together are only temporary. That, when we get back to our separate restaurants, we'll need to pretend that our lives have no bearing on each other. When it's the opposite.

He takes my hand and we start walking back. I imagine a time when we don't have to hold hands in the dark, when we can visit each other on lunch breaks without having to find a secluded park.

"We'll find another moment," Bảo says, reading my expression. "We still haven't had a first date yet."

"If you think about it, haven't we've gone on many dates already—between the restaurants that we went to and our meetings in the art room?" I say, even though the word "date" causes my stomach to tumble.

We stand at the intersection between Larkin and Sylvester, knowing we'll need to let go. By day, the plaza is packed with cars, but the parking lot is empty now. A neon sign saying CLOSED burns brightly in the dark, casting a metallic sheen against Bảo's face. It's silent save for grasshoppers hiding in nearby bushes.

"This is going to be different. Let's go somewhere where I can hold your hand like this." He squeezes my hand. "Brush aside your hair when it falls in front of your eyes." Like now. "Kiss you." He leans in, capturing my lips.

"Our first date will be ours alone," he declares.

On a Saturday, my parents and I attend a two-part wedding: the traditional Vietnamese ceremony and the American reception—all in one day. The bride, Fay, is the oldest granddaughter of Bác Xuân. I've talked to Fay a couple of times, our circles of family and friends overlapping because of our business, and liked her. Rather than being involved in the food business, she went to dental school and later opened up her own practice in southern California. Her partner is her soon-to-be husband.

Attending a wedding ceremony means I'll need to squeeze into my *áo dài*, which grows tighter each passing year. It means seeing strangers who know everything about me through information shared over various phone calls, store errands, and house get-togethers. It also means there's a high possibility of me sitting at the kids' tables at the reception—with the actual ages ranging from two to college students. Since Evie's back at college, I'll be the only teenager at the table, but for the first time ever, it won't matter.

This wedding is an opportunity.

My mind latched on to Bảo's suggestion as I fell asleep last night. Is it possible that there's more to our families' feud besides our competitive restaurants? Is there something else that might have driven them apart and made our families this way?

I can't ask my parents outright; I'm not even sure there's a way to ask them subtly.

But, as all Vietnamese know, information gets around. At least one person has to know the truth. In my parents' network, there's only one viable person who might know more about my family—and Bảo's. The best connection that we have so far is Bác Xuân, Fay's grandfather, who gave my mom a chance with the restaurant. And who helped most of the businesses around here, including Bảo's family restaurant.

Mẹ and I are getting ready in her bedroom. She's just put on her *áo dài*, a yellow-and-white floral pattern adorning it from top to bottom. She needs me to hook together the sides so that skin there doesn't show.

Apparently Fay and her husband are not going to last, my mom confides in me. They'd picked the wrong dates, didn't consult the right calendar, or something like that. I don't think those things actually have a real bearing on the outcome of their marriage, but my mom—and her friends—certainly do.

The ceremony at Fay's house proceeds smoothly. First the men and the women from each side of the family exchange gifts in red tin baskets covered by red velvet. It's a way of the husband asking permission from the bride's family to see her. Both families line up at the shrine, also decorated in red. Fay, radiant in her traditional red *áo dài*, emerges from upstairs, her arm looped through her already crying mother's. When she joins her soon-to-be husband, Dũng, who's wearing the traditional blue *áo dài* for men, the image of them is striking. They're the most colorful people in the room, and their happiness only makes them glow brighter.

I imagine the murmurs from the crowd fade when Fay and Dũng face each other to exchange vows. Dũng, so nervous, bumbles his way through his speech, his words earnest and sincere, and Fay reaches out for his hand when he pauses, holding back tears. We're all smiling by the end of the ceremony.

Later, the wedding transitions into a modern American wedding. The *áo dài* disappear—though Fay's mom opts out of changing—and we move for the American ceremony to a Catholic church, the reception to follow in its courtyard right after. I've changed into a periwinkle dress that stops above my knees.

I do my best to avoid the women in Fay's family. They like to tease. They think, *Well, there's one Vietnamese woman off the market! Let's see who else has potential*, so they crowd the young ones and joke about their boyfriends. I can just imagine the fury on my parents' faces if I were to ever answer the question honestly. That me and Bảo are finally together.

I try to fight back my smile when I get the question for the fourth time tonight. I guess it feels less tedious when you actually have a perfect answer.

Fay and her husband, Dũng, couldn't look any happier. Probably both from the relief of finally seeing their wedding go off without a hitch and from the actual idea that they're just starting a new life together.

By now, food and lots of alcohol have sated the guests. The elderly ones sit clumped off, chattering away about past and present grievances. My parents are sitting with Fay's parents, chatting.

The younger generation are tearing up the floor, moving along to the American music blasting from the speakers. They're heedless of the expressions of shock, and some amusement, from their parents and family members watching. But there's also a few braver older Vietnamese guests who've joined the floor, and I think I can pass the night away just watching it happen. The strobe lights are blinding, disorienting. I almost forget about Bác Xuân, until I see him a couple tables away, seated in a wheelchair on the edge of the dance floor. My heart wrings at the sight of him; it's been so many years since I've seen him in person.

I escape the flailing elbow of a seven-year-old to my right and make my way over. "*Thưa*, Bác Xuân."

Bác Xuân looks up slowly and reveals a nearly toothless smile. "Ah, *cháu*."

"Do you remember me?" I ask cautiously in Vietnamese.

"Of course. Liên Phạm's daughter," he replies. "You look just like her now. What a beautiful young woman you've become."

I laugh, sitting down across from him. Age spots outline his cheek. His hands sandwich mine, trembling faintly. There's a glossiness in his eyes that I mostly see in my family's elderly customers. They're past the point of worrying, their lives already fulfilled. I think it's a look of satisfaction, or I hope it is.

"How are you doing? What are you doing in school? And where is your sister—you have a sister, don't you? I remember she was very smart. And you still draw?" He seems happy to talk to someone, finally. I smile with relief, just glad that he remembers me.

"Evie's away at UC Davis, studying biology."

"Ah!"

"And I still draw. I'm a painter, in fact."

"So I can see." He gestures to my hands. I really thought I washed them well, but I missed a spot on my pinkie finger. *Giống y hệt dì của cháu,* he mutters, amused.

"My aunt?" I ask in English, jostled by the comparison. Then I remember she visited him when she was over here. "Dì Vàng, you mean."

"Of course. Ever since she was little, she would have her hands in something messy. Mud. Then clay. Sculpting was her true passion."

The disorientation comes back and now it has nothing to do with the lights. "You knew my mom and aunt back in Vietnam?"

"I lived just a few houses down from them. In Nha Trang."

I lean back into my seat. That's why my aunt had been so familiar with him on her last visit. They weren't just meeting; they were *reuniting*. I glance past Bác Xuân, feeling as if the ground shifted underneath me.

Back in Nha Trang. *Before me.*

Bảo's right. There's more to the story than we've been given.

"Oh, your mother and your aunt! They were inseparable, especially after your grandparents passed. It was always interesting seeing your mother act like the older sister." Bác Xuân shifts in his wheelchair, his pillow slipping sideways. I get up and fix it quickly, earning a pat on the shoulder. "Thank you. The community, just like here, was important in our neighborhood. Individually we didn't have much, but together, we had everything we would need,

266

even as the *Cộng sản* were starting to take everything we had. We looked out for each other. Mẹ, your mother and aunt, the Lês, especially after the fall of Saigon." He pauses.

"Ah, forgive me. She's no longer a Lê; she's now a Nguyễn."

Nguyễn.

"It was a miracle that we all found each other again when we made it over here. It took longer than we all imagined."

Nguyễn as in Bảo Nguyễn?

"Bác Xuân," I say, interrupting him midsentence, "by Nguyễn and by 'she,' do you mean the woman who owns the restaurant across from ours?"

"Of course, who else? She runs her restaurant like a true entrepreneur. Just like her own mother. I thought that by encouraging her and your mother to see each other again—the restaurants facing each other—they would be able to move on from the past." He shakes his head. "Ah, terrible what happened."

"What happened?" I ask immediately, though I wish I hadn't, because it signals a change in Bác's expression. He actually looks uncomfortable now.

"You don't know?"

I shake my head.

"Ah, well. It is not my story to tell. If my wife were here"—Bác Xuân's wife had passed before I remember meeting him— "she would tell you everything, but I don't think I can. I don't think I have any right to."

"I won't tell my parents, I swear. I've been wondering about the other family, why they've never spoken to each other. Why they seem to hate each other." I place a hand on his arm, but he only pats it again, this time with sympathy.

He chews on his lip, deep in conflict. "We went through many things to get here, *cháu*. Things that we do not speak of because it might pain us too much. Show some respect. It will all come out in due time." He nods to another person over my shoulder, then wheels himself away, oblivious to the thoughts roiling inside me.

I stalk the room, deep in thought, the wedding fading in the background. My mom and Ba have now included Bác in their conversation with Fay's parents. Mẹ is smiling and Ba throws back his head, laughing. They're both red from the wine at the table. Looking at the group, I wouldn't have been able to see the shared history with Bác; I always assumed they'd met in California. But there's a story between them—and between my mom and Bảo's mom.

The bride and groom do their rounds around the room, trailed by a red-eyed, pale photographer who looks like he doesn't know what sleeping means. When they get to my table, where I'm now sitting, the kids all hold up their fourth glasses of soda that their parents, under the dim lighting, and amid the noise of celebration, don't know they're having.

Fay spots me and gives me a quick hug. I push the revelation from Bác Xuân to the back of my mind. She introduces me to Dũng. Up close, dressed in a chic white dress and crisp black-and-white suit, they really do look like models.

"How'd you guys meet?" I ask.

At my question, Fay and Dũng exchange one look and a small

smile, full of meaning, full of secrets only the two of them can know. "Well, we were in college and in the library cramming like usual."

"It was the first time I stepped into the library, actually," Dũng jokes.

"We checked out books at the same time. Mine was a chemistry book."

Dũng glances down in mock shame. "And mine was a manga book."

"Something I'll never stop teasing you about." Her husband pulls her close, planting a quick kiss on her forehead.

"Our first date, because we were poor college students, was actually on campus."

First date. Bảo said we'd have one soon, but will that all change when I tell him what I've found out? That the history between our families goes even further back than we realized, to a time that neither of us belonged to?

Turns out Dũng had been the one to ask her out first. "We had a picnic on the quad, then walked around campus, ended up at the library, where I made dinner in one of the study rooms."

Fay gazes up at Dũng with a soft smile, so tender I feel like I'm intruding. "And did your parents approve of you two?" Then, the DJ decides to turn up the music, drowning out most, if not all, of my question. In Vietnamese, he asks if everyone is having fun.

Fay leans over, asking me to repeat myself. The photographer snaps a photo of us. I shake my head.

"This wedding is so much fun. Congrats!"

CHAPTER THIRTY-ONE

BẢO

I die. Again and again and again.

"Damn it," I say, throwing Việt's console to the ground. I've played *Apex* before, but not as badly, but I guess that's what happens when my mind isn't on the game. Instead, it's on a certain painter, and that date I was so confident to suggest.

We're at Việt's house on our day off from work. Việt is ensconced in his beanbag chair, looking like he was browsing the Internet rather than systematically destroying me and my team. "You suck more than usual," he says oh-so-observantly.

"Thanks. Sorry, let's try it again."

"Okay, whatever you say."

I haven't had a chance to see Linh, only text her. She said the wedding had gone okay, and that she needed to tell me something, though it might be important since she didn't text me what the thing was, just that she'd see me soon. A small part of me wonders if she's regretting everything that happened—if I'm putting more hope into a relationship that can't work out. But that kiss Linh had given me, the texts since then—and the promise that we would see each other—made it sound like she was in this, all the way. What did she need to talk to me about?

When I think of romance and dating, my mind plays out the South Korean dramas that get Mẹ giddy: You know, the kind with the impossibly good-looking guy and the impossibly good-looking girl who's disguised as an awkward person. Cue scenes with intermittent slow-motion physical contact, gauzy romantic music. Then they somehow end up trapped in an elevator and fall asleep slumped together. These things don't happen in real life.

I never thought that I'd be staying up late reading *Seventeen* and *Marie Claire* articles on first date ideas. I never thought I'd be reading those magazines, period. So far, the options are boring and generic, but I keep trying because my other option is to ask the person who knows Linh best for ideas and that's Ali, and I don't want to go there.

One thing that's consistent in the articles is that dates should be activities that two people would want to do together. We've done the restaurant thing. Movies could work, but we've already had six years of silence, once I think about it, so that's off the list. I thought of Phước Lộc Thọ, but a local mall crawling with people who know either set of parents would make us paranoid the whole time.

I am so desperate for an idea that I consult Việt in between games. All I get is a blank stare.

"But you watch *The Bachelor*!"

"I do. But his dates actually suck!"

Not helpful.

The next day, I resolve to find another source: Chef Lê's place, which is just starting to switch from late afternoon to dinner service. It works out well, since it's the same day Linh has resolved to submit her paintings to the Gold Keys; she just needs to choose between her final pieces.

Linh disappears into the back to grab a fresh paint mixer, and that's when I bring up the whole date issue.

"First date?" Chef Lê shouts across the room at Saffron. "Babe, they're going on their first date!"

"I heard you; you don't need to shout," she sings back to him, joining us at the center with a sparkling water with lemon in hand.

"So what, Bảo, you need some tips?"

"Yeah, kind of."

Saffron says, "Any date you think of will be fine. As long as you don't do what Bry did."

His head swivels in her direction. "What do you mean by that? Mine was the pinnacle of romantic dates."

"You took me to the Eiffel Tower."

Ohhhh. But Chef Lê is less than quick to get it, apparently. "Yeah, it's beautiful."

"Honey, I'm French. Seeing the Tower is like Americans visiting Washington, DC."

Chef Lê leans forward now, elbows on the table. "So what made you want to go out with me again?"

Amused, Saffron takes a sip of her sparkling water. "I guess it was the day we went shopping. Which we didn't really call a date, but it was one."

"To buy the floor lamp for your apartment? Going *shopping* was what convinced you?"

"I thought it was sweet that you decided to go somewhere that you had zero interest in just because I said I wanted to go. I'm not about big gestures. So when you volunteered to come with me, I loved you even more."

"So if I took you to the bridge with all those locks, we wouldn't have ended up together?"

"I would have left you right away."

"Regular comedian today, aren't you," Chef Lê grumbles before disappearing into the kitchen.

Saffron winks at me and with laughter still in her voice, says, "It was actually three dates before I decided I liked him. But don't let him know."

I grin, thinking back to what Saffron just said. It wasn't the date's destination that really mattered to her; it was the gesture. She seemed to appreciate something less extravagant, as long as it felt real.

At that exact moment, Linh comes back, mixer in hand. "Don't let him know what?"

"Nothing," Saffron and I pipe back.

An hour later, an idea catches on. I'm sitting down, my back pressed against the heaters emitting air that's neither hot nor cold. Seeing that I had nothing to do, Chef Lê asked if I could look over his brief speech. As comfortable as I've grown with writing, it's still a shock that someone would trust me with their writing like this.

Hell, I still can't believe *Ali* put some semblance of trust in me.

After journalism class today, Ali updated me about Ernie, who handed over his first television review about a *Black Mirror* episode. It was like another person had penned it. The writing was strong, energetic, and went deeper into the narrative than I'd ever be capable of doing.

Now, Linh is just a few feet away, wearing her usual paint gear, nestled comfortably on the top of a ladder as she outlines parts of the mural with chalk.

She has a sketch clipped to her mini canvas and every minute or so, she squints at it, then stares hard at the mural. As if she's imprinting the image with her mind. Not for the first time, I'm not in her orbit anymore.

If I walk out, will she even notice?

I set down my laptop and stand, fighting back a smile.

"You'll go blind if you squint that much."

"You sound like my mom."

"I'm channeling mine." I grin once I'm by the mural.

"*Shut up,*" Linh answers, refusing to look at me.

I wish I could lean up, steal a kiss. It's been a few minutes since our last.

"Bảo," she says, still focused on her design. "I can feel you. You're hovering."

"Just . . . making sure the ladder's secure."

Linh rolls her eyes at me, then shakes her head so that her ponytail slides off her shoulder, back to a free hang.

"What photo do you have?"

"It's called reference photo. Chef Lê gave it to me."

"Oh."

I know I should let her concentrate. And that she needs to get this mural done. But I also can't wait to ask my question.

I clear my throat. "So are you—"

"I haven't figured out a way—"

We stare at each other, laughing nervously as we talk over each other's sentences.

"No, you go. You haven't figured out a way to . . . what?"

"At the wedding, I ran into Bác Xuân, who gave us the restaurant. And he actually knew my mom before they ever lived here. He knew her back in Vietnam."

I blink at her sudden statement.

Linh blows out air. "*And* that's not the only person he knows." She gazes down at me. "He also knows your mom from Vietnam."

"Whoa," I say. I sit down by the foot of the ladder. Linh eventually comes down, gesturing for me to scoot over as she sits right next to me. I think the air circulation has somehow gotten cut off, because suddenly I'm dizzy and barely feel the surface beneath me.

Linh goes on, maybe too lost in her own thoughts to notice my reaction. "So I'm starting to think that this feud goes way back—

before we were alive. It happened back *there*, and it must have been bad if our moms aren't talking to this day."

"That's—"

"Exactly."

"And you don't know what caused it?"

Linh nods and shrugs at the same time. "Bác Xuân wouldn't say another word. He said it's not his story to tell."

Linh tells me what Bác said about their neighborhood being close, how they all helped each other in need. Almost as if they'd become a family. So whatever happened between them had to be capable of breaking apart a family. Based on gossip from my mom's circle, that could be anything. They'd mentioned a family whose youngest son had gotten into drugs, which got him banned from ever entering his childhood home. A man who was sixty years old went back to Vietnam to find a wife half his age, leaving his ex-wife and two kids to basically fend for themselves. The wrongs done to the family seemed limitless.

"Okay, we're getting somewhere," I say numbly. We are, but what if we eventually find something that's bigger than we ever imagined? What if it turns out it's nothing we can ever fix? What would that do to our families? To me and Linh?

Linh slips her hand into mine. "I'm still here, you know. Nothing's changing the way I feel about you. Whatever we find out, we'll find out together."

CHAPTER THIRTY-TWO

LINH

Bảo kisses my hand, making me blush. Obviously the fact that our parents had known each other in Vietnam scared him, just as it scared me, and yet he's still here. Holding my hand. Our break is interrupted by Chef Lê. He's been so grateful that I'm taking on his mural, that in addition to paying me commission later on, he's been feeding us whenever we come by. He's also calling me "Miss Mai"—and Bảo likes it so much that he teases me whenever we're alone.

"Yo, you two are like an old married couple," Chef Lê's voice booms across the room. He's carrying two plates of *bánh cam* over to us, a towel slung over one shoulder. Even if I didn't see him walk over, I would have smelled it: thick, glutinous rice balls fried till crispy, with sugary mung bean nested within—a soft surprise once you bite through the outside.

Chef Lê has a big, smug grin plastered on his face. "Time for a break."

I try to turn it down; it's the polite way as my parents taught me. "No, I have to finish this sketch for the mural."

"The mural can wait a few minutes. I'm not going to have someone faint on the job. Come here." Bảo shoots me a grin and heaves himself off the floor, going to reach for one sesame ball.

His phone, though, rings at the wrong moment. He grimaces at me. "My mom."

"Better pick that up before your mom calls again," Chef Lê says seriously, perhaps remembering his own experience with his parents at our age.

Bảo presses Accept. "Hi, Mẹ ... Uh, yeah, I'm with Việt, just shopping." Which is half true. Việt's out shopping, just with his track friends, I'm told. Bảo glances at me before turning away, still talking to his mom. Apparently he needs to run to the store to get something.

"Are you two not supposed to be here?" Chef Lê asks.

"Kind of. I'm not supposed to be here with *him*."

"What'd he do?"

"Nothing. It's just ... complicated. Our families hate each other. Restaurant rivalry." At one point, that had been accurate. But now ...

"No shit. That's rough. So I don't imagine you have a lot of chances to hang out."

"We've been finding time to steal. Sometimes at school and after school. And here. And we're going on a date soon, I think."

Or I know, since Ali texted me earlier saying that she had a "talk" with Việt, who apparently told Ali that Bảo was doing research.

"First date, that's big. But he hasn't asked yet?"

"I think he was about to."

"I can remind him." Chef Lê nudges me by the shoulder. If I had a brother, I think he'd be like him.

"What are you going on about?" Bảo asks, pocketing his phone.

"Oh, you know. Deep emotional stuff," Chef Lê says casually.

A harried line cook surfaces from the kitchen, yelling Chef Lê's name with equal parts annoyance and authority. Her hair has reached maximum frizz capacity. It's obvious this isn't a new thing—Chef Lê wandering during duty when he's really supposed to be manning the kitchen. He wouldn't last a day in my mom's kitchen.

"Oops, I guess I have to go back there." He heaves himself to his feet and slings the towel back onto his shoulder. "Now eat before the sesame balls get cold."

"Here you go, Miss Mai," Bảo says, handing me one. It's still warm.

"Thank you, Mr. Nguyễn."

I grin, loving his sudden shyness. For a wordsmith, he clearly doesn't have the right ones lined up now. So I answer for him, put him out of his misery.

"Let's go on a date."

"Good, because I have an idea."

In a modern art class in freshman or sophomore year, we looked at a Van Gogh painting from his time spent at Arles. He was always a tragic figure, someone who went through so much difficulty, only to receive fame years after his death.

He'd capture a simple rendition of his room: his bed, two empty chairs, portraits of unnamed subjects that seemed to stare right at the bed where he would usually go to sleep. As if his world had turned inward. As if there was nothing outside for him.

Van Gogh's room is my mom's kitchen.

After my shift, right before we start to lock down, I find my mom alone in the kitchen, stirring a ladle in a large pot. She's not committed to it, just turning the spoon, slowly and slowly. Something must be bothering her, just as Bác Xuân's statement has been bothering me.

I don't know how to bring it up. How can I even start a conversation and transition it smoothly over to the past—a past that my mom seems to volunteer to talk about less and less? What right do I have to bring something up that may be painful to her?

Let it go. It will all come out in due time, Bác Xuân said.

Will it be too late then?

Mẹ comes back to life; she picks up her stirring, then takes a sip. After adding a handful of sugar, she turns, jumping at the sight of me.

"You scared me, con."

"Sorry," I finally said. "What were you thinking about?"

"Dì Vàng. She's coming very soon. I wonder if I'll have everything ready by then."

"Are you excited?"

"Of course. She's my sister. It's been far too long."

This is an opening. I should ask, shouldn't I? But perhaps it's my mom's mood, perhaps it's the feeling that I'm trespassing somewhere, but I keep the question to myself. I'll ask next time.

I will.

I'm in the art room after school the next day. I don't have to work today, so I'm taking the extra time to just paint. Paint without needing to worry about what to submit since I did it right after stopping at Chef Lê's. I know I chose the right paintings in the end, the ones that mattered the most to me and best represented the theme I was capturing: memories. Memories about my parents and growing up. About my journey as an artist. About Bảo and the discoveries I'm making as we have more time to ourselves.

I only stop painting when Yamamoto comes in, announcing her appearance with a dumbfounded, "Huh." I turn on my stool, facing Yamamoto, who's behind me, and wait for an explanation.

But it doesn't come, not right away.

"What are you thinking about?"

"I'm not sure. Your colors are the same, but something about this is . . . lighter." Yamamoto regards my canvas, tilting her head.

Lighter? I try looking at the canvas the way she is. But it doesn't seem out of the norm of what I usually paint.

"Like, what gives?"

I bite my lip. "I *might* be seeing someone."

"You're kidding me!" She smiles, pulls up a stool beside me. "Wait, let me guess. Tall, lanky kid? Kind of good-looking? Who conveniently comes into the art room at lunch, but someone I've never had in art class before?"

I smile at the thought of Bảo hearing how he was described . . . until her words catch up with me. I nearly drop my paint brush, but Yamamoto only laughs. "Saw him the other day. It's fine, of course. I remember being your age. And from what I can tell"—she gestures to the canvas, still seeing what I can't— "spending time with him is making you happy. And your art's never been better. At the same time, I'm still supposed to be your teacher. So if it happens again, you'll get sent to the principal's office." The threat's diminished by her subsequent wink.

Yamamoto turns to leave, throwing me another grin that makes her look years younger. "This is the type of thing they like to see."

"Who?"

"Scholastic. Gold Key."

"Thanks," I say, blushing.

"I know it's going to be a long time until you find out the results. So, to hold you over, I'm giving you an early holiday gift."

Now I'm dubious. "You've never given me a gift before."

"I will now." She beams. "Guess who I want to spotlight at the end of the year Art Fair?"

So caught in more looming deadlines—and crises—I'd forgotten about the Art Fair. Only one person gets spotlighted in their own exhibition. And all previous artists who were lucky enough to get picked had also won various Scholastic awards. Yamamoto has said again and again that this was just a coincidence and that what happened at school had no bearing on Scholastic results. But the myth is there, and in the past I'd even believed it.

I just never believed it could happen to me.

As if the world is conspiring to help us make up for lost time, Bảo and I get a day to ourselves one Sunday. Mẹ left early to visit a friend's house to cut herbs and bring home fruit, which translated to a daylong affair of gossiping and catching up about their families. Mẹ will drop Evie's name a few times, I'm sure of it. That also meant Dad would want to make his own outing to visit friends at their restaurants and cafés.

I'd always imagined going on a first date would be the most nerve-racking thing, an event that would set my stomach alight with butterflies. A time for two people who like each other to be alone. But for me and Bảo, we've only known *how* to be alone. So as I'm walking toward our meeting spot, I feel no different from when I'm with him in the art room.

Until I see him: standing in the middle of the park, fresh from the shower since his hair is still wet. He's wearing a button-up red-and-black plaid shirt and loose jeans, and smiles cheekily once he's spotted me. The butterflies kick up in flight.

He points to my camera. 'I wasn't aware you wanted to

document this. Should I sign a form of consent?" he teases me.

"I capture memories, remember?" I snap a photo of him—he covers his eyes. "And it's been ages since I've used it."

He poses, lifting his chin up. "I guess I'll volunteer to be your model. I'm a great model."

"Says who?"

"No one." Bảo grins. "Absolutely no one."

"Yeah, that's what I thought."

Laughter and movement from behind catches my eye.

Perfect.

"Hold still," I whisper.

"What?" I laugh as his eyes widen.

A family celebrating a birthday has taken over a table, filling it with mouthwatering food and presents. Some brought balloons of all colors, weighing them with a rock. Cerulean, canary yellow, and cherry red bump and bob next to each other. But from where Bảo is standing, it's almost as if the balloons are sprouting from his head. Smiling, I look through my camera. *Click.*

Then Bảo is free to move, whirling around. "If it's a bee, I'll run."

"No, look." I move closer to him and he dips his head down to see my camera screen. He smells as fresh and clean as cotton.

"Nice." Our eyes meet—an indescribable *whoosh* passes between us, so strong I feel the need to look away.

"So where to?" I ask.

We pass a squad of elderly Asian women, coordinated by their visors, oversize sunglasses, and faces whitened with 80 SPF sunscreen. They're windmilling their arms. They look at us as if we're in the way—and for one small moment, I wonder if any of them have come to either of our restaurants or know our parents—and imagine how quickly this would travel.

And how possible it'd be for everything to unravel in an instant.

"Judging by your look," Bảo says, interrupting my spiral of thoughts, "you're thinking that we probably shouldn't have our first date so close to home."

"Spies."

"Exactly what Việt said. So, I have a place in mind that I think you'll like. Do you trust me?"

I thread my fingers through his.

"Let's go."

CHAPTER THIRTY-THREE

BẢO

As I'm driving, doubt creeps in. Did I really pick the right place to go on a date? An ad for Ellen's Studio appeared during a search—as if the universe was taking pity on me as I considered different date ideas. It was far away enough that no one would know us. And it was something creative, perfect for Linh.

Confidence in my plan dimmed when I made the mistake of telling Việt about it. He replied with a straight face, "Aren't you supposed to impress your date? Not embarrass yourself?" We were in the kitchen then, so the line cooks and other servers—Eddie and Trần included—then offered their own dating advice that seemed borderline illegal and might have been fun, I don't know, back in the nineties.

I sneak a look at Linh. She's wearing a jean skirt and a white flowy blouse, a part of it tucked in. A picture of comfort. She catches me looking and I will myself to stay put and not look away like I would've months ago. A bright smile graces her face like we haven't seen each other in days. A thrill shudders through me.

Once we stop at the plaza, Linh leans her head out the window and makes a noise of surprise at the storefront. "Pottery?"

She unbuckles her seat belt and slips out. I follow her, watching with some hesitation. Her eyes go soft and she slips her arms around my middle, almost mirroring her impromptu hug that day we decided to start all of this. "Where did you find out about this place?"

"Oh, I heard it was good. I love . . . er, ceramics."

"Liar," she whispers, before fitting her hand into mine, leading me inside. I'm content to follow her. Inside, my veins are like highways and all cells rushing through me like high-speed cars.

"Wheel-throwing," that's what it's called, the instructor tells us, but we can't throw the wheel? Her voice, melodious and deep, demands our attention, and for a few minutes Linh and I watch as she demonstrates how to handle the clay and gently shape it. The wheel should be at a medium pace, and she makes us practice. But I might be doing it wrong, because the clay wobbles unevenly. Laughter sounds from next to me.

Linh's been watching me, but now she's purposefully focusing on the teacher. Her lips twitch.

"Oh, shut up."

"I didn't say anything."

"Your face says it all."

I stop pretending to be mad when Linh has her turn at the wheel. Her hands merely guide the clay into the shape it's meant to be—no frantic movements to force it one way or another. "Of course you're good at this."

"I'm really not. I'm just okay. My aunt, though, does this for a living."

"The one in Vietnam."

"Yeah, I haven't seen her in ages. But she's coming over because some of her international friends are displaying their work around the country." You had to be pretty smart to navigate a foreign country like that. "My mom's already worried about her. She's acting like the older sister and all that."

The mention of her mom prompts my question. "So do you think your aunt knows what happened between our families?"

"Oh, that's nice!" the instructor interjects. At Linh or someone else; we're not paying attention.

"I don't think it's possible that she wouldn't. I mean, if my mom and your mom were actually friends, surely they would have known each other. Hung out together."

"Do you think you'll get a chance to talk to her about it? When she's here?"

"Still figuring out how to approach that. But yeah." Linh gets tired of her hair falling into her face and hurriedly brushes it away with the back of her hand. In her rush, clay that caught on her wrist swipes across her cheek. I wait a few seconds. She still doesn't notice. Of course.

Our instructor stops by, examining Linh's work: a small teacup. Mine's just a cylinder, like the cardboard that's left over when toilet paper runs out.

"My, you've done this before, haven't you?"

Linh smiles politely. "A few times."

The instructor nods her head in approval and her eyes slide over to mine.

"And yours . . ." She quickly assesses it and takes a breath. "Well, I'm glad you could come by today."

She walks away, leaving Linh in a fit of laughter and me trying to hold my dignity intact.

"I tried."

"Oh, you did." She shakes her head. "Though this is fun for me, you must be bored out of your mind. We could have done something else, you know."

"But I chose this place because I thought you'd like it. Also, I'd never use the word 'boring' to describe what it's like being around you."

"Oh? And what words would you use instead, Mr. Wordsmith?"

"Honestly, my vocabulary isn't big enough for what you're asking."

I won't tire from that look in her eyes. Soft amusement, a moment where the worries slide from her mind. Her hand rests on mine. "Thanks. I'm having fun. But it's because I'm with you. Next time, we'll go where you want."

Next time.

I refuse to let go of her hand until the instructor tells us to place our ceramics on a shelf.

"Let's trade," Linh says suddenly. "Mine for yours."

"Really?"

"Yes."

"But then you're stuck with mine."

"I don't care. It's one of a kind. It's something that you made." She tilts her head, sending me a dazzling smile. "So I like it."

"Okay, one more thing, then. Need to mark it with something."

On the bottom of each ceramic—the teacup and the whatever-the-hell-it-is—I etch our initials: *BN + LM*.

I get a kiss for that.

CHAPTER THIRTY-FOUR

LINH

One of the places I'd pick to represent California, the real California, where people grew up their whole lives, planted their roots, and left things behind for their family to take over, would be Huntington Beach. People know colors here, with their skateboards, parasailers, and sunglasses screaming out their personality. Hip-hop beats from boomboxes and live musicians, mostly guitarists, clash in the air. Everything is alive here.

When we were kids, Evie and I could have spent all day here if it weren't for my parents, who were wary of too much time in the sun. Never mind that they always slathered the both of us in too much sunscreen. Never mind that we were mostly sitting under umbrellas. We'd beg them to buy us cotton candy, but would get a lecture about cavities and bad teeth. I'm glad I'm getting the chance to enjoy things now.

Bảo offers me his hand, and I take it.

"I like your face today."

I laugh. "I believe you'd call that a *non sequitur*."

"You're speaking my language." Bảo pulls me in by the waist. He doesn't explain right away, just holds me close. "I meant that I like how calm you look right now. You're not worried. The thing between your eyebrows"—he pokes me at that spot— "isn't there."

"The wrinkle's not always there."

"Not always, but I notice it when it appears." He swings our arms.

"Well, I have one less thing to worry about—my application's sent off. So I guess it *is* better than before. But that's been replaced now by something else to worry about, right?"

"Our moms, yeah. And however your aunt might fit in."

I nod. "I know we have to ask. I know. But a part of me doesn't want to. To find out something that might change everything."

"It's scary. I think we have to ask the question eventually. If we really want this"—he holds up our clasped hands— "to work. I hate hiding. I hate not being able to kiss you before we go to work, right across from each other. I hate not being able to walk in the park near our homes, just because I might be seen with you."

"I hate that too," I say. The feeling of lying has become all too familiar. It's not the nervousness of hiding something now—it's the shame that weighs me down, more and more. "But you know how our parents are with the past. What if, by asking questions, we make things worse? With our parents? With us?"

"But if we don't start asking these questions . . ." He shakes his head. "Remember what Chef Lê said? About having these questions he wants to ask his mom but knowing he can't because she's gone?"

"How it's too late?"

"That could be us one day. One day, they're not going to be around as much. That's what's happening next year—we're going to college and they'll be living out their lives—and in no time, it'll happen. The chance to ask will pass."

On our way back, dusk is our cover. Me and Bảo hold hands—his clean, mine still stained with paint no matter how clean I tried to make them. I mention that to Bảo, but he only shrugs. "Feels like a hand. Feels like mine." He reaches our clasped hands up, kissing mine, then smiling, knowing I was watching, probably blushing. "Plus, you wouldn't be you without it."

Together we walk into the ocean and take in the waters that stretch ahead of us.

"What?" I ask, looking up at him.

"Nothing. Just . . ." He trails off as he leans forward, and our lips touch again. I slip my fingers into his hair. My heart beats double-time, and the way he's looking at me sends a rush of heat through me.

I meet him there when he ducks his head to kiss me. It's him making a strange sound when I stand up so that I'm flush against him. I can feel all of him, him me. A small wave crashes against us and I stumble until he catches me at just the right time. We laugh together, our sound mingling with nearby notes of happiness: kids shrieking as they splash up a storm, squawking seagulls flying and dipping into the ocean, lazy guitar music tickling our ears. The most perfect day.

A phone call wakes me up. I hear murmuring from down the hall, until I hear an exclamation. I stop mid-stretch, waiting to hear more, but the whispers return and then nothing. *Am I dreaming?* It happens sometimes, whenever I shut off my iPhone alarm, feeling a false confidence that I'll get up, and I descend into a dream where I do just that: wake up, eat breakfast, go to school, as if everything was normal.

I drift above myself until the cabinet door slamming shut wakes me up completely. I'm still in bed.

This time, I walk to the kitchen, clearing away the gunk from my eyes. Mẹ is washing dishes, her shoulders tense.

"You're up early."

I look to my dad for an explanation of her mood, but Ba is determinedly concentrating on his issue of *Người Việt*. It all feels . . . off, wrong . . . angry. What did she find out just now?

"What is it?" I ask hesitantly.

Mẹ twists the water handle closed. "I got a call. Someone is spreading bad rumors about us."

"Rumors?" I sit down, nerves on edge. "What kind of rumors?"

"*Con chuột,*" Ba answers shortly. Then, making me jump, "*Rats!*"

"What?" I yelp. "We don't have rats in our restaurant."

"That horrible restaurant. That *woman*," Ba mutters, directing his rant at Mẹ. Ba ignores me, his newspaper forgotten, and punches in some numbers on his cell phone. He disappears from the room; I can sense his anger but I can't hear it.

He mentioned a woman. Only one person can get Ba this riled up. But rats—is Bảo's mom truly capable of spreading this damaging rumor? The rumors before had been trivial—easily dismissible— aside from the one about Bác Xuân. But rats . . .

"Apparently *someone* noticed that we'd changed our tablecloths and place mats and *somehow* that led to the idea of us having rats. A customer called me and said so. Said she was trying to warn us. She said it was the Nguyễns spreading this rumor."

"But that's not true," I say. "It can't be."

"You know how rumors go. We've discussed this."

"No, I mean about the rats. Will people really fall for it?"

Mẹ turns, her mouth set in a thin line. "It will be hard to convince people that it's all lies."

"So what are you going to do?"

My mom merely shakes her head. "Go to school. This is not your issue."

"Will everything be okay?" I ask.

"Ba is talking to the Health Department. They've already called us wanting to schedule an inspection, but we are trying to clear things up . . ."

"Will everything be okay?" I repeat. She doesn't answer, only leans against the counter, waiting for Ba to get off the phone with whomever he's speaking to.

CHAPTER THIRTY-FIVE

BẢO

In the morning, a half hour before classes start, I head to the art room, where Linh texted me to meet her. The lights are on low, the sun straining for passage through the blinders. Long shadows cast against the floor. Motes of dust drift lazily across the room. At first I can't find Linh, but she's there, on the center stool, facing a blank canvas. She sits empty-handed.

"Why's it so dark in here?" I ask, approaching her. I lean down, aiming for a kiss, but her lips are stiff against mine. I tilt my head in question. "Everything okay?" A sense of foreboding washes over me.

"Your parents spread a rumor about our restaurant."

"What rumor?"

She gnaws on her bottom lip. "Rats."

"*What?*"

"They said rats are in our restaurant."

"And you think my parents did it." The fact that she doesn't answer right away tells me. A spark of annoyance flares up inside me. "They *wouldn't*, though. No way. Linh, they might be harsh sometimes, but to spread a rumor like that ... that's *just—*"

They're my parents. This rumor ... it's beyond my mom. She isn't cruel. They wouldn't jeopardize Linh's family restaurant just because of the feud—or whatever happened in the past—would they?

"A customer told my parents they heard it from you."

Some of the hot air leaves Linh and she leans against me. "I'm only telling you what my parents told me. And they're pissed, Bảo. I don't know what to believe. This is serious."

"She wouldn't do it," I answer tersely.

"I'm sorry." Her apology sounds hollow to me. How would she feel if I came out attacking her mother? "I'm only saying what my mom says. And I can't help but wonder—about the time we took over the restaurant, if—"

"*I'll talk to them,*" I say, cutting her off. Angry at the accusation. Angry at how possible might it be, given the past offenses my mom had against Oh Mai Mai. "I'll just ask them."

She folds into me, apologizing again. "I'm sorry, I really don't want to believe it. I'm just so, so confused. And angry. And—" I instantly wrap my arms around her waist, trying to calm us both down. "I'm just *so* tired of this, Bảo," she mumbles into my chest. "How is this ever going to work?"

I'd like to think my parents are good people. They've gotten us this far. They have friends, a network of people. They can't go so far as to create this rumor to destroy competition. They wouldn't ... would they?

"I'll talk to them," I repeat, wanting to make it sound like that will solve everything.

School passes in a blur, my thoughts occupied by Linh, by the rats, by my parents' potential hand in it. Even Ali, perhaps after texting or talking with Linh, leaves me relatively alone in journalism class. And then I get a text from Linh saying they need to close down the restaurant for a day. The inspector is still coming by, regardless of her parents' efforts to dispel the rumor.

One day gone; one day of potential profits gone.

When I get to the restaurant, Mẹ's circle is there at the usual booth. Ba is elsewhere; he might have gone to visit his friends—the husbands of the very wives his own wife befriended. Friends. Followers. Whatever they call themselves. As annoying as their laughs were before, it's even more grating today, since I know what they may be laughing about. They're celebrating. Hyenas laughing.

"Mẹ, can I see you for a second?"

"Oh, hi, con. Are you hungry? I just made a new batch of phở and can get it ready for you."

"Not hungry." Not while Linh's—or her mother's—accusation clings to me like a cloying cologne. I sense the General's eyes on me, as well as the other women's. "Can we go to the back?"

In the kitchen, alone with me, my mom moves around as if nothing is wrong. She flicks on the stovetop, reheating a stock pot of broth, seemingly ignoring what I said before about not being hungry.

"I heard there's rats going around. Not here but at the restaurant across the street. Have you heard anything like that?"

Something passes over my mom's face, too quickly for me to catch. But her tone, as she answers, is even and as hard as flint. "Yes, I think I heard that too."

"But they don't have rats."

"How do you know?"

I sag against the counter behind me. I hear the challenge in her voice and it confirms it all. I wanted Linh to be wrong. So badly. But this is a deflection. My mom's purposefully not answering my question, which can only mean . . .

The rumors. My mom *did* spread them.

The headache from earlier today comes back full force. Maybe that's why my next questions come out louder than I expected, louder than I'd ever spoken—dared to speak—to my mom. "Why is it always *them*, Mẹ? Why are you always trying to ruin *them*? What, like they're not people, too? They're like you, Mẹ. They have this job, it's what they do to put food on the table, pay for their oldest daughter's tuition. Linh's graduating soon, too. This rumor could really ruin things for them."

Mẹ's mouth falls open. Then closes. Opens again. Stunned. "How do you know all of this?"

"Know *what*?"

"Linh. It sounds like you know her."

This is it. Maybe if she accused me of this earlier in the year, before I knew how I really felt about Linh, I'd waver and deny being close to Linh. I remember Linh in my arms, trembling from anger and worry.

"I know Linh because I'm friends with her. Been friends with her for a few months now." *And we're more than that now.*

"*Gì?*" she asks me to repeat myself.

A river of laughter from her circle reaches the edges of our space, but it dies down, engulfed by the tension between me and my mom.

"We were partnered up for an assignment," I continue, watching her expression. "The newspaper. And I've been spending time with her. The articles I've been writing—the one about the Vietnamese chef, and other places—I've been going with her and she's been making the sketches. We're partners."

"How's that possible?" she asks almost in wonder, before her tone switches up, reprimanding me. "I told you never to talk to them. Never to interact with them."

"Which never made sense to me. It's impossible to avoid them."

"Yes, it is possible if you make it so. If you listen to what I told you."

"Well, I'm sorry, I didn't listen to you," I say, my voice gathering strength. I've gone this far, and I don't see a way back. "But I like Linh, Mẹ. I realize she's just like me. With a family just like ours. She's one of the nicest people you've ever met. And I don't know what you have against her family—"

"What has she said? About our family?"

Her question throws me off. I cross my arms, suspicious. Instead of chewing me out for admitting that I was friends with her, she asks *that* question? "Why does she have to say anything about us?"

Mẹ closes her mouth. "Never mind." She swiftly turns. A line cook steps into the kitchen, AirPods in. She barks at him, bringing him out of his musical reverie, to clean up the prep table a bit more. I could feel her anger, even if it were miles away. Most of the time I keep it separate, observing it from afar. Sometimes my dad and I can laugh it off. Simply steer clear. But now, the anger is like tar. I'm a part of it. I'm the reason for it. I feel what she feels.

"What *do* they know about us? What aren't you telling me?"

"Nothing for you to worry about." She turns her back, busying herself with moving around pots and pans. The line cook, sensing the mood of the room, quickly departs, leaving me to ask:

"Mẹ, is this about what happened in Vietnam? What Bác Xuân knows?"

She slams an empty pot against the stovetop before whirling around. Before I know it, she's around the table, yanking me toward the back entrance to our alley, until we're both outside, standing between a heap of black trash bags and broken-down cardboard boxes. "How did you—*why* are you asking these questions?"

"Because I'm trying to figure all of this shit out!" I yell freely. "All of the secrets. The way you're acting. Why I can't even mention Linh and her family's name without getting this kind of reaction from you! Or maybe it's because I don't want to think that you, Mẹ, could do this to another family. This can't be you, Mẹ. I didn't think you could be this cruel."

"Cruel?" My mom sucks in a breath. A movement catches my attention, rendering me speechless.

Tears.

Falling like snowy specks.

I look to the side, hating to see them. My body screams at me, my heart thudding at the idea of betraying her—*you made her cry; you did this!* But another voice inside me protests: *She is crying because she's guilty.*

"It wasn't me who said it," she finally whispers. "It was Dì Nhi. It was said inside this restaurant; I didn't think anyone would take it seriously. It wasn't meant to leave here. I'll talk to her."

The admission doesn't help. Not one bit. "That won't help. This is Dì Nhi we're talking about. Everything she says takes on a life of its own. And you should have stopped her. And now their restaurant's in danger."

"Con being dramatic. It will go away. Like all rumors. So Mẹ not sure why con being so—"

"Linh told me a health inspector's coming by. Making them close down for the whole day. Imagine if you had to do that, Mẹ." I turn my back on her. "Linh's just like me. And she's scared of what's going to happen to *her* parents, to *their* restaurant. It's their only means of living."

I can't be near her, not right now. I almost turn to go back into the restaurant, when suddenly her voice stops me.

"Your uncle died because of that girl's family. My brother died . . . because of *them*. They are murderers." Her voice cracks at the very end.

I pivot, reaching for the words to lead me back to my mother, who brushes past me, escaping into the depths of the kitchen. In my imagination, her words keep echoing back at me.

What the hell?

What the hell is going on?

CHAPTER THIRTY-SIX

LINH

It's crushing to see my parents look scared. Because when they're frightened they're no longer the people who raised me to be strong, but strangers who look older than they really are.

The inspector came by. He's Vietnamese as well. He gave my parents a brisk handshake, clipboard under his armpit, but before stepping into the dining area, he gave a good sweep of the room, eyes calculating. I wondered if he was judging us, how we lived. I wanted to yell that this was all a cruel joke. It was embarrassing to have him rummaging through the kitchen cabinets, bending over and checking under the tables, feeling along the walls for cracks and damages.

Despite the Health Department clearing us, I see how the rumor has done damage afterward—small, but damage nonetheless. Customers who'd visited us daily dropped off until Ba, turning on his charisma, appealed to them, explained the situation, offered them discounts on future meals. The favors that my parents were so reluctant to ask for are used now to recoup whatever unquantifiable loss the rumor had cost us. Luckily, it seems like the stream of new customers hasn't been affected.

There's no way to tell if Bảo's talk with his mom helped in that matter, but the next time I saw him, he said his mother promised to have a word with Nhi Trưng, the real culprit. He doesn't say much more, though. Sometimes I catch him spacing out, eyebrows furrowed. I'm prone to daydreams, but not Bảo. So he must be bothered by something.

I would hate it if his relationship with his mother was tainted by this. Even if she did play a part in spreading the rumor—even if—I don't want to demonize her. Just like I wouldn't want Bảo to demonize my own parents for their prejudice.

He feels maybe more unreachable, even as we spend most of our free time at Chef Lê's restaurant, finishing up the mural. I like painting from this height; I'm untouchable, unreachable, too . . . and everything below is smaller. Issues farther away.

That same distance seems to overtake my parents. I rarely see them in the morning, and when I work after school, they're preoccupied at the restaurant. Dì Vàng's visit is only a few days away, too. It'd be impossible to bring up what I heard from Bác Xuân.

Lately, Bảo doesn't seem as intent on finding out more about our families' shared past.

I feel, somehow, that me and Bảo are running out of time. That the both of us are being pushed toward an edge, but we won't know if we'll go over until the very moment it happens.

CHAPTER THIRTY-SEVEN

BẢO

In the next two weeks, my mom makes herself scarce. She talks to me, but pretends that she didn't drop a bomb on me about Linh's family being possible murderers. We don't even discuss my friendship with Linh, and I don't know if she really thinks I'll follow her request to not see Linh. At this point, I can't. I won't.

I don't tell Linh, either, secure in the knowledge that Mẹ wouldn't want to tell anyone. Even her gossip group. They still come in, and when they see me, they still treat me with the same level of disinterest. Their laughter is the same as I retreat to the back.

When I'm not at work or at home, conscious of this weird shift in my relationship with my mom, I find refuge at Chef Lê's. I watch as Linh's mural blooms to life. At her request, we're not letting Chef Lê past the curtains anymore; she wants to surprise him with a reveal. Saffron's gotten a peek at it, though.

She'd carried her ten-month-old son Philippe against her hip. He was yanking at the handkerchief wrapped snug around her neck, but she paid him no mind, taking in Linh's work of art. Beaming. "He'll love it. He'll absolutely love it."

In exchange, Chef Lê said he wants to invite a few friends over for the reveal and close down the restaurant for the night. It'll be small, he said, and it'll be a chance to "debut Miss Mai" and "share her talents with the world." Well, Fountain Valley, at least. Linh tried to protest but she was up against four people—Chef Lê counts as two. She really had no choice.

CHAPTER THIRTY-EIGHT

LINH

Soon enough, it comes time for Chef Lê to reveal his mural to his friends and family. His missive to me and Bảo, as well as Việt and Ali, is to dress "fancy." I'm not sure what that means coming from a man who wears T-shirts underneath his chef's jacket.

I'm not expected to work tonight and Mẹ and Ba are already at the restaurant. *It'll be a late night. Food is in the fridge*, reads the sticky note in my mom's neat cursive.

I'm about leave for Chơi Ơi, finally settling on a strapless black dress paired with an old burgundy shawl I found my in my mom's closet.

As I'm in the closet, curious, I see old boxes of photos. My parents always tell me they'll put these photos into neat scrapbooks. First it was planned for the weekend, then during the holidays when things died down, and now they've pushed it to retirement age. But my dad, in his defense, did start the project.

Not in his defense, he got tired by the time the photos started showing Evie at age four and me age three.

My parents keep the photos in bulging shoeboxes from Payless, Ann Taylor, and Adidas. But the sepia photos from Vietnam are stored in pocketbooks, underneath crinkling plastic. There are a lot of beach photos—a given, since Nha Trang's known for its beaches.

In one photo, my mom lounges on the beach in a one-piece, sunglasses tangled up in her hair. Behind her is my aunt, who might have just pushed her from behind—their smiles are identical, even with five years in between them. It seems impossible to think that outside the frame of this photo, the country they knew was changing rapidly. And yet here they were: joyful. The next photo appears to be from the same day, only now they're standing. Same with the next handful of photos. I've never seen my mom smile so much.

And I stop.

Bảo is in this photo, still at the beach, standing right next to my aunt. But that can't be. I was just thinking of Bảo right this second; that's why my mind brought him to mind. That must be why, as I come across this photo, his face appears on the photo.

It's him.

And yet it's not. Of course. This was before he was born. The man's hair is far longer than Bảo's has ever been.

I find the answer on the other side of not-Bảo. I've seen her only in glimpses—coincidental looks as she leaves the restaurant for some reason or another—including that time at the Vietnamese supermarket.

Bảo's mother is in this photo, indisputably confirming what Bác Xuân shared with me.

Two women, who supposedly hated each other, and did everything to avoid each other, are embracing like they're sisters. So that must be Bảo's uncle, the one who died at sea.

Back before the second Phở Day happened, Mẹ mentioned my aunt had a fiancé, didn't she? Someone who died.

Of course.

It's *him*.

My aunt and his uncle had been together. Until . . . what was it? He left, causing his family to lash out and blame my family. What did they say in their defense?

And how the hell did all of that bring us here?

I take the bus instead of driving, not trusting myself to navigate in this confused, somewhat dizzying state. I bring the photo along, tucked inside one of my dress's pockets. It crinkles as I walk a certain way, reminding me of its existence.

Our parents knew each other back then—or at least our mothers. And, even though it would have seemed impossible before this photo—they were good friends. My aunt was in the group as well. Does my aunt know about the Nguyễns' restaurant too? Know that they now hate each other?

Bảo and I were wrong, absolutely wrong. It was something

entirely bigger than just the businesses. And far bigger than we'd feared.

I stop. Bảo. *What am I going to say to Bảo? With everything going on!*

The dining room is closed for the public tonight, and one of the waiters standing at the door grins when I tell him my name, playfully gesturing me forward. Inside, the room is awash in soft lighting. Jazzy music plays in the background. Ali is dressed up in all black with red shiny-but-sensible heels that still make a statement, and she waves excitedly. Việt stands next to her, his excitement level less obvious, of course, but he still gives me a small wave, one hand in his pocket. And Bảo . . .

Now I know what books and old movies mean by *dapper*. Like Ali, he's dressed in black. He looks far older, and for a moment, a vision of an older Bảo—someone like his uncle in the photo—supplants itself over my vision. One blink and it's the Bảo I know again. Once I'm close enough, he hugs me, lifting me off my feet. I laugh as his kiss meets my crown.

"You're way more excited than you should be," I mumble as I retighten my ponytail.

"How can I *not* be? You have a mural. This is *your* reveal."

"I'm nervous."

He brushes my cheek. "Don't be."

Putting aside the last few weeks, I want to tell him about the photo, but the way he's looking around the room, pointing out the size of it—the way he just looks so *proud* of me makes my throat tighten up. I ignore the photo for a moment.

312

"Local genius displays award-winning art," Ali says with her Banner Move, which I approve only in this instance. "Linh, this is . . . I don't know, I'm out of words."

"For once," Việt quips. But he's grinning and adds his own congratulations. "You think they can tell we're all, like, two decades younger?"

Focused on finding my friends, I forgot to really look around. The other guests must be Chef Lê's friends—people in the restaurant circuit. A couple are dressed in bright colors—artists? Fashion designers? The idea of Chef Lê having all sorts of friends from different crowds feels right.

"Miss Mai!" Chef Lê shouts, barreling through the crowd like an overgrown puppy. He gives me his signature bear hug, and I feel a wave of affection wash over me. "You ready for this?"

"Did you have to invite this many people?"

"*This many people*. This is the smallest gathering I've ever had. Didn't want to overwhelm you." He playfully pushes me by the shoulder, crashing me into Bảo, who catches me and grins. "C'mon, the mural's so great. Everyone in Orange County has to see it." And with that, he pulls me by the elbow into the center of the crowd. My friends laugh, trailing behind.

"Friends, you know this place is my baby and I love showing it off. I want everyone to be reminded of why they're here. For me, it's a reminder of why I'm here, how I'm the chef right now. It's a reminder of everything that my parents have done. Especially my mom." He clears his throat as a somber look passes over him. His father, or who I assume to be his father, clasps him on the shoulder,

313

showing his support. "I wish Mẹ could have been here to see what the restaurant's become, and I hope to God that she knows she doesn't have to worry about little me anymore."

A respectful silence settles in the room. A few people clap in encouragement.

"Well, not *little* me, because, you know." The mood shifts again—laughter. "Anyway, I'm intentional in everything that goes into this restaurant. It's Vietnamese, one hundred percent, and I like to think the decorations are reflective of that. But this column"—he points— "I couldn't figure it out. I needed something." He pauses dramatically.

"That's why I was so excited to meet a special artist who came in here with a young man. Before they met me, believe it or not, they were *just friends*, but you know how I like to meddle—"

Bảo clears his throat. "Um, Chef Lê—"

"Okay, okay. Long story short: I'm the only reason they got together and they should thank me," he adds in a rush, despite Bảo's suggestion. The crowd laughs and I glance in mock suffering at Bảo, but instead of embarrassment, the look in his eyes is soft like the warm glow of the light above us. "All I want to say is I told you so. Anyway, they wrote this bomb piece for their school newspaper but it was better than anything I've ever read. And it led me to discover the extraordinary talent that is Linh."

He gestures for me to stand next to him and I'm emboldened by the applause. "Is everyone ready?"

The wrap falls with a *whoosh*. A flash blinds me for a split second. I haven't seen the mural from afar in this kind of lighting. I'd only been up close, using the smallest brushes imaginable, observing for all kinds of imperfections, and so I rarely stood aside to see what I was building layer by layer, color by color. The crowd eases forward, murmuring to one another. Bảo slips his hand into mine, squeezing, and a few feet away, Chef Lê is pointing out details of the mural to the friends closest to him.

It's a collage of him and his mother, based on photos that he gave me: her hugging him on his first day of school, him standing on a stool to help his parents roll out *bánh bao* doughs, all the way up to a scene from last year, of them together in the kitchen. It's celebrating her and everything she gave him—and more.

A round of guests come by to congratulate me.

"A high school student did this?"

"Is she available for other work?"

I duck my head at some of the praise, but I can't deny how they make me warm all over. "Beautiful," Bảo says, kissing my temple and hugging me from behind. I lean back against him, my mind running on imagination. Somewhere, far into the future, people might come to my exhibition and feel the same amount of awe that I've had toward other artists growing up.

I want to stay like this forever.

"If this writing thing doesn't work out, I'll be your manager."

"Sorry, Ali's going to be my manager."

"PR, then. I'll write the best PR," Bảo says as he pulls up a few houses away from mine.

I laugh. "You don't know a thing about art."

"But I know a few things about you," he returns cheekily. He leans in as smoothly as he can with his seat belt keeping him back and kisses me twice. He doesn't pull away, his eyes roving over my face. Looking for something. "I'll let you go—you're probably tired from the all-star treatment that you got."

A satisfied laugh bubbles in my throat, and I want to protest, but he's right. We can't push it. I slide out of the passenger seat, careful not to close the door too loudly. The movement reminds me of the photo in my pocket, which slips out, catching Bảo's attention. I grab it, wanting to keep it out of sight, out of mind, just for tonight.

"What's that?" he asks, resting a hand on the steering wheel.

"Look closer."

He squints and leans forward, assesses the man's head full of hair, his lean frame, his smile—and disbelief dawns on his face. "That's my uncle."

"Yes."

"How . . .? Isn't that . . .?"

"My mom and my aunt." I exhale. "Bảo, there is more to the story. First it was my mom and your mom. Then there was the question about my aunt, but here it is. Proof. My aunt and your uncle were together at some point."

Bảo releases his hold on the steering wheel, dragging both hands through his hair.

"What do you know about him?"

"He died," he says, staring straight ahead. "He tried to escape by boat first, but he died. And my mom doesn't talk about him much. Hurts too much, I think."

"Of course. It was her brother." I try to think, try to connect the dots between my mom, my aunt, his mom, and his uncle, and I know there *is* something, but everything feels unfocused. Just out of reach. "I think he was the one my aunt almost married. But he left. For some reason he left."

Bảo is tight-lipped. I feel his mind working itself into a frenzy.

"I told my mom about you."

"What?"

"I told her how we became friends, how we worked together. I didn't mention *what* we are, but I think she knows. But she didn't really blow up about that. It was what she said after, and I didn't tell you right away because I didn't want to ruin things. I didn't want there to be another reason for us not to be together."

"Bảo?" I slip my hand back into his. "It's okay. You can tell me." I don't care that he didn't tell me right away; I tried hiding the picture from him. We both didn't want to ruin things. Now, even if we don't have all the pieces, we're gravitating closer to the truth.

"My mom said that it's your family's fault that my uncle died." He turns his head, meeting my eyes. "She called your family murderers."

I suck in sharply. Moths dance around one of my neighbor's porch lights. Behind shaded windows, multicolored lights from their television pulse. My gaze falls on my house, dark save for the light from the back of the kitchen, shining half its usual luminosity.

"Murderers," I whisper. What a horrible word. An impossible reality.

What does this all mean? How could my mom, my aunt—or both—have played a hand in his uncle's death? Had they gone with him? Did he drown, then? And where was Bảo's mother in all of this? "They couldn't have—" Killed. Murdered. Done whatever they were rumored to have done.

"Linh, I have no clue what that means. I'm just saying what she said, but . . . fuck, this is all messed up." The desperation in his voice pulls me back into the car, and I reach for his hand. "I really don't know what to think."

"I don't know either, Bảo. I really don't."

"We have to talk to them. At least we have something tangible in front of us. They can't deny it now."

"I can only nod.

Tomorrow. The truth will come out tomorrow.

Bảo kisses me goodbye. We linger, noses touching, breathing in and out again. Then, he gives me one last kiss. He backs up and drives off, leaving me wondering how I'll be able to go to sleep tonight.

But then my living room lights snap on, the curtains part sharply, and two silhouettes appear, facing me.

My parents are home.

The exaltation from tonight's showing, the peace that I felt being with Bảo—it all gradually disappeared as details of the photo came out and Bảo told me what his mother said. Any good feeling that was left bursts into nonexistence the moment I step into the house.

My parents' shoes are by the front door, neatly against the wall

318

as always. The room feels colder than usual, but maybe it's me, shivering at the prospect of my parents, who'd come home early to find an empty house, when I said I'd be home.

I hear them exchange sharp whispers, and they stop when I get to the kitchen threshold. My mom's at the kitchen sink, washing dishes. Ba sits at the table, mandarin peels sitting in front of him. Neither looks at me.

"I'm sorry. I realized that I needed to finish up a project. And I sort of lost track of time." I force out the lie, instantly hating myself. "I'm really sorry."

My mother still doesn't turn around. Ba's focused on something on his phone.

"I'm really sorry," I say again, hating how stale it sounds.

"We don't care that you're late. Not now," my mom says. Her voice sounds clogged, like she'd just been crying a few minutes before.

Ba abruptly pushes away his chair, as if ready to storm from the kitchen. But he doesn't; he just paces, his steps heavy. "Are you going to tell us where you really were for the past hour? Or will you lie again?"

Oh no.

Ba turns his phone, slides it toward me. His Messages app is open, showing a photo that was received a half hour ago.

The photo is of me and Bảo. At the mural reveal, the moment the curtains had fallen. I remember there'd been a flash, and I guess whoever had taken the picture had sent it his way. "The person who puts our ads in the newsletters. She was there and told us how proud we should be. To have our talented daughter showcase her first mural!" Ba shakes his head. "I should have answered, 'What daughter?' After all, what daughter hides this from us?"

I feel cold all over. I swallow hard, trying to summon the right words to explain everything. I know I have many things to defend; I don't even know where to start. How can I explain meeting Bảo? Wanting to do art, not engineering? Being at the reveal, rather than at home? Words are out before I know what to say. "Mẹ, I know I'm not supposed to talk to the Nguyễns—"

"Bảo, you know him," Ba says.

"We're friends. Good friends. I didn't expect it to—"

"This isn't just about the boy or his family. *Con này nói láo từ hồi nào tới giờ*," my mother interjects, directing her anger at Ba. She twists the water off, wrenches her gloves from her hands. They smack against the sink. Her sharp voice stuns me, jumps out into the space between us like a flame on the stove turned up too high.

"It's the lies. All of them. How long were you seeing this boy? How long have you been doing this painting for that restaurant? How long were you lying to us about *everything*? *Tại sao mày dám làm như vậy tới cha mẹ.*"

How dare you.

How dare you do this to us, your parents.

"I didn't know how to tell you," I say weakly. About everything. "Ba, Mẹ, I've always wanted to be an artist. But I couldn't tell you that because you were always saying things about Dì Vàng, about how that kind of life will be hard. You'd never approve.

"And with Bảo . . . I didn't know what to think at first, but I got to know him and he's nothing like I always thought he'd be. He's a friend—a great friend—and as much as his family has gone out of its way to hurt us—he's not them.

"By the time I was getting further along with my work, by the time I . . . spent more time with Bảo, I couldn't explain it."

"So you thought you'd go on like this. Never telling us about *any* of this," Ba finishes.

"No!" I quickly reply. I shake my head. That's not it. But what do I want to say? What can I say? "I didn't want to do this forever. I was *just* starting to find a way—"

Mẹ overrides me. "So you didn't trust us. Your parents."

I'm so tired. "That's not it. It's not that."

"You lied about the boy."

"Yes."

"You lied about your painting job."

"Yes."

"You were elsewhere today."

So many lies. I pinch my eyes closed. "Yes."

"I wanted you to have a good life. A safe life. A happy life, by raising you the right way."

It's confusing—her words, how suddenly they come, how sad my mom sounds.

"But we hardly know you anymore," Mẹ says. "And you never thought of us as you were making these lies."

"That's not true, Mẹ."

"Tomorrow," Ba adds, ignoring me. "You will go home right

after school. No more staying after school to paint. No more seeing *thằng đó*."

"I can't—"

"*Cha mẹ nói sao, con phải làm*," Ba says with finality.

"I don't understand!" I shout, finally, hating that I'm beginning to cry. I sound like a baby. I sound like a kid. "I'm not the only one lying, am I? You're lying too, aren't you?" I shakily reach for the photo that I found in the shoeboxes. "What's this, then? Why didn't you tell me you knew the Nguyễns? That you were close with them, too?" I smack the photo against the center of the table. "And why they're saying you're murderers."

My mom barely glances at it. "I don't have to tell you anything," Mẹ finally snaps at me. "There are things that only adults know. This is one of them. You are a child, con. *Nhiều thứ con không cần biết.* The pain that will happen to you. Everything I've done in America, I have done for you. To give you a good life. To raise you well so that one day, you will not need us anymore." Mẹ angrily wipes away a lone tear running down her cheek. "*Ba mẹ nói thì con phải nghe.* Art will get you nowhere, con, because I've seen it for my sister, your aunt. *Nó sẽ làm của con rất là nghèo khổ.* And I can't let that happen to you Not after everything Mẹ—*my family*—has gone through."

The sight of her tears makes my heart feel as if it's being gnawed on from the inside. I want to tell her to listen to me, listen to what I'm saying. But she's shaking with anger. Her hair has fallen loose from her clip. And her eyes . . . I look down. I think this is the first time she's doubted that I love her.

My mom storms out of the kitchen and a few seconds later, her bedroom door thuds against its frame.

I brace myself, wait for my dad to scream as well. His gaze is on me. Yet, he's calm. I think I want him to yell now, because it'll show he's feeling *something* toward me. But the quiet between us is cold and cut off. Like I'm beyond reproach, like I'm worthless.

He snatches up the photo I showed Mẹ. He turns his back on me. "If you don't honor your parents and listen to us—after all that we have done for you—then we have failed. We have failed as your parents."

"I didn't mean to lie so much," I say weakly.

Ba doesn't say more. He walks away from me.

The next morning, I wake to an empty house. My cheeks are dry and tight from crying. In the kitchen, I splash cold water on my face. My parents have already left for the restaurant. No note or anything, no breakfast Saran-wrapped in the fridge. I wonder what hurt more: the yelling match we had last night or the resulting silence. Disquieting. Unforgiving.

My walk to school is slow and painful, as if my body is also hurting. I keep my head down too, because if I pass someone I know, the polite thing to do is smile, but it's not something I can muster. Neither does sitting in class interest me.

Bảo's at my locker, holding on to his backpack by one strap. I see the worry on his face, then his eyes rove over me, and his eyebrows quickly furrow. Of course I know why; I saw my face in the mirror. It's blotchy, my eyes are swollen, and the bags underneath create the illusion that I smeared gray paint below them.

"What happened?"

His look of concern hurts rather than helps. "I can't. Not right now," I say. I put in my combination.

I don't comprehend right away why my touch is slippery, why my vision starts blurring. Then Bảo's arms are around me, and he's mumbling "What's wrong?" again and I'm saying things into his chest and he can't hear me.

Soon enough I'm half walking, half leaning on Bảo as he moves us into an empty classroom. Empty for how long, we're not sure. I hate how I'm a cliché, crying in the middle of the hallway. People are probably thinking we broke up. They're going to go to class and gossip. Roll their eyes, but then forget about it next period.

I tell Bảo everything as I nestle against him, last night's ugly words between me and my mom flowing out of me in a furious, murky stream. If I could take back last night, I would. If I could go back to the beginning of this year—before *everything*—I would.

Even if it means never meeting Bảo?

CHAPTER THIRTY-NINE

BẢO

I don't know what else to do but hold Linh. Drop a kiss on her head now and then. And just hold her more. She's trembling, her voice breaks, and I don't have anything to give her but physical comfort. Still, it feels empty, temporary, and Linh needs more than that.

"I mean, I've never seen them look at me that way. Especially my mother. It looked like I broke her heart." Linh sniffs. "And maybe I was too honest toward the end. Throwing that photo in their faces only complicated things more."

"Don't think that. You got it out there. All the things you were holding back for months. It's there." I wouldn't say that telling my mom about Linh made things better—but it didn't make things worse. Just uncomfortable. I'm more disturbed that she pretends as if we never had that conversation, as if she hopes I'll forget about it.

"But now everything's a mess!" Linh gestures to the ground, as if the argument with her parents were physical things just scattered below our feet. "It's all out there, but tangled up, messy, and—"

"*It's out there*," I try saying. "You don't have to lie anymore."

That's not the right thing to say. I can tell by her face falling, her voice turning dull. "I guess that was the actual problem for them. Lying. Me, lying. You saw it from the beginning."

"Hey, don't go there," I counter as gently as possible. "If you're a liar, I am too. And parents blow up. They say things in the heat of the moment. I've argued before with my parents. You have too, probably."

"Not like this, Bảo. Never like this." She slides off the desk, sniffing and wiping back stray tears, looking so defeated.

"It hurts, Linh. I know it does. But there's always a way out."

"How?" Linh asks, an edge to her voice. "Tell me how. Because I don't think I can keep doing this, Bảo. Trying to defend what I've been doing. And what we were about to do, digging into the past." I read between the lines. Does she want to give up?

"Don't you want to know?" I ask, reaching for her hands. "Don't you want us?"

She doesn't move.

"Oh." I never thought a nonresponse could hurt me so much. Not a word, but that look on her face. Empty.

"I don't think I can keep doing this, Bảo."

"You're scared, Linh. I know you are."

"Ever since we started *this* . . . no, even met, I think, my life has been about putting one fire out after the next."

"So, what? You think it'd be better if we'd never met? Never spoke to each other again?"

The bell ringing to announce first period cuts through our silence.

"Maybe, Bảo. Maybe."

CHAPTER FORTY

LINH

Everyone is just about settled in class and any minute now a school aide will start her rounds, trying to catch kids playing hooky from class. The noise in each classroom—chattering, laughing, the droning of a documentary—reaches me. I'm not sure where I'm going until I stop by rote.

Ali, to no surprise, sits at the front of her AP History class. She sees me through the door window, a smile ready on her face. She stops mid-wave. Then her hand shoots straight up.

"Mrs. DuBois?" she says, the sound muffled.

"Yes, Allison."

"Can I go to the bathroom?"

"Why didn't you go before? We're just about to—"

"Thanks!" Ali bolts from her chair, swiping the bathroom pass from the whiteboard's frame.

Out in the hall, she pulls me aside and lays her hands on my shoulders. "Linh?"

And I just cry.

CHAPTER FORTY-ONE

BẢO

I'm not sure how long I stay seated in the classroom, but the period bell ringing makes me stand. I don't feel like myself as I walk out, the teacher looking curiously after me.

Linh doesn't want us.

Somehow I make it to another classroom, and only when Việt arrives do I realize it's Forensic Science today. He offers a packet of Orbit gum. When I don't take it, that somehow draws his concern. He waves his hand and I'm forced to look at him, really look at him.

"What's with you?"

I might have spoken in sentence fragments. Or rambled on and on. Or shouted. Not so sure, but Việt listens the whole time. Today our teacher's routine lateness is to our advantage, and our class-mates are clumped together to one side, watching a YouTube video or something that makes them snicker now and again.

"Do you think she means it?" I ask.

Việt chews his gum slowly. He plays with the corner of his worksheet, which was filled out—reminding me that I left mine at home. Great.

It's not like I haven't been rejected before. It's not like I haven't disappointed my parents in some ways—and will continue to do so—for a lifetime. But I guess it fucking sucks when I hear it from Linh.

I thought she saw something in me. And I wanted to believe in whatever she saw. I thought we would figure out the truth of us together.

Mr. Lynch enters the room, hungover by the looks of his mussed hair and wrinkled polo. He yawns a "Good morning" while the other students snicker knowingly. I don't care about that.

I put my head down, feeling just exhausted.

I don't care about anything.

CHAPTER FORTY-TWO

LINH

Doing as I was told, I skip work and head home, lying in bed, facedown, pillow over my head. I try to drown out my thoughts, my worries, scenes from last night and today pounding inside my mind. I would have tried to take a nap, but my phone rings. Someone's calling on Viber.

"Oh, Linh," Dì Vàng says when the visual stabilizes, sounding like I was the one to call. She's at an airport, sitting in a packed waiting area. Beside her is a nosy grandmother who stares suspiciously at my aunt, then looks away. "Five more hours until I land in Cali!"

I summon all of my energy into a smile and tell her how excited I am to finally see her. I must look like something's wrong because the next moment she leans in, squinting, and asks, "What's wrong? Were you crying?"

What a way to welcome my aunt to the States after seven years.

Before I know it, I'm telling her everything that's happened in the past few months. It pours out of me. Maybe a screen separating us makes it easier for me to speak freely. Or maybe because Dì Vàng looks a bit like my mom now, and I wish I could explain this all to her. I start from the beginning—and for me, the real beginning was when Bảo crossed the street because he saw I needed comfort. I start with *him*, not mentioning him as the son of my parents' nemeses or as the nephew of her former fiancé, but the boy who offered to help when he didn't have to. I tell her about him and his writing and my painting—how our relationship had formed and blossomed along with the art I'm finally making.

I tell my aunt about our meetups, and then our dates. About that happiness that came in revealing my mural—that initial silence, then uproarious applause from strangers who loved what I'd put out there. And then I tell her about the moment things went wrong with my parents, everything that I had hidden from them coming out and me having no real way to explain myself.

I should have known where I would end up. I knew that lying was wrong, but I'd thought it was the only way to do the things that I wanted. Wasn't it? I finish my story with that question, one that my aunt needs to look away to ponder.

Then she sighs and sips her coffee, which she got from Auntie Anne's. "This doesn't sound good, Linh."

"I know," I say miserably.

'It's a lot to take apart, but I think it's the act of lying that hurt my sister the most. She loves you, Linh. And I don't think she feels great about being left out of your life."

'I didn't mean to do that."

'Oh, I know you didn't," she says sympathetically.

'I'm sorry, I don't mean to unload on you right before you even land here."

'I can think about it on the plane ride over." She leans back in her seat. 'So this boy," she says almost wistfully. 'I remember being your age—what that was like." She smiles quickly before it disappears. 'From what it sounds like, this boy seems very *đàng hoàng*."

I inhale. I'm on the precipice here, and once I say this, once I hear her reaction, I really can't go back. 'That's something else I need to tell you. You know Bảo, kind of. Because you know his parents, or his mother. And his uncle. The one who died."

Her lips part, the sun from the far-left window, facing the planes, touches her face, obscuring her expression from me. *Trời ơi."*

She knows. She remembers.

The kiosk attendant starts calling people to board.

'Dì Vàng—" I start to apologize, knowing that this thought will occupy her mind over the plane ride, and there won't be anything she can do to stop it.

So in shock, she only manages a goodbye before telling me she needs to step in line. 'It's been so long. But I guess we all have to face this, once and for all. I will see you soon."

334

The drive is excruciating. A song plays in the background, the kind to lull me and Evie asleep during rare road trips. This was before Mẹ and Ba opened the restaurant, when their work hours were slightly more forgivable. We'd drive within California—to a park or to visit a relative. In intermittent moments, my mom would reach her hand back and my sister or I, giggling, would put our hand in, asking her to guess whose it was.

"Tay của ai vậy?"

Mẹ would pretend to think, squeezing the hand, fingers, guessing whose hand she's holding. Of course, my mom had the rearview mirror and could easily see who, but I thought it was just a superpower she had because she was a mom.

In the arrivals wing, my parents and I sit with three seats in between us. Every few minutes, Ba gets up to stretch his legs, then stand by the window, hands clasped, to observe the planes taking off. The area is alive with vibrant clothing and languages mingling and flying right over my head. The walls are wide and white, and tired passengers flow from the customs gate, their dull faces turning into laughter, surprise, eagerness as they reunite with their families. Then the most colorful person emerges—a woman with her hair piled atop her head, for convenience, rather than looks. Her neck scarf, blouse, and pants show a bizarre spectrum of shades of green, pink, and yellow, though they all seem to mesh. She's here.

My aunt shrieks, causing the other off-loading passengers to look back at her, some with shock, some with amusement. Leaving her bag there momentarily—a woven bag that's seen better days—

335

she and my mom, who's suddenly come to life, embrace. Her hug is strong and tight. I feel it myself.

"You look so skinny!" my aunt exclaims, squeezing my mom's cheeks, shoulders, hips, but she bats her hands away.

"What are you wearing?" my mom asks dubiously, in the same way my sister asks when something doesn't compute with her right away.

"The latest Vietnamese fashion," she retorts pompously. "I bought you the same scarf."

"You shouldn't have."

"Fine. I'll give it to Linh." She turns to me, opens up her arms. "Look at you, all grown up! You're so beautiful." I stay there for a moment and I hear Mẹ tell Ba to pick up the bag Dì Vàng left behind.

I don't know why, but I start crying. Maybe I was exhausted by this energy in the house, by what I did to get us here, or that I didn't expect my aunt to hold me for this long. Or that it would make me miss the way Mẹ used to hug me. My aunt's arms tighten around me.

CHAPTER FORTY-THREE

BẢO

I'm glad that Việt is not someone to press me. He knows what's happening with Linh, but he doesn't force me to explain. Doesn't tell me to stop moping. Just lets me deal with this my own way. At work, he keeps chattering on about his TV shows, not caring that I'm not listening to half the words. At school, in Forensic Science, he does most of the work, telling me to write this and that down.

But one morning, I think he may have had enough. He's calling my name as I'm zoning out, and when I don't answer him right away, he punches me in the shoulder—the pain jerking me awake from my daze.

"Look. Someone screenshotted these Yelp reviews."

I pull his laptop closer. It turns out Jared, the guy who accused my mom of scamming him, had been making rounds, based on these online Yelp profiles all under different names. He was hitting several businesses with the same message:

> *Fucking FOBS—if they're going to open businesses here, they should speak in English, since they can't even do that, they should go back to where they belong.*

I click on my parents' restaurant. Similar message.

My first thought? *Run-on sentence.* Then I hear Jared's self-righteous voice. It may or may not be him, but since he was the most recent person to say things like this, my mind uses him as the person sitting in front of a PC, trolling because he doesn't have better things to do with his life. I see his wife hovering over his shoulder in their home somewhere, pleading for him not to hit that Post button, then walking away, shaking her head, when he fully ignores her.

Go back where? Where else would Linh's parents go? My parents? By now, half of their lives have been spent here. The country they remember is not the one that exists today. So why should they go when they so clearly belong here?

This guy doesn't know shit.

"He's everywhere," Việt says. He clicks through other names from our neighborhood shops. Nail salons, *bánh mì* places. Jared, or whoever it is, has really been hitting up every prominent Vietnamese place nearby.

"Do you think a lot of people have seen this?"

Việt just shrugs. "For this douche's sake, let's hope not."

The community did see it. Not through electronic means, but something more reliable for our parents: word of mouth. And who hears it first? Mẹ's group. Her circle, including Nhi Trưng, convened in their booth, bickering quietly among themselves, printed pages of those reviews spread out across the table. Mẹ examines one of them, her glasses at the bridge of her nose. She doesn't look happy.

"So you guys saw it too?"

"Bảo?"

"The reviews."

Mẹ purses her lips, answering my question. "They're ridiculous. Racists."

Leaving the group, she strides to the back where Eddie, Trần, and others are goofing around again. I don't see Ba, until I realize he's in the restaurant too, with the husbands. They've come here about the review as well. In the kitchen, one of the line cooks wordlessly slides down a tin of Café du Monde and Mẹ receives it smoothly, spooning it into a single-cup filter.

"Con muốn cà phê không?" she asks breezily, and starts making one for me before I can answer. I realize that this is the first real one-on-one since our argument a few weeks ago about Linh. We're exactly where we were before. This time, I round the prep table, try to reason with her.

"Are we going to do anything about the review?"

My mom doesn't answer me right away. Instead, she busies

herself with the filter, fiddling with the dripper, twisting it so that the drips run at the right pace.

"Do what?"

My parents have never been the type to make a fuss. They save their comments for the kitchen after hours or the safety of our home. If their opinions are to be shared, they do it with others like them—Vietnamese who've fled home for the same reasons, who read the same newspapers about the home they once knew. I wonder if it's because of what they've gone through; how easily they could have been punished for speaking a word against the communist government. How they saw their friends and families punished for doing exactly that.

It could all be that. But it's not like they'll ever tell me.

I try again. "This review is ridiculous."

"So?"

"It's basically talking shit about every business in our community! We need to do something."

"Why do you keep bothering? What can we do? Hm?"

Her anger rises like a quick flame, knocking me off guard. And also because I don't have an answer. How can we fight someone who's anonymous? Or the lies that they spread online about us?

"What is it that Americans say? It's not your battle."

I shake my head. An antithesis to basically everything she's said to me my whole life. It's always about us. Not one person—us. Together. And I'm not going to let her start saying things like that now.

"These words," I slowly say. "They have consequences. Yeah,

340

sometimes, you don't think they will do much, especially when they're said among friends—within the safety of one place." Her face shifts; she remembers our argument. "But some words, like this, sometimes they win. We can't let that happen. We can't let anyone just see these words on our page and not defend ourselves."

Now my mom just looks tired, decades older than she really is.

"I'm not going to let this person get away with saying things like that. I'm not."

I'm tired.

Of all of it. Of all this useless gossip that never dies, only comes back in different forms. Causes people to hide certain things, then when it comes out it hurts all of us at once.

Someone needs to finally say something in our defense. Even if it hurts.

Later that night, instead of sleeping, I'm up with the lamp on, my computer in front of me. Considering the blinking cursor for a few minutes, I place my fingers on the keyboard, and before I know it, words and sentences fly from my mind to the keys. With each word I type I'm hoping to erase the vile reviews that those shitheads left on our pages. I'm writing this for not just my family, but other restaurants—and I pause—and the Mais' restaurant. As much as our restaurants have clashed, as much as their weird battle has gone on, we still live in the same place. And hasn't Linh always encouraged me to write what I feel? What I'm passionate about?

I sit up straight, stretching my back and arms. A look at the clock shows that I've been typing for an hour. It's the first long piece I've written that wasn't an assignment. It's me on the page, and looking at it, I almost feel lighter.

The first person I want to share it with is Linh, but at the memory of our last talk, seeing her at her breaking point, my energy stills for a moment. That's not an option, so I go to the next person I can trust.

I almost hesitate to show Ali the next day. Who knows what she's thinking about what happened between me and Linh, whether she'll take Linh's side and cold-shoulder me, too, because that's where her loyalty should be. But when I text her for help on the article during lunch, she sends back a quick "yeah, sure," telling me to find her now in the newsroom like usual.

I pack my things from the lunch table and Việt sends me a quick nod. He's been my friend for so long that he knows when to shut up. I haven't heard *SVU* recaps from him in what seems like ages and I've got to give his cross-country friends credit for following his lead, their conversation a little less boring than usual.

Then, because I can't help it, I seek Linh out, wondering if she'll be here or in her art room, cooped up as usual. But she's here, eating lunch with some friends. I stare harder at her, willing her to turn around, to see me, but she doesn't notice.

Swallowing hard, I leave.

"It's not bad?"

"Not bad so far."

"Really?"

"Hey, I said 'so far.' Your next sentence is probably going to be shitty."

We're quiet as she keeps reading as promised. I scroll through Twitter on the computer. She marks up some words and nods sometimes.

"So Linh told me what happened. Well, kind of. Not the whole story. But she did tell me what happened."

My hand freezes on the mouse, but I keep quiet.

"She's been really stressed. I mean, you know she probably didn't mean any of it?"

Ali sits next to me, looking unusually somber. "See, the thing with Linh is that she was alone for a while. Not physically, but alone inside her head. I'm a journalist and she's a painter and though they're both creative things, she never really had someone on that level with her. But you, Bảo, you made her open up a little. Her art has changed. It's transformed. It's been freed." Ali pauses. "I've never seen her that happy, and it's because you walked into her life. I'm grateful for that."

Words are stuck in my throat. This wasn't what I expected when I came to Ali for help.

"I'm not just talking about Linh who's changed. You've become the writer you're meant to be." She nods, like she's confirming the fact to herself.

"Despite what's happening, Linh's just scared. Because it *is* scary. Her world—both of your worlds—have been upturned." Ali shrugs. "Let it settle a little. And don't doubt what she feels for you. Or what you feel for her."

343

After a few beats, Ali stiffens her back, morphing into the journalist I know and am terrified of.

"You won't ever repeat that to anyone," she says, in her signature *I will cut you* voice. Right after, she smiles. A genuine smile that she'd share only with Linh. "This is great. I actually think it's your best."

"Really?" I say again, like a broken record.

"So good," she says, pushing herself off the counter, "that I think you should try for something bigger than just our newspaper. Because it's not really about the school. It's about the community. Your community. Your home. And if you need help with that, I have the right contacts."

Hearing the word "contacts" come from her mouth still sounds ominous, but out of everyone, she's the best person to help me.

And she does.

WE ARE HOME

To the man posting anonymous flame reviews of several Little Saigon restaurants, to the same man who came into my parents' restaurant insulting everything they stand for:

Didn't you hear your children begging you to stop? Didn't you notice how embarrassed your wife was? Didn't you see the stunned look of everyone around you as you left in a fit of rage, without paying?

There's a lot I can break down here. There are many assumptions I can make about you and where you come from.

But I won't state them here because I don't want to be like you.

Here's a fact, though:

You clearly don't know us.

So let me teach you something.

In Bolsa, everyone you've brushed shoulders with—the very people you dismissed—probably knows more suffering than you will fortunately ever know. They saw their beloved country destroyed by colonialism, then civil war. They left everything they knew for the unknown. They left for a chance at freedom, a chance for their family and their future.

One hand would never be sufficient to count their losses.

But this loss, I think, has made them the fiercest, strongest people I will ever know.

It saddens me that you don't recognize this. It's an unfortunate reminder that as much as my community represents the true American Dream—building a foundation out of uncertain hopes and dreams—people like you would rather be ignorant or spread hate than accept this reality.

But your racism has no power here. Your words mean nothing in Little Saigon. So whatever you hoped to accomplish—in person and online—you have failed.

A person close to me—one of the most passionate, talented people I'm proud to know—once told me that I needed to write about what I really care about. It goes without saying that it's this community. It's my home. It's my family. So it's not cool what you're doing.

I would like to think that you will learn from this and become a better person.

But again, I can't make assumptions.

Thank you,

Bảo Nguyễn

Proud son of Vietnamese immigrants

◇ ◇ ◇

I don't think it hits me what exactly I did by writing the op-ed, until the first customer this morning walks in with her husband. She looks vaguely familiar; maybe she doesn't come here with her husband but with other friends.

"Your son is Bảo, yes?" she asks in Vietnamese.

Mẹ and I stand at the front desk, going over reservations for lunch. Hearing my name, she squints at me, as if to ask, *What did you do?* Her attention turns to the woman, who slides a folded newspaper her way, a perfectly manicured finger pointing at something.

My name.

My *byline*.

Turns out it's in the *Người Việt* morning edition with a translated version.

"When I read what happened, about that awful review, and then this beautiful response, I had to come over first thing. You must be so proud of your son."

My heart leaps at the praise. A stranger, complimenting me? "Thank you." Mẹ pauses, still hesitant.

"It was really touching. Those reviews were vile. I've been here so many times and I've never had a bad meal. So whatever happens, you have my full support."

After getting the woman settled into a booth, my mom takes the newspaper with her to the back, bringing along her grocery-store glasses. I wait tables all the while, my focus split between the back and the customers—many of whom have actually come by because of my article, to my shock.

An hour later, Mẹ emerges from wherever she was, her glasses hanging by her shirt collar. She brings the newspaper back with her, but she doesn't look for me. She takes her spot by the front desk, straight-backed, busying herself with the cash register. And I thought that this was it. The article was written. It's out there.

Then she stops. I approach her, not sure how she'll react, what she'll say about what I wrote. Before I can get a word out, she speaks.

"You wrote this?"

"Dạ."

"By yourself?"

"Yes."

"Are you lying?"

Okay, really? Have some faith in me.

"That's my name, isn't it," I answer, measured.

Mẹ nods. "I didn't know that you would feel this way. Especially about the gossip."

"I only hate the gossip when it's bad. When it really hurts someone else."

"You mean the Mai family." Her voice isn't angry. It's curious.

I shake my head. "I meant what I wrote. This wasn't just about the Mais. It's really about all of us. I didn't like that we were just going to let some guy on the Internet win."

"The article was good. Very good." Reaching out, she cups my cheek. *"Giỏi, con."*

A few minutes later, after getting back to work, I look back and see Mẹ holding up the newspaper against the wall, like she's checking to see how it'll look.

The next day, there *is* a framed picture of my article hanging on our wall of fame: articles about the restaurant when it first opened, the great reviews that have come in. My mom probably pulled in a favor with friends to get it made so quickly.

According to Ali, the article has gone viral, shared by local news sites. She had that gleam in her eyes when she explained: "They love underdog stories, you know. People fighting back against assholes like this guy." And because of the reach, we're getting more and more customers, even from outside Bolsa.

There's a small collective of people in our community taking it upon themselves to look out for future racist incidents—online and in real time. Walking into work one day, I see my mom's friends crowded around someone's laptop, systematically scrolling through old reviews to report them. The General, ironically, might have established herself as the leader.

I can't be sure that this will help stop the gossip wars, but it's still a welcome change. And it was one article that started it. Mine.

At school only the kids whose parents run businesses in the area paid attention to the news—and I didn't realize that it was actually a lot of people. Some classmates came by to high-five me or say "Nice article" and things like that. Lunchtime surprised me too:

Apparently Việt looped in some of his cross-country friends into the whole deal, and they were nice about it, joking around about me being famous now. Even Steve was so curious that he forgot about his banana.

I tried to look for Linh. Not that I would know what to say, but I wanted to know if she read what I wrote. If she knew that I, in my own way, was reaching out.

There are flyers now showcasing the upcoming Art Fair, so Linh's picture is verywhere that's eye level. I want to tell her how happy I am for her, really. Even though she doesn't seem to want to talk to me anymore.

Ali's become my pseudo-publicist, in a way. When a local station wanted to interview me on camera for a brief segment, she demanded that they send her the questions for approval. I'm 100 percent sure that she added some questions that would involve me mentioning the school newspaper and my role in it.

And that's what's happening now as I'm in front of the restaurant, fiddling with the collar of my dress shirt that my mom forced me to wear. *"Đẹp trai,"* she said this morning when inspecting me, ultimately approving the look. My dad let me borrow his belt for my pants.

The female news anchor prepping me reminds me not to move so much because the microphone is sensitive and will pick up extraneous noise.

"You have to zoom out," I hear Ali telling Tim, the cameraman. A professional. "Just like—yeah, there it is. Perfect."

"Kid, I know."

After the countdown, I can't even hear myself talking. I just see the host nodding intently, and her mouth forming words, then she addresses my parents directly. They keep shifting behind me, uncomfortable, fidgeting in the spotlight.

"You must be so proud of your son," the reporter finally says.

I almost chime in, wanting to tell her, "Well, that might be a stretch." But my mother answers first. She looks directly at me and nods silently, seriously. It makes me stand straighter.

"Of course I am proud. All of this makes me wonder how he turned out like this."

"It was all because of me," Dad says from the other side. His joking side has come out, though the reporter looks confused, not sure if he's serious, so she just laughs nervously.

Finally, she signs off and the record light dims. I guess I *did* do okay—or maybe my eyes are screaming *I SUCK!* and she just feels bad for me—because the interviewer shakes my hand, telling me, "Good job," before telling her coworkers to pack up.

Later, when all the cameras have gone and customers have dwindled enough that everyone can catch their breath, I spy my dad Windexing my framed article, even though I'm sure it's already spotless. He steps back to inspect his work.

Ba notices me a beat later. "Gì?"

"Nothing." I fight back a smile.

"Okay," Ba says. "Get back to work. Stop being so lazy."

I happen to look up, out to the Mais' restaurant. It looks as busy as it was when I first crossed the street, first had the courage to speak to Linh. It's busy, too, perhaps because of the article, but that's not what caught my eye.

I saw a movement from behind the window.

A flash of long dark brown hair.

I miss her.

CHAPTER FORTY-FOUR

LINH

I miss him. There are so many things I want to tell Bảo after reading his letter. I'm so proud of him.

I wish I could be like you.

You're speaking the truth, without worrying about consequences.

But I'm ashamed of how I ran away—not just from our last conversation, but before. It was him always having to pull afloat, reminding me that I can't hide from problems. Because it'll build up and bury me until I can't breathe.

The house is made less tense with Dì Vàng's arrival. The past few nights have been light and fun, full of laughter. It was almost as if the argument in the kitchen never happened. But take her presence away and we're back to square one between my parents and me. Terse. Cold. Punishing. Dì Vàng has been visiting friends in Washington—perhaps even Bác Xuân—and she comes home late, or not at all, staying at her friends' places. She'll have to leave again and miss my exhibition at the Art Fair in a couple of days.

But the one night Dì Vàng does stay, she comes to me to talk. She's just showered and is dressed in pale green pajamas. My drawers are packed with similar clothing, gifts from her across the years. Her long hair rests on her left shoulder in a beautiful clean braid and she's peering closely at the artwork above my desk. Her eyes linger on Bảo's sculpture of whatever from our first date and she tilts her head in puzzlement before moving on. It was shipped here a couple of days ago.

"You are just as talented as your mom always tells me."

"Thank you," I say quietly, suddenly nervous. I'm still adjusting to seeing her in person—unpixelated and in real time.

"I'm not lying. Your mom's so proud of you. Your dad is, too, but you know how it is; he says it from the background." She throws a grin over her shoulder as she pulls back the bedcovers and slips in, looking right at home. Far from sleeping, my aunt props her head up. "Is everything okay now? Since we last spoke."

I pause. "There's been no change."

She stretches her hand toward me and I reach for her, the space between us only an illusion. "I'm sorry."

"Has Mẹ said anything to you?" I ask hopefully. She shakes her head.

I stare at the ceiling for a moment, listening to the low hum of the air conditioner turning on, the hush of sprinklers in our lawn. A car passes by, headlights shining into the room before disappearing. I want to ask about Bảo's uncle, but she's not offering to tell me herself. Does she want to ignore it too?

"I will tell you everything, Linh," she says.

I look at her in surprise. She must have read my mind.

"I will, I promise. But I have to sort things out, too. My sister doesn't even know that I know, so just give me some time. It'll all come out."

Bác Xuân had said the same thing.

"Mẹ always talked about you like you're some sort of tragedy. Like your art was a punishment."

"I was in a bad way after all that happened. But what my sister doesn't understand ..." Dì Vàng pauses. "Or maybe, one day, what you can *help* her understand, is that for people like us, sadness is part of our inspiration. Others might bottle up their sadness and pour it out on certain occasions, but we let it pour from us and into our medium. It's the same for most emotions, and we do it so that we can make room for more."

I nod, remembering how my art was the only thing to calm me when things with my parents and Bảo were collapsing.

She then adds softly, "We all lost something precious during that time."

I think Ba has grown tired of the tension between me and my mom, despite Dì Vàng being there to cut through it all. Now she's off visiting a friend in San Francisco, scheduled to come back later

355

this week. Ba's kind of annoyance takes only a day or two, much like when he sprained his back. But whether it's the food, or the silence, or being in-between, I won't ever figure out why Ba shows up outside my bedroom as I type out the captions to my Art Fair display. Just a few more days to go. Ba doesn't come in, like my mom; instead he hovers, like he's waiting for my permission to enter.

"Homework?"

"Kind of." A half-truth, not a full lie. His attention is on the paper in front me, the scraps on the floor as well.

"Come eat. I made soup. *Canh sườn bí*."

His signature, bland dish.

"Mẹ's not coming home?"

"Working late," he says.

I guess even if he were mad, he wouldn't starve me. Without another word, Ba turns left, back toward the kitchen, where he's already set the table. Two bowls are stacked on top of each other by the rice cooker. He fluffs the rice with chopsticks, but doesn't fill the bowls. I sit down, sensing he doesn't want me here just to eat. Maybe he wants to tell me again how disappointed he is, and I feel my stomach drop.

Ba settles in his usual seat. One of the light bulbs above us is dead, washing the top of Ba's head in a dim glow. It highlights his white hairs—he has so many these days. And it doesn't look like he's shaved, the hair on his chin appearing as if it's just sponged-on black paint.

"Mẹ and Ba are disappointed, con," he starts. "We didn't think we would raise a daughter who would lie to us so much. Lie and think we wouldn't figure it out."

I bite my lip, thinking of how I tried to argue with Mẹ and how poorly that turned out.

"It is not just that: disappointment. You hurt us." I shift in my seat now, unaccustomed to hearing that word from him. Come to think of it, I'm not sure I've ever heard it said here. The concept is unfathomable—how could Ba be hurt? He's always so forceful, so set in his ways. One of those Roman marble sculptures that miraculously never chip.

I whisper at his pause. "I'm sorry." I repeat it in Vietnamese, though it doesn't seem to register with him because he says right away:

"But a part of me wonders. Ba and Mẹ should have noticed more why you were acting strangely. Noticed that you looked . . . sadder than we are used to. I noticed that right here, in this kitchen that night." He gestures to the spot where I'd been. He leans forward. "*Ba không muốn* con be sad."

I don't want you to be sad.

"But you are happy here." It's then that I notice Ba had something in his other hand. A clipping of a newsletter, the kind that businesses pass around door to door, and it had the photo of me and Bảo that someone had texted. Was that only two weeks ago? The Linh there is proud, proud of herself, and also happy in Bảo's arms as they look on at the mural, her work, her art. Ba's right. I was happy.

But why is he showing this to me now? Will he say something

357

about Bảo? There's no denying what we are in this pic. Instead, he seems to be ignoring him, literally putting him out of the picture.

"We want you to be happy, but we don't want you to suffer."

"Like Dì Vàng," I whisper, recalling my mom's words repeated over and over.

He shakes his head. "Like we did. *Khi Ba tới nước này*," he starts, before switching to English. "When I came here, my English was not good. Still isn't good. But back in Vietnam, I could stand in front of a classroom and speak without fear. My teachers told me I would be a great businessman. That I would make everyone broke because everyone would want to buy whatever I sold!" He smiles at the memory, proud. "After escaping, after coming here, I wanted to try that. I wanted to try marketing and advertising because it was something I loved to do, and before you were born, I went to school for it."

A thought tickles my brain, and I go searching for it, finding it in a few seconds. In the box of photos, there was one showing Ba in a classroom. Maybe it was from that time? I knew Ba didn't have a degree, but I didn't know that he tried for it.

"But because of my English, I sounded unpolished in presentations. I couldn't speak to even my classmates. It was hard, and I started to hate it. I started to hate doing what I loved to do, which I never thought would happen.

"I know other people could have moved on despite this. Your mother is someone who would, because she is strong. I wasn't. And then Evelyn was born. And then you were born, and there was no more time for school. We had too much to worry about. We had to survive."

I reach for his hand. A strange sense of understanding comes over me. He went after what he loved to do and couldn't do it, or finish it, as hard as he tried. But that didn't mean he was a failure.

"You can go back to school. There's time."

Ba waves away the suggestion. "I am happy at the restaurant now. In a way, I still do marketing and advertising." Like the phở specials and how every time a new customer comes in he flashes his smile, his charisma. "But I am scared for you, con." Another word I don't often hear from Ba. "Art will be a hard life."

I hold my breath.

Will. He might not know the significance—maybe he *does*—but this is the first time I heard it as a possibility.

I grab on to it, squeezing his hand. "Ba, I know it will always be hard. But I *can* do this. I *am* doing this, now." I remember his words before, about how other people might have continued, unlike him. "Don't you think I'm *strong enough*?"

"Of course con strong. You are Linh Mai," he answers quickly.

I smile faintly. "I want to do this. I *can* do this. I know I can. Because I have you and . . . Mẹ. You guys did the surviving for me and Evie," I say, bringing up his words from before. I wonder if Mẹ feels this way as well, and maybe that is why she's never seen art as a path for me. She is scared, too, her own history tinged with so many struggles in Vietnam and after. It might be with her forever.

I know if I close my eyes now, I will see Mẹ, in this kitchen, tears in her eyes. I see her at my age, when she came here, when she didn't have what I have now, which is opportunity. All because of them.

'Ba, all the struggles that you went through. You've surpassed them. Now you just deserve to live."

Ba glances at the table, blinking. Holding back tears. I've never seen him cry, and I don't think I will, but to see him this close unleashes my tears. I fall apart; I understand, now, just a bit more of what he's gone through, mourning his life that he never got to really have. He's tired. We sit there, hand in hand for a few minutes, until I feel Ba's squeeze.

'Does it really make you happy? Painting?"

'Yes."

'Are you *sure* you don't want to do engineering?" he asks.

I laugh now, shaking my head so that my tears fall to the table. 'Definitely sure."

"*Thoî*," he says after clearing his throat. His voice is gruff. *Đừng khóc nữa. Rửa mặt đi, xong xuống ăn cơm."*

I laugh. *Wash your face.* The Vietnamese dismissal that I got as a child whenever I'd cry after getting yelled at. I rush down the hall to the bathroom, splash cold water on my face, and glance into the mirror. The redness is still there, but I feel different.

For the first time in weeks, I'm a bit lighter.

I return to the kitchen to a bowl now full with fluffy rice, *nước mắm,* and a bowl of *canh bí* between us. I scoop a spoonful, tasting it. 'No salt."

Ba tsks his tongue. 'You try cooking it, and we'll see how well you do."

Our chopsticks hit the insides of our bowls, us eating our meal quietly, comfortably, even. When Ba finishes his first bowl, he sets it down.

"That boy across the street from us. The one who wrote the article that everyone is talking about." Ba points to the photo with his chopsticks. "So you do know him."

I take a large gulp, hoping that we're not going to head into another argument, because that would break me. I nod.

"Is he your friend?"

Another nod.

"Bạn trai?"

Boyfriend. Not anymore. I'd hurt him. The urge to cry comes back, the corners of my eyes prickling. It's not only Mom I'll need to apologize to, but also Bảo. "We . . . we haven't seen each other in a while. And I'm not sure if we will again."

"Okay," he answers simply. Perhaps remembering that it is Mẹ I would talk to more often than Ba, he merely returns to his meal. A part of me wonders if he's realized that he's never showed me this much emotion, so he may be reaching his limit in one night.

I still miss him.

As mean as I was to him, as hurtful as my words were—even if I didn't mean it—he still wrote that article defending us, our community, including my family.

Linh, you really messed things up.

Things at home are not much better, but not worse. A plan came just at dawn, at breakfast, watching my mom cut coupons and my dad read the crime section of the paper. Ba has been trying to cool Mẹ down, smooth things over between us, but my mom's stubborn.

Every cold shoulder, every glance past me, hurts me more than I realize. Maybe I can't fix that right away. I did lie to her. But there's something else I can try fixing now, and maybe some good will come out of it.

I stop just before the front facade of Bảo's restaurant. Suddenly the alley door opens; a mop of black hair appears—and it's Việt. I freeze in my steps, and he does the same. Unsure of his reaction—if he'll just ignore me—I feel relief coursing through me when Việt speaks to me.

"You saw the article?"

"I did. It was great. I'm really proud of him."

"Does he know that?"

Both of us know that we haven't spoken since that day in the art room.

"I'm gonna be blunt, Linh. You're a friend now, you know." How matter-of-factly he says this, and I almost start crying. Unbelievably, Bảo's weird best friend has also become someone I can trust, too. And he's still speaking to me. "So I'm saying this as a friend to a friend. If you don't really like Bảo anymore and you don't want to date him, I'm okay with what you did." Every bit of me wants to scream *NO*. "But if you did it because you're scared or something . . . don't you think Bảo's feeling the same way? I mean, he knows that everything is stacked against you two."

"I'm sorry."

"You know he did all of this for you." In typical Việt fashion, he

362

only shrugs. "Ultimately, it's between you and him. If you choose to end the relationship, just do it the right way."

He expects me to agree, to let him go.

"Is that what you want?"

I don't move. That's the last thing I want to do, but I don't say that. Instead, I ask, "Is Bảo's mom inside?"

Something lets up in his eyes. And he nods, as if saying, *Good choice*.

I wince at the jolting ring of the front door bell. The sun hits the wall differently, revealing even more of its imperfections—cracks in certain places, discoloration under constant sunlight. Bảo has said that wall was always an eyesore. My eyes drift from the wall to the front desk, where Bảo's mother stands and stares at me, her glasses at the end of her nose. It isn't as severe as I expected, but I still take a deep breath.

Her reaction is strange, like she's seeing something I can't. Maybe there was something else there, but it disappears in a moment and she's emerging from behind the front desk. Will she make me leave?

"You're one of their daughters. You're a Mai."

"Dạ, chào cô. Tên con là Linh." I figure answering in Vietnamese might be polite. I suppose it works, since she just nods. Waits for me to take the lead.

I switch to English. "I saw what Bảo wrote in the paper." I point to the frame on the wall. "It was really nice of him to defend our community."

'It was good, yes.'

'He's so good at writing. I'm sure you're proud of him.'

'And you know he writes?'

'We're friends. We'd never spoken to each other before until this year and we've become . . . close.'

'Friends.' Her eyes widen like someone learning what it means for the first time.

'Yes.' *There, that's out in the open.*

'Anyway, what he did meant a lot. That he'd write something nice about our family. I don't . . . pretend to know what happened. To make you hate us"—I rush through my words when I see her open her mouth— 'and I know I'm not a part of it, and that's fine and all. I don't think my parents would even want me here.'

I breathe out. 'But they were glad to have someone defend them. It meant a lot. So . . . thank you.' I take a step forward, but Bảo's mother doesn't back away or anything. I unroll the paper I'd worked on, slowly. I feel her gaze on me, taking stock of me, unsure why I'm even here. 'It was so nice of Bảo, especially since . . ." I gulp—no need to give her another reason to kick me out.

It feels like a weird dream being here. It's just me and her. Like me and Bảo, we've existed in the same place, a few feet away, and now we're here in front of each other.

I glance at the wall that Bảo had brought up in some of our conversations. 'I want to do something for you. You see, I'm a painter.'

'An artist?' she asks numbly.

I tilt my head, not expecting that reaction. It sounds like she's in disbelief. 'Yes, that's kind of how me and Bảo first started working together. And I had a vision for this wall. It's beautiful as it is, with all the photos, but I wonder—" I bite my lip before unfurling the paper fully.

Essentially it's a mural I'm proposing. One of Nha Trang from a bird's-eye view. The waters, the streets crowded with motorcycles. An ode to where they'd come from. They'd keep the picture frames, but it'd be like the faces in the landscape. A nice reminder of the past—even though it wasn't all that nice. As I gesture to different parts of the mural, I'm hyperaware of her hands, slightly pink like they were just washed under warm water.

"I'd like to do it for you one day."

"Why?" she asks, incredulous.

"Bảo told me the next thing you wanted for the restaurant was a new wall." My voice trembles. "He really loves you. You're his mom." Now I'm just babbling, so I summon my remaining courage. "I want to apologize to Bảo, but I don't know how. He's the most honest person out there, more honest than me. Because he cares. Because he's special. He means a lot to me." I break off before I start to get too emotional. I put on a brave face, starting to back away. "Anyway, thank you for your time. And please let me know if I can help in the future."

"Why don't you tell him all of this yourself?"

I smile sadly. "Because he was right: I'm still scared."

CHAPTER FORTY-FIVE

BẢO

The door rings in the next customer and I say hello without looking, counting a customer's change before handing it over. "Thanks for coming by." Plastering another smile on my face, I focus on the newcomer, only to realize it's not a regular customer.

It's Linh's father. Years of spotting him by the window looking out at us, of his profile just before disappearing into his store, tells me it's him. He stands with his arms crossed behind his back—Vietnamese style. I instantly sense disapproval from him—as if Vietnamese fathers underwent the same aura training before having children—but it's more of a gut reaction than anything else.

"Tên con là Bảo?"

"Dạ. Chào, Bác."

He nods. Probably noticing how atrocious my Vietnamese is but accepting my attempt, at least. His eyes sweep the room, and my mom's panicked voice sounds choked up inside my brain, *Why is he here?!*

He switches over to English. "Your article is very good." He holds out the latest edition of *Người Việt* where it's folded to show my op-ed. "And you defended us well."

Us.

"Are you a writer?" he asks.

If I answered *I think so*, he'd probably think even less of me. "Yes, I am. I'm thinking of doing it in college."

He shakes the newspaper at me—not in a threatening way, thank God. "I think it would be very good for you."

"Th-thank you," I manage to get out.

Again the silence falls heavily and I try not to squirm under his scrutiny. I wonder if he knows I was seeing Linh before everything blew up.

"You are Linh's friend."

It's not going to stop just because of the argument. At least, I hope. "I am . . . Do you want to talk to my parents or . . ."

His face changes. "No, no." He shakes his head. "Don't let them know I was here." A corner of his lips turns up. "I'll get in trouble."

Ah, the terror of Vietnamese wives. I just nod and wave as Linh's father backs out, hurrying across the street so quickly that I must have hallucinated his entire visit. I don't know how long I stand there, watching the restaurant across from us, mirroring my dad's

367

own surveillance stance. Is it possible that my article managed to bridge some gap? Can forgiveness be born from this?

I dip my hand into my back pocket, brushing up against the folded-up flyer for the Art Fair. I hold on to it as I cross the street.

CHAPTER FORTY-SIX

LINH

I snuck out for the Art Fair. No, that wasn't exactly it. My parents had to have known I was leaving. I made noise walking down the hallway, made sure my keys jangled loud enough, before shutting the door. All done to see if they would say anything. But there was nothing. Them not monitoring where I'm going is so much worse.

The auditorium isn't filled to capacity like it is for sports events, but when I walk in, I'm surprised by the number of people here for the Art Fair. But farther in the back, ribboned off—dramatic!— is my display. I see some other classmates, like Eric and Spencer, exhibiting their art.

Spending so much time nose-to-canvas, obsessing over the littlest details, I forget to see the whole picture. I forget what everything looks like when it's all put together. And now, easel set up like this, I feel like I can see a story.

I did all of this. Everything here I can call mine. Despite being alone tonight, I'm latching on to this.

I don't think I've ever smiled so much. As I wait for people to come by, I reread my statement. I had Ali look at it, but what I really wanted was for Bảo to see it. He was always good at things like that. But it's my fault that I can't, I know that. I pushed him away, hurt him. And now I'm paying for it.

The compliments are nice and heart-warming, but temporary. My smile fades once each exhibitor leaves my display. I watch a classmate and his parents pose for some pictures. His dads look so proud of him. I turn around, fighting back a burning sensation in the back of my eyes. I wish Mẹ and Ba could be here, but I couldn't bring myself to mention the fair, even if Ba is starting to come around to my art. I wish I could have told the truth from the very beginning. Maybe then they'd be proud enough to be here, just this one time, for me.

Soon enough, the Art Fair crowd has dwindled, people are leaving, and some other artists are already taking down their canvases, to store here or bring home.

"Linh!" I see Ali's curly hair before her face. She squeezes me to death, rambling about how proud she is of me. "Total masterpieces! How are you feeling?"

She'll be worried if I answer honestly: that I feel alone and I can't seem to stop it, even if everyone's responding well to my artwork. The people whose opinions matter the most . . . just aren't here.

Offering me some comfort, whether she knows it or not, Yamamoto quickly passes by, squeezing me tight, whispering about how proud she is of me. That if I don't get the Gold Key scholarship, she'll visit their headquarters, wherever they are, and protest.

I force a smile, which fades as I spot *him*.

I think I say hello or some version of it, right as he does the same. He's stumbling over his words now before he finally stops himself, fixated on the floor. Will it be like this from now on?

"You look nice. Professional," I offer.

"I needed to impress someone." A smile plays on his lips. My heart leaps at his answer but I try not to show it, waiting. Then I notice the bouquet that he's offering me sheepishly. "I heard about your mural idea. My mom told me."

I accept the flowers. "She was really shocked when I came by."

"She could barely speak. That's not a common thing." He pauses before turning to my paintings. "So, tell me about them."

He's not walking away. He's here and his presence gives me a small semblance of hope. In this moment, it's enough. I slip my hand into his, relishing in his warmth, and pull him toward my work. The earliest of them depicts a common scene from my childhood, me waiting for my parents to finish prepping for the next day. I painted my ten-year-old self into a booth, preoccupied with blowing bubbles into my water. Mẹ has popped her head out from the serving window and is likely trying to talk to Ba, who's at the front desk.

I show them my family restaurant's facade, that night Phở Day ended with a success. I tried to infuse the contentment I felt at seeing Mẹ's face through the yellow haze of the streetlights shining down, the glistening of puddles left from the storm.

I lead Bảo to my painting of the art room the first time he visited me. An idyllic scene, the afternoon light streaming from the window, touching the desks and stools, and my back as I faced the canvas. I painted in Bảo's backpack and a hint of his shoes peeking out as one table blocked the view of his body.

These memories grew out of me over time and in the last few weeks. The act of painting them is now a blur; I was so focused on my canvas that I barely kept track of time. Maybe because I'd never desired more to escape. Seeing my paintings now, displayed like this, is somewhat of an out-of-body experience, but it's also hollow. I wish my parents could see them, too, see how much my art and my life with them, here, are so deeply intertwined that it's no longer about trying to undo these ties.

The concept of me being an artist *without* them doesn't exist.

I peek at Bảo's reaction as he leans forward to study the details of the art room. He still hasn't let go. I realize that my hands, despite the hard scrubbing, still show residues of paint. But the sight of it against his clean skin is comforting. Normal.

"I thought I knew what you were capable of, but this is beyond that. I don't think I can pick a favorite. I love all of it." He's looking at me now, and perhaps it's foolish hope that makes me spot a familiar wistful gleam in his eyes. The kind he'd send me before bringing me in for a kiss, before brushing aside a strand of my hair.

And I know I should just say it. "I'm sorry, Bảo. More sorry than I can ever express. The mural was just one attempt to try to make up for what I said."

"Linh, you don't have to—"

"Your article was honest—the exact opposite of the way I'd been acting. I was scared of telling my parents the truth. So I lied, and those lies just kept piling up. I hurt you. I hurt them, and now—this, while it's all that I can ever dream of—it just feels empty." I gesture to the paintings behind me, with colors and emotions that were painted, in a way, for them. "I can't really celebrate because I hurt so many people to get here."

He stops trying to protest, bringing his arms around me. I don't understand how much I needed his full touch until my nose is pressed up against his shoulders and comforted by his familiar scent. "I was hurting. I didn't know how to deal with all the secrets coming up. But I lied to you, Bảo. I want us. I've always wanted us."

"I think I knew that. At least, I hoped what I was thinking was right." He leans back slightly to catch my eye, his thumb caressing my cheek.

"Thank you for being brave, Bảo Nguyễn."

"Ahem."

Ali, surprising me, hugs the two of us from behind. "Finally, Romeo and Juliet are back together. I thought you'd be mad at me for letting him see you."

"Letting me?" Bảo asks, but Ali ignores him.

"But I have to admit, these past few weeks have brought me and

373

this guy closer. If we paired together, we could really change the newspaper-making business."

I hold back a laugh at Bảo's grimace, which Ali can't see since she's facing away from him. Yet that laughter turns into confusion when she asks him, "Are they outside?"

"I was getting there." He's almost . . . shy? "Linh, I know there are important people you want to be here, who are missing here. But they're not, not right now." Bảo tilts his head, gestures to the exit. "They're outside."

"What—" *They?*

Who . . .?

I leave a trail of flower petals as I dash out of the auditorium, down the long streak of hallway with loitering parents and younger siblings amusing themselves with whatever they can touch. I find my aunt at the very end of it, alone. She welcomes me with a smile.

"Dì Vàng!" I fly into her arms and she returns my hug with a deep chuckle. Her shoulder purse slides off and falls to the ground.

"Surprised?"

"Shocked. How—"

"Well, I was always planning to come. The thing about visiting a friend—that was a lie. I wanted to surprise you." She looks at a point over my shoulder. When I follow her gaze, I don't see anyone. I pivot, confused. "That was him, wasn't it?"

Not finding the right words, I merely nod.

"He's the spitting image of his uncle." She says this lightly, but there's a whole story behind her eyes. What she'd already told me was likely only half of it.

374

She shakes the look away and pushes me gently out of her arms. She steers me to face the exit. "What—"

"Go. Some important people are waiting just outside for you. I'll meet you back inside. Apparently there's a superstar who's displayed her work here. Be the brave, honest person that I know you are."

My steps outside are far more hesitant. The scent of cigarettes clings to the cool air. They've dressed up. My dad with his polo neatly tucked into his belted dress pants. He stands with his back to me, arms crossed behind him, head tipped back like he's watching for a sign from the sky. Next to him is my mom, always favoring softer floral patterns, in a red-and-white knee-length dress that I've never seen her wear.

It's possible that she bought it just for tonight's exhibition—and the thought makes me hopeful.

"Ba. Mẹ." I clutch the flowers to my chest. They're ruined by now. "I didn't think you'd come." My steps toward them seem unusually disruptive and it's only because my parents are so quiet and still. Such lifelike statues.

"We didn't know this was happening until today. Con didn't say anything directly." Accusation rings clear in her voice.

"So how did you know to be here?"

"Someone slipped a flyer under our door," Ba explains evenly.

Someone. "Ali?"

"Maybe," Ba says. He stares unblinkingly, but doesn't say anything. Now's the time he's going to try for subtle? What could he . . .?

Bảo.

So that's what his smile was for.

"After what happened, I knew you wouldn't want to come."

"Con knew? How could con know that?" Mẹ fires back. The red in her dress seems to take on a life of its own, a fire in the night. Ba interrupts her, telling her in Vietnamese to lower her voice. He's playing the opposite role today; his eyes beseech me, reminding me of when I cried and cried. He's on my side, but he can't do much if I don't explain myself.

If I don't finally tell the truth about myself.

"Mẹ, I don't want to lie to you anymore. And I know I've lied. About what I wanted. About my art. About Bảo, too, and our ... friendship. At the time, I thought all of this was necessary."

My voice cracks. "I'm a painter. And I really love what I do. Nothing makes me happier. When everything in the world seems tough and harsh, painting's where I go. It's like you and your cooking, Mẹ. Don't you ever feel like you can disappear in it?"

Mẹ folds her arms, and keeps her eyes fixed to the ground.

"I still wanted to make you proud and show that everything I was doing was *because* of you, not despite you."

"There are other ways to make Ba Mẹ proud. Above everything, you should not lie to us."

"But I didn't mean it like that. Mẹ, please. I draw *because* of you. Because you've always tried your best to raise me right. Because you work so hard, never find time for yourself, so I'm doing this for you, for both of you. Everything you're doing has allowed me to be happy. I wish you had that when you were younger. You worked so hard, you gave everything of yourself away just so that I could have a good life. And I believe that. I have a good life. I have a happy one."

"Please. I want to show you what I mean. Can I show you?" I hold her hand. The fact that she doesn't pull away encourages me.

I lead her back into the school like I did at Huntington Beach, that time we saw my first real artist. It wasn't just because I wanted to see; it was because I wanted my mom to see it too.

Distantly, I hear Yamamoto greeting my parents. I don't eavesdrop, but I stand aside and observe their faces. A bit of confusion. A bit of disbelief. They must be overwhelmed because it's not just Yamamoto gravitating toward them; it's other parents whose kids also displayed their work.

What surprises me more, though, is the quiet awe burgeoning in their eyes, a reaction they would have to my pieces from elementary school art classes.

Taking my mom's hand again, I point to a scene that I hadn't shown Bảo yet, hadn't gotten to. I painted it because I was remembering how much simpler life was a few months ago.

It's a nine-by-eleven-inch piece depicting the hours following our first special: the three of us celebrating in the kitchen. It might have been dark outside, but inside the kitchen, under the bright ceiling lights, we were exhausted and hopeful. My mom bends closer to the canvas. I hope she sees the look in her eyes that I tried to capture, that tired contentedness. I hope she sees me leaning against her, shoulder to shoulder. And I hope she sees my dad and how tall he sits. Most of all, I want her to see how the three of us are together, a family. We are strongest only together.

"I really love this one," Yamamoto remarks, standing just behind me. I spot my mom squinting at the tattoos along her arms, more curious than horrified.

"Why?" my dad finally asks.

"Because I've come to know Linh over the years, Mr. Mai and Mrs. Phạm. I've seen how much she cares about what you think. But I've also seen how present and alive she is through her art—probably more than she realizes. And just a few minutes ago, watching you walk into the auditorium, I saw how Linh lights up knowing that you're here to support her." Bảo's right; my expressions give me away. "All of this"—she gestures to the paintings— "this is Linh and what she values the most. In one exhibition."

"Being an artist . . . it's hard," Mẹ says slowly. I wonder if she's cautious to voice this opinion in front of a teacher.

"Oh, it is. You know it is. And from my brief conversation with your sister"—Yamamoto tips her head at my aunt, who's mingling with people at the opposite side of the room— "she knows, too. But in anything you love, isn't there always some bit of sadness, some essence of suffering? That, to me, is what makes art worth it. Suffer through it—mine the emotions you keep inside yourself, face whatever's emotionally burdensome, take control of it—then emerge reborn in the end."

She speaks directly to me. "This is what Linh is doing. It's such an honor to be her teacher. I hope you know that Linh's one of a kind."

◇ ◇ ◇

Yamamoto squeezes my arm, before drifting back into the crowd, like a kind spirit. Other classmates and their parents surround me and for the first time tonight, I bask in their warm glow. I keep an eye on my parents simultaneously. They're walking around, peering at other artwork. My aunt soon joins them and points at certain canvases and sculptures, perhaps explaining the different media. Ali's been going around the room interviewing other artists, explaining that she couldn't show bias in her reporting. Bảo, though, seems to have disappeared, understanding that I needed more time with my parents.

The auditorium clears out and only five or six families linger. My parents rejoin me along with my aunt, and all I can do is follow them as they wordlessly head back out into the hallway. Our footsteps squeak and echo into the empty space. I'm sandwiched between my aunt and my mom. I'm struck by the need to clutch Mẹ's hand again.

Mẹ's voice startles me from my thoughts. "From now on, con can't tell more lies. *Đừng nói láo nữa nghe không?*"

I nod, promising that there won't be any more lies between us.

"Art is what you want? It makes you happy?"

Ba had asked the same question.

"The happiest, Mẹ."

We walk some more, now standing in the parking lot. The faint smell of grass, barbeque smoke, and asphalt surrounds us. "Mẹ *còn* mad at you," Mẹ answers calmly.

"I know. But I promise, I won't—"

379

In a split second, I'm crushed against my mother. Her arms leave no room for escape. "You know you are my life, con," Mẹ whispers fiercely into my hair.

I blink away tears, my head buried in her shoulder. I feel Ba patting my back, and my mind flashes back to a younger me, a sleepy me, who's carried up to bed by my parents.

"Don't cry," Dì Vàng says, happiness pure in her voice.

I'm not sure which one of us she is talking to.

In the car, as we're pulling out of the lot, Mẹ reaches back with her hand. I grasp, asking whose hand it is.

"What a silly game," my aunt mutters with a smile. My mom and I grin at each other through the mirror.

My family spends the rest of the ride bashing other artists, even though I think they're all great. Dad called them *"dở quá."*

"So how much better am I as an artist?" I tease Ba.

And his answer surprises me in the best way possible, as he sends me a big, fat smile in the rearview mirror.

"Một trăm percent."

CHAPTER FORTY-SEVEN

BẢO

Tết in Little Saigon means tons of road closures. The few police officers who didn't grow up around here look befuddled by our penchant for bouncy music, performances from dojos, and bedazzled floats filled with flowers—lots of them. The American flag and South Vietnamese flag hang along light poles.

The air is filled with the smell of fried sweets—bananas, I think—and the crowd ranges from young to old. Little kids run along, some struggling in their bright silky *áo dài*, followed by a parent looking stressed out and clutching their child's mini *khăn đóng*. But the hate of hats is universal in kids their age. Old dads try locating their wives, who've abandoned them for friends; today's their day off. I sputter when some stray balloons collide with my face. A sunshine-y version of *"Xuân đã về,"* celebrating the arrival of spring, blasts from a float made out of straw. Miss Teen Vietnam, California, sits perched at the front, waving prettily from it. People holler from the crowd.

"Look at how skinny she is," Mom mutters, clutching her purse to herself. She then nastily eyes a pack of girls who inadvertently pushed her to take pictures of the passing float. As much as she hates crowds, she always makes a point of attending the celebrations. I think it reminds her of her childhood. And she always manages to run into some Vietnamese friends.

The cash prize is the other draw, ranging from five hundred to five grand. "How else will we pay for college?" Ba replied when I asked why we entered with little chance to win.

Scarily, there was no joke in his tone whatsoever.

The usual float from Vietnam America TV 57.3 passes. Another float comes by, some local florist shop, and they're launching bouquets into the crowds. Mẹ smacks my dad on the shoulder. "Look at the flowers!"

Lo and behold, she isn't the only middle-aged Asian oohing and ahhing at the flowers being thrown to the crowd. With swiftness that surprises me, my mom jumps to grab a bunch, holding them over her head victoriously. Ba makes some joke, though I can tell he's proud of her.

Just then, I see the familiar swish of hair across the street, standing behind the fence. Linh. She leans over, peering for the next float to come by, and she's smiling. That's my girlfriend across the street.

382

A real girlfriend. *As opposed to ...?* says a voice strangely like Việt's in my head.

Could she be more beautiful? This time, she's tied her hair in a side braid and is clapping along to the music.

Linh is with her parents and another woman who must be her aunt. She has long hair just like Linh. She mentioned she was visiting. I push my way up to the front, earning some elbow jabs along the way, but I can't help but feel as if something is pulling me toward her. I wave my arms wide, yell out her name.

She notices.

What are you doing? her panicked eyes seem to say.

There's nothing to be scared of anymore! Our parents know we're seeing each other, I say back with my eyes. When nothing changes in her expression, I realize that we haven't mastered telepathy just yet. Behind me, I hear my parents calling my name, confused.

The crowd is so ferocious that it crushes me against the fence. Linh still looks scared. At this point, neither her parents or her aunt have noticed me ... but then she does. The aunt, at least. Her face goes slack, stopping me in my tracks. I've never seen anyone turn white that quickly, but why at me? But her eyes don't lock on me; they slide right past me ... zooming in on my parents, who, I turn and realize, froze in the middle as well.

It's like the meeting at the Buddha temple again.

Then something weird happens. Linh's aunt turns ...

And runs.

CHAPTER FORTY-EIGHT

LINH

I never expected Bảo to be at my doorstep.

Or that he'd be able to come into the house at all. But that's what's happening now. He's sitting next to me in the living room, as if we do this every week.

"You okay?" he asks, tucking a hair strand behind my ear, which makes me panic. My eyes go to my dad, who's sitting in his usual chair; he keeps shooting us inquisitive glances, but if he disapproves of our proximity, he doesn't say much. My mother, who let Bảo inside in the first place, is more preoccupied with my aunt, who, upon returning from the parade, walked straight into the master bedroom, locking the door. Not answering anyone, even my mother as she pleads for her to come out.

"What's happening? Are you okay?" she asks through the door.

The bedroom door creeps open and we all stand when my aunt appears, red-eyed but otherwise composed.

"Sorry, I needed to collect myself." Her eyes sweep the room before landing on Bảo, the only one who doesn't belong. Seconds pass, the silence grows disconcerting. "I saw you at the fair, but to see you in the daylight like that . . . you really do look like your uncle."

"So I've been told."

"How much do you know?"

I speak for myself and Bảo, explaining how Bác had told me about our families knowing each other back in Vietnam. About the photo I found, which was when Bảo sheepishly recounted his story about what his mother said—not the accusation—but the distress that she expressed when she found out we knew each other.

Mẹ sits silently, nervously, as Ba stands by the living room window, watching us.

My aunt turns back to Mẹ. "I already knew they were here."

"How?"

"Does it matter?" my aunt counters. "Now why didn't you tell me all of this?"

"I didn't want to hurt you again. I didn't want to bring up memories that were meant to be forgotten."

Dì Vàng shakes her head. "That was a long time ago. I'm an adult now."

"You were in love with him," Mẹ says. "And he left you without a thought. That was his fault. And his family's. And it was all unforgivable."

"Do you know why he left?" my aunt asks sharply. "He was to inherit the family business."

"That's a reason to celebrate, not abandon you. He should have been taking care of you."

Dì Vàng scoffs, throwing her hands up. "Of course! Because I was destined to be poor just because I'm an artist."

"We all know the struggle. You couldn't just ignore it. It was the reality." My mother looks to me now, only this isn't about me. "Our parents were just doing their part and looking out for you."

"But I'm here. And I'm fine, you didn't need to protect me. You don't have to."

"You're lying to yourself. I knew you were sad after he left. And I could barely speak to his family after that. How could I? When they were the ones who drove him away, convinced him of a better match."

"They're not to blame at all," Dì Vàng says.

"How? How do you know?" Mẹ demands. My dad mutters something; I suspect it's to tell her to calm down, but he's silenced with a withering glance.

"Because I was the one to tell him to leave."

The puzzle dislodges again, my understanding of this very weird situation disappearing in a millisecond. My eyes move between my mom and Dì Vàng, a staring contest in play, both willing the other to speak first. Ba sits silently, arms crossed, his expression emotionless.

"What?" my mom whispers.

"What no one knows, no one but me and Bảo's uncle, is that we were never together."

"Gì? Nói lại," my mother says, confused.

386

"We were a distraction. He liked Huyền."

"Huyền?" Mẹ looked away, a hardened version scoffing at the name. Now I wonder what that woman did to get on my mother's bad side.

"Yes, Huyền."

"Who was she?" I ask.

"Neighborhood girl," Dì Vàng explains quickly. "But her family was poorer than both of ours and Cam's family would have never approved of the match."

"Hmm," my mom mutters dismissively. "Because they were prejudiced." Bảo stiffens beside me. First time over and he's indirectly insulted by my mother.

"I could say the same about ours," my aunt retorts, her tone severe enough to rival my mom's. "Financial security, wasn't it? Ultimately that's why our parents approved of us so much.

"But Cam was my best friend. And he loved my other friend, so I pretended that I was seeing him whenever we left the neighborhood, but I was really bringing him to see Huyền." Once the last words leave her, her secret finally released, she sits down. She touches her necklace in thought. "Then the whole engagement happened and we were swept up with family expectations, trying to make things work out.

"Remember, Huyền had to leave because her parents fled first. And then he was so sad. I couldn't get a word out of him. I couldn't make him happy, even as his best friend. So I told him to go after her. Life was already miserable back home because of Viet Cong, you know that. Having a broken heart as well?" My aunt shakes her head. "So I told him to go. Find her wherever she is and tell her the truth. Start a new life together."

She exhales shakily. "I didn't think he would lose his life along the way."

I look over at Bảo, his mouth slightly opened at the revelations emerging in our living room. He'd been in the dark just like I was, and now things are just beginning to make sense. These decades of blame from our families manifesting in what we thought was just a silly competition.

"That can't be true," Mẹ says.

"It is."

"Why didn't you say anything?"

"How would I even *begin* to explain myself? It was, to everyone, a perfect match. Mẹ and Ba"—hearing my aunt mention her parents makes her sound young again— "It was something they were happy about too."

"But Cam's family—they blame you. Don't you remember how angry you were at each other? The yelling that happened. His sister said horrible things."

"She'd lost her brother."

"Still! They shouldn't have said you were heartless. Worthless."

Is that when things went sour? I remember my mom's reaction when she saw the picture of me and Bảo. Her anger overpowered me, overpowered any logic. I can only imagine the ugly words that flew between our families.

"My family doesn't know the truth, do they?" Bảo asks. Mẹ's eyes fly to him, widening before narrowing, as if she's just realized who

388

she actually let in. "That's why they're still angry at your family."

"The things that were said were hurtful. But they didn't hurt me. *They* were hurt. They'd just lost a son. A brother." She turns to my parents. "If you lost me, wouldn't you react the same way, look for someone to blame?

"There's only so much anger you can hold. But I'm hopeful, because here are Linh and Bảo, willing to move past this."

"Bảo's great," I say. "And his family cares about him just as much as you care about me."

He squeezes my hand, a smile playing on his lips. This time I don't blush; I'm bolstered by his silent agreement. "When a bunch of racists hounded our place and nearly everywhere else in Bolsa, he wrote an article, for all of us. Because it's right."

My aunt appraises him and, based on her smile, seems to think more of him. "He wrote what he thought was best. He didn't let a little history get in the way of what's right."

Bảo shifts in his seat. "What if you spoke to my family?"

My mom sits up straight. "What? No, no, no, it's too much. I don't want to see them. It's . . . too much has happened."

"All because I held back the truth for years. And now look at what happened. I have to take the blame for that. We're going," my aunt says.

"But—"

My aunt turns to me, then brings her gaze up to Bảo. "Call your parents."

Even though he suggested it, his Adam's apple nervously bobs as he nods.

CHAPTER FORTY-NINE

BẢO

My mom paces the restaurant, nervously smoothing out her dress, the same one she wore for our on-camera interview. She's pretending to mutter to herself—meaning, very out loud at me and Ba—about how Linh's family has the nerve to come over uninvited, like uncultured swine.

Never mind the fact that Linh's family called to explain their visit.

Or that I told them Linh's aunt would be here too.

Or that the time was one that my mom decided.

Not knowing what to do with myself, I join my father in the kitchen, where he uses a ladle to pour *chanh muối*—salty limeade—

from a large jar into six drinking glasses. Limes are packed tightly for months, then finished off with a bit of sugar, water, and ice. I find myself salivating; I haven't had it since I was little.

Ba looks up briefly, finishing the last glass. "They made the best lemon tea. Linh's grandmother. After school, we would all go to her grandmother's house for a glass. It was refreshing."

"Oh," I say, unsure how to respond to the comment, a memory about the other family, whom they'd hated for so long, shared so willingly. I'm saved from answering as he gestures for me to bring the glasses out and place them on the table.

The light falls on our family's black-and-white photos, which have watched over me as long as memory serves me. The sight of them sends me some hope. Whatever happens today, they will be our witnesses.

As I wait at the front desk, tuning out my mother's dark thoughts, eager for a glimpse of movement outside the windows, I can't help but feel a strange sort of calm, too. An inevitability that started the moment my mother let Linh into the restaurant, despite her family and who she is.

I hold on to the feeling when I see Linh leading her family over.

"They're coming."

"So what!" my mom calls out, but she leaves the kitchen, starts fretting with the dishware and silverware.

"How are things over here?" Linh murmurs once inside. We stay back as our families file into the dining room.

"Frickin' weird." I don't take my eyes off our families, together in one place. It's like I'm watching my favorite television show live for the first time: familiar players but unknown outcomes. "I checked my mom for weapons and she's clean."

Linh stifles a laugh, then squeezes my hand before letting go too early. I run my hand down her back in a fleeting gesture of comfort—for the both of us—before focusing on our respective parents in the dining area. My mom saw this interaction, brief shock sparking in her eyes, but says nothing.

She stands stiffly next to Ba

"It's been a while," Linh's mother says.

"It has." My mom nods at Linh's aunt. "I didn't know you were visiting." Her familiar brisk tone has given way to a different sound. I realize then that her voice is wavering.

At Ba's gesture, we all sit at once: three on each side of the booth, with Linh's aunt pulling up a chair at the head. I can't remember how to move my hands, where to put them. Linh throws me a hesitant smile across the table. Her ankle brushes up against mine.

"Are you staying in America for long?" Mẹ asks.

"Yes, only a few weeks. I've been planning on visiting for a while. So far things have been exciting." Linh's aunt keeps her tone light and airy; she's treating this like a regular occurrence.

"And what do you do now over in Vietnam?"

"I'm still an artist. I sculpt. I make jewelry and vases." She reaches into her bag and places down a figurine—a red dragon with yellow spots along its body. My mom doesn't touch it. Ba's the one to take it in hand.

He nods solemnly. "A beautiful dragon." Still he pushes it an inch back to Linh's aunt.

"Don't you know why it's a dragon?"

Here I'm lost and fascinated at once—nameless emotions cloud, then disappear from my mom's face.

Dì Vàng's smile is wry. "Year of the Dragon. Cam's year."

My mom glances down once at the dragon before clearing her throat. "Why is it that you're here?"

"I was surprised to see you at the parade. Linh had mentioned you, but seeing you so abruptly, I ran. I remembered our last encounter. I remembered what we said. And now I think it's time we put this all to bed."

"What is there to say?"

Linh's aunt inhales. "I know you blame me and my family for your brother's death. That you think I somehow hurt him and made him leave the country, and that's how he died. And what I want to say is that I am guilty. But not in the way you think."

My mom leans forward, the chair creaking.

"Before he left, Cam wasn't in love with me. He was in love with someone else."

"Are you saying he was unfaithful?" My mom starts rising from her seat, ready to defend her brother's honor, yet Linh's aunt remains seated, shoulders squared—just like Linh when she has her mind set. Even though we've barely spoken to each other, I'm beginning to like her. This is someone who, long ago, knew how to stand her ground against my mom, a force of nature even though she was younger.

"I'm telling you the truth. My truth. And his."

"It's not his truth, since he is not here."

393

"He was in love with Huyền. Remember her? The granddaughter of the woman who always sold fish to the neighborhood on Saturday mornings? The freshest kind! Didn't we all used to admire how neatly she was able to braid her hair?"

My mom's brow is creased. "She told us her grandfather would braid it. Because her grandmother's hands always smelled of fish." She sounds far away, her mind's eye sifting through memories.

"Yes! Huyền. She was a lovely girl. So smart. So beautiful." Linh's aunt pauses. "The only strike against her was that she was poor and her parents had abandoned her.

"Cam and I were close, so I knew of his feelings. I always knew. The whole time, I was the one orchestrating their visits, giving them time to spend with each other while you all thought we were together."

"Why?" my mom breathes.

"Because I did love him. And because I knew he was happy with her."

"But the engagement—why . . . how?" Ba asks.

"Like I told my sister, we were just swept away by it. We couldn't get out of it. I saw that Cam was miserable. But everyone was so stuck in their ways. And so Cam resigned himself to it."

"If he was so resigned—you would have been married," my mom says harshly.

"I told him to go. You know how vocal he was? How miserable he would have been in that country? Even if she hadn't gone, he would have eventually left."

"And he died."

"And that's something I'll never forget. But then I think of it:

394

Who controls the storm? How can anyone divine the seas?

"Don't you know that I feel the same way? That if I could *make* him love me that would be enough? But that's impossible. You can't control who you love, any more than anyone can control the seas that took him from you. From me." Her voice cracks. "From all of us."

Linh looks at me.

I hold Linh's gaze.

"Không bao giờ em không nhớ Cam."

There's not a day that goes by that I don't remember him.

A pause so long that we can hear the kitchen fan rumble and the clock in the back of the room tick away. The air returns, allowing us to move. In this moment, we're all standing on a precipice.

I hold my breath as Linh's aunt reaches over, clasping my mom's hand. She doesn't pull away. "Cam is gone." But she gestures to everyone. "And don't you think he would be even more upset to see how our families turned out in the end? We were once so close.

"We were like family. We suffered together. We celebrated together. To hear what has happened all these years in between— which I only found out because Linh told me—it's just wrong. This . . . rivalry."

My mom raises her chin. "It's natural for restaurants to compete against each other."

"Ours was not natural," Linh's mom interjects.

"What did you expect? Your mother was always the better chef and she was the one to teach you how to cook. Of course I felt intimidated when you arrived on the scene." Never in a million years did I think my mom would admit her recipe was inferior.

"We didn't know you were across from us when we agreed to buy the restaurant from Bác Xuân. We never meant to compete; it was a way to provide for our daughters."

"Who turned out brilliantly," Linh's aunt adds, throwing a proud look at Linh, who tucks a strand of hair behind her ear. I'm briefly distracted by the blush on her cheeks. "And it seems like your son has grown up admirably because of your hard work, too." I scratch the back of my head as Linh playfully kicks me under the table. "We can all agree on that."

She softens her tone. "But isn't always competing with each other tiring? At what point will you have won? Either of you?"

I'm not sure if my parents have ever asked themselves that question. But I know the answer. There is no point to it. There's no winning if all this competition has been masking a war on matters unrelated to the number of customers that come in, the number of bowls sold each day.

By the way my mom sags into her seat, she's probably just reached the same conclusion. Her eyes skirt over to our wall. She might be looking at her brother, having a silent conversation with him.

"Bác Xuân ... By selling the restaurant to you, I sense he was trying to get us to forgive each other."

"Very unsuccessful," Linh's mom says.

"He was always nosy."

"So nosy."

"Ông tò mò," Linh's aunt says, and she turns to her sister. "Wasn't that what our mother always called him?"

"My parents called him much worse names." *Wait. Is my mom hiding a smile? It can't be.* I turn to Linh, who appears just as shocked by what's unfolding now.

"*Thôi, không nói nữa,*" my dad says, his bones creaking as he rolls back his hunched shoulders.

"*Mình làm gì được bây giờ?*" her dad mutters in agreement.

What can we do now?

Our dads arrive at an agreement first and now it's up to our mothers.

Our parents glance down at the plates, pushing around their food, running out of words.

Dì Vàng takes a sip and winces. "*Chua quá, chị.*" Too sour.

I gulp. This is it. Everything will be derailed.

Then, unbelievably, a full-blown smile appears on her face. "Some things really don't change."

Instead, my mom sniffs in a way that tells me she's not really mad. "Blame your mother. She never wanted to give me her recipe."

Our families have a lot of catching up to do. Their reminiscences continue, pushing me and Linh out of the conversation. But it's fine, because at least everything is out there, finally out there. Sharing one look, we rise from the table, and me and Linh head outside. We find a spot by the curb and sit down—right across from the very spot where we shared our very first laugh.

Linh rests her head on my shoulder. "Is this a dream?"

I laugh before dropping a kiss on her crown. "If it is, let's stay inside it for just a little while longer."

"Do you think everything's going to be okay?"

Linh turns her head to look back at our families and says, "They can't really forget the past, though. With one like theirs it's too impossible. But will they be able to move forward now?" Her gaze lands on me again. "I think so."

I squeeze her hand in agreement.

CHAPTER FIFTY

LINH

The Mais and the Nguyễns will never be the best of friends they once were decades ago. Too much history clouds the waters we share. But at least there are fewer words left unsaid. In a spirit of forgiveness, the Lunar New Year passed with ease.

My mom and Bảo's mom have taken to sharing their home-style recipes, updating each other with each culinary treat they make at home. Sometimes they visit each other at their respective restaurants. My dad and his dad mesh well; if anyone looks closer, it would seem that they were brothers. My aunt now calls Bảo's mom—whether she wants to hear from her or not. Bảo's still trying to figure that out.

I know things will be all right. Because each visit, each moment spent together, each laugh shared repairs what's been broken, like a brush of gesso gently rejuvenating something precious from long ago.

I don't think Chef Lê understood what he was getting into when he invited me and Bảo *and* our families to his restaurant. He apologized profusely, saying he meant to do it right after my mural was unveiled, but his son, Philippe, had gotten sick and there wasn't enough time.

Faced with two strong women with strong opinions on cooking, I almost expect Chef Lê to melt under their interrogation. But of course, he had his own Vietnamese mother to contend with growing up, and he easily deflects the heat. I would even say they are impressed by the kitchen workflow and some of his dishes—maybe even curious to get their hands on his recipes.

In the dining room, I glance across the table, watching Bảo try to fend off his mother's insistence that he needs to eat more rice. My own mother warns me to watch for bones from one of the plates of *cá chiên* sitting at the center of the table, even though I've eaten this kind of fish my entire life. Meanwhile, our respective fathers sit across from each other in companionable silence, preoccupied by their own bowls of rice.

Bảo's hair is still slightly wet. Seeing Chef Lê and Saffron's son across from him, he tries to make the poor kid laugh, but Philippe is completely unamused. Once in a while, from his position on his father's lap, he glances confusedly for help from his mother. He only smiles when Saffron mutters an endearment in French, then crawls into her arms.

Ali had jokingly said that this was the dinner of the century, and I'm sure if I told her where I was going, she'd probably follow. Lately, she's had this ridiculous idea that she'll write a novel about two warring Vietnamese families whose respective son and daughter fall in love. I don't know how she'll do it, but I guess Ali can do anything once she puts her mind to it.

Under the table, I feel Bảo squeeze my hand. We don't quite hide it from our families—us dating, even though "no dating until you're married" is a common refrain from our parents. And when I do leave the house or take a break to visit Bảo at his restaurant, my dad's always saying, "Ah, her *bạn*." Her "friend."

We'll get there . . . like everything else.

Our dinner finally ends and the laughter in our throats—courtesy of Chef Lê's comedic timing—finally settles. Toothpicks are distributed and there is momentary silence as each adult digs into their teeth.

A server sidles up to the table, setting down the bill.

A quiet "Oh shit" slips out from Chef Lê's lips as he remembers *exactly* who's at the table and the accompanying struggle of Vietnamese families fighting over the bill. He mutters about checking on the kitchen and scurries away. Saffron and Philippe soon join him.

"Let me get this," my mom says first, using the tone that commands the line cooks and servers.

A glint appears in Bảo's mom's eyes. "Oh no, let me."

"*Thôi, được rồi*. Please, let me."

Who will win?

I jump when Bảo whispers in my left ear, "Let's get out of here? Before they really kill each other?"

I nod and leave the table. So focused on the bill, our parents don't notice our departure.

Outside, we find ourselves in an alley, a familiar meeting spot for us, I suppose.

"Last time we were in an alley, you almost turned me away," Bảo says.

"Oh really?" I arch an eyebrow.

"Are you going to turn me away again?"

Grinning mischievously, I press him against the wall and plant a loud smack on his lips. We burst out laughing the moment we part. "Smooth." The grin stays on his face. "Linh?"

I sigh, content. "Hmm?"

"You have paint in your hair again."

I really did try to stay clean. I shrug. "So?" I say, challenging him.

He gives no response, a glint appearing in his eyes, and he reaches for me, pulling me to him by the loops of my jeans. His thumb caresses my cheek, and his eyes are soft.

Now we kiss for real.

ACKNOWLEDGMENTS

I have so many people to thank. Ba, I am thankful for your quiet love, comfort, and encouragement. I will always remember your patience as I scoured the bookshelves at the Cheshire Public Library—and later earned too many fines. Mẹ, you are the strongest person I know and I would be lost without you. I've grown to understand your strength and sacrifices more and more. I think my love of storytelling started with you—those nights when you'd tell stories about your childhood, squished between me and Chị An after we'd pushed our beds together.

Ba, Mẹ, I love you, I love you, I love you. I can't imagine not being your daughter. I don't think either of you ever tried stopping me from reading and writing, and I am glad for that.

An, our lives take us on different trajectories—*very* different, lol. Your brilliance, your strength, and your love have gotten me through so many things. You are truly my big sister. I love you, and I want the best for you. I'm glad to be your sister-in-law, Kevin, and I can't think of a better life partner for An! I am also proud to be Calhoun's aunt.

Dan, you are a rare human in every way possible and I do love you.

I'd like to thank my extended family as well because when I was really young, we lived or were always together. Now we're scattered across America and Vietnam. I don't take their struggles, unseen and unsaid, lightly: Dì Chín, Anh Bé, Chị Ty, Chị Quỳnh, Anh Sơn, Chị Như, Chị Nhi, Bon Bon, Tin Tin, Gigi, Anh Thông, Ben, Lilly, Eric, Ý Vy, Chị Huyền, Anh Thiện, Jasmine. Dì 10 Lớn, Cậu Đức, Chị By, Anh Hoàng, David, Noah, Sam, and Hannah. Even though we've only seen each other a handful of times, I want to send love to the West Coast fam (it's definitely been more than seven years), and to my family in Vietnam.

Jen Ung, this book literally wouldn't have existed without you. I admire you as an editor and I admire you for being my editor. Thank you for bearing with my lateness, for your insightful notes, for your enthusiasm. I have learned so much from you; you are beloved. Jim McCarthy, you're such an astounding agent, and I'm forever thankful for the support you've shown me from the very beginning. You're the best in the business. To the publishing team behind me, thank you: Mara Anastas, Liesa Abrams, Laura Eckes, Elizabeth Mims, Sara Berko, Brenna Franzitta, Mandy Veloso, Kathleen Smith, Caitlin Sweeny, Lisa Quach, Savannah Breckenridge, Nicole Russo, Lauren Carr, Jenny Lu, Lauren Hoffman, Anna Jarzab, Christina Pecorale, Victor Iannone, Emily Hutton, Michelle Leo, and Stephanie Voros.

I don't think I have enough space to thank everyone in my life, and I'm actually afraid of forgetting people. Please don't be offended if you're not here. Some may know their impact and some may not (surprise!), but I wanted to thank you regardless because you've enriched my life as a person, as a writer, and as an editor: Ali Famigletti—not the Ali in this book—I'm glad to have found a soul sister in you. From the moment we bonded over *Fringe*, from that snowy day in Fairfield, I knew we'd be friends for a long time. Eric Lynch, Spencer Colpitts, and Clara de Frutos—Look at us! We are all so different from each other, and we've done a lot of growing up. I love you. Love and hugs to the Tran family, Mariah Stovall (Beans!), Stephanie Jimenez (Beans!), Luigi DiMeglio, Melissa Bendixen, Lara Jones, Melanie Igelias Pérez, Wendolyne Sabrozo, Chelcee Johns, my Atria colleagues, Fiora Elbers-Tibbitts, Sean deLone, Nick Ciani, Daniella Wexler, Rakesh Satyal, Jhanteigh Kupihea, Amar Doel, Lindsay Sagnette, Libby McGuire, Dr. Tommy Xie, Gretchen and Jeff Messer, Kelly and Stephen Barry, Rebecca Faith Heyman, Bryan Crandall, Caitlyn Cardetti, Steve Breslin, and BTS (sorry, I had to).

Thank you to The Hastings—my MFA "sisters": Ellyn Gelman, Stacey Holmes, Sam Keller, Kerry McKay, Alix Purcell, Sam Sullivan, and Jessica Tumio. I'm eternally grateful to the Fairfield University English Department and the Fairfield MFA faculty who taught there during my time: Elizabeth Hastings, Hollis Seamon, Eugenia Kim, Al Davis, Rachel Basch, Karen Osborn, Sonya Huber, Elizabeth Hastings, Carol Ann Davis, Baron Wormser, Susan Darraj Maddaj, Michael White, and Bill Patrick.

Friends and teachers from Cheshire: I think you know who you are. We may not be in each other's lives anymore, but I see you and I'm proud of you. Ms. Yamamoto, you left the world as I was writing this manuscript. I was imagining the day I visited CHS and dropped off a copy in your office—the same office where our class, even after we were done, shared more Occasional Papers and proudly hung up our college acceptances. I just want to thank you for inspiring me, for being so kind to many, many, many people.

Thank you,

Loan

ABOUT THE AUTHOR

Loan Le holds an MFA degree in fiction from Fairfield University, where she also earned her bachelor's degree. A Pushcart Prize–nominated writer, Loan has had her short stories appear in *CRAFT Literary*, *Mud Season Review*, and *Angel City Review*. Loan works in book publishing and lives in Manhattan. *A Phở Love Story* is her first novel. Visit her website at writerloanle.com and find her on Twitter @loanloan.